Casualty of War

Casualty of War

Kim Moore

Writers Club Press
San Jose New York Lincoln Shanghai

Casualty of War

Writers Club Press
an imprint of iUniverse, Inc.

For information address:
iUniverse, Inc.
5220 S. 16th St., Suite 200
Lincoln, NE 68512
www.iuniverse.com

ISBN: 0-595-20925-4

Printed in the United States of America

For my family
Tom, Mary Lou, Beth, Tom, Steve
and
Bear

Preface

I am a face of the I.R.A. That's Irish Republican Army, not Individual Retirement Account. I plant daffodils outside my house to beautify the neighborhood. I chat with you as your children ride their bikes in the street. I help you carry your groceries to your front door. You think I am quiet, keep to myself, even, dare I say, pleasant. I'm sure you wonder about me, the single, childless woman. Well, wonder this. Wonder what it is like to live a life in uncommunicative silence. What it is like to have numerous close friends who are completely unaware of what holds my soul hostage. I am a casualty of war.

Accidental Terrorist
Eileen Eliot

Acknowledgements

Some of life's greatest gifts are the people we meet. This project is a result of many who are not named, yet still so important. Special recognition to: Anne Mitchell, my dear friend and advisor; Col. Martin Egan, USMC (Ret.), a fan before and after being my first reviewer and critic; the owner and staff of Ireland's Own/Pat Troy's Restaurant and Pub for constant motivation and a place to write; Sandra Remey of Remey Communications, my first editor; and Steven Moore, my husband and biggest fan even when I don't put away my shoes.

1
October 1998

Sweeping through the restaurant, running her hand along the dark wood as she passed through the bar, Eileen approached Janet who was sitting at "their" table. Janet had been there long enough to have one merlot under her cinched belt and was working on her second. Eileen had called her at 9:00 that morning rambling about how they "absolutely had to have lunch today." Eileen pulled back her chair—she never waited for the maitre'd to assist—dropped a manila envelope on the table and sat down. She looked great—a good hair day. Her eyeliner wasn't flaking yet, and her navy pants and cream colored bodysuit hugged her figure exactly as it should. She loved walking through a crowded room, dressed to the nines, and showing off the body that had taken two successful divorces, a hint of psychoanalysis and lots of step aerobics classes to achieve.

At 34 she'd married well, both times, only to find later on that Husband #1 had a penchant for 22 year-old women, and Husband #2 developed one for 22 year-old men. Both settlements afforded her the luxury of keeping her cottage in Eastham, Cape

Cod, complementing it with a rowhome in Boston on Beacon Hill, and a rental property in Alexandria, Virginia. One of her engagement rings managed to cover the cost of renovating both bathrooms and building a terrific bricked-in patio at the Beacon Hill house. Despite the traffic, noise, and tourists, Husband #2 was kind enough to fulfill her dream of a home off Cambridge Street, just a few blocks from the Commons. When Eileen found his stash of home video tapes with a variety of fraternity hunks, he handed over just about anything she wanted as long as she didn't tell his mother. It must have been the video filmed in Mommy's bedroom that would have really pushed her over the edge. Needless to say, Husband #2's trust fund experienced a serious withdrawal, and Eileen's mutual funds got a significant cash infusion.

Eileen was not of the mindset to spend her days wandering through the boutiques of Newbury Street, although she knew the streets of Boston based on the location of particular stores. For example, a meeting at the corner of Milk and Devonshire Streets meant that she had to get to that great little wine merchant's place—the one that delivers—then find parking in the garage across from CVS. Granted, she afforded herself one afternoon every two weeks either to get her hair done, have a manicure, or browse through the Armani and BeBe stores on Newbury. Shopping was a controlled habit. Not because the money was tight, but more because her weight had fluctuated so much in the last two-and-a-half years that it was pointless to spend so much cash on clothes that would only fit for a couple of months. Eileen had one of those frames that when in great shape, she was a knockout, but it didn't take much to rescind from knockout to okay looking. Ten pounds in the wrong place and the image was blown. At 5'6" she could not afford too much extra baggage on her body, even though she was comfortable with her figure. She tried to stay a size 10, an 8 was too hard to maintain, and a 12 was just too close to maximum density for her own comfort. This month, her hair was a dirty blond. Hair was one of those few things that could be easily changed, so she colored it every three months. Depending on her mood, the dye job would be subtle or drastic. Just before her blond stage, she was a deep brunette (her natural color) and was now thinking of heading for the red zone. The style was never too dramatic. She liked the basic all-one-length cut with a few wisps around the frame of her face. It afforded lots of versatility, translating to a reason to buy hair accessories galore. Whether conservative, subtly glamorous, or downright striking, she had the look and the necessary accoutrements.

Today she'd taken a shuttle to New York for a meeting and to get together with Janet. Eileen had been so happy to get out of New York following the demise of Husband #1, then wound up back there when Husband #2 was transferred to the headquarters of Marsh-Magee Investments and closer to his mommy. She and Janet had been friends for over 10 years, and used to lunch at Cafe a Largo at least twice a week. This reunion of sorts was the icing on Eileen's cake.

"I couldn't believe it when you called this morning," Janet started, following a hug. Janet had actually managed to get out of her seat. Janet never stood for anyone unless there was a chance that a member of the press would catch her on video, or she might make Liz Smith's gossip column. "I didn't think I'd see you again unless I flew north. Dear, you look fabulous. Promise me you'll never re-marry. It gives you wrinkles." She giggled, and sipped her wine.

Eileen waved at Victor, their server. Victor had been at the cafe longer than the women had been patrons there. Victor must be eligible for a gold watch, and a hell of a 401(k) package at this point, she thought to herself. "Hi Victor. It is so nice to see you. How've you been?" They exchanged approximately 25 seconds worth of niceties when Eileen cut to the chase, "Victor, could I please have a sauvignon blanc, an iced tea, and the chicken Caesar salad? Oh, and some of those terrific breadsticks, and lots of butter."

"Butter?!" Janet was stunned. "Okay, what's the deal? You must be celebrating something."

"Maybe." Eileen loved having the dirt when Janet was in the dark. Janet thrived on gossip. She had to know everything about everyone. She probably knew about Eileen's husbands' antics before Eileen did. Eileen's smirk told Janet that yes, something was up, and if you are a good girl, I will tell you a little secret.

"What is it? Come on, sing it girlfriend." Janet's hand was holding her wine glass a little tighter, a clear sign of angst over being out of the loop. She tapped on her glass with her professionally glued-on fingernails.

Victor returned, placing the drinks to Eileen's right and the breadsticks in the center of the table. Eileen picked one up and began spreading butter all over it. The knife moving back and forth, her wrist delicately turning, steering the blade like a sailboat rudder. She was thinking of how to make her presentation. She took a bite of the breadstick, crumbs falling all over the table as she began to talk a little bit through her crunching. This was Janet. Manners on some level were necessary, but the Amy Vanderbilt approach to dining was not required.

"Okay. Remember about a year ago when I bought a computer? Well, since then, I have written a manuscript, and—"

"Oh my God, you're getting published!" Janet gulped down the rest of her wine and ordered another.

"Better. You remember Jack Marston don't you? Anyway, Jack was over for dinner one evening, and we were talking, and—"

"Did you fuck him?"

"No!"

"Why not? Has he gained weight?"

"I am not interested, he looks great, and shut up and let me finish. You are unbelievable." Eileen was never quite sure why she and Janet were friends. Janet was good for giggles, but she was no confidante. She was of the big-hair mentality; relatively shallow, never without a purse-size bottle of hair spray, and she had this annoying habit of fixing her make-up at the table. Eileen was continually revolted by Janet's custom of pulling out her lip liner and lipstick in a restaurant and repairing her face between courses. Somehow, Eileen's depth blended with Janet's lack thereof so that the two learned from each other.

"So Jack and I were in the living room, having a few cognacs debating the various angry situations around the world, when I told him about my manuscript. He browsed through it. As he put it, he 'goddamn loved it.' I thought it was the cognac talking, but he took another look at it about a week later, and shopped it around to a few publishing houses. Jack's met a couple of publishing lawyers through his firm. He's been helping me through the whole process, and he put me in touch with the people at Empire."

"Empire! Ooh, they put out such great stuff. Barnes&Noble is running a big promotion of all of their books. I wish they put out Judith Krantz. I could've gotten her latest book for half price then." Janet was enthralled that she was now dining with a soon-to-be-published author, and felt an intense urge to whip out her cell phone and call Liz Smith herself.

"Wait. I haven't told you the best part. Empire has been looking at it for the last few months. I've been through two hair colors since then and am trying like crazy not to dive into a box of Oreo cookies on a daily basis. They finally called me last week and Jack and I came into town today to wrap up the negotiations. I have

excerpts of the manuscript with me." Eileen patted the envelope
sitting on the table.

"Did you ever think that I would be an author!" Eileen's wine
was nearly gone, and Victor, with his eagle eye, had already
ordered another one for her. What a guy. "Here, take a look at it."
Eileen handed over the envelope to her lunch partner. This was a
relatively dangerous thing. Janet was not a quick reader, but
Eileen was ready to share her good fortune with just about anyone, and did not mind spending the time in silence as Janet
perused the pages. Janet opened the envelope, fingered through
the pages, and began to read:

The Accidental Terrorist
        —Eileen Eliot

"Oh how neat! Look, that's your name! I can't get over it."
Janet turned the cover page back toward Eileen, tapping her finger
next to Eileen's name. "Eileen, I just want to pass this all around
the room, and say, 'See this, that's her.'" Janet thrived on the
brush-with-greatness approach to dining. Actually, Eileen was
thrilled too, but restrained her elation. She hadn't adjusted to the
concept of someone paying her to write.

                *   *   *   *

Two weeks ago I was feeling abandoned, convinced that my
head was going to explode if I didn't talk to someone, and I'd been
having too many conversations with myself for too long. February
sweeps month had just finished up and everything on television
was a rerun. My meetings had just wrapped up and I therefore
had no more work to take home with me. Now I was forced to
live the life of a normal person. You know the deal, work, friends,
home, good nutrition, going to the gym, and wondering if Mark
would call that night. We're all pretty much the same when it

comes right down to it. We thrive on relationships, complaining about the lack of girth in our paychecks, and running errands. It's kind of entertaining to sit on my couch and to think that even the President and the First Lady have probably had one or two nights in the last week or so when they've been pissed off at each other. See, no matter who you are, it's all the same. Except for me. My relationship is on the line. The love that I've carried in my heart for over six years is teetering on the edge because of the confidence I broke, and the thoughts I've had. I still can't tell if it was out of anger or revenge or stress.

I was home from the end of a very stressful day, one in which every phone call I received at the office was not from Mark, and every analysis I'd written was subsequently red-inked by my boss with pointless changes in verbiage and comments clearly indicating he had not read the memo or listened to my reasoning.

Mark was somewhere, and whether it was business or his so-called hobby that was keeping him away, my patience was running thin and I hardly could sit still anymore. Or was it just that I'd had too much coffee? Two nights ago, I'd called his new apartment in Atlanta, and he'd asked if he could call me later. He was not alone. I was so proud of myself for "understanding" and for not getting upset. Then, as I rinsed my chamomile shampoo (good for those with color-treated hair) from my head and reached for the mint conditioner, the voices were pouring through my head, and rational thought was going down the drain faster than the sham-poo suds. Maybe she was there. She, the imaginary girlfriend, who had been stalking my mind for months. Just who was there? Mark never phoned back. I dwelled on it all day long.

No wonder he wanted us to maintain our long-distance rela-tionship. Maybe work was as much of a front as the imaginary girlfriend. I was losing my mind. One cannot go for so many years without telling anyone about the truth to my love life. I was tired of hearing my friends tell me that I should start dating other people. They wanted to know why we hadn't gotten married yet. Clearly, they did not hear me when I said, "because I don't want to." Okay, so maybe that isn't *entirely* truthful. I am unconventional. I prefer to be on my own but still hopelessly in love, and to be loved by a man who knows every last detail of my life, even if he sometimes acts as if he knows nothing of me. I didn't want to share my house with anyone else. I didn't want to have to race home to get dinner ready—like he'd ever be there. I was not prepared to share my remote control. Maybe someday, but, please, not yet. I'm too young, and duty calls.

Joe, my best friend since junior high school, won the booby prize when I called him. The couch cushions were feeling too thin, so I walked to the phone and dialed his number. Okay, maybe I didn't walk. Maybe I slid my slippered feet across my dirty hardwood floors. I kind of like that sound the dust makes under socks and slippers. It reminds me of being a kid in my grandmother's house. Her floors were always clean, but age had softened the wood so that it emanated the same dusty sound. As I held the phone, I was running my hand along the inside of the waistband on my sweatpants, and trying to decide if I'd really lost weight or just was feeling a high level of self-confidence.

"Joe?"

"Hey, what's up? Did you see *Melrose* last night? What a disappointment. It has gotten just way out of control." Joe and I usually swapped commentary on the latest *Melrose Place* episodes if we didn't watch them together. Yeah, it's a childish activity, being over 30 and putting so much weight on a TV show, but it was fun.

"Joe, I have got to get out of the house. Will you please go out with me? I don't feel like sitting in a bar by myself." It's not that anyone would have tried to pick me up. It was that I would've taken either my journal or the newspaper with me and neither were beneficial diversions that night.

"Oh jeeze, Sophie I'm beat, and I'm totally tapped out. Can we go on Friday? I'll have cash then." This was not the response I'd needed.

"Joe. I'm losing my mind." I was wrapping the phone cord around my right index finger, trying to see how tight I could get it. I was up to eleven rotations and my fingernail was completely hidden. I wanted to make it to twelve. I started over. "I have got to go out. I'll buy. Please come with me. You know I wouldn't buy unless I was really desperate."

He thought for a minute. By this time I was standing in the living room with the phone cord wrapped around the wall and my thighs and was channel surfing via remote control. No more C-SPAN, no more C-SPAN—that was my latest mantra—no more C-, "Okay. I'll go. What's wrong? You're being goofy."

"I'm just really wound up, and I can't sit here alone. I'm aching for social interaction. It's just one of those days when I'm not comfortable being in my own skin. How's Jack and Bud's?" J&B's was a dive near our houses. The name of the place reminded me of Christmas at my aunt and uncle's house. Uncle Mike never drank anything other than J&B on the rocks with a splash.

Joe lived two streets away from me, just off Commonwealth Avenue. Don't ask how it happened, 'cause we still can't figure it out. Talk about a need to cut the proverbial cord.

Joe and his 1992 Toyota Camry pulled up in front of my house ten minutes later. He'd had a CD player installed in it recently, so it was understood that anywhere we went he drove; even if it was only a 1/4-mile.

We took a table in the back corner, ordered a pitcher of Killians and I fired up the first of many Marlboro Lights. "I wish you'd quit smoking. It makes it too difficult for me to stay away from them," he picked up my pack of smokes and pulled one out. I lit it for him.

"So, how's it goin'? Any word from Suzanne?" Joe's fiancée was traveling on business with the senator she worked for. For all I knew, she was in Mark's apartment earlier this week. At this point, nothing would shock me. I hadn't taken Joe's engagement well. It meant that I'd be the last of the single people in our crowd, and I couldn't compete with all of the gripping discussions about babysitters and kiddie videos that were now creeping into the realm of our social gatherings.

"Suzanne's fine. What's wrong with you? Soph, you have 'big picture' written all over your face. Spill it." Joe has spent the last year trying to train me to stop thinking about the big picture. He says I try to tackle issues that are too broad rather than just appreciate the small things. For a month, I had to call him every day and list five small things that made me happy. I was also barred from using the term "pisses me off." I apparently was using it too often. I thrive on the downward spiral. No angst? Then I'm just not happy.

"Oh, I'm fine. The house just was seeming really small. I've had too much on my mind. You're right, the big picture is coming into play, and I've got to get rid of it."

"Well, what are you thinking about?"

"First, I'm thinking that you shouldn't end your sentences with prepositions. Second, I'm dwelling on the fact that Mark and I will never be married. It's not going to happen. Before, I could be happy with that. I love him, and the fact that we are together is all I've ever wanted, but now I want more. At least, I think I do. I mean, this long distance thing has gone on for six years, and I don't see an end to it. Even if we moved closer to each other, I would assume that we'd live together, or get married, but that's not going to happen."

"Have you talked to him about it?"

"No."

"Why not? That's it, you're too busy worrying yourself by answering for him rather than asking his opinion."

"You don't get it. We don't talk about 'us' or the future. The future as far as we're concerned is next week. It's just not the done thing." I was rolling the cigarette box end over end, stopping briefly each time the box was upended. Is that compulsive? "Besides, I know that we will never be married, and I'm really not sure if that bothers me or not. I'm more worried about being away from him and these disjointed feelings, than I am about a life-long commitment."

I continued for about fifteen minutes, throwing back my beer and lighting another cigarette as I pontificated about how I wanted to grow with him, but wasn't sure if that meant that I wanted to get married, and I was thinking about kids, but didn't know if I wanted them either, and what if we had the kids but still didn't live together OR get married, and how sometimes that would work for me, and how I really had no idea what I was feeling, but that I knew that he did not want to get married. I was thoroughly confusing Joe. Clearly, I'd had too much caffeine at work. Then it hit.

"I'm tired of being supportive and understanding, and patient. I am at his beck-and-call, but he's not at mine. You know, I really tend to wonder if he'd be there if something really awful happened and I needed him, or if something really fabulous happened. I mean, he would, if work didn't get in the way. But I am the last of the priorities. I could walk naked through his kitchen and he'd still tell me that he had to work and he'd call me later. I am probably the only woman in metropolitan Washington who does not protest when her lover gets up from the couch, announces that he has to make a phone call, walks into the bedroom, and closes the door. Most people would assume he's either calling some 976-FUCK line, or setting up a date with the other woman. I can't be bothered with either concern anymore. Besides, it's not even an issue."

"You know Soph, you've been complaining about his work schedule, and frankly you don't deserve this. Are you sure he isn't, and I'm not trying to be mean, but, are you sure he isn't screwing around with someone else?" Joe told me that at first Mark's schedule was understandable, but that after six years, it was clear that respect was not coming into play, and that maybe I should consider leaving him. How can I leave someone who is 600 miles away? Isn't he already gone? It was the respect comment that set me off. The one thing I know is that even when he's working he's thinking of me. Mark is as loyal as the day is long, and if we go for two or three months apart, we are both suffering. We are crazy about each other. There's never been anyone else, at least I don't think there has, but I never will admit that fear to anyone. "You've got to put your foot down and tell him that the job issue has to change."

"I can't do that." I sipped my beer. "It could kill him."

"I doubt if it would kill him."

"No, I'm serious." At that moment, the lid was blown from my love life. Joe couldn't understand, and I couldn't stop. I ordered another pitcher.

Shortly after Mark and I met on the Cape, we were lying on the beach at the edge of Pleasant Bay in Harwichport. There was nothing. No noise except our breathing and the wind in the marsh grass behind us. I had one leg draped over his, with my head on his shoulder. We had an empty twelve-pack in the sand, and an unopened bottle of whiskey. Back then, I couldn't understand how anyone could drink the stuff. Now I think it's got to be a gift from the heavens. He was only here for a few months, on a temporary visa, and was leaving in the next two weeks. He did not want to return. He started telling me about how his sympathies and ideas had changed and he did not want to go back to the way things had been.

"What are you talking about?" Joe was having a very difficult time following me.

"Joe, Mark is, for all intents and purposes, a terrorist, but frankly that doesn't matter to me. Besides, I think he's right."

"You are lying." He leaned back in his chair, folding his arms in front of him.

Why was I not surprised by that response? I continued to tell him that I did not know any details, but that I've been living in my own support group for the last few years, since we'd started seeing each other. "I mean, they don't really put out self-help books on this subject, you know? And it's been a while since Oprah has run her episode on 'what to do when you're involved with a political insurgent.'"

I have spent virtually every weekend alone and in silence. My phone rings, but I always knows that it's not Mark. He spends his weekends in undisclosed houses somewhere in cities all over the country. Boston is his home now. At least it was until he moved, but I know he's still going back there. He's spent thousands of dollars decorating houses that weren't his, but had served as home for various stretches of time. Too bad he couldn't get tax deductions on them.

"For the last six years, I have not known where he spends his time, from where he is calling me, and when I might see him. In the same breath, no one knows about me. I do not exist, and that apparently is for my protection. Somedays I'd like to chuck the concept of 'protection' and just come clean. I mean, these people must have families or significant others, yet they get to go about their business. Sometimes I am ready to just come out of the proverbial closet, but other times it frightens me. Jesus, sometimes I feel like I could be carrying just as much liability. Can't you see it? 'No your honor, I was not aware of that threat. I mean, sure I knew he was in, and I knew it was a federal offense, but come on, he's so cute, and I didn't know any of the details, and he always remembers my birthday.'" I was teetering back and forth between complete agony to an almost scary sense of sarcasm, "Can spouses still be prohibited from ratting on each other in court," my eyes were wide open, but I was not seeing Joe. Another beer was finished, and another poured.

– – – – – – – – – –

Mark failed to see that Sophie had become involved in his work from almost day one of their being together. He could not understand that despite her not participating in his plans and tasks, the I.R.A. was her life. She has surrendered her life's plans for the good of the organization just as much as he had, though she'd never dared to make that statement to Mark. He would have gone through the roof. At least, that's what she'd thought for years. After two years together, Sophie finally dropped her own bomb of sorts on Mark. He was scheduled to be away for two weeks on assorted business trips, with some organizational responsibilities thrown into the mix. Since his plans were essentially set in stone, Sophie had planned a little time away. The conversation with Mark was not pleasant, but he seemed to try and understand.

On a Saturday night in September, four years ago, they were in Sophie's aging Chevrolet Cavalier driving home from dinner. There was little traffic on the expressway, but for some reason, the fog was thick. It was almost never foggy in Washington, but the cold front rolling in was stealing the warmth from the afternoon. Sophie hoped that Mark's need to focus on the road, she always let him drive her car, would help him to maintain composure. "Honey, I put in for some time off and have decided to take a vacation," she said as she was casually leaning in toward the radio, searching for a better station.

He was lighting a cigarette, replacing the car's lighter in the socket, "That's great, Babe. When are going? Got any plans? You've been needing some time away for a while." He didn't tell her, but he had wondered why she hadn't prefaced her announcement with the traditional urging that they take some time off together. She had stopped asking that question months ago. Too many invitations had been turned down, and she refused to set herself up for the fantasy of going away together only to have him kill the illusion with his refusal.

"I leave in three weeks. I'm taking two and a half weeks off." She was picking at her fingernails, clearly getting increasingly uncomfortable with the impending discussion. Mark turned the car into the parking lot outside her apartment.

Closing the car door and putting out his cigarette butt on the ground beneath his boot, he casually asked her, "Where are you going? Up to your parents' place?" Sophie's parents had purchased a beach house on Maryland's Eastern Shore as a tax shelter, when such shelters were still included in the tax code.

"No." She was pulling her handbag from the backseat of the car, dragging it between the two front seats as she emerged from the car. "Derry."

"What did you say?" He stopped walking toward the house, turned, and looked her square in the face for the first time in weeks. He was listening, and preparing to light into her with all force if necessary.

"Derry...I'm taking two and a half weeks, my camera, my journal, and a few changes of clothes. I'm staying four days in Belfast, renting a car, going out to Giant's Causeway, Donegal, and the countryside, staying in B&Bs, then working my way through Derry and anywhere else I feel like going. I will not wait any longer. I've got the time and the money, and I know that you will never go with me, so it's now or never." She continued walking to the front door, and put her key in the lock.

He walked in behind her and shut the door. After she flipped the light switch, he grabbed her shoulders so that she could do nothing but look at him as he spoke at her. "I cannot allow you to go. It's too dangerous. I will not allow it."

She laughed at him, "You what? What are you, my father? Even he knows better than to use those kinds of phrases with me. What's your point sweetheart? And please let go of me. I'm not going anywhere, and I want to talk about this. I've wanted to talk about this for years."

"I can't let you take that kind of a risk, Soph." He kept talking as he walked to the kitchen, removed two crystal glasses from the cabinet, and poured them each a Bushmills single malt. "You know how things are right now. We've just gotten behind another July of Orange marches and rioting. No sane person would go there, and I cannot run the risk of your being there. Internal rumblings are getting really bad right now. You could be putting yourself at grave risk. It's too hot."

His comments were not the least bit consoling to her, nor did she feel any sense of reconsideration. If she'd felt that he was asking her not to go out of fear for her own safety, she would have thought it somewhat romantic and sweet. He was forbidding her from going for fear that it would screw up the organization's plans. Leaning against the doorway of the kitchen, she watched him fingering the top of the glass. "How can this possibly be a problem for you? No one knows about me. How could I be at risk? Things have settled down. Besides," she smiled, "don't you guys give advance warnings? I'll have plenty of time to bolt out of there if necessary." Unquestionably, she was yanking his chain, rattling his cage, pushing him over the edge, and frankly, enjoying it. This was her vacation, her choice, and he was not going to stand in the way of this, as he'd been standing in the way of so many of her other plans.

He pondered chucking the glass at the wall but found restraint. "That's it." Watching him cross the kitchen floor into the dining room, she knew that the grandstanding was about to begin. "You just don't get it do you? This is not a game, Soph. This is real life, and it's not your life. It's mine. Spending a few days trying to immerse yourself in the culture and politics is not going to make you some de facto member, or any better of a sympathizer. It's not your war. You're being ridiculous, and I won't hear any more of it." He was yelling, screaming, shaking her. She'd expected this, but had not anticipated the ensuing discussion.

"No, Mark. You are the one who does not understand. This is my fight. This is my life. And it's time I got a grip on it. You have been fighting and planning and plotting for as long as I've known you. I've lost my freedom in this battle just as much as you have, so don't sit here and try to play the martyr to me." Her voice was wavering. Mark sat down on the couch, placed his drink on the coffee table and looked up at her. This discussion warranted his attention. "Perhaps I am at the disadvantage of never having lived there. But Honey, you haven't either. You lived in the Republic, not the occupied territory, or six hostage counties, or whatever the fuck is the phrase of the moment. I don't know the land, and I don't know the culture. But this war has taken away my life. I see you when we can squeeze it in. None of your friends or co-workers knows about me. Half of our life is a mystery because you can't tell me about it. Most days, you are distant and preoccupied, and it's all I can do to get a glimmer of emotion from you. Yet, I know that you love me. I remind myself of that every day. I even remember the last time you told me so. It was in April. April 12. That's five months and 8 days ago. Don't you get it? I never asked to be drafted, I've pondered becoming involved, though I know you wouldn't let me. I have nothing to gain other than the warm feeling that one day all of Ireland will be governed by Sinn Fein, and that Protestants all over Ulster will be unemployed and living in crappy houses. This is my life, Mark and I don't even know what much of my life consists of these days. I need to go. I need to see it for myself. I just need a small point of reference and some time to absorb it for my own satisfaction. Can't you see that I have made sacrifices for 'The Cause' that I know in my heart is right, yet I have no way of understanding right now?"

"Sophie," he moved toward her on the couch, wiped away one of her tears, and stroked her hair. "Hon, I understand what you are feeling and I am sorry I didn't see it on my own. I don't want you to feel this way, but I also don't want you to go. I promise, we'll go someday. I want to be there with you, but I cannot risk anything happening to you. I know how you are. You'll go wandering into some neighborhood with your camera and your curiosity, and you'll keep snapping photos until you piss off some stupid bastard who thinks he's a renegade and really lets you have it." She was laughing now. Good sign. "I'll try to tell you more about my work, and I'll try not to shut you out so much. You're right. I have been completely wrong to treat you this way, and from tonight forward, I promise to be better." Famous last words.

Mark convinced Sophie to reroute her plans, take four days in London, a week in Edinburgh and a few days in Dublin. He called her everyday at her respective hotel to ask how she was faring, and to make sure that she hadn't sneaked off to Belfast for a lark. Upon her return, she had no greeting at the airport, no phone call from Mark for four days, and did not see him for another five weeks. But when he called, he whispered "I love you" and spoke of how much he missed her and promised they'd be together soon. Anything to keep her sated until she came off the high of her extended vacation. He truly did love her and wanted only to be with her, but the organization came first. That's how it had been, and that's how it would stay for as long as necessary.

– – – – – – – – – – –

"This is ridiculous." Joe was on his fourth Marlboro Light, and I couldn't tell if he was realizing the weight that I had been carrying. He was listening, but I don't think it was sinking in.

"I think I'm going to be sick." My hands were shaking, my stomach turning, and my eyes couldn't focus. I had wanted to tell someone so badly, but now I was physically reacting to my infidelity. Mark had told me about this so many years ago. I was breaking my silence, and risking everything I had with him. What had I done? Why do you always realize the gravity of your mistakes after you've made them? Why couldn't I just have spent tonight at home on the couch with *People* magazine and a bottle of scotch? It would've been so much safer. I poured another glass of beer and decided that I would just talk about myself. After all, that was the point of this discussion. This was the "Joe-I'm-Losing-My-Mind Talk."

"Everyone has been commenting about how great I look. How I look thinner, and my hair is great, and I'm just in so much better shape. No kidding. Fitness relieves stress, you know? Well Honey, it doesn't get much worse than this." The fact that I had all but pickled myself in booze for the last year helped preserve my looks too, for now.

"Sophie, if you've been carrying this around for all these years, why are you telling me this? You're a mess." Joe liked Mark, but his concerns were for Sophie. He would die for her if necessary; just as he'd rescued her from drunk, advancing rugby players at numerous college parties, and convinced her not to go down the aisle on her wedding day nine years ago. Tom, her former fiancé, was dead wood who was only going to drag her down. Standing in her raw silk gown, surrounded by four bridesmaids, a flower girl, and 225 friends and relatives waiting on the other side of the sacristy door, Joe had forced her to admit that she couldn't go through with it. Her father had loved Tom, and it was only in the last five years that he could bring himself to speak to Joe without recalling all of those non-refundable dollars he'd spent to celebrate his only daughter's march down the aisle to a life of tax-deferred investments, a vacation home, and a lucrative corporate real estate firm.

"No shit. I think it's an early mid-life crisis." I was picking at my fingernails, just as I always do when nervous. For some reason, when I'm nervous, I have this sense that my cuticles are ridiculously overgrown and must be tugged at, peeled, or bitten off.

"What? Sophie, you're 31."

"Yes, and the man I love and want will never have me. Not because he doesn't want us to be together but because there's an international terrorist organization dictating how he's to live his life, and they can't know about me. Do you believe this? Can't you just see me marrying into the I.R.A.? 'Oh, hi guys. Yeah, come on in. So, what's on for tonight? Planning any good gun-running? Hey, did you see that explosion in Argentina this morning? Very clean. Anyone want a beer, or a cup of tea?'" I stopped. I knew it would never be that way, even if we did marry. I was coming completely unglued. I gathered my senses and spoke slower even though I wanted to run screaming from the bar and had no idea in which direction I'd run. I would have run home and called Mark and pretended as if nothing happened, but he was somewhere in New York for the night and of course, I didn't have a number. I felt lucky for that. He would have been disgusted to see me in my current state.

"Joe, I'm being excessive. But, can you see my point? Most women lie in bed at night thinking of which clothes to take to the dry cleaners, and who to remember to call in the morning, or they're mad about something their husband or boyfriend did or didn't say. I get in bed at night—this is my latest ritual—" I extended my hands toward him to add to the description. "Okay, I do the anti-wrinkle oil around my eyes and forehead, and I wonder if Mark will call. Then I debate about whether or not I want to know what he's doing. Then I channel surf and tell myself how lucky he is to have me because I'm so understanding. Then I curse the 'corporation' for all of the time it demands and revel in a fantasy of having a good face-to-face discussion with at least one or two of them so that they can see that I'm no threat, but that I'm also no pushover. This, naturally, is all taking place as I am slathering lilac moisturizer over my feet and legs because we women are supposed to care about that kind of crap. This sucks. Joe, I don't want the house in the country, or the quiet life. I'm not even sure if I want kids, but I'll tell you that I know that I want him. I want to be with him in some manner. I need him. Mark is it for me. No question. I'm not going anywhere. I mean, I'll stand by everything he does, and I will not allow my life to be governed by the group. Then again, maybe I will. At this point, I don't know anymore. If this relationship hits problems, it will be because we have a problem between the two of us; not because the corporation is too demanding. I will not give in. Ever."

I realized I was engulfed by this, whether I liked it or not in February 1996; the day the ceasefire ended. Most people can tell you where they were when President Kennedy died, or President Reagan was shot, or the Oklahoma bombing occurred. I can tell you where I was when the ceasefire was announced, when the findings of the Mitchell Commission Report were announced, when the ceasefire ended, and when the Ulster Volunteer Force set off simultaneous explosives in London, Dublin and Belfast when the all-party talks seemed to be going too far in favor of the "other side." I was studying in the Madison Building of the Library of Congress when the ceasefire happened. I was elated. I'd hoped that Mark's life would become a little easier, that our lives would be a little more normal, but I also knew that the fun was only beginning. He was with me when CNN broke the Mitchell Commission findings, but I had the impression that he already knew what was in it. He tells me nothing. We don't really talk about it. It takes up enough of our lives. He knows that I worry, and he tells me not to. That's our deal. I'd like to think that he keeps quiet simply to protect me, but I know that he says nothing because he can't. I would be a "breach of security," a fate punishable by death. I, in his world, am a liability, and he treats me as such. Ain't that a comfort? Some women want to be supportive, or be stay-at-home moms, or be gourmet cooks. I strive to move, like an accounting entry, to the asset column from the liability column. I am not a positive. I am not even a zero-balance. I am a negative. My mother would be so proud.

I was at home when the ceasefire ended. And the bombs, oh hell, that was just the icing on the fucking cake. I'd taken the afternoon off from work to take a little well-deserved quiet time. I was emptying my dishwasher and dropped one of my four dinner plates on the floor when I heard the news on the television from the living room. I wanted to run somewhere, or call someone, but I couldn't. I shook. I stood there, grabbing onto the countertop surrounded by shards of broken porcelain and just shook. Even if Mark had known that any of this was going to happen, he wouldn't have told me and I will never ask. I really have learned my place. The first few years were rough. Now I don't bat an eyelash at much of anything.

Here I am with a man who keeps me in the dark about most of his life. He could be doing anything, with anyone and I would never know. I have no way of checking up on him. A long time ago, I used to dream of following him and finding out what he was doing and who he was doing it with, and wondering if I really had reason to worry. But I've learned, and I think just because I've matured and not because I've actually gathered any information, that there is no reason to worry. Mark could do whatever he wanted, and he has the capability of keeping it from me, but I also know that he loves and respects me and that quite simply put, he would not do that to me.

A warm glass of whiskey in my crystal Waterford highball glass, spring breezes through the branches of my dead maple tree and nearly dead rose bushes, and it all falls into place. I need that support group, even if it's just a few people sitting in a bar having a few pints of Sam Adams, debating why the boys think that they are so busy and so indispensable that we girls get stuck learning about home repairs and car maintenance. Honest to God, Mark wouldn't know how to operate a washing machine if I held a gun to his head. He would, however, know how to disarm me inside of two seconds.

My biggest fear is that Mark will die, and all of these people who have already stolen him from me will have stolen those moments that I will long for as well. I know it sounds melodramatic, but when you are me, and he does what he does, these things cross my mind. I leaned back in my chair, pushing the front legs off the ground as I stared at my smoldering cigarette ash. Leaning back into the table, I slammed my hands down, looked Joe square in the face and pronounced, "I, am a god-damn nut." It was almost a perfect Jack Nicholson impression, save for the tears in my eyes.

Joe listened to me rant about all of this, and after I mentioned my concerns about funerals and being a pawn, he suddenly looked very nervous. The bar had gotten darker as the hours passed. Why do bars always turn the lights down as the sun goes down? Booze makes you drowsier anyway and putting the clientele to sleep would only cut into a bar's profit-making potential.

Joe had the look of someone absorbed in the last 20 minutes of the last night of the world's greatest mini-series. He was floored that I could keep such a secret from him for so long, until he figured out that he now knew something highly illegal.

"Come on, Soph. Do you realize that the Justice Department could really hit us if they knew."

"Honey, if you even tried to make some kind of accusation, Mark would have a better chance of suing you for slander than you would of screwing him over. Just keep your mouth shut. It's not that big a deal."

"Sophie, this is a big deal. I don't know how you can think otherwise. Do you realize what you are in to? Has it occurred to you that marriage might be your best defense? At least if he were caught, you wouldn't be able to testify against him."

"Bullshit. I'd be a hostile witness. Don't think that this hasn't crossed my mind. They'd get me, and I'd go down too. I've also wondered if I could be extradited to a country where I'm not even a citizen. Thanks very much, but I am not crazy about the prospect of being incarcerated in a British prison as an Irish Republican sympathizer. Marriage might be a good defense, but frankly, if we ever get married, I want it to be because we are totally hot for each other and can't stand to be apart any longer."

I'd failed to tell Joe that I have perhaps become only slightly paranoid. I didn't tell him that my Saturday morning cooking classes were actually target practice. I bought a gun three months ago and have kept it with me at all times. It's one of the beauties of living in a concealed weapon state. Mark, who is also unaware of my new toy, says that the only purpose for guns is to kill people and he doesn't think anyone should have them. After the ceasefire ended, I knew that Mark could be in a very sensitive situation, and I was not about to let anyone try and use me in the process. I've become a one-woman counter-terrorist operative.

"Joe, last fall I had an abortion." Joe nearly dropped his beer glass when I quickly whispered this to him. Dazed, he couldn't understand how I could have kept this from him for almost a year.

"You what?"

"You heard me." I hesitated, "I had an abortion last year." I'd never told anyone, and my mouth could hardly form the words to tell him. The muscles around my lower jaw were almost too stiff for me to speak.

"Why? When?"

Shaking my cigarette box to hear for any Marlboro Lights rolling between the foil lining, I looked at Joe. "I saw Mark on Labor Day weekend. It was the first time in two years that we had gone away together."

"I remember. You went to Nags Head, right?"

"Yeah. It seemed like a safe time and we hated using condoms, so we didn't then. Now, I am never unarmed." I asked the waiter for another pack of smokes, and slipped him five bucks plus the cost of the cigarettes. He wasted no time fulfilling my request. "By Columbus Day, I was a week late, and within a week of that, 2 EPTs, one First Response, and a ClearBlue Easy confirmed that I was pregnant."

"What did Mark say?"

"I didn't tell him."

"You what?!" Joe was beyond concerned. "Soph, that's not right."

"I tried. I really tried. I asked him one night on the phone about kids. He said that he couldn't consider such an idea right now even speaking hypothetically. Let's be honest, what would I tell the kid? 'Oh Sweetheart, Daddy loved the video of your soccer game, and he can't wait to see you, but he's bringing democracy to the whole of Ireland, and he'll call soon.'"

I wanted to cry, but I had spent too many months on my couch, talking to Mark even though he wasn't there. He had secrets that he kept from me for my protection. If I'd told him my secret, it would've brought the cause smack into my living room.

"You know what," I said, "I really wanted that baby. I'd even named it. I could feel it. I thought of raising it on my own, but I knew that Mark would not have let me, and I couldn't do that to him. Maybe I'm selfish, but if he and I ever have kids, I'd want for us to have spent some time together first. It was the wrong time."

"Aw geeze, Soph. You've always been so pro-life. I can't believe you faced that on your own."

"Joe, I'll say two things and then I'll stop. First, I am pro-life, but I thank God and the Supreme Court that I had an option. Maybe I did it for a poor reason and maybe that makes me pro-choice now. Second, I've never experienced a more intense physical or emotional pain, and I wouldn't wish it on my worst enemy. So, what's new with Suzanne?"

I tried to think of something else to talk about. I was hearing the sound of the nurse explaining everything to me back then, the sucking sound of the machine and feeling convinced that I would be turned inside out by the equipment. It was not an abortion. It was beyond punishment. It personified the Rah sucking the life out of me. I was convinced of it. Did every woman feel this way, or was I receiving care from an incompetent doctor? I had been sure that this was the way it always felt after I had spent two days at home recovering. On the first one, I prayed for death; anything to make the pain go away. Anyone who claims that it feels like really bad PMS cramps is either male or has never had PMS and wouldn't know a cramp if it walked up, introduced itself, and socked them in the gut. On the second day, I still hurt but felt slightly less dramatic than the day before.

Joe was becoming increasingly uneasy about our discussion, and asked me to stop. "Sophie, I am fearful for you, and I really don't want to know any more. I've always liked Mark, although I have believed that he doesn't treat you as well as he should. He's hardly ever there for you, and seeing each other once every 4 to 6 weeks does not, in my opinion, breed a healthy relationship. I really think, given all that you have said, that you should consider ending it with him." I almost flipped our table, but managed to remain calm. "I know that you are both crazy about each other, and that you've been friends for years, but come on. What does the guy have to offer you? Can he ever marry you? I know that's what you want. Can you ever have kids? Will he ever be around to make it a true partnership, or will you be left holding the bag in an empty house while he's off working through the night, staying in an undisclosed location?"

Joe had made a lot of good points. Many of which were issues that I had run through my own head, but to be honest, I didn't know if I wanted to get married. I know that I want to spend my life with Mark and that nothing would make me happier than to be 70 years old and living with him, sharing our lives. I don't want to date forever, but I would also be much happier to be with him as things are now than to lose our relationship. It's worth too much.

"You know," he said, holding his beer glass just a few inches from his mouth. He took a sip, and returned it to the table. "For all these months I've been on your case about 'the big picture.' Telling you that you worry about too many things and need to harness your concerns. You finally lay all these cards on the table, and I am trying to figure out how you kept your head screwed on straight. I'm almost sorry, like I should have realized that something much bigger was happening, and I missed it."

"You have no idea how happy I am to hear that. If I hadn't been able to keep this from the one person who knows me as well as you do, then I would have failed. This has almost eaten me alive on more than one occasion, but I never let it win. Tonight I feel as though I have defeated my enemy, and I have created my own little support group, per se."

Then, Joe dropped his trump card, and I felt that my best friend now was my worst nightmare. "Sophie, you have got to get out. Get out now. Mark will not leave them. He's in too deep and has been in too long. I don't care what he says. I want you to promise me that you will leave him."

"I can't do that."

"I'm telling you, I know it's hard, but it'll be the best thing for you in the long run." We sat in silence for a few seconds, both staring at the table or the ashtray, or anything other than each other. Then he took my hand in his and looked at me like a man who was about to propose marriage. Joe had never conveyed any type of interest in me, and I was a little frightened by his posture. "Sophie, I love you. I always have and you know that. I'm telling you for your own good. If you don't give up Mark, I will do everything I can to turn him in. I don't agree with his political leanings. He can blame the British government all he wants, but if his group disbanded, I don't believe that the issues he is railing against would continue. He's going to kill you if you continue to let him pull you into his lifestyle."

As Joe laid down his ultimatum, I felt a growing sense of betrayal. Joe was my oldest and closest friend. He was the older brother that I'd never had and always wanted. He was my hero and my perpetual head case. He always needed my help, and I always gave it, and now he was turning the tables.

"Okay," my eyes were swelling. I was almost talking into my beer glass. I couldn't look at him. "Okay. I'll do it. Just give me a little time."

Joe got our check, paid the bill and helped me put on my coat. We walked down the street along the windows of the dry cleaner, video store, and bike shop. He draped his arm over my shoulders and pulled me against him. He'd never displayed affection like this before. His hand was pressing against my upper arm so that I couldn't move very much. "Joe, loosen up a little," I whispered. I felt his other hand resting on top of the waistband of my jeans, and his finger holding one of my belt loops. I could feel his fingertips digging into my arm.

I couldn't think of anything other than what I had just done. Joe would not be silent. He would track me down, and if necessary, in his own twisted, seemingly protective way, he would fuck me over. I had opened the door to ruining my own life, but he was going to be the one to push me in and lock it behind me. He was holding me closer, leading me into an alley behind the dry cleaner. No dumpsters or empty boxes like you see in the movies. Just a stark alley, no lights, no obstacles. This was not a short-cut back to the car, and I noticed that Joe was breathing heavily. He stopped, turned me toward him and began railing into me about my indiscretions.

"What are you, stupid? You cannot see or talk to him ever again! I will not permit it." He was holding both of my arms, shaking me, yelling, but never raising his voice above a loud whisper. "Why did you do this? Why didn't you leave when he told you? It was so long ago. I could've taken care of you. I could've had you. We could have been happy. You've ruined everything." He pushed me against the back of the building, my head smacked the wall, as he pinned me into the concrete with his body. He held my face with one hand, gripping my chin, pressing his mouth over mine, and kissing me so hard that he bit my lower lip. Joe had never, in all the years I'd known him, ever had displayed an interest in me, and this behavior was no change in that line of thinking. This could not be happening.

I could hardly believe that this night was ending as it was, but I'd abandoned fear long ago. I was still thinking. Joe was going to betray me, betray Mark. I returned his kisses, slipping my tongue in his mouth with all I could possibly muster without throwing up all over him. I put my arms around him, but he responded by reaching inside my sweater, tearing my T-shirt from the neck to my left shoulder. He put his arm around me, pulled my shirt out of my jeans, and that's when he found it. My revolver, a Smith and Wesson Airweight .38 was in the back of my jeans. He felt it, but wasn't sure what it was at first. When I realized what he'd discovered, I tried to continue kissing him, but he removed it from the small of my back, took a few steps away from me, and pointed it at the ground.

"Soph, what is this? What are you doing with this thing?" If I'd known that the gun would have stopped him, I should've just handed it to him in the first place.

"I don't know." I shook my head, staring at the ground, then looking up at him. It was so dark that neither of us could see the other very well. He was little more than a black outline standing before me. I couldn't even see his mouth move as he spoke at me. I put my hands against the wall behind me, dropped my head and began to cry again, my back sliding against the wall as my knees hit the ground. "Joe, I'm losing my mind. I have no control anymore. Please help me. I don't know if I can leave him. Joey, how did this happen? How did I get here? Oh my God." I was sobbing, my hair hanging in my face. As Joe took a few steps closer to me, he extended his hand and helped me up. He held me in his arms. So close, so gentle. I thrust my left knee into Joe's groin, and watched him double over in agony. I hadn't kicked a guy like that since the third grade. He dropped the gun.

I picked it up without thinking, and pointed it at the black figure that was beginning to stand up and pulled the trigger. Joe hit the ground. I'd hit him in the gut, and he was still very much alive. Joe was threatening to ruin me, to ruin Mark, to ruin everything that I'd spent years to protecting. I could not let him destroy that. He could not demand that I do anything. My decisions are none of his business. I straddled myself over his body. His breathing was rapid. I looked down at him, aimed for his heart, and fired. Joe may have been my friend before the night began, but by the time it ended, he was my mortal enemy.

The police didn't question me in too much detail. Joe, I explained, was very upset about getting married because he had apparently concluded that I was the love of his life, and he had to have me at least once. His rationale was that if we had sex just once, he could decide whether or not he really loved me or if I was some fantasy he could not release. I told them that I had given in to him long enough for him to relax a little then I took the gun from him and shot him in self-defense. The bruises and scratches that he had inflicted in his twisted display of passion, and the cut on the back of my head were testaments to my story's validity. After a night in jail, and some investigation, they released me on bail until a hearing was set to determine if I should be charged with manslaughter. No charges were filed.

I gave Mark the same story that I'd given the police. There was no need to give him more information than necessary. Joe had attacked. He had wedding jitters. I just didn't tell him why Joe got so upset. What would that have helped?

      *   *   *   *

"Oh my God, Eileen, it's amazing! I want to read the whole thing." This was a serious compliment. Janet rarely read anything more than a book excerpt in *Cosmopolitan*.

Janet stopped reading and looked at Eileen. "This is unbeliev-able. Eileen, I'm so impressed. So, how did Sophie and Mark meet? Is it in here? I'm dying to know." Janet was now nursing her wine, which for those who knew Janet, were acutely aware that such a lack of attention to a good cabernet, especially a Silverado Reserve, never happened.

2

Shortly before her book went to press, two agents from the FBI's Boston office came to Eileen's house on a cold, cloudy March morning. No trench coats, no dark glasses. They'd called her the day before and scheduled their appointment. She prepared for the meeting by stopping in at Haute Coiffure, her salon on Newbury Street to touch up her recent hair color. She was still a red head. She'd had the color when the picture for the book jacket was taken and figured that for the tour she had better be recognizable. If people were going to pay $22.95 to read her fluff, the least she could do was look like the chick on the back of the book jacket.

"Good morning, gentlemen. Won't you please come in." She took their coats, and showed them into the living room where a tray of coffee and pastries were already placed on the coffee table next to a copy of her book.

"Ms. Eliot," Agent Lloyd began. "It is a policy of the Bureau that we interview any individual who writes any type of material containing seemingly classified or sensitive information about counter-political organizations. Because of the subject matter of your novel, we are required to discuss with you your reasoning behind selecting this topic, and how you acquired your information."

As he spoke, the front door opened and Jack let himself into the foyer. As she walked across the room to greet him, Eileen felt intensely gratified that the FBI would feel the need to interview her. What a hoot. She introduced Jack to Agent Lloyd and his rookie assistant. "Gentlemen, after I spoke with you yesterday and scheduled this meeting, I was unsure of the purpose of your visit and requested that Mr. Marston, my good friend and attorney, sit in on our conversation if you have no objections."

Jack had warned Eileen that there was a high probability that the FBI would pay her a friendly visit before the book went to press. "It's no big deal," he said, "But you might want me to stick by just in case they've changed their tactics. Eileen, I have to say, you've got some pretty timely stuff in that little story of yours. I don't know where you found all those details, but I hope you did it legally."

"Oh Jack," she'd said to him, "Yee have so little faith."

She returned to the couch and picked up her coffee cup, as Agent Lloyd continued. "Ms. Eliot, as I said, I was wondering if you might tell me what gave you the idea to write this novel?"

"Well Agent, Lloyd is it?"

"Yes."

"Well, Agent Lloyd, I can tell you that the topic of Irish politics and the behaviors of the British government in Northern Ireland have been a personal interest for many years. When I chose to write a book, I wrote about what I cared for. You see, I come from a family that prides itself on information. I thrive on news and details, don't I Jack," she giggled as she turned to face him.

"To say the least," he mumbled.

"If you are asking me if I socialize with what some people refer to as terrorists, I can assure you that you could not be farther from reality. In truth, I developed an interest in this subject matter as a child. As I grew older and the situations evolved from progression to digression and, oh who knows where it is now, I began to consider some of the sociological sides to this intensely personal problem. As Americans, we cannot truly enjoy the kind of familiarity required to understand the issues at hand, but whether in the U.S. or abroad, there are those individuals who hold concern for the Troubles, are personally affected, yet who also are removed from the immediate activities." Her voice had taken on the inflection of a college professor as she continued. "As I am sure you are well-aware, most people think of the typical 'terrorist' as a relatively young man. To write about such an individual would have been run-of-the-mill. I wanted a different perspective, without the smash 'em up approach of so many spy novels. I simply do not think in that context. When I decided to devise this story, I wanted to take a woman's perspective and combine the thrill of passion with the roller coaster of political intrigue.

"There must be so many people who feel displaced in this most unfortunate and devastating issue. I suppose I wanted to bring them to the forefront for a little while." She sipped her coffee and held it in her hand just over her knee, and looked him square in the face as she concluded her soliloquy.

"Yes, but Ms. Eliot, many of the items in this book were highly confidential and not of public knowledge. To this day, they are not publicly known. You may have written a fictitious novel, but you also managed to include in your dialogue many surprisingly accurate comments and details."

"Agent Lloyd, please take a look at my bookcase." She got up and walked to the other side of the room where she ran her hand along the jackets of one shelf of books in her recessed cases. "These books are all on the same topic, spanning years of coverage." She stopped at Schelling's *The Strategy of Conflict*, J. Bowyer Bell's *The Troubles*, Tim Pat Coogan's *The I.R.A.: A*

History, not to mention numerous books of Irish poetry and literature. Among over 300 books on her shelves, Eileen had at least forty on Irish history and politics that she'd ordered from Kenny's Bookshop in Galway, Ireland. "Finally, Agent Lloyd, I wonder if you and your colleague would be so kind as to join me at my computer?" They followed her to her desk, and stood just over her shoulder as she sat down and powered-up her PC. While it was starting, she noted, "I don't know how to tell you this, but many of the details I obtained are from various Internet resources, including the libraries of the White House, State Department and your own Bureau." The PC was up and running and she was on-line entering a variety of Internet addresses to illuminate their somewhat dim familiarity with on-line information gathering.

"You see, these are not easy addresses to access, but if you have the patience and the know-how, virtually any search engine on the net will provide the correct address to offer whatever information a person may require. In addition," she clicked to her e-mailbox, "I am a subscriber of numerous mailing lists, both political and trivial. As I said, I thrive on news, and therefore I have signed on to some of the most obscure publications." Scrolling through her list of mail, it was clear that she received transmissions from An Phlobacht/Republican News, the Irish Republican Information Service, Sinn Fein, the SDLP, and even the UVF's home page just to be fair. Her lists also included every major newspaper from the UK and the Republic of Ireland. Her crowning glories were the direct access into the libraries of the National Security Advisor and the State Department.

"I acquired these addresses from basic Internet search programs. It seems to me Sir, that if any breech of information occurred, it was only of the fact that perhaps proper security was not instituted when certain systems were developed."

Lloyd stood perplexed, sipping his coffee as he thought of an appropriate response. She was right. She'd done nothing wrong. As sensitive as the issues were, her information was completely legitimate. "Ms. Eliot, it is clear that there is no cause for concern here. We merely are required to contact you, as I indicated earlier." Lloyd continued with his diatribe about policy, etc., all the while thinking of how excited his Director will be to find that the average American legally can scan the files of the National Security Advisor. "By the way," he asked, "Would you mind telling me just what are your leanings in this debate? I too have pondered the topic."

Liar, she thought. "Mr. Lloyd, I have learned never to discuss two things, religion and politics. I am not about to delve into an issue addressing both taboo topics. Besides, I think my opinions should be rather simple to assess." If not, she thought, you are in the wrong career.

Eileen noted how nice it had been to meet them, and showed them both to the door. Pulling their umbrellas from the rack just inside the foyer, they thanked her for her time, descended the stairs to the street level and walked off in the direction of Cambridge Street, back toward the T Station.

"Well, that was quite an interesting exchange," Jack chuckled as he headed back to the living room and lit a cigarette.

Eileen locked the front door and crossed the foyer, "Yes, well, thank goodness you were here, otherwise I'm sure I would've put my foot in it."

"In what way?" He leaned forward on the couch toward the crystal ashtray he'd picked up for her on his last trip to Switzerland, and flicked the tip of his Benson&Hedges into the bowl. Benson&Hedges. Eileen hated that one feature about him. Why did such a powerful, extroverted, well-regarded man smoke such a pansy brand of cigarettes? The men Eileen went for were always Marlboro, Marlboro Light or Camel smokers. Perhaps it wouldn't have been such a mark against Jack's quality if Husband #2 hadn't also enjoyed the same brand. Sure, that jerk had smoked the Deluxe Ultra Lights Menthols, but in her mind, a B&H was a B&H.

"Oh, you know," she poured another cup of coffee and replaced the china pot on the silver tray, "Situations like that always tend to make me feel cornered and the likelihood is too great that I will recoil and fire back with some flippant remark. Honestly, can you believe that that Junior Birdman had the audacity to ask me about my political leanings! Is that legal?"

"Considering the circumstances, probably not, but I think he liked you and was trying to make small talk. Believe me, if he'd pushed, I would have pushed back."

"Fuck that."

"Hey," Jack walked toward Eileen. He took her coffee cup from her hand and put it on the mantle behind her. "What's all this," he asked putting his hands on her shoulders, "There's no need to get bitter. You just had to jump through a bureaucratic hoop. It's over and done with. No big deal. Unless," he raised his eyebrows and said sarcastically, "You have something to hide."

"Oh Jack, don't be silly. I'm sorry. I'm just in a mood. After all, it's not everyday that the Feds come to your door and ask to see your records." She picked the cigarettes up off the table. "Can I have one of these?"

"Sure. But I know you hate those kind."

"I don't care. I'm out, and this coffee is sparking my addiction, so to speak."

"Listen Dear, I need to get moving. I have a meeting with a client whose trying to prove that his used car business isn't turning back the odometers on his inventory."

"Is he?"

"A lawyer never tells, but I have to say that there seem to be more little old ladies driving their BMW 750s to churches all around Newton and Wellesley than there are little old ladies in Fort Lauderdale."

"Lovely."

Jack pulled his overcoat from the closet and picked up his brief-case. "Okay Sweetie, I'll talk to you tomorrow."

"Thanks Jack. Good luck with Mr. Turn-Back-the-Clock." She closed the door behind him then walked up the stairs to her bed-room and opened the antique trunk against the far wall. The trunk held a chronology of every major event in her life since she was four years old. Eileen opened it only when she was in an exceptionally good mood or feeling completely alone. On top of the piles of papers and mementos sat a photo of her at 20, with medium length natural brown hair and an enormous smile, wear-ing a thick sweater and leaning against a young man close to her age. Even so many years later, his blue eyes still spoke to her. The expression on the student's face showed no signs of anything other than his thrill at being able to hold her in his arms. They were in the Nineteen O'Connell Pub in Dublin in December 1986. "Frannie, my sweet Frannie. I still miss you so much." Eileen held the picture against her chest, then looked at it again. "What have I done? What will this mean? Oh Frannie, Frannie, have I made a mistake? I need you. I can't keep doing this by myself." She moved to the desk by the bay window, placed the photo in front of her and put her face in her hands with her elbows resting on the table.

3
July 1986

She met him by accident; roped into another family dinner of the $13.95 blue plate special, cheesecake and coffee. It was the first summer that she ordered coffee in restaurants. It had become a new staple in her diet thanks to college exam weeks and a job working too many double shifts waiting tables. Despite the fact that it was 80 degrees she wore her khaki shorts, a blue T-shirt and her denim jacket with a pack of Virginia Slims in her inside jacket pocket. She only smoked them when her parents wouldn't catch her.

After finishing her coffee served in a styrofoam cup, and her father paid the bill, her younger brothers, much younger than she, wanted to play miniature golf at the course adjacent to the restaurant. It was tradition. This was their ninth summer in Eastham. They had dinner at Martin's Lobster Bar at least once a week during each season, and the kiddies always played mini-golf. After dinner the previous week, her father had met a kid named Mullen. He was a biology student from Cork, Ireland, and since her father was a physician, he found Mullen to be a very nice fellow. She had spoken briefly with him and figured she'd talk with him a little more while the kids battled spinning windmills on the course. This night presented her with something altogether different.

He stood behind the counter, inside the mini-golf hut, five foot six, charismatic, smart, thick brown hair, and terrific eyes. She wasn't sure what color they were. It was a little too dark to tell. Her cousin was with her, so the three of them talked throughout the kids' eighteen-hole bonanza.

"Hi, I'm Eileen," she said. "This is my cousin, Sarah."

"Francis," he responded.

They shook hands even though the introductions came 15 minutes into the conversation, Eileen suddenly felt as though she were in a movie. After all, didn't all women always introduce themselves after the quaint discussion, then act aloof and uninterested? She also felt sure that Sarah was more interesting, so and thought it better to let her cousin claim the prize and not feel the let down.

Sarah and Francis chatted about the party he and his housemates had thrown the previous weekend. They were the same age and had more experience with throwing bashes. Eileen's background was limited to fraternity parties on a small Washington, DC campus. It was an environment where the object of the game was to go to a frat house, drink all you could, and stumble home…alone. She almost chimed that she was known for winding up in the dorm bathroom at 3AM every Saturday night, getting sick, swearing that she'd never drink again, but decided that it was more than she wished to reveal. Francis said that they would be having another party the upcoming weekend and that Eileen and Sarah should attend.

"I'm leaving Saturday morning," Sarah said.

"Eileen, come on over."

"Oh, I don't know. Maybe." Go alone to a party, she thought. You must be joking. She did not yet have enough self-confidence to tackle such a challenge.

Sunday morning, after Sarah left, Eileen went to church with her family. She noticed Francis in the back of the church with another guy, then stopped after mass to talk with him as he was getting on his bike. She had to giggle to herself. She thought of that saying, "on your bike," and felt as though she were the goofy one who should be rolling out on her proverbial two-wheeler.

"So, how was the party," she asked.

They talked for a few more minutes. He told her that he was working at the mini-golf that night and she said that she might stop around. It became a nightly habit when after his shifts, they'd lock up the mini-golf hut together and she'd toss his bike in the back of her father's 1982 Buick Century sedan. Some nights they sat outside the post office, under the street light in the corner of the parking lot debating the differences between the US and Ireland, or swapping stories about their friends or concerts they'd been to and which band was better. Other nights, they drove to the harbor and hung their legs over the pier and talked some more. On their second night at the harbor she was laying with her head in his lap and her hand on his thigh. He stroked her hair as he spoke. "One of these days, I'm going to build a monument in your honor, right here."

Eileen sat up and laughed, "You are ridiculous."

Fran put his hand behind her head and leaned in to her, kissing her cheek, then moving his mouth to hers. They stayed there for another hour and a half, talking and kissing. She didn't know that she was only the second girl he'd ever kissed, and he didn't know that she had a semi-serious boyfriend back at school.

On the last night before her family was closing up the house for the season, Eileen found her courage to go to a party at Frannie's house. Frannie made her stomach jump and dominated her thoughts. She wasn't feeling the kind of anxiety that often came with new boyfriends. This was an entirely different anxiety, the kind when you realize that someone else knows you to your core, where if you didn't trust him, he could shred you.

They disappeared from the party, up to his room in the back corner. Yelling and laughing from the party downstairs came up through the floorboards. They lay on his bed and talked for a few minutes until the point of grace of decorum had passed and neither could wait any longer. Fran's tongue filled her mouth, she sucked on his lips as he pulled her shirt out from inside her jeans. Eileen lifted his T-shirt over his head. He unhooked her bra and placed both hands on her breasts. Fran slid down her stomach and Eileen felt a gnawing of sorts on her pants. "Francis, what are you doing?"

He looked up at her, "Nothing."

She looked down into his eyes, then at the tops of her jeans. Her belt was undone. She laughed quietly, then said in a stern but comical manner, "Francis Sullivan are you telling me that you opened my pants with your teeth?"

He put on his 'I'm just a shy little Irishman in a foreign land' look and said, "Kinda."

"Would you mind if we held off on that?"

"Sure, no matter." He moved back up to her face, put his arm under her neck, pressed his body against hers, and whispered in her ear, "Come 'ere to me." They lay on the bed in silence running their hands over each other's bodies and listened to the police officer downstairs breaking up the party.

Eileen stayed until the sun rose, though neither of them slept all night. They stood in the driveway looking at each other, trying to figure out how to keep the end from happening. "So, when are you leaving," she asked even though she knew the answer.

"A month. My classes start in the beginning of October."

"Oh, right. I go back to school in two weeks."

"Give me your address."

They swapped address and phone information, then he put his arms around her. "Eliot, I'm gonna miss you."

"I know," she was starting to cry, "I'm going to miss you too." She stood back from him, wiped her eyes and laughed, "Man, this really sucks."

"I'll talk to you soon. Be well. God, I hate this." He kissed her.

"Oh Sully, don't you worry, I'll see you again." Eileen nodded her head and gave him a very coy look. She kissed him back.

"Okay, you'd better go. You'll be late." Eileen got in her car and drove up the driveway back to her parents' house. On the family's drive back to Boston, she lay in the back of her mother's station wagon, half-sleeping from exhaustion and half sick from missing him.

4
August 1986

The school year began in its usual mayhem of moving into a new dorm room, and reuniting with friends. Eileen's boyfriend Steven was relieved to see her back at school, and to have her all to himself again. The summer apart had bothered him, and he'd made a deal with himself that he never would let her out of his sight again. Steven and Eileen began dating during their first year of college. The chemistry of freshman year love coupled with freshman hormones launched them into a seven-semester involvement that probably should have been put down long before they'd each chosen their majors. In late September, Eileen decided to go to New York City to spend Fran's last weekend in the US with him. They had been talking about it for weeks and exchanged numerous letters detailing the hotel plans and meeting times. Steven was livid when Eileen announced that she'd be away for the weekend. "Eileen, why didn't you tell me? Who are you going with?"

"Friends. It's all of my friends who I met over the summer. They are all leaving to go back to school, so we're having a reunion this weekend, just before they fly home."

"So, you're going to spend a weekend in a hotel with guys?"

"And girls," she responded. "We're only getting two rooms. There are nine of us. And please, you were all I talked about to them over the summer, so I'm sure I'll be getting the third degree on how the beginning of the school year has been for us." She smiled at him and tugged on his T-shirt.

"Do you want me to go with you? I'd feel better."

"No. I don't think so. Really, they're friends, and you don't know any of them, and I know how uncomfortable you get when you don't know anyone. It's only for two nights, and I'd really like to enjoy myself with my friends. It's no big deal. Besides, I'll be spending half of my time consoling Debbie as she counts down the hours to Michael's departure."

"So there ARE couples."

"Oh for crying out loud! Steven, if you must know, there is one. One couple. One couple out of the entire group will be in New York. Is that okay with you or should I call Deb and ask her to keep her hands off Mike because it would make YOU feel better? Honestly Steven, you are beginning to irritate me." Eileen was standing in the corner of her room, leaning against her desk, where pictures of Fran were hidden in the back of her top drawer in an envelope marked "Cable TV Bills."

"I'm sorry. I just love you, and I want you all to myself; and okay, I'm jealous." Steven had an uncanny ability to play the martyr when necessary. What other man would utter the words, "sorry" and "jealous" in the same breath and keep a straight face? He hugged her and gave her a kiss before they left for the grocery store.

Three days later, Eileen was on a bus to New York City to meet Fran. He'd spoken to her the night before from Eastham and would be arriving in the City about two hours before her. The rest of the housemates had decided to stay in Boston with the girls, at their dorms. All four of them went to Northeastern University. Eileen had no idea how many times this weekend would resurface in her mind and just how much it would change her life.

In the non-descript Hilton hotel room, after they'd spent the day seeing the sights and sat on the floor of Grand Central Station eating pizza and people-watching, Francis stood in the dark as she sat on the bed. The words came out, one by one, each one separated by hesitation. He wasn't sure why he was telling her. It had been eating him alive, and he was afraid to go home. He trusted her. He had his hand on the back of the chair in the corner of the room. He was holding a glass of Jameson and couldn't look at her.

"Fran, what is it? Fran, what are you trying to tell me?"

"I, I'm in the I-R-A." He waited, silent, afraid to see her reaction. Eileen didn't tell him what she thought then; she was afraid it would sound naive or overly supportive. She'd seen stories about the group on the news, but to her, it was just the name of an organization. She had nothing to compare it to.

"Why? How? I'm confused."

"It started when I was 15. I wasn't leading the most reputable life—and well, I got noticed."

"What do you do?"

"I can't say. I'm sorry, but I really can't tell you. I've already broken the oath. I could be killed for this." He walked across the room, then over to her.

"Sit down." She put her hand down on the bed just to her left.

"Really?"

"Yes," she said. "Sit down and talk to me." She didn't smile. She didn't know what to do. Fran sat down next to her and continued to speak. He had his right elbow on his knee and his forehead resting on his hand.

Looking down at the carpet, he continued. "Ya wanna know something really fucked up about this? A priest gave me the oath. A priest, can you believe that?"

"Frannie, there has to be something you can do about this. Look at you, you're a wreck. I'm afraid for you. I don't understand this, but I can see that it's ripping you up. Christ Francis, I have never seen you in a state like this."

"Shit. Leen, you wouldn't believe the things I've seen. The things I've done. God. How could I do it?" He got up from the bed, lit a cigarette and poured another glass of whiskey. "They suck ya in, and they tell ya how much everythin' needs to change. Each time they tell you a little bit more. They tell you what you want to hear, and convince you that unless you become a part of it and work for change, everything will get worse." Eileen listened to horrible tales. Night after night, they'd taken Fran to places like that so he could see how bad it was. He had to be shown the seriousness of the problem. They showed him what happened to British sympathizers. There'd been a man who'd been known to talk to an RUC officer, the Royal Ulster Constabulary. Local police force in the North," he explained. Fran stood by, 16 years old, watching them beat him for his betrayal. "Leen, I handed them the fucking hammer. I stood there watching, listening to the screams."

"Oh my God." Eileen was frightened, but not of Fran. Her stomach felt emptier, and she felt the bile mixing with the tobacco she'd been inhaling. "Does your family know?"

He was astounded by that thought. "God no. It'd kill my mother. No one knows. You're the only one, and I never should have told you."

"Then, why did you?"

"I don't know. He sounded like he was going to cry, but instead his voice was halting out of panic. "I like school. I want to go back to my classes, but I don't want to go back to that. I'm scared."

They talked until 3AM then got into bed. Eileen was already under the covers when Fran asked, "Is it okay if I take my pants off tonight?" The night before, he'd slept next to her, in his jeans. Eileen had never asked him why he was doing it.

"Yeah. No problem."

He got under the covers and lay on his back facing the ceiling. A few minutes passed before he asked, "You okay?"

Eileen rolled over on her side and faced him. "I'm fine. I just, I don't know what to say. I mean, you're in this horrible situation, you've done some horrible things, but it's also so hard for me to understand. I see you in so much pain. Fran, this is about the last thing I would've expected to hear from anyone. This isn't you. I mean, I know you. You're a good person. I trust you. I care about you, and now I find that this has been going on. The two sides don't mesh. I want to help you, but I don't know how."

"You can't. There's nothing you can do, but I am going to figure something out. You're too good for me, and I'm not going to be that kind of person anymore. You shouldn't be with someone like that." He was still looking at the ceiling.

"Come here to me." She reached for his hand and Francis moved toward her where she held his head against her collarbone and put an arm around him.

They left the hotel the following morning. Eileen took the bus back to school, and Fran headed north to meet with rest of his classmates for their flight back to Dublin. It was two years before anything about their discussion of the night before was mentioned again. They continued to exchange letters and phone calls and Eileen went to Ireland for Christmas two months later. The following summer, she rented the house Fran had been in, and he returned shortly after she moved in. She was 20, and the photo of the two of them from the night in Dublin sat in a frame on a milk crate in the living room that served as an end table. By his letters, Eileen could tell that Fran was tortured by his decision. He wanted to get out, but his words on paper contained continuous references to the opinions that either he had formed or someone else had formed for him.

17 Sept. 86

"All I know is that you have given me extreme happiness, and anytime I am with you I have no worries, I feel relaxed, so happy just to be with you and am confident in what I say because I know you know me and I feel as if I can trust you with my life and tell you anything. I even feel better about my Boston ties and am ultimately determined to totally get away from that.

14 Oct. 86

"...There is a postal strike. God knows when I can post this. If there is a letter from you in that post office just lying there then I am going to kneecap the postman, or even worse, let my dog deal with him.

I miss you like hell.

I love you.

Yours, Frannie"

November 1986

But seriously dearest, I miss you a hell of a lot and I can't imagine the scene waiting for you at the airport. I'll be so nervous the security men will think that I've just planted a bomb."

21 January 1987

"I just thought I'd take a break from studying to tell you that I MISS YOU-I want you here, and that I'm still in love with you. Believe me, it's fucking amazing how I can love anybody or anything after studying macro-economics..."

I love you

Francis

5 February 1987

"*I'm somewhat buzzed—I've had a few drinks. The cross border bandits ride again. It was a hell of a laugh. Being true alcoholics, we couldn't leave the land that is rightfully ours without any of the cheap beer. Lashed down two cases on the way home. When we hit the south, Billy, the bold fucker, gets the idea to horse a can every mile. He nearly drowned. He says that I'm totally better off out of it until I want to go back because it takes total commitment.*"

Feb. 14, 1987

Telegram

LOVE YOU

ALL YOURS

FRANNIE

3 March 1987

"*You said once that you didn't think that you helped me with the old problem, but believe me, you did, and you still are. Now I have something to believe in. Even if everything falls apart—God forbid—the thoughts and feelings for you remain. Sometimes the thought occurs, why don't I just go back, Christ I loved it so much. But then again you say that you saw something different in me, I don't know. No matter because pretty soon I have the best chance of getting out totally for good.*

I miss you Eileen, something bad. Believe me that I really do love you."

He'd wanted to get out but his words on paper contained continuous references to the opinions that either he had formed on his own, or had been instilled for him. Within a year, too many of the stories he'd told in his letters didn't fit together, except for his one about being picked in the lottery for a green card. The day the approval came, Fran phoned Eileen at her room in the sorority house. She'd just gotten through another round with Steven.

Steven, at first, was a sweet, quiet boy. Eileen had liked his reserved nature, the way his tall frame seemed to envelop her; and thought of him as almost a strong presence she could rely on. As the months passed, his confidence grew from knocking down Eileen's. To him, everything she did was wrong. She ate the wrong foods, wore the wrong clothes, talked to the wrong people and thought stupid things. Eileen was led by her guilt. Steven had been so kind in the beginning, and she had rewarded him by sitting up until the middle of the night crafting love letters to another man. She could not let go of Fran and knew that if she were going to keep Steven happy, she would have to put up with his moods.

The night before Parents' Weekend in October 1987, Eileen went to Steve's room to get some of the books she'd left there. They hadn't been speaking for the last two days, but that was typical. By Sunday, Steven would be pledging undying love for her. Eileen knocked on the door and walked in when she heard his roommate Jason yell, "Enter."

"Hey Jason."

"Hi Leen. Steven's not here."

"That's fine. I just need the books I left over here the other day."

"Oh, help yourself." Jason never went out on weekends before 11:30. He didn't think the parties were worth checking out until they'd been going on for a few hours.

Eileen was standing in the doorway preparing to leave when she saw Steven, in his boxer shorts and a sweatshirt sneaking back up the stairs outside their room. "See ya, Jason." She turned and went up the stairs to the landing above. There were only four rooms above, and she could hear his voice through the door to her left. It wasn't quite closed, so she knocked just hard enough to push it further open. Steven sat on the couch, in his underwear with Jill Schwartz's head leaning against his shoulder. She was in a T-shirt and boxers. Steven looked at Eileen and yelled, "What do you want?" She turned and went down the stairs toward the door six flights below. Steven followed her, grabbing her arm and stopping her on the landing outside his room. "What is the problem?"

"Just stay away from me," she said.

"Eileen, I wasn't doing anything."

"Please."

"I wasn't. I've been talking to her because I'm so upset about you and me."

"Steven, I've had it. Stay away from me. We're done." Eileen felt her strength draining to her toes, but kept going.

"You can't be serious. I know about you and your little Irish friend. So don't even try to make me out to be the bad guy."

"Spare me. First of all, my little Irish friend as you put it, is a friend," she knew she was lying. "I am not lying in my underwear on his couch, am I? No, as a matter of fact he's 3,000 miles away from here, and no threat to you except that maybe he's a little smarter and a whole lot nicer than you. He's NORMAL, STEVEN!" At that, he pushed her against the wall, and pinned her into the corner near the door.

"You are a pathetic, little waste of space. I've tried to help you straighten yourself out, but you just don't listen. I've tried to be patient, but you just don't listen TO ME!" He held her chin with his right hand and stared into her eyes, "We are finished Eliot. I'm done with you. You sorry, pathetic, little slut." He stood back from her and told her to leave.

"Do not ever speak to me again," she was picking up her books that had fallen on the floor in corner, not looking up at him.

Steven pushed his foot into her shoulder and knocked her onto the tile floor, "I'll speak to you however and whenever I want," and closed himself in his dorm room.

The following morning, he appeared at her door with a bouquet of flowers. "I'm sorry. Eileen, I'm so sorry." He was tearful, but not crying.

"Come in." Her roommate Robin was sleeping at her boyfriend's.

"These are for you." He handed her the flowers, and she lay them on her desk. "Please, talk to me. We need to talk."

"Fine. Talk."

Steven told her that he couldn't bear the thought of losing her and that she was all he wanted. "I keep having this fear that you're going to leave me, and it's making me crazy."

They talked for an hour, and Steven agreed to put more trust in her. He also promised to stop visiting the neighbors in his underwear. Eileen told him that if he ever laid a hand on her again, there would be no future to their relationship. She felt that she'd pushed him too far. By her letters, she was more in love with Fran than she could begin to say. She never again mentioned his name.

Steven and Eileen fell easily back into the role of the perfect couple as long as he always knew where she was. He met her for lunch and dinner every day, telling her what to eat, not to use salt, and calling her "fats" if she went for seconds of anything, including broccoli.

A month later, Eileen's sorority co-hosted a party with the Phi Zeta fraternity welcoming each of their pledge classes to Greek life. Michael Davis, pledge master for the Zetas hooked up the taps in the frat house, rolling kegs of Natural Light under the bar. Eileen carried bags of chips to the kitchen and stacked the CDs next to the sound system on the stage. "Thirty-seven pledges. You guys did pretty well this rush season."

"Yeah," Michael answered from underneath the bar. His head reappeared but only just above the edge of the wood. "We planned on thirty-five, but two of the guys are really cool and they should be good additions. Besides, you have to count on one guy in the class to drop out. Someone always falls under the agony of pledging." He smiled at her.

"Well, beat your boys into the ground if you want, but we don't believe in doing that to our girls. I don't understand you guys. I've never been able to understand the idea of insulting and abusing guys for twelve weeks, then saying, 'Okay, we're brothers now. Let's be best friends.'"

"It's not like that."

"Well then, what's it like?"

"The taps are hooked up. You want a beer?" Michael grabbed for two plastic cups.

"Sure." He handed her a beer, sat down on the stage and tried to explain to her the rites of passage into fraternity life. The pledges arrived an hour later in their matching t-shirts, escorted by the sisters and brothers from the two houses. It was a private party. Steven avoided Greek life on campus, except for the free beer at the open parties. By 10:30, the basement floor of the Phi Zeta house was covered in spilled beer, and the third keg had been tapped. Eileen danced with her pledges, watching 28 19-year-old girls feel special and elite, being in the presence of the fraternity and sorority brothers and sisters who for the next three years would be their links to belonging to a fold; being popular. The crowd dwindled after midnight. Some passed out in the bathroom. One senior year Zeta slept on top of the pool table. Most staggered back to their dorms carrying plastic cups full of Natural Light that they would find on their desks in the morning, trying to remember where the beer came from.

Michael and Eileen stood in the kitchen where 30 empty bags of chips and 10 quart-containers of dip littered the countertops. "Well," she slurred, "I think the evening has been a success."

"I would say so too." Her glassy eyes looked up at him. Mike put an arm around her and kissed her. Slow at first, then he shoved his tongue in her mouth.

"Wait. Wait." Eileen backed away a few inches from his face, and put her hand to her forehead.

"Come on. It's just a little kiss for a job well done." Mike pulled her against him again.

"Well, okay, I suppose. But, just a kiss." Eileen returned his sloppy kiss and slid down against the cabinets on the floor with him. Michael put his hand up the back of her shirt and tried to slide it around to her breasts. "Hey. Stop. Come on. That's enough," she murmured through the kiss. Michael took his hand out of her shirt and kept kissing her. He turned her body away from the cabinets and pushed her down to the floor, still kissing her, biting her lip. His torso pressed into hers, and he moved his hands down to her jeans, undoing her belt.

Eileen squirmed underneath him, half-conscious. "Michael, no. This isn't right. We shouldn't do this."

"Shhhh. Come on. I like you Eileen. We should do it. We need to do it. I want you." He lay on top her and pushed her jeans down to her ankles. Eileen squirmed under him, yelling at him to stop. He opened his pants, and pulled himself out of his zipper, not bothering to take his pants down. Eileen looked up at the ceiling, begging him to get off of her, trying to push him off of her. She felt his hand slip between her legs and he bent her knees enough to allow him room to push himself into her.

"Stop it!"

The music blared through the floor from the basement. Muffled voices yelling along the staircase blended with the rhythm drowning out her words. Michael thrust into her then rocked on top of her for a minute. His speed increased until he was banging into her so hard that her right shoulder caught under the cabinet and the baseboard. He came inside her, saying, "Yeah baby, that's it," arching his back a little and moaning toward the ceiling. His face contorted, and when he was done, he didn't look at her. He backed off of her, closed his jeans and stood up. "Let's go get a beer."

"Get out," she replied. Michael left her on the floor. Eileen pulled up her jeans and walked from the party back to her sorority house. Two of her pledges were ahead of her yelling to each other in drunk-speak about how cool the guys were, and how "Michael Davis is soooo cute. Do you think he has a girlfriend?"

Eileen unlocked her bedroom door. Robin was gone again. Eileen took off her clothes and threw her jeans into the trash. She staggered to the bathroom and sat on the toilet. Her hand gripped the windowsill as she forced Michael's semen out of her body. She washed her face and looked horrified at the suck mark he'd left on her neck. Fran had given her one once by accident, but then it was a "luv bite," he called it with his accent. She'd laughed about it with him, and he'd promised to never do it again.

The light blinked on her answering machine. She pressed the play button and fell onto her bed drifting into a restless, inebriated sleep. Steven's voice played twice. One telling her which frat house he and Jason would be at that night and the second asking her to call him when she got in. She didn't bother to call him back. Fran's voice followed. "Hi Babe. It's nearly daylight here. Just wanted to ring and say that I'm thinking of you." Eileen clutched her pillow, begging to be anywhere else but on campus.

She cut her classes and avoided Steven for four days, unable to tell him what had happened. Wednesday afternoon, he stopped her on the walk to the business school. He asked if something was wrong. Eileen couldn't focus on his face. Instead, she looked toward the ground. Steven became angry, finishing the conversation with, "Fine. Behave however you want, but don't plan on talking to me later."

"Please, Steve, I need to talk to you. But not now."

"Why not?"

"We have class."

"So. We can cut it. What's the matter? Is your other boyfriend coming to visit?"

"I don't have another boyfriend."

"Sure you do," his eyes were empty. "Your Irish fried, remember?"

"Let's go." She turned to head back toward his room.

Steven sat in his desk chair and watched a re-run of *Hogan's Heroes*, not looking at her as she told him about Michael, and showed him the cuts on her shoulder from the cabinet. When she finished crying through her story about what happened on the floor of Phi Zeta kitchen, Steven never bothered to look at Eileen. He simply said, "Leave."

"What?"

"You are pathetic. You go out and get drunk and screw some guy and then tell me you didn't want it. Leave." Eileen continued to cry, begging him to believe her, but he never looked at her. "Go tell your other boyfriend. I don't want to hear your excuses."

Steven called her two hours later, telling her what a loser he was, asking her if she was all right and could he come talk to her. He brought her two burritos and a Diet Coke from Taco Bell as a peace offering.

Eileen re-played the rape over and over in her mind, trying to remind herself that she had said, "No," and that she hadn't wanted it. On her first visit to the campus psychologist, when Dr. Nelson asked, "Did you say 'No'," she hesitated for a minute, listening for her voice on the floor to make sure that she had. She had no trouble recalling the feel of the corner of the cabinet bearing into her shoulder, or the sound of Michael's breathing over her face as he did it to her. Remembering her own voice was the hardest part.

For the next year and a half Steven never hesitated to cut her with questions like, "How's your third boyfriend," or, "Why don't you have a drink and go see Mr. Davis?" Eileen never included anything about Michael in her letters to Fran. She was afraid he'd have him killed. She hated Michael, but murder was not the answer.

5
July 1988

Frannie's letters kept coming, keeping Eileen's lifeline open. They'd planned their second summer together, and Eileen had booked the Cape house by the beginning of February. She did not care what Steven thought. She wanted her life. She wanted her happiness, and Steven would be working all summer. To him, working was everything. He wanted the cash to be able to buy expensive stereo equipment and clothes. During their previous vacations, Eileen always had been the one to drive to his parents' home in Delaware for visits. She would arrive late at night in time to meet him at the end of his shift of whatever job he held on any given break. Eileen knew there was no risk that he would try to come to Eastham. Frannie's school year ended later than hers and he would not be able to join her before July. By then, Steven would be counting down the weeks until school was to start and amassing every last penny he could.

Eileen told Steven that she was renting the house with friends, which she was. She was rejoining the girls from her holiday in Dublin. If Fran was there, she didn't care about the consequences.

She would lie her way through any situation in order to protect her time with him. Steven never bothered to ask to come up to the house, but continually asked Eileen to drive to Delaware for the weekend.

"No," she'd say, "I've only rented this house for the summer, and I cannot afford to take the time off. I need to pay the rent. I've told you, come up here if you want, but I cannot get away. Besides, you're working half the weekend. I'd drive all of that way and hardly see you. School will be starting soon."

Steven's typical response included venomous comments about her "other boyfriend," whom to his knowledge, hadn't even arrived in Eastham yet, and how she should just do whatever she wanted because he didn't care. He didn't care so much that he called her every night and tried to keep her on the phone for an hour, guilting her into staying home and talking to him while her housemates went out. It didn't work. Eileen knew that this summer was her few weeks of freedom and that it would have to carry her through the rest of the school year because Steven would make her life a living nightmare. She was too unsure, too afraid and too guilty to leave him.

Twice during the school year, Fran surprised her. The first time, he'd sent her a letter telling her that he'd phone on Saturday evening so that she'd be sure to be there. Rather than a ringing phone, she received a knock at the door to see him and his duffel bag standing in the doorframe.

On the second, he'd surprised her in the Black Rose during her spring break. She was home, out with some of the girls from Eastham who were attending Northeastern. Fran arranged with the barman to let him get behind the bar and take their drink order. Instead, he poured each their favorite pint, and put it in front of the girls before they even could order. Eileen brought the bar to a dead silence when she looked at him and screamed uncontrollably. Karrie had to take her outside onto the corner of Chatham Row just past the front door until she'd calmed. Fran had run out of the bar after her, holding her, laughing, rocking her back and forth in his arms as she laughed, cried, and occasionally yelled. Each time he only stayed for three or four days; just enough to ease the craziness that swelled in the months they had spent apart. Eileen never asked how he managed to pay for all of his airfares. She didn't care.

A year later, Eileen realized that she had to give up Fran in order to end Steven's abuse and graduate with some semblance of sanity left. She had to give up Fran to try and keep hold of one steady part of her life. College was her sorry, little world and getting through the rest of the year would mean that she had to focus. She would withstand Steven, putting all of her effort into making him happy. His insecurities had been the reason for his moodswings. Eileen wanted to put them to rest and do so with a clear conscience. She wrote to Fran, telling him that they no longer could go on.

January 10, 1989

I've tried to listen to your stories and to believe every single word you've ever said to me, but all I can see are lies. I don't believe the reasons you've given me, and I don't believe that you ever will be out of your 'game.' Frankly, I've tried to research everything you've told me about your friends, even the ones who you say are not part of the madness, and I don't have any reason to believe that they exist.

You tell me that you love me, and that things will change, but I have seen none of that. I cannot take the ups and downs of not being with you or of being with you and not knowing what's truly going on with you. It's too much for me and I have to make the decision to let you go. Do whatever you think you have to. I know, having read your letters that you will not change. If what you told me is the truth then I pity you. If what you told me is a lie, then God help you for what you've put me through. I simply am not strong enough to continue to go on with you. I always will love you, but being with you, I know, will destroy me.

Fran read the letter for the fourth time as he rode the T into Boston. It would have been the fifth time, but first time he was unable to finish it. He'd been living in the city for a few months since finishing college and considered returning home after receiving Eileen's letter, but decided to stay and hang on for a little while longer. Maybe she would change her mind. He would give her time, let her think things through, get through the end of the school year and see if there was a way to salvage everything. He considered writing back to her but could not bring himself to ever mail the drafts that he scribbled. *You accused me of some awful things and standing back and looking at things I can see how you arrived at these points of view and that I am totally guilty of them. I purposely kept from telling you that things were not going well, but what did you want, a letter saying that life was dreadful since I left you? I know you Eliot and you have a habit of blaming yourself for everything.*

He sat on the mattress in his studio apartment with the tablet of paper on his lap and stared at the words he'd written to her the night before. He crumpled the page in his hands knowing that he could not reply, even though his senses flipped back and forth between being silent to sending something apologetic to begging her to reconsider to calling her every name in the book then sealing it with a kiss. He never replied.

6
August 1993

Fran was not gone by a longshot. They managed to always know exactly where the other was living, what they were doing, and on a few occasions each year, he would phone her. He always had the best intentions of being nice, trying to be her friend, but like each previous call, his anger would surface, presenting itself as his way of letting her know how much money he was making, and how many women he'd been dating. Eileen would listen to him spit venom at her, sometimes turning the phone away from her ear, tired of hearing his ranting, but she never could bring herself to say, "Look, just don't ever call me again." Her feelings for him remained strong, and if he hadn't gone off about all of the women in his life, and his obvious disdain for her, she would have begged him for forgiveness and asked him to take her back.

Eileen found herself on her first major business trip to the West Coast for her financial firm. She had stayed in DC after college and joined an outfit in the District, doing corporate research for their mutual fund division. She'd met her second husband there within weeks of joining the group, and only two months after her six-month marriage to Steven was dissolved in the Alexandria Courthouse. Jason, soon-to-be husband #2, was a Senior VP. Once they'd decided to marry, he was transferred to the New York office. She liked the work, but wasn't thrilled enough with it to want to make a career out of it.

Eileen hadn't thought much about the changes ahead, focusing only on the chance to get away from the office for a few days. The opportunity to let her own sense of business take the front seat exhilarated her. Going to San Diego meant seeing the other side of the U.S. for the first time. It meant frequent flier miles, and expense accounts. She knew that to most people, hopping on a plane, jetting around for business, did not mean much. For Eileen, sitting in her cubicle by the elevator, next to the laser printer, receiving that ticket to San Diego was like being accepted into some exclusive club. Her lust for traveling subsided shortly after boarding the 737 on the first leg of the cross-country flight. It was bound for Kansas City.

During their conversations, between subtle jabs to each other's egos, Francis had told her how much he liked Kansas City. Somehow, the boy who Eileen worked so hard to bring to the U.S., was seeing more of her country in a matter of sales calls than she had in a lifetime. Inflight, Eileen found herself running absurd scenarios through her head. What if he was in Kansas City that day too, she wondered. Tossing in her seat with various newspapers piled on the tray table in front of the empty seat on her right, she kept hoping that some act of God would put Frannie in the Kansas City Airport at the same time she would be there. She knew it was a stupid thought but couldn't help holding on to the fantasy. What would she say, if while walking through the terminal, he ran into her? Would he be as anxious as she felt at that moment? Eileen dwelled on the images as the USAir flight crossed the Mississippi into what is referred to as "America's Heartland."

Eileen exited the plane during the 40-minute layover and was shocked by the size of the terminal. Kansas City airport almost made the interim terminal at National Airport look like JFK. It was so small; almost intimate with exits only feet from the gates and the baggage claim areas placed at random between ticket check-ins. Eileen saw this as a bonus. A diminutive airport meant that Francis would be easier to find. The fantasies were winning, and until she was back on the plane for the final leg of the flight, Eileen would continue to hope that Francis, by a miraculous act, would appear at one of the concession areas in the airport. She felt him so strongly, despite not having seen him in four years, that for 10 minutes she stood in the middle of the concourse, travelers passing with their rolling suitcases in tow, hoping that at some moment, she would see him. She didn't want to talk to him anymore; the fantasy and the missing him were so ignited that merely seeing his face was all she wanted. The computerized voice announcing flight arrivals and departures crackled over her head. Eileen thought that with all of its woodwork, the airport needed a steakhouse or some farm-oriented cocktail lounge.

Suitcases and the heels of rushing dress shoes clacked on the tiles between each gate. None of the bags or shoes belonged to Francis, but for some distant, inane reason Eileen felt a closeness knowing that at one time, they had been in the same place. When the thought struck, she considered ordering a drink to flush the silliness from her mind, but since it was only 11:00 a.m. in Kansas City, she likely would be considered a major lush as opposed to a borderline basket case.

7
April 1994

Jason was not pleased when shortly after their move to New York, Eileen announced that she was leaving the financial industry. Despite his independent wealth, none of which he'd worked for, he liked the comfort of knowing that more cash would be rolling in on a consistent basis. He liked his mother's money and the allowance she'd funneled to him every month since his thirteenth birthday. He liked his grandmother's money and the trust funds she'd established for him since the day he'd hit the planet. It was Eileen's duty as a woman in his life to continue the tradition of supporting him. His own work was a direct result of wanting to control other people's money. The commissions required work, but he hadn't had to go out and actually earn the money that fed the investments that fed his checkbook. Call it passive-aggression or passive-accumulation. His key accounts, the million dollar babies, were all family members and wealthy friends of family members. He was a rainmaker for the firm, and lucky enough to have been born during monsoon season.

"What do you mean you're quitting the business," he'd whined over dinner at Café a Largo.

He was stirring his martini with his finger. Eileen hated that. Since when, she thought, was Stoli a finger food? He was pulling his finger out of his mouth, then going back for the olive when she replied, "I'm going to try doing some freelance writing."

"What?" Freelance meant non-steady income.

"I talked with the communications director at the firm, and he's willing to give me a shot with a few articles for the newsletters and work on the semi-annual reports."

"But, Eileen, you've never written anything."

"Jason, I've written for years. I wrote before I knew you. Besides, I have a few friends in the medical industry who are dying for extra help covering meetings and writing articles for their membership publications."

"What friends? Do I know them?" Translation: Can I open accounts for them?

"Friends from college. Remember Jennifer MacLean? She was at our wedding. She works with the Academy of Ophthalmology Surgeons in Chicago. I talked with her a couple of weeks ago. New York is a huge town for medical news, and they could use extra hands covering it. I've got a small, trial assignment at NYU Medical Center on Wednesday."

"What's the pay?"

"Nothing." She was waiting for him to choke on the pimento.

"Nothing?"

"I told you. It's a trial run. If they like my style, then it'll be about $250 per article, depending on the length."

He scoffed, "$250. Two-fifty wouldn't cover our weekly dinner bills."

"Jason, get over it. I want to give this a try." She looked down at her crab bisque then asked, "How's the frat house? How much are you spending there?"

Jason reached for the fresh martini, his third, trying to seem unphased, "Frat house? What are you talking about?"

"You look great on the video, Dear." Eileen had been dying to find the right time to let him know that she knew about his secret life, and wasting the moment over a chat at home just didn't seem right. "Then again, I always did say that you have a nice ass. By the way, try and lay a hand on me again, and I'll knee your balls to Brooklyn."

"Eileen," he leaned closer to her and whispered, praying that the couple at the table next to them couldn't hear their conversation.

"Jason, do not even try to give me any excuses. Christ, at least they wear condoms in porno movies now. I've already called Jack, and he put me in touch with a lawyer here. No pun intended," she sipped her wine, "but, you're fucked." She waited a second, watching the color drain from his face before calling over Victor, who happened to be filling in for one of the dinner servers that evening. "Victor, may we have our check please?" He nodded in the affirmative. "Oh, wait one second." She turned back to her husband, "Jason, give him your AmEx card." It was the one credit card in his name only. "My husband's mother is taking us to dinner tonight." She reached over the table and held Jason's hand. "She's a wonderful woman."

Victor, unaware, asked, "Are you celebrating something tonight, Mrs. Levitan?"

"So to speak," she answered.

8
May 1994

Fran's reappearance in her life came unexpectedly and the pace picked up to a fever pitch within weeks. Eileen had been in Boston visiting Karrie. It had been years since they'd managed to find a weekend to get together rather than random phone conversations every three or four months. Shortly after Easter weekend, Eileen hopped a shuttle from LaGuardia, landing on Karrie's doorstep on Commonwealth Avenue in Brighton. It was Wednesday and she'd planned to stay through Friday. Karrie would call in sick, and the girls would relive their youth without having to put up with the college crowds that jammed the streets on weekends. They took a nostalgic visit to the Kinvara Pub in Allston. The Kinvara, if caught at the right hour, was good for a few darts games and conversation with the boys; most of whom hailed from Dublin, Galway, Tyrone and every other area in Ireland. More patrons showed their passports to get in to the place than driver's licenses. It had been the same way in '89, and the tradition remained.

After two beers the crowd grew too thick and they moved to the Black Rose near Quincy Market. Halfway through their first drinks, Andrew Grealy injected himself into their conversation. He worked with Fran. Andrew's intention had been to pick-up Eileen, and he thought he had a sure chance with her when she mentioned that Fran worked at the same company at one time. Shortly after college, she learned that Fran had taken a job at MARTENZ, but wasn't sure if he still worked there. Andrew, an extra-starch, blue-shirted, pin-stripe-suited sales rep thought he'd hit pay dirt when he told Eileen that he not only knew of Fran, but worked with him. Francis, he said, covered the southeast territory. Andrew prided himself on being the number one sales rep of the Midwest region. MARTENZ was the number two supplier of PVC valves for construction companies all over the US. "You probably have a few in your own home and don't even know it," Andrew joked.

"Gosh. I couldn't tell you," Eileen replied. "I'll have to ask my husband about that when I get back to New York." Andrew's face dropped, and Karrie poked her finger in Eileen's side. Andrew spoke with them for a few more minutes then made his excuses and begged off.

"You are brutal!" Karrie was astounded as she held Eileen's left hand in hers. "How could he not see these rocks?" Eileen's two-carat engagement ring and a diamond wedding band stood out on her finger.

"Easy," she said waving her fingers in the air, "I had my hand in my pocket." Eileen put her left hand back in her jeans and laughed.

"You are so bad," Karrie joked and ordered another round.

Eileen returned home to New York and the emptiness of her already dead marriage. Francis phoned her at 1:15 PM the following Wednesday afternoon.

"Hello?"

"Eileen? Eileen Eliot?"

"Uh, yes." She hesitated then said, "Francis?"

"Hey!" He was nervous, sitting at his desk motioning as though he were cold-calling a potential client in order to throw his colleagues off from the scent of his personal life. "Leen, I understand you met one of me co-workers." He was trying to play it cool. Her voice ran through his ear, filling his gut and almost made his shoes feel tight.

"Hi." She didn't know what to say. His voice stunned her.

"Yeah, can you believe it? Small world. How are you? I hear you look terrific." He laughed into the phone.

"Excuse me?"

"Andrew. You met him in the Rose. So you're married, huh? Again. Didn't you just get divorced?"

"Yes, well, that's a long story. It's good to hear from you."

"I hope you don't mind my calling. When Andrew said he'd met you and that you lived in New York, I called Karrie and asked her for your number. Do you have any idea how difficult it was for me to speak to that woman?" Francis and Karrie had had an enormous argument years ago; one so bad that they still refused to speak to each other unless for a life-altering reason. Neither of them seemed to be able to recall what it was about, but a mutual disgust for one another was now understood. Eileen still hated that the two of them could not patch up their differences. It had forced her to edit her conversations with Karrie so as not to mention *his* name, and sometimes made her feel stupid around Karrie for having been involved with someone who Karrie regarded as being patently evil.

"I can't believe you actually called Karrie," she laughed and felt her face getting warm, "And I'm happy that you did."

"What do you mean long story? Was it an arranged marriage, or something?"

"No, just a momentary lapse of reason." Why was she telling him her story without question? "The long and short of it is that I'm married, have been for all of seven months, and hopefully won't be for much longer. We've filed the papers, and I'm counting the minutes to get out. Now, I'm waiting for him to move out, which should be coming any day now. What a crock this turned out to be. So, PVC pipes, huh? How'd you get into that?" She wanted to change the subject.

"Oh, you know how it goes. You need a job, and some guy walks up to you and says, 'Hey buddy, wanna make a few bucks?' And so, I've been here for four years." They talked for 10 minutes more, catching up on trivial details.

"Frannie—"

"No one's called me that in years."

"Sorry."

"No. It's nice to hear." He leaned back in his chair not caring what his colleagues saw.

"Frannie, it's good to hear your voice. I hope we'll talk again soon. Please, let's not let it be for so long in between, okay?"

"Sure. I suppose fate says we should take advantage of the opportunity." He gave her his office and home phone numbers. "I travel an awful lot, so you'll have better luck with the office number and the voice mail."

"Sounds good. Give Andrew a hug for me," she joked.

"Um, no. I'll talk to you tomorrow."

"Sounds even better." Eileen replaced the antique phone on the cradle next to her bed.

9
June 1994

Near the end of the month, Eileen's phone rang at 12:30 Sunday afternoon just before her parents were leaving to return to Eastham. Fran's voice came through when she picked up the receiver. He never called on weekends. He was always working then. That was an understood thing. Eileen walked further into the kitchen listening to him speak. He was in Chicago.

"What's up," she asked.

"I miss you. I'm here in this big hotel room, and I miss you. God Leen, you wouldn't believe what they want me to do."

Eileen tried answering in short, quiet phrases not wanting to attract her parents' attention. "What is it? Are you okay?"

"I'm fine." This was the first step in his letting her into the state of his affairs with the Rah. "There's to be a big meeting soon, Leen. I mean huge."

"I know. You told me."

"No. Bigger than I thought. They're going full force with it, and I don't know what the hell I'm doing."

"What do you mean? I thought you were there for real work."

"Jesus," he digressed, "Not a decent soccer game anywhere." Francis lay on the bed in the Renaissance Hotel wearing dirty jeans, his ages-old "Never Mind the Bollocks, We're the Sex Pistols" T-shirt, channel surfing. "Shit. The only game I can find is on Telemundo." He turned down the volume and watched it anyway.

"Fran, that's great. Are you okay? You're weirding out on me."

"Yeah." He was silent. "Yeah. Fine. It's happening, Babe. It's really going to happen. I've got to be back here soon for another meeting."

"Why?"

"Everyone's coming in to town. Boston, New York, KC, San Francisco," he rattled off at least 10 cities; cities where the boys had "chapters." They were coming in to talk about the ceasefire, but he hadn't revealed that yet and wouldn't say so into the phone.

They spoke for another few minutes. Fran told her again that he missed her. Lately, he'd been doing that a lot, but he still had yet to see her and the angst was growing.

"Stop it." Eileen peered into the living room checking on her parents. "I can't talk like that now." Her breathing became slow and shallow.

"Oh, come onnnn." She hated when he whispered to her with that inflection that begged her to be what he used to call a "naughty, naughty girl." He could make her crazy in a matter of seconds.

"No. I'm serious. It's not a good time."

"Is he there?"

"No! He's been gone for ages, probably off picking up frat boys, but my parents are here."

"Okay, but I'll just lie here and think about you."

"Francis, you haven't seen me in five years. You are living on an outdated fantasy." Eileen smiled and twirled the phone cord around her forearm.

"Dear, you are an unforgettable vision."

"Perhaps, but don't be surprised if the packaging has changed. She ran her hand over the back of her head, wondering how different she'd look to him. "Look I've got to go. When will you be back in Boston?"

"Tuesday."

"Then hold that thought. I'll call you Tuesday. Don't worry. We'll arrange something soon enough."

Two weeks later Frannie called her from work for their typical afternoon chat. "Hey, what's up?"

"Oh, same old stuff. I talked to my lawyer. The divorce is proceeding nicely, so it looks like I'll be able to get out of the marriage and New York pretty easily. So, I guess that means it's been a pretty good day. Oh, and I'm going to Chicago on the 26th to write up a meeting."

"Oh you are. Hold on one second. Jane, Jane, shut up!" A noisy co-worker was drowning out their discussion. "Sorry." He returned his attention to her as he bounced a miniature soccer ball off the wall in front of him.

It had been over five years since they'd last seen each other and the thought of laying eyes on him again made her heart race. Nothing else mattered. Could he make it out there, or would a weekend in Chicago seem like an even worse experience than the 40 minutes in Kansas City Airport? "Well, can you be there?"

"Hon, I honestly don't know. There's so much happening right now, and I can't just disappear for a few days."

"Please Frannie, I'm meeting with AOS' editor. This is my first time away from New York in so long. Please don't make me go by myself." She couldn't remember the last time she'd pleaded for anything. "Let's meet somewhere, even if it's only for dinner. I will fly you to Chicago for the evening if I have to. You'd be home by midnight."

He laughed into the phone. "All right. All right. Let me see what I can do." He didn't tell her that he'd already had plans to be in Chicago that same week. The 26th would be the day after the meeting.

The following week, Francis called announcing that, ironically, he would be there too, and for the week prior. She knew he had business to tend to, but did it really require his being there for over a week, or did he, like she, find a way to extend the stay? Years later, she hadn't asked that question, and no longer cared about the answer.

On the evening of the 26th, they met in the bar at the Hilton O'Hare. Her flight had arrived a short time earlier, and he'd had a MARTENZ meeting there in the afternoon. It had been years since a day seemed so long to her. Eileen changed her clothes twice in the ladies room, opting finally for the black skirt suit and silver silk blouse she'd worn on the flight. She arrived in the bar 20 minutes before he was expected. Perhaps a drink would make the time move faster. She had a book with her, but couldn't read it, unable to concentrate on the words.

He strolled into the bar, "Hey." She stood and he hugged her. "Sam Adams and a shot of Bushmills," he said to the bartender. "I have had it with MARTENZ." He rambled on about useless managers and stupid customers, wound up by an awful day. Or, was his day as long as hers and the release too overwhelming? She never asked that question either, and again, the answer did not matter.

Neither made any reference to re-acquainting themselves. Instead, he rested his hand on her back, behaving as though he'd seen her just the other day. He was Frannie. Her Frannie.

Eileen commented, touching the dashboard of his Nissan Maxima while he drove to dinner, "Not a bad set of wheels. You must have a hell of an expense account.".

"Yea, they treat me pretty well." Fran flicked his cigarette out the driver's side window. Eileen sat nervous, unsure of what to say to the man with whom she'd spoken almost daily. Her eyes shifted from a direct gaze out the windshield to the side of his face as he spoke, then to the back of his neck. His hair had gone just the slightest bit gray on each side, and she felt her right hand holding down her left so as not to stroke the base of his head. She spoke, "How did the week go?"

"Fine."

"Great. Just fine?"

"What do you mean?"

"Francis Sullivan, I know you. Your tone of voice says that there's something on your mind but you are refusing to tell me. Fine. Don't tell me if you don't want to, but to be honest, you suck at hiding your moods."

"I have to ask you something." He kept his eyes on the road.

"Anything."

He turned to her for a second without losing his attention to the highway. "Are you wearing any sort of recording device? Is this conversation in any way being recorded?"

"Aw Honey, you say the sweetest things."

"I'm serious." His response startled her. Never in their years together or phone calls when they were apart had he ever asked her such a question.

"Of course not." Normal women would have been frightened by such an inquiry.

"We're getting close, Leen. It's coming soon. God, what a meeting." He banged his right hand on the steering wheel.

"What happened?" They passed the sign for Diversey St. and neared downtown Chicago.

"Everyone was there. Every major city is here, plus a few from home. Shit, it was a bloody reunion. We're bringing them all on board. We're close to a ceasefire."

"Are you serious? Oh Frannie, that would be incredible!" Eileen stopped thinking about his neck and centered on his words.

"I know." He looked amazed and smiled, "I never thought I would see this happen."

"Frannie, I have to ask you something now." Eileen felt a twinge, but the curiosity was killing her.

"Anything," he glanced at her then took her hand and kissed it.

"Are you armed?"

"Yes, and legged. But if we're out late enough, I may be legless."

"I'm serious." She looked directly at him.

He returned her glance, looking at her from the side of his eyes. "I know you are, hon. I'm sorry. That was not a fair response. No dear. I am not. Guns are for killing people, and I would not keep one anywhere near you. I hate them." He went silent.

"What is it?" The darkness inside the car was brightened by the small orange glow coming off of her cigarette lighter. Eileen lowered her car window just a bit to let the smoke escape.

"Nothing. I'm starving." Fran looked at the digital speedometer. He had the Maxima going 72 miles an hour down the Kennedy Expressway.

They valeted the car outside of Trattoria Parma, a small traditional Italian restaurant off of State Street. Throughout dinner and so much of the evening, Eileen felt so young, so uninteresting. As he spoke about clients he had visited that week, and places he was scheduled to go next, she wondered if she was boring. Was he happy to see her? Was being with her what he had expected, or was it some kind of disappointment? Years ago, she had felt this strange combination of being his equal but also learning so much from him. Now, she knew that she could keep up with him, but honestly hadn't the foggiest idea how, or if he'd want her to. Standing in the restaurant bar, waiting for their table, he told her that she looked terrific and that she hadn't changed. "Neither have you."

He laughed, "Oh yes I have." His eyes lit up, opened wide like they always did when he laughed, and his smile got bigger. "You, on the other hand, look exactly the same."

He had to be kidding. She was 15 pounds heavier, wore her hair straight rather than the curly way it used to be, and felt sure that the look on her face screamed "deer caught in the headlights!" It was not the expression of a woman, who at one point in her life, would have rows with him, so fierce that they'd clear rooms, and he'd begin to speak Irish so as not to let her know what he was thinking. "Don't pull that Gaelic shit with me," she'd yell. Tonight, she couldn't have yelled if she'd taken five minutes alone in a room to conjure every ounce of force in her body.

10

They stepped off the elevator at the 21st floor of the Marriott on Michigan Avenue to Eileen's room, 2105, just 10 paces from the elevator. Fran took her keycard, unlocked the door and pushed it open for her to enter the room. Eileen felt her body temperature rise having him in her room. They hadn't been in a room alone together in over five years. She hung her coat in the closet and walked to the desk unsure of what to do next. Fran stood at the foot of the bed looking at her. Neither knew where to move or what to say. Suddenly, they behaved like children waiting for the music to stop during the last round of musical chairs. Eileen made the bold move of unlocking the mini-bar. "Wanna drink?"

Frannie leaned over the door of the refrigerator with his head just over her shoulder. His breath, smelling of cabernet, Bushmills and Marlboros wafted through her hair onto the back of her neck. "Heineken."

Eileen pulled the green bottle and a Miller Lite from the shelf, removed the caps and handed him his drink. A look of shame washed over his face as he focused on the top of the beer bottle until he managed to turn back to Eileen. "Is something wrong Frannie? I mean, I certainly hope it's not everyday that you are in a married woman's room, but I didn't think it would hit you this hard." She was trying to make light of the situation.

"Yes. No. No, it's not being here with you. God no, that's not it. I don't know."

They sat down on the side of the bed. "You see, it's this kind of direct response that I've always found so attractive in you. What is it, sweetie? Talk to me." Eileen touched his knee then pulled away her hand.

"I used a gun this week. Leen, it gave me a rush. I haven't fired a gun since I was a kid."

"You what?" There was no fear; just a blank curiosity.

"Some fool questioned who I was. I arrived here, and he took me for a drive to the middle of nowhere. Some young punk who's seen too many Clint Eastwood movies and hasn't been home in a while. He said I had to prove that I was who I said I was. I was one of the assholes running the fucking meeting!"

"My God. What did you do?"

"I was armed. Given what was happening last week, I had to be. So, I made the fucker drop to his knees."

"You shot him?" Eileen's stomach flipped and she prayed his next response would be the one she wanted to hear.

"No. I fired two shots on either side of his head, then told him to run like hell. I sent him into the darkness. I left him out there. Stupid fucker."

"Fran! You just left him there?!"

"Honey, the man wanted to kill me. Do you not understand that?"

"Yes, I, I don't know." Eileen crossed the room looking out the window at the city lights. "I'm just glad you are okay. I don't know."

A normal woman would have kicked Francis out of her hotel room. Eileen leaned against the desk with a vision of Fran in pitch darkness with a crying man on his knees and Fran standing over him telling him how things were going to be. Eileen saw Fran for the first time for what he was, a terrorist. Plain and simple. The I.R.A. was alive and well in the Chicago Marriott. Her Fran was back in her life, in living tri-colour, in a way unlike any other way known before. They talked until 4 am, until they both fell asleep on top of the bedspread, fully clothed and too exhausted to care.

Fran phoned her everyday, sometimes three times a day after their weekend. He'd check in during the afternoon often putting her on hold between clients, and again at the end of the day with a long chat some time after midnight. His evenings, when normal people would go for dinner or catch up on the events of each other's days, were spent in South Boston, Southie, with "the boys." The ceasefire was so close but still so fragile. Too many volunteers refused to sign on.

"I thought we'd resolved most of the problems in Chicago, but glitches keep coming up."

"What kind," Eileen asked him with her head pressed against her pillow.

"Sorry Babe. I can't say, but most of them are from these idiots in the States who just aren't copping on."

"Well, what difference does it make if the U.S. boys aren't on board? How much of an impact can they have?"

Fran lay on his couch smoking, and laughed, "Babe, I'd love to explain it all to you but I can't. Basically, it wouldn't take much for the dissenters to upset the entire process. It's not all a done deal. Everyone has to be on board. Leadership, mostly, but the masses need to support the decision as well." He was exhausted. Drained from too may long days being the king of PVC valves, and nights trying to organize the madness. Eileen never would understand that it was the U.S. boys who worked everything from fundraising to weapons proliferating. If she knew some of the connections he'd made over the last two years, she'd freak. U.S. and international government representatives were behind them, and his ties had managed to misdirect more than a few shipments of U.S. weapons to them. The U.S. Rah boys harbored the ones on the run from home. They were almost the heart and soul of the operation, minus the actual warfare. If members in New York or Chicago didn't support the deal, then nothing would hold.

On Monday, August 28, 1994, he called Eileen from work, sounding awful. He hadn't phoned her since the previous Thursday and never called on weekends. On weekends he always was off "working" in Southie or New York or God knows where. She never wanted to know where he was. If he'd been in New York and knew he was somewhere in the city, not seeing him would have frustrated her to no end.

Once, she'd said, "Honey, if you're down here in the city, you definitely should stay with me. I don't care what time you come home, I'd just like to have you with me for a little while."

He almost breathed fire into the phone, "Absolutely not! No one will ever know about you! You will never be near them. I don't care what it takes. Dear, I want to see you, and if I could, I would spend every night with you, but I never would risk exposing you to them."

"Why not, I'm not going to hurt anybody?"

"Honey, you don't understand. These people are dangerous and you would be a liability. Things change in the matter of hours and if they wanted to, they wouldn't hesitate to use you to get to me. I will not allow there ever to be a chance of that happening."

She listened to him talking to her from his office, whispering, "We're close Leen. We're right there."

"What do you mean close? How close?"

"Before the end of the week, Hon. We'll see an end before the end of the week."

"Sweetie that's great!" Eileen was looking through her mail as they spoke. "Oh my God! Oh my God!"

Fran sat up in his chair frightened by her yells. "What's the matter? Are you okay?"

Eileen started to cry. "It's, it's over. It's wonderful!" She was jumping around the kitchen, spinning until the phone cord wouldn't let her spin any further.

"Leen, what are you talking about!" Usually, he had all of the info and she was in the dark. He didn't like having the tables turned on him.

"It's final. My divorce came through. The certified papers are here. I'm completely free! Goodbye, New York!"

"Honey, congratulations. But you gave me a fuckin' scare with all that screamin', woman! Seems like we're both having a good week."

"Yeah. Unbelievable isn't it? I'm free, and maybe with some luck, you will be too."

He couldn't answer that wish. He just said, "We'll see."

On Thursday, August 31, Eileen came home from her real estate agent's office and played the message on her answering machine. It was Fran, singing one line from U2's *Sunday Bloody Sunday*, "I can't believe the news today." The cease-fire had gone into effect at midnight.

11
October 1994

Settlement on Eileen's new home in Beacon Hill still was six weeks away, and she hadn't seen Fran for nearly a month. The phone bills would have been astronomical save for his 800 number at work, and their propensity to talk well after midnight when the rates dropped. After *Leno* and before *Late Night*, they were five minutes into their third chat of the day. "Hey, I'm thinking of coming up for a long weekend on the seventh. Will you be available?" Eileen hadn't realized what this request would entail. Though he'd never clued her in, she'd learn how much he needed to stretch his availability while she was there.

"It sounds okay, but let me check." He called her back three hours later. "Okay, the seventh will be great. I've got it all worked out. We'll do dinner, movies, sleep late, the whole nine yards."

"Oh, sweetie. This is almost too good to be true. I'll see you next Thursday." Her eyes were closed as she spoke.

"Excellent."

Eileen booked a flight out of Newark. Like a sick joke, Continental Airlines delayed her plane for over an hour, forcing her to check her hair a hundred times more than she'd planned, and read far more than she'd had any interest. This would be their first time together since Chicago. She'd never seen his apartment, and he'd never seen her home. They knew what went on in each other's minds but had no idea what their favorite clothes were, or what kind of food they kept in their refrigerators. Eileen felt a rush at the thought of stretching out on the same couch he sat on when he'd talk to her at night. She wanted to sleep in the sheets that smelled like him. More than that, she was nearly crazy by the prospect of lying in bed and actually being able to extend her toes and run them along his legs.

She arrived in Boston, but he wasn't there. She was to meet him at his office. She put herself in the back of a cab and took a $35 ride out to the suburbs, the land of MARTENZ. Eileen was miffed by his inability to meet her, but expected that it was better for him to get all of his work done than to leave the office early and be a stress case all weekend.

They arrived at his apartment, a third floor walkup in Woburn. It was almost bare; only a couch, an end table, a halogen lamp, stereo system and television. She looked around and wondered, why is every guy the same? They can go for months without a set of forks in the house, but they ALWAYS have a wicked stereo system. Every man's first paycheck must have some subliminal message embedded in it whispering, "You need a 99-CD changer and new speakers. Oh, and your tuner sucks, so get one of those too." The hardwood floors were bare but nicely finished. Fran made the bold move of buying her a bottle of Diet Coke, and a six-pack of Sam Adams for the two of them. He put them in the refrigerator, then met her in the living room, coming up from behind her, putting his arms around her, spinning her to face him and dancing around the living room. No music necessary. He sang Frank Sinatra's "World on a String" softly into her ear, finishing with "What a world, what a life, I'm in love…"

Eileen walked into the bedroom to unpack her bag. Fran said he had to make a call. Within weeks, the term "Gotta make a few calls," was said more often than "I love you," "I miss you" or "How was your day." He closed the bedroom door with her in it, and walked to the phone in the kitchen. Three minutes later he came back to the bedroom. "Honey, you're going to kill me."

"You have to work don't you?"

"Yes."

"All night?" She threw a pillow at him in over-dramatic disgust, trying to hide her disdain.

"I don't know. I hope not. Probably not." He walked to her, apologizing, kissing her, and begging her to touch him the way she'd described over the phone so many times. They rolled around in the sheets for a little while until he looked at the clock and said, "I need to get in the shower. I'm due in the city by 7:00."

While he was showering, the phone rang, but she didn't answer it. A woman left a message on the phone. "Frannie, it's Nuala, I forgot to tell you, bring TV's." What? TV's? What the hell were they planning?

He stepped out of the shower with the towel around his waist, combing his hair. Eileen walked to him and they stood in the hall. "You had a phone call."

"Did you answer it?" She caught the panic on his face.

"No."

"Good. I don't want anyone to know you're here. I'm sorry, Babe."

"That's okay. She said to bring TV's."

"TV's?"

"Yeah," she said, 'I forgot to tell you, bring TV's."

"Oh, CDs! Bring CDs."

"Are you going to work or to a party?"

He stood in front of the mirror, not really putting much effort into his answer. "These are long nights. Lately, sometimes it's quiet and sometimes it's not, so we bring whatever we can think of."

"Oh, can you think of this while you're working tonight?" Eileen put one arm around him and kissed him then let her other hand move under his towel until it fell to the floor.

"Stop. I can't. I'll be late."

"Come on, so what," her hand slid back and forth. He moved her back onto the mattress and made it to Boston 40 minutes late. Eileen had no indication of where he was going, but he said he'd be home in the middle of the night.

She spent the evening watching television, flipping through magazines and looking at the postcards on his refrigerator; Palm Springs, Amelia Island, Miami. All definitely were from a woman but her name was difficult to make out. Just a big "N" followed by some squiggling. Eileen noticed the pile on top of the refrigerator. There must have been 25 more postcards all from "N." Who the fuck is "N," Eileen wondered, angry. Was he out with "N" tonight? She drank the Sam Adams and smoked a pack of cigarettes before going to sleep.

He reappeared at 11:00 the following morning. "Where the hell have you been?" Eileen sat on the couch with a cup of tea and an ashtray full of cigarette butts on the table next to her.

"I'm sorry. Someone came in to town last night. We had to keep him company and make sure he didn't go anywhere. This morning he announced that he wanted breakfast, so, we had to take the son of a bitch to breakfast." Frannie shrugged his shoulders.

"Who was he?" Eileen had read two newspapers, gone for coffee twice, and considered packing her bags and going home to New York.

"I can't say. Just someone who we absolutely were not expect-ing to see."

"Honey, I don't care if Whitey Bulger shows up at your door with a bag full of cash, and says he wants to knock back a few pints. I'm sitting here like a fool, waiting for you, stranded with no car, and you go for flapjacks with the boys. That's great. And by the way, I picked up your mail this morning. I thought it would be a nice gesture, ya know, go get the paper, buy the milk and pick up the mail. You got another postcard from, 'N' whomever that is. So, I suggest you call her and tell her how your night went unless she already knows, because I'm out of here."

"What?!"

"The postcards, Fran. They're all over the goddamn house. If you're seeing someone else then tell me right now so that I can get the hell out of here, because as far as I'm concerned, you've been lying to me."

"Oh Jesus. Eileen, sit down, please." She sat on the couch. He sat on the coffee table with his hands on her knees. "She's one of the boys. She's in the crew. She's a front."

"What? Explain."

He took a deep breath and proceeded. "Well, I'm never here, I never have people in and out of the apartment, and as far as the neighbors or anyone else can tell, I have no social life. I have no alibis for my whereabouts, or my who-abouts, so, they gave me a girlfriend. She never comes here, but the postcards show up all the time for all of the neighbors to see when they walk in the build-ing." The mailslots in the building were open. "I keep them just in case I need them. It was supposed to be a joke. It was supposed to be part of some drunken joke, and it's all spun out of control. I'm sorry, Babe. I should have told you, but I'd completely forgotten about them."

"Well, you have a social life, and you have a lovelife, and I want this shit to stop right now. This goes no further. I'm not kidding." Eileen still was debating about leaving.

"Okay." He got up to stop in the bathroom and saw her bag packed on the floor. "Jesus, you weren't kidding."

"No. I wasn't. I'm not."

"I'm sorry." He was silent, staring at the floor. "Eileen, I'm so sorry. I wanted this weekend so badly. You have to understand that. Luv, I don't have a choice. I have to go when they call, and you were hurt by this stupid joke of theirs. I'm so sorry. I wish I could come out with it all and say, 'Hey guys, check her out. Isn't she great,' but if they knew you were here, it could put both of us at risk."

"I know I know. I'm just frustrated." She calmed to an abnormal level of understanding. "Just don't do it tonight. I don't care if you have to call in sick. We leave the lights off, and we don't answer the phone. "

"Okay. It's a deal. And Hon," he pulled her off the couch, clutching her against him.

"Yes?"

"I didn't have the flapjacks. I had eggs, sausage and toast."

"Fuck off."

That evening, they stayed in, and as promised, Fran turned off the phone. "Frannie," Eileen asked sprawled on his couch as he held her feet in his hand.

"What?"

"Have you ever killed anyone?"

"No. I shouldn't answer the question, but no."

"Good," she answered not moving her feet from his grip.

"Would it make a difference? If I had said yes, would it change your view of me?" His face was deadpan. His fingers continued to massage her toes as panic swirled in his gut.

She put a hand over her eyes. "Truly, I cannot say either way. It's a hell of a hypothetical"

He sat up and let go of her feet. "Why? Do you not think that what I do is wrong?"

Eileen sat upright against the side edge of the couch. Her knees were bent. "Honey, I can't honestly say. I've loved you for so long. Frannie, I know you. I know how you treat me. I know how much you care for your family. I suppose if I knew more about your business, I would have a more definite opinion. It's like knowing that two worlds are colliding but only seeing one of them. I cannot imagine your doing something like that, but on the other hand, it's not like you boys are goodwill ambassadors for Ireland."

"Well said." Fran walked to the kitchen to grab a Sam Adams from the fridge. His mind centered on the nights at home when he'd terrorized Protestants merely because they thought of God in a different perspective. He could almost feel the heat of a bala-clava's wool on his cheeks as he and two others beat a known UVF supporter so badly he was put into hospital with two broken legs, four cracked ribs, and broken wrist, and his nose so mangled he was nearly unrecognizable.

Last week's meeting with the military contact floated in his mind as he handed Eileen her beer. What would she say if she knew that her own armed forces was indirectly funneling arms to the I.R.A. thanks to inside info from a few former soldiers. Worse, Fran thought, lighting Eileen's cigarette, I've held a gun to the head of British embassy staff. He recalled the night in Dublin as he followed the ambassador's secretary down the block. Fran, sporting a baseball cap pulled down over his face, yanked Stephen into an alley and whispered, "Back off," as he held a photo of Stephen's family in front of him.

"Thanks," Eileen whispered when he handed her the beer. She dragged on her cigarette.

"You're welcome." Fran leaned from behind and kissed her cheek before taking his seat on the couch. "Feel better?"

"Why? To know that my soul mate is not a heartless murderer and merely a career insurgent?" She tried to be pleasantly sarcastic. "Sweetie, when we met, I loved you instantly. When you told me about all of this, I was confused, but pleased that you saw fit to tell me. Now, I know you even better and love you even more. I support you as much as I can. I trust you to be honest with me and to tell me what you can. I love you, Fran. Maybe I'm crazy, but I do. Very much."

He put down his beer and lay on top of her, "You are everything to me." He ran his fingers through her hair, "Everything." No, he thought, I merely compromise your nation's military personnel, use our supporters' money to buy guns and support republican families, and would kill John Major at the drop of a hat. "I love you, Dear."

"And I you. So much."

12

In November, Fran showed up at her house, completely unexpected. Eileen felt like a lottery-winner. She hadn't bothered to put on any make-up and was dressed in ratty jeans and a T-shirt from scrubbing the kitchen floor and cleaning out the basement apartment. "Honey, you wouldn't believe the apartment down there. I hadn't paid much attention to it, but it's really pretty great. Come on down and take a look at what I've done."

"Wait." He gently grabbed her by the elbow. "Let's go sit down." They walked into the kitchen, and he reached for two crystal glasses and the Bushmills.

"Sweetie, what is it? What's wrong?" She was getting scared. Had the police learned something? Was he in trouble? Was there someone else? Was there…she couldn't take it. "Francis, what is going on?"

"You are not going to believe this," he rubbed his forehead.

"What amn't I going to believe?" Her chest was constricting, raising the temperature in her face.

"MARTENZ."

"You lost your job?"

"No. They are so pleased with my work that they are moving me to Chicago. I told them I'd have to think about it."

"Oh." Eileen could not think for a second.

"Exactly."

"Well, it sounds like a wonderful opportunity, and God knows you deserve the recognition. What about everything else?"

"I don't care about everything else. I want to know how you feel about it. I want you to be a part of this decision." He shocked her. Frannie always did whatever he wanted to. He made decisions without her input, spent time in places where she never could find him, and now he was asking her for her opinion on a major decision.

She started to cry a little. "Well, I think you have to do it. I mean, this could be really good for you. You'd be away from the boys, you'd be doing something that you are really really good at, and you could be establishing yourself for a major promotion. You've worked hard for this. I don't want you to go." She cried harder. "I don't want to be without you, but on the other hand, how much time have we been able to spend together lately? Fran, money is not an issue. It's not as if I can't hop a plane and visit you whenever I want, or that you can't do the same. Would we really be much different than we are now?" She started bawling. "I don't want you to go, but I think you should." They'd been sitting across from each other at the small table under the window across from the refrigerator. He left his chair, getting down on one knee in front of her and pulled her head to his shoulder.

"We'll be fine, Babe. I promise. It'll be fine. I don't want to go either, but I think you're right. Besides, Chicago has been good to us, right?" He looked at her and smiled, tilting his head with the hint of a suggestive look.

"Well then," she reached for the bottle to refill her glass and lit a cigarette, "What's your timeline?"

"Six weeks. I need to get out there, find a place to live, get rid of my place and move."

"Well, give your notice now and move in here with me."

"Can't do it. The work is not quieting down. Shit, I can't wait to tell the boys that I'll be moving. Wonder how they'll take it."

"Will they let you?"

"They have to. I'm the boss." He'd never said that before. "I'll kind of miss those guys, ya know."

"Oh sure!" She threw her hands in the air in mock-disgust. "You're packing up and leaving, telling me that we'll be fine, but it's THEY who you say you'll miss????? Francis, please. Shall I throw a little dinner party for you so you can invite your friends over to play? I'll do all the cooking then go disappear down to the Kinvara so you can do whatever it is you guys do."

·"Stop it."

"I know. I'm over-reacting. No, you'd better go break the news. I'll listen for the wails of misery wafting up here from Southie. Good luck, Sweetie. I know this might not be a pretty sight."

Fran stubbed out his cigarette, knocked back the rest of his whiskey and walked to the front door with Eileen's hand in his. "Hey Leen," he hugged her, "I love you." He was looking at her as though the emotion surprised him.

"I love you too."

"No," he held her hands in his, "I mean it. I haven't said it to you in so long. I truly love you. I don't know what I'd do without you. And I don't care what happens, I'm coming back here tonight. I'll try and be here by midnight."

"Okay." Her eyes were still twitching from crying, and random tears settled in her lower eyelids, but the smile on her face showed emotion completely separate from the one above her nose. The tightening in her chest had relaxed and her hands weren't swelling anymore.

He put one foot out the door, then leaned back in to kiss her again, "And keep your mitts off the whiskey. I don't want to come home to you passed-out on the couch, and too much of a dead-weight to carry up to bed. "

"Very well. I shall be on my best behavior, and naked as a jay-bird by the time you get back. So hurry up, wildman!"

With his back turned to her, he walked down the stairs saying, "Oooh baby, whatcha do t'me!"

"Uh, I heard that," she said, making him stop near the bottom stair, "And it's not, whatcha do t'me. It's 'Oooh baby, what I'll do t'you." She pointed a finger at him, smirked and closed the door.

Fran walked down Hancock Street, heading for his car that he'd parked near Arlington Street. A Marlboro in his hand, he thought of Eileen, his "naughty, naughty girl," and then of how he'd tell the boys that he would be moving to Chicago. This, by no means would cut him out of the business. If anything, he likely would become even busier, working both groups on either end, and straddling weekends in Boston and wherever else he'd need to be. Eileen was going to pay dearly for this decision, but he could not think of that. She knew that it was going to be rough some-times, and she'd been patient so far. She can hold on a little longer, he rationalized.

13

Fran was settled in Lincoln Park, Chicago by early January. Moving to Chicago in January was about the stupidest time of year to do it, but as he put it to Eileen, "I'll just have a few of the boys handle it." He said there was no need for her to come out there until he'd gotten settled. Translation: he needed to meet the Chicago group and find out what their situation was. As it was put to him before he left Boston, "They're a bunch of fuckin' renegades and need a bit of control put on them. Sort them out."

After the February 1996 Docklands bomb in London, Francis virtually disappeared. Every conversation was work, or exhaustion mixed with sexual innuendo. She felt useless. "Frannie, I want you to talk to me. Look at yourself. You're a wreck."

His eyes became more vacant, and she felt him looking for things to say to her. He behaved as though he only knew how to either sell an idea or defend one. Human nature was slipping from his possession. "Did you know about this?"

"You know I couldn't tell you that, even if I did. This is bad, Leen. This is really bad."

"No shit." She was angry that they'd betrayed the ceasefire, and the seeming normalcy that she and Francis had managed to assemble over the year and half. This meant that it all would have to start over again. They talked for a few minutes, but he was at work, and already running late for a meeting.

14
September 1996

They managed to secure a routine of at least every third or fourth weekend together, with a mid-week rendezvous thrown in when possible. This month, Francis returned to Boston a few days early. He picked at his salmon steak and baked potato not bothering to look at Eileen. She finally had figured out how to broil salmon without charring the top and leaving the inside cold. How is it that a woman can be raised by a gourmet cook, come from a long line of champion cooks and still have difficulty microwaving popcorn? She didn't even like salmon all that much, but it was Frannie's favorite. She'd even mastered a mean dill sauce to go with it. He sipped at the Saintsbury chardonnay she picked up for the evening.

The raw salmon had been laughing at her from the cutting board earlier in the day, taunting her like an ornery 12 year-old boy to a 9 year-old on a playground, each time she picked up one spice or another to season the thing. She uncorked the first bottle of wine before going into battle. The carving knife felt better in her hand knowing that the cavalry was standing sentry in a

Waterford wine glass only two feet from her. The sense of triumph, removing the perfectly cooked salmon from the oven was almost too much for her to bear. Fran stood in the kitchen watching her, applauding as she lay the salmon on the plates.

Eileen poured the dill sauce over hers. Fran ate his plain. She noticed his absence, listening to the tinny beat of his fork beating against the plate, spearing at this meal. "Hon, is there a problem? Is the food okay?"

He looked up. "Great," he spoke with his food packed against the inside of his right cheek. His fork was turned with the tines downward. He waved it back and forth as he continued. "It's wonderful. You've outdone yourself." He gulped down the mouthful and reached for his glass.

"Then what's yer deal, man?" A feeble attempt at bringing levity to the table.

His fork met the plate with a mild force and he looked right at her. "Tomorrow's my review."

"Your what? Tomorrow's Saturday?"

"No. My other review. My annual assessment, you might say."

Eileen ripped at a dinner roll, shoving the piece into her mouth and washing it back with the Saintsbury. "So, what does that mean?"

"I wish I could tell you, but basically, it'll be a full weekend of physical exams, a psychological analysis and a bunch of interviews."

"Well, a physical will be good for you."

"Yeah, but if they actually find that I have a beating heart, they may drum me out for being too human." He gave a quiet chuckle.

"Promise?" Eileen smiled.

"Unfortunately, no."

"If it'll help, I'll read love sonnets to you all night and you'll go in there flitting around like TinkerBell."

"Doubt it would work, Babe." She felt sorry for him, watching for a sign of positivism in his eyes. Fran rarely displayed real emotion about the Rah. Non-chalant, poker-faced, no-matter responses were the norm.

"Alright. Well, you can't say I didn't offer."

"I know," he reached across the table and held her hand. "Babe, dinner was great. I'm sure better than what they served at the Last Supper."

"Lovely. I'll be sure to include that as the reviewer's quote in the guidebooks when I open my restaurant."

He pushed back his chair, still holding her hand and pulled her up from her seat. "Aw, come onnn." Frannie kissed her then picked up their wine glasses. He tilted his head toward the doorway, "Let's go in the living room."

They left the lights off and Fran did his Ricco Sauve saunter to the fireplace. "How 'bout a little mood lighting?" He flipped the switch next to the mantle and turned on the gas-powered flames.

"Perfect." Eileen sat on the floor and leaned against the leather chair just to the left of the fireplace.

"I still can't believe you put in a fake fireplace." He sat next to her with his arm around her.

Eileen slumped down a bit, resting her head against his shoulder. "It's not fake!" She slapped her hand on his knee. "It's cleaner, it's cheaper, it means that I don't have to lug wood into the house, and it enhances your capabilities as a stud, so shut up, darlin'." She kissed his jaw and sipped her wine.

"God, this is nice." Fran stroked her hair with one hand and held a cigarette with another. "Leen, thanks for a terrific dinner. This has been more than I deserve."

"Deserve?" She rubbed his leg as if consoling him. "Honey, you deserve much more than silly piece of salmon and a spud. One of these days, we'll be on the beach in Bermuda, staying in a posh hotel and having a whole week to ourselves." The fantasy was one Eileen lived on over and over. "Someday," she wanted to say to him, "Someday, I will be number one in your life." They'd talked about it numerous times but always as a far-away dream that Fran would never dare to encourage. Talk of beaches and vacations were met with responses like, "Hmmmm, yeah. It'd be nice."

"Leen, I'm scared. I'm fuckin' scared."

"Why? Don't you do this review thing all the time?"

"This one will be different." He was speaking so quietly she almost couldn't hear him.

"Tell me why."

"Ei-leen." He drew out her name in frustration as if to say, "You know better than to ask that."

She sat up and put her hands on his shoulders. "Fran. As you've said to me over again, 'Talk to me.' Sure, you always want to hear what goes on in my head. Well, I don't care about protocol. Fuck sake, Frannie! You're a mess. What will be different! I want to help you through this."

His hand shook as he took a drag on the Marlboro. He rubbed his other hand over his jeans to try and stop his palm from sweating. "I can't! I want to, but," he put out the cigarette, ran his hand through his hair and took a deep breath. "I fucked up, Leen. They think I failed."

"How?"

"The ceasefire. The whole bloody thing. I pushed so hard for them to go along with it and it failed. This was my one shot and now I have to pay for it. I don't know what's going to happen. I can tell you one thing, I won't be a leader for much longer. It doesn't look good. I don't want to scare you." He looked at her, watching her face twitch trying to keep from crying. "Oh Honey, come 'ere t'me." His arm wrapped around her shoulders pulling her to him. "I promise. I'll be okay."

"You don't know that. I'm sitting here listening to you tell me how awful it all could be, and I'm frightened for you. Now, you're telling me that it'll all be fine."

He kissed her. "I don't know what will happen, or how it'll all go, but I can promise you that I'll be o-kay. I'll be okay. You'll be okay, and we, we will be okay. Leen, you are my sanity, and my only source of real happiness. Protecting that small portion of what's left of me is worth fighting for. I can still be scared, but I'll be fine. Besides, a little fear is healthy."

"How come you're not there tonight?" She wasn't going to ask him that, but he never mixed weekend work with her, especially when it seemed to be this big a deal for him. "Why did you come here instead of going straight to Southie?"

"I wanted to be with you. I've missed you, and I needed to see you. Plus, we deserve some time together. They think I'm in Des Moines. I'll have to give them a call in a bit. I hate to ask, but can you run me to the airport in the morning?"

"Sure." Involving her in any kind of scheme, no matter how minor, reverberated his desperation to be near her. He could have just called a cab in the morning. He didn't have to say, "I love you." He rarely ever did anymore. This small action was proof of it. He was eluding the Southie crew to be with her. Who needed hearts and flowers with proof like that?

"We'll figure something out, but probably, you should drop me at international departures and I'll walk over to United arrivals."

"Whatever you want. God, I wouldn't mind going to international departures and us just getting out of here."

"I know. Leen, please don't talk like that now. I need to keep my wits. Though, you'd love Paris." He stood up. "I have to stop." He rubbed his hands over his face and grunted.

"Frannie."

"Yes Dear."
"Take me to bed."
"Yes Dear."

15

They woke at 7, showered together and dressed in relative quiet. Francis' nerves were stretching thinner. Eileen thought she'd noticed him develop more wrinkles in his forehead overnight. They drove to the airport, barely speaking, oftentimes looking for something to talk about. She pulled up to the door at Swissair departures, hesitant to speak.

"Well Hon, I uh, I hope you have a good weekend," her face twisted in a confused expression knowing that she was not saying the right thing.

"Thanks." He had his hand on the door handle. "Look, Babe, I'll be fine. Don't worry about me. It'll be okay."

"I know." Eileen nodded her head and felt tears rushing through her sinuses, into her eye sockets. She did not cry. The tears dripped without the typical sniffling and voice crackling that she had become so accustomed to battling.

"Hey, hey. Come on," Fran held her and pushed away her hair. "Look, I'll be back in Chicago on Monday. I'll call you Monday night and we'll talk, and this weekend will be behind us and everything will be the same as it always has."

"Okay. You can't come back before you leave?"

"No. They'll drive me to the airport, and I know that I'll be exhausted. You shouldn't be around me afterward. I'll be in a less than pleasant mood." He laughed a bit.

"Alright." She'd heard the same excuse loads of times before and knew better than to push.

Fran let go of the door handle and leaned over the gear box to hug her. He kissed her quickly, the way a husband kisses his wife when she drops him at the train station every Monday through Friday. Almost rote behavior. Eileen laughed at his actions.

"Okay Dear," she said, "Have a good day at the office. Don't forget to pick up lotto tickets on the way home."

"What?" She confused him.

"Frannie. This is so weird. It's like I'm dropping you off at work and should be saying, 'Okay Honey. Have a good one. I'll have dinner ready by 7.' Instead, I'm saying, "Okay Hon, have a good day; watch your back; don't let them break your spirit; and make sure you're not followed. Now, do you have your lunch money?"

"Woman," he held the door handle and looked at her, "Sometimes you are so strange, but I do love that about you. Okay. I've gotta go. Have a good weekend, and DON'T WORRY about me. I know you. Don't do it. There's no need." He kissed her again. This time with more passion than a train-station drop-off peck on the cheek. He grunted as he backed away from her. "Thank God it's a long walk to arrivals. I need to walk off the thoughts I'm having of you right now."

"Bastard." She slapped the steering wheel. "Oh sure. Leave me with parting thoughts like that. I'm going to have to go home and sit on the washer." Eileen giggled, smiling at him as she ran her hand through his hair. "I love you."

"I love you too, Babe." He was stepping out of the car. "I'll talk to you Monday night." Fran closed the door and she stayed there until she watched him walk into the terminal. She thought of following him down to United arrivals to see who was collecting him. She could have followed him/them to Southie. She could have satisfied her curiosity and just at least seen where it was that he spent all of his time. Eileen thought about it, rolling the possibility over and over in her head before she pulled away from the airport. Fran trusted her. Their relationship was the only one she'd ever had where trust was an understood thing. From the night in the New York hotel when he let her in to his secret, to every other letter and conversation and moment they'd shared. He knew everything about her, and she knew everything he could tell her. Breaking that trust would have destroyed the core of their relationship. Knowing an address, or seeing the faces of a few strangers wasn't worth the destruction it would do.

Eileen had become a champion at self-preservation. Lying to her friends and family about Fran's schedule and whereabouts wore thin. Eileen was living a secret life, just as much as Frannie was. A sane person, living two lives. She equated it to being the perfect test-case for a shrink in search of a schizophrenic completely aware of her personalities, and always in complete control of them.

Eileen invited Jack over for dinner that evening. They hadn't gotten together for a while. No *Now Voyager*, or any other films. Tonight they sat at the bar at Brendan Behan's, an old hangout in Jamaica Plain, drinking, smoking, and lamenting Eileen's lovelife. Jack never was a huge fan of Fran's, but he'd also never seen Eileen happier with anyone else, so he had to give him that much. "Jack, there are so many times when I wonder to myself, 'Just what am I doing?' I mean, this is bullshit. I consider all of it, but then I consider what it would all be like without him?"

"I never thought I'd say this, but you've got to get away from him. Eileen, this is ridiculous." The conversation continued on an ebb and flow like a pathetic game of badminton, for at least 20 minutes, or however long it took to consume two pints a piece. As Jack rambled about why Eileen should subject herself to another break-up with Francis, Eileen observed the couple at the end of the bar. They were having a heart to heart, or the woman was having at him while the man expressed his mea culpas. Why, Eileen wondered, did they choose to get into it in a bar? Could she only convey her feelings with a few drinks in her? Was it a "sperm of the moment" debate about one or the other not being happy with their sex life? The woman, visibly distressed, needed to tell him what was on her mind between sips of chardonnay. Was she aware that on a good day the house white was a run-of-the-mill chardonnay? She looked like the type who only drank Kendall Jackson when absolutely necessary, yet preferred the vintages of smaller, lesser known Sonoma County vineyards. The neighborhood was becoming increasingly yuppified, and wine snobs now were blending in at Stop&Shop with the kids from Mission Hill. Eileen gathered all of this from the woman's impeccably tailored suit and perfectly selected accessories. The man, a young one of roughly twenty-five, was doing everything possible to keep her happy. As her facial expressions grew more tense, his right hand reached for hers on the bar, and his left arm found its way, yet gingerly, around her waist. His body language screamed, "I'll do anything to keep you happy—for now," in unison with her words of "If you love me, here's watcha gotta do." It was typical, and priceless. Frannie was always telling her to stop watching people, but then he would throw in his own two cents about the situation she was surveying.

"Eileen," Jack asked again, "Why do you put up with it?"

"Jack, I can't explain it, but trust me, I'm very happy." Jack would not have believed her, except for the accompanying smile on Eileen's face, backing up her words.

16
May 1997

Eileen sat on United flight 642 to Chicago with a mix of excitement and fear. A weekend with Fran, after three weeks of
repressed emotion peppered with pornographic phone calls in the
middle of the might. They'd become so used to phone sex that
Eileen considered bringing her cell phone and lying next to him in
bed while they held their phones to their ears and talked about
what they were doing to each other. Yes, the first few days in
weeks when he could pull himself away from the boys, and the
girls, though she chose not to think of them. One other small
thought struck her; the positive pregnancy test stick in her handbag. The little blue stick housed in a zip-lock bag would make for
interesting conversation.

"Would you like anything to drink?" Eileen hadn't noticed the
flight attendant until she smacked her elbow with the drink cart.
She didn't want the useless bag of honey-roasted peanuts and a
spit-worth of Diet Coke. She thought, a double Jameson neat for
my nerves, and a bag of ice for my throbbing arm.

She turned to the 21 year-old artificially blonde, pixie-stick of a woman and said, "Just an orange juice, please." Four whole ounces of juice. Good thing those airlines give you so much ice, 'cause I might hurt myself on all that vitamin C, she wanted to yell.

"Fran, I'm pregnant," she mouthed the words to herself. She'd yet to say them out loud. She preferred to count the days on the calendar, call the test a mistake and tell herself she was "running late."

"'Scuse me," she looked back at the attendant's navy blue ass and white apron strings. The attendant was bent over the passenger on her right. Jeeze, with a pointy ass like that it must hurt when she sits down. Eileen was in a mood today. No doubt about it. The toddler behind her was kicking the back of her seat. Please, can't we open a window and send him off? The high-altitude bartender turned around to her. No "Yes, may I help you," just eye-to-eye contact. "May I have a white wine please," Eileen asked.

"Chardonnay?"

"Perfect." Eileen hated most chardonnays. They were never dry enough for her. She couldn't tell Fran without a little booze in her blood. Too many thoughts, visions and potential conversations had over-taken her life for the last two weeks. This child would have 10 cousins, all in Ireland. Two years they'd been together. Two years of lost holidays, lost weekends, letters and phone calls. What would the other passengers think if they knew that I.R.A. off-spring was on board? Okay, she thought, enough with the mental torture.

"Ma, look what Daddy gave me!" Christmas mornings would be soccer balls and long-distance phone calls. The child behind her was getting louder, kicking faster than a Riverdancer, escalating to a tantrum. Eileen had watched the army of strollers and diaper bags board the flight. Would this be me? Never. I will be a much more fashionable parent. The conversation in her head continued. I might never travel alone again. I might be escorted everywhere. After all, I am the mother of an Army Council child. Great, she continued, now I can move through a gauntlet of barmen, taxi drivers, construction workers and business managers between airports across the country. Bridget and I (Eileen knew she was having a girl) will be fine. We'll be with Fran. He can bring the boys to her soccer games if necessary, but she will be ours and just ours.

Rap! Rap-rap-rap rap-rap. Bang. Bang. Bang. BANG! The toddler was in full tantrum. Eileen turned around, wrapping her neck into the aisle and behind her seat. She looked at him, then at his mother who had one hand on his right leg while reading Jackie Collins' *Hollywood Wives*. Her black, straight, Cher-like hair covered her face so that she could not see Eileen.

The child, about two, focused on Leen for a bit like he hadn't realized that the seat in front of him was a life size jack-in-the-box. She touched his little Air Jordan Nikes, looked at him, then put her finger to her lips. His silence caused his mother to look up from her book, and put her hair behind her ear. Eileen smiled at them, then turned back to her seat. I'll be a great mother, she thought.

Against every guidebook's recommendations, she drank the wine—her first drink since doing the test. This night was special. Surely God would give her special dispensation for it. Would Fran be there for the delivery, or would he be on the phone from Chicago or New York or wherever coaching her through it. Eileen drank her wine. She wanted another. The baby must have grown legs in those 10 seconds just so it could kick her for having that thought.

The plane arrived at O'Hare Airport on time but still went through the interminable taxiing to the gate. Her nerves soared to a new level of tension. A part of her wished she was sitting closer to the front of the plane so she could get off sooner. Another part considered hiding in the bathroom until the plane turned back around to Boston. Rational thought won out, and Eileen gathered her bag from the overhead bin, steadying herself for seeing Fran. She always hated the first and last few hours with him. Those were the times when, in her mind, she was supposed to first be grateful, then ultimately understanding of his limited availability. She made the decision about half-way up the jetway to maintain control of the weekend's events. This time, the boys would have to take a backseat to our life. Eileen felt almost powerful.

Fran stood at the edge of the gate where the carpeting met the tile. Eileen came alive in his arms. The smell of his neck as she pressed her body into his made all of the time apart disappear. Every time she envisioned these moments, she'd cry, but never did in real life. Wheeled suitcases whipped past them in the terminal. Eileen noticed another couple, both in grey business suits sharing a similar embrace. Were there three of them too? She closed her eyes as Fran pulled her head closer to him and whispered, "Hi Babe. God, I've missed you." He kissed her ear, let go a bit and pressed his lips to hers.

"Me too," Eileen gave him a kiss. He picked up her bag, and they walked to the parking garage. He didn't hold her hand. He never did anymore. Eileen forgot when the change came, but they'd reached the point where affection was expressed in three situations: after and before flights, and in bed. Eileen had watched him shut down over the years. Frannie had reached the point where he called her his "sanity." Did that mean that she was his only remaining link to humanity? With her, he had to show emotion. At work, that was almost frowned upon.

"You want to get some dinner," he asked her approaching the toll exiting the airport.

"Sure." Eileen was looking at the billboards on the highway trying to figure out how to tell him.

"Hey," he reached over and took her hand then kissed it. He shocked her. Is it pathetic that I am elated by this small display, or have I become 'understanding,' Eileen thought. They went to a small steak house near his apartment, but she could not bring it up.

On the drive home, Eileen knew that it had to be done. "Hon, can we stop at Walgreen's?"

"Sure. What do you need?"

"Tampax," with that one word, Eileen was guaranteed that he'd leave her to shop on her own.

"I'll wait in the car." A 35 year-old career terrorist intimidated by a wad of cotton in a plastic tube. Were John Major and Tony Blair aware of this and simply not exercising a plan? Forget intelligence gathering, Eileen thought strolling through the aisles. MI-6 could eliminate the Rah by carpet-bombing Ireland with tampons. Regulars in the less volatile areas, and supers in the high-risk regions. The entire era of the Troubles could be brought to a grinding halt. No man in Ireland would be capable of going outdoors. It'd give a whole new meaning to the term PTSD—Post-Tampon Stress Disorder.

Eileen put aside her twisted notion as she paid for two EPTs, and yet another ClearBlue Easy. Frannie, like her, was a stickler—no pun intended—for detail. Until it's been verified by another source, it isn't necessarily true; three verifiable sources and it's gospel. Eileen paid for the tests and returned to the car.

"All set," he asked.

"Yeah."

"Well, guess I know what kind of weekend we'll be having," Fran joked to her, but still sounding disappointed that she was "off the team" for the weekend.

"Aw Honey," Eileen leaned over and ran her hand over his crotch, "I'm sure we'll find plenty of things to do." Frannie moaned and shifted himself in his seat.

They returned to his sparsely decorated apartment in Lincoln Park, managing to get a parking space only a block from his place. Fran carried her duffel bag. Eileen clutched the Walgreen's bag. He opened the door to the second-floor apartment, flipped the light switch on the wall to the right of the doorway and gestured her to enter ahead of him. They stood in the living room staring at each other. Eileen picked up her bag and tossed it in the bedroom. "I'm going to get ready for bed. "

"Excellent," Fran replied. As she walked toward the bathroom he picked up the bag, "Hey, you need this?" He felt the boxes jumble in the cellophane bag. "Leen, what is all this?" He opened the bag and looked inside.

"Oh God."

Fran reached into the bag and pulled out the ClearBlue Easy. He tipped the box back and forth looking at each side of the packaging, confused. "I thought you needed tampons."

"Frannie," Eileen sat on the bed, "I'm late."

"How late?"

"A few weeks," she tried to sound unaffected by the delay.

Fran stood silent then began searching for rational excuses, "Well, you've had so much going on, Babe. You've been working hard, getting the house together, and things between us haven't necessarily been a walk in the park lately."

"That's true, but," Eileen pulled the zip-lock bag from her purse, "I got a positive test the other day."

"You did?" He stood barefoot on the carpet, leaning against the closet door.

"Yes, but I had another that was negative, so I really don't know what the story is. I shouldn't have said anything."

"You bought more tests tonight?" He pointed at the bag now sitting on the bed.

"Three."

"Go do them." He handed her the bags, and she walked into the bathroom. After she'd shut the door, he leaned against it. "But, do them each separately. You want three different samples otherwise who knows what we'll get."

Eileen sat on the toilet opening the first box. She didn't need to read the directions. She'd done the same damn thing just the other day. First the ClearBlue. She peed on the stick without thinking of Fran on the other side of the door. Usually, when she was in his apartment, she was especially nervous about her bathroom activities. Did she spend too much time in there? Could he hear her? Even after all of these years she hadn't overcome the bathroom phobias so common with new relationships. He, on the other hand, never hesitated to pop into the room while she was in the shower, sit on the toilet and fire up a cigarette. Eileen stood watching the second-hand on her watch, staring back and forth between the clock and the stick. She looked in the mirror, opened his medicine cabinet for no reason other than to do something with her time, and recalled the morning he lit the cigarette while she was in the shower. The steam and the smoke wafted over the shower. "Jesus! Are you trying to kill me? Get that thing out of here!" She had to laugh at the memory.

Eileen emerged from the bathroom with the stick in her hand and a smile on her face.

"Well?" Fran was sprawled in the chair in the living room. David Letterman's laugh track emanated from the TV.

"Negative."

"You sure?"

"Yeah," she said. "Yeah."

"Do the other one." He needed confirmation from the second test. Force of habit. "Come on Hon. You had a positive one, and a negative one. Let's go for two out of three."

"Okay." Eileen drank a Diet Coke, watched Letterman for a few minutes then returned to the bathroom. This time she used another brand. As she waited for the test to be done, she noticed the massage oil on the shelf above the toilet. Now was not the time to worry about it, but she had to wonder why he had it. They'd never used massage oil. Her attention shifted back to the test. "Oh God." She opened the door and handed him the stick. "Fran. It's positive. It's positive!" Eileen began to cry. She'd never thought of having a family with him. In the back of her mind, she thought it would happen down the road, but not with both of them in two different cities, and in these circumstances.

"Okay. Okay. Let me take a look at it." He held the stick in his hand, looking at the plus sign in the circle on the center of the stick.

Eileen sat on the edge of the bed and began to half-laugh half-cry. "Frannie. I just can't believe this."

He put the stick on the bathroom counter, came back into the bedroom, business as usual, and took off his clothes. He stepped out of his boxer shorts, the ones she'd given him, and got under the covers. Eileen had already crawled under the sheets on her side of the bed. They lay in the dark silent until Fran spoke. "You'll have to get rid of it."

"What?"

"Eileen, I can't be a father right now. I'm in no position to have a family."

Eileen faced the wall away from him and listened to his words float to the ceiling. "Uh-huh."

"Leen, this isn't the time. You can't keep it." He didn't say, "We can't keep it," or, "Are you okay," or "Let's talk about this, but realistically we can't keep it." This was an inconvenience for him. Fran rambled on about the way things were going with the boys. Eileen grew angry, crying into her pillow without making any noise. Frannie moved toward her, pressing his body against hers and stroking her hair. Eileen watched the lights fall down the mini-blinds as cars drove past his apartment building. "We'll be okay. C'mere t'me." She wiped her eyes and remained silent, rolling toward him and letting her face fall into his chest. They fell asleep until 2 AM when he woke and began making love to her. Eileen woke to his touch until they both were fully engaged for another two hours, more than likely waking the neighbors.

Sunday morning they lay in bed until 10:00. Her flight was at 12:15. "Please, can't I switch it and take the 3:00? I want to spend some time with you," she pleaded.

"No. I'm sorry, dear, but I've got people coming into town, and I have to work." Frannie was busy Sunday afternoon, as he was nearly every Friday, Saturday, Sunday, and whatever other day in the week there was to be busy. There was no room for Eileen in his plans. He prodded her to get in the shower and get ready to go. Fran drove her to O'Hare, holding her hand throughout the drive up the Kennedy Expressway. He stopped the car outside the United departures door and pulled her bag from the back seat. "Okay Hon, have a good flight."

"Thanks. Tell me what I want to hear," she whispered in his ear as he held her.

"I love you," he whispered back. He had to be asked. She knew that he was thinking of the rest of the day's business and had noticed him checking the clock on the dashboard as though he'd barely make it to wherever he had to be.

"I love you too." Eileen carried her bag into the airport and headed for the gate with 25 minutes to kill before boarding began for the trip back to Boston. Eileen sat on the flight infuriated, feeling as though she'd spent the night with an entirely different man. She'd met the self-absorbed Fran. No, she said to herself, rationalizing, he has no choice. We have no choice. This is our life. But, no matter what his excuses or reasoning, Frannie Sullivan was leaving her to handle the "problem." She couldn't call any-one, couldn't tell anyone about her disappointment and was afraid of the prospect of having to have an abortion. She couldn't care for a child on her own, and if this was how Francis had taken the news of her pregnancy, she had no confidence in him if she'd chosen to keep it. She rode home in the cab from Logan paying no attention to the traffic or the fact that the leaves were coming out on the trees around the city. Eileen carried her bag into the house, and heard it echo in the foyer when she dropped it on the floor. She couldn't call Jack. That would require telling him everything, and she didn't want Jack to think badly of Fran. Frannie was working so hard. No one possibly could understand their situation. Eileen lay on her bed with her hand over her stomach, apologizing to Bridget. "I'm so sorry Sweetheart. Your father really is a good man."

At 8:30, Eileen woke, took off her clothes and got in the shower. As she shaved her legs she watched the water swirling on the bathtub. It was pink. Her period had happened. Most days, it never was noticeable in the shower, or even in the tub. This time, it was almost violent. Bridget, stronger than her mother, had made the decision to leave on her own volition. Eileen got out of the shower, clutching her stomach from the ensuing cramps, put on her robe and retrieved a beer from the refrigerator. She raised the bottle in the air and said to Fran, "Well, once again, it works in your favor." Eileen never could be sure as to whether or not she was pregnant, but for weeks she felt guilty for not having defended their child to its father. She was angry for never having pushed Fran to the wall, never forcing him to accept what they both could be facing. She only saw herself lying on her side in his bed, watching the lights flow downward on the mini-blinds.

17
Nuala

Nuala had been a joke. A big night of ugly drinking, and her note had been a follow-up joke of the inferred need for them to get together. Except, Nuala was in. Nuala was part of Frannie's world. The part that he swore Eileen never would know. She came to Eileen in her sleep. On one occasion, Eileen had taken great satisfaction in dreaming of driving Nuala's silver Volkswagen Jetta into the river, and just standing on the dock watching it sink. Unfortunately, in the dream, Nuala hadn't been in the car. Perhaps in the next chapter of her dream, Eileen thought the morning after the dream, Nuala will be strapped and glued to the drivers seat with all of the car windows open on one of the Charles River's dirtiest days. For that, Eileen would welcome seeing the horrifying look of Nuala's algae-covered body, bloated face, and bulging eyeballs in her sleep. Eileen didn't tell Frannie that she felt pretty sure he had been fucking Nuala at one point in time. Surely not lately. He has been on his best behavior and for virtually all of the years they'd been together, he had always treated her with the utmost respect. No, he wasn't cheating now, but at one point early on, he had been getting a piece of the action on both sides of the prover-bial fence. She knew he'd lied. He committed the cardinal sin of cover-ups; he'd made his opinion of Nuala far too vile, and his laziness far too obvious.

Men have learned that women are suckers for statements like, "If I had something to hide, would I have left this sitting out in such an obvious place for you to see it?" Frankly, yes. Frannie had made that mistake three times, and each time his excuse was worse than the one before. First there was the greeting card perched on his coffee table. "Honey, if I had something to hide, would I have left this sitting out in such an obvious place for you to see it?"

Then, there was the wedding invitation addressed to the two of them. "We have common friends, and were invited to go together. Besides Honey, if I had something to hide, would I have left this sitting out in such an obvious place for you to see it?"

It capped off six months earlier with the discovery of Nuala's business card on his bedroom floor, a really lousy place to find another woman's calling card. "I have got to be more careful. This kind of stuff laying around could be really damaging to my work." Frannie took the card from Eileen as she held it out to him asking where it came from, "Besides Honey, if I had something to hide, would I have left it in such an obvious place?" Frannie should never have uttered that statement, because his fate had been sealed. Eileen had stood in the shower that morning after a few hours of making love with him, and immediately after, stepped on Nuala's business card (Ophtech, Morlat Health Products, Director of Regional Sales, New England Region, Framingham, MA). She'd considered throwing up, packing her bags and leaving, but could not find the strength to walk away from him. Nuala hadn't been mentioned in well over a year since the postcard discussion. A smarter woman would have said that

Frannie had become better at hiding. Eileen hadn't even thought of her, and the drowning dreams never resurfaced. After the morning's activities, the business card had been equivalent to being pistol whipped in the jaw, in a fine restaurant. Eileen gave Frannie the benefit of the doubt. She believed that it was more than likely the case of having seen Nuala at some meeting in some undisclosed location. She probably gave him her card from her new job, and they probably had to talk to finalize some plans before the latest round of peace talks.

Calm reasoning made the business card seem only slightly explainable. Stepping from the shower and drying her legs on the edge of the tub, Eileen set out on her own mission. Wrapped in her towel, she kissed Frannie, gave him a big "good morning Sweetheart smile," smacked him on the ass and told him to get in the shower. Once she could hear the changing timbre of the water on the floor of the tub as his body moved under the showerhead, she walked into his closet and made a beeline for the confirmation she needed. He had 17 golf shirts. Three were ones that she had given him, two were from his own company, three with the logos of unknown golf courses, one from one of his company's competitors, and eight were from various Morlat golf tournaments. One with the logo of the newest subsidiary of Morlat hung just below the empty box that Eileen's Valentine's Day gift, a black teddy, came in. That tournament had only taken place a month ago. Eileen knew because she'd watched it on ESPN. She held the sleeve of the shirt in her hand and thought, she has no creativity when it comes to giving gifts. A golf shirt or two is fine, but eight of them? Be serious. What she had really wanted to do was drop to the floor in the fetal position, clutching the shirt and the business card, wrapped in her wet bath towel and cry. "Honey, if I had something to hide, would I have left this sitting out in such an obvious place for you to see it?" She felt that statement stinging her brain. Yes, you asshole, you would.

Frannie still felt the guilt of having lied to Eileen. It had been so long since he had seen Nuala. They met through mutual friends, comrades, co-workers, whatever the appropriate term may be. She had tended to work on gathering information from the Western areas of the Republic. Frannie specialized in getting it from Armagh and Monaghan in the North. Upon first sight, he considered her to be an intimidating woman whose strength was not an attractive quality, rather something to fear. She was in jeans and a white T-shirt when they met in June of '93. She had been in Boston for 10 years, was 36, single, 5'9" and had eyes so dark that it was impossible to imagine what she was thinking. The eyes are the windows of the soul, and either she had no soul, or the curtains were closed. Her black hair was all one length, pulled back in a low ponytail. She had a small chest for a woman her size, but of course her purpose was not to entertain the boys, but to oversee them. Through numerous weeks and late nights, Nuala, who had once been a relative outsider, established herself as an essential leader and proved to be more than capable of taking their shit and giving it right back to them. Perhaps she brought gender equity to the I.R.A.. Perhaps she merely put the fear of God in them. When Eileen asked him about the card on his coffee table, Frannie had told her that he found Nuala completely frightening.

On that point he had not lied; however, he had failed to tell Eileen that those impressions did not last long, and while it might have been only for the sake of relieving stress or letting off steam, he and Nuala found themselves engaging in a wildly sexual relationship that lasted nearly six months. At the height of the final negotiations to call the I.R.A. ceasefire and pursue meaningful negotiations on the future of Northern Ireland, Frannie and Nuala had, in their respective areas of expertise, been working almost round the clock at coordinating intelligence on the ability to quell those on the fringes of the organization so that a ceasefire would be not only attainable but maintainable. Too many in the organization were eager to continue with campaigns of violence, disbelieving that any laying down of arms possibly could lead the British government to viable discussions. Frannie had achieved some incredible contacts in the U.S. Congress and the State Department who were willing to push the President to place Northern Ireland on his list of foreign policy priorities. With the backing of the U.S. Government behind Northern Irish actions to resolve the conflicts, the British would be more inclined to respond, or at least that was the thought. For 25 years, Britain had continually handled the situation on its own recourse. Such recourse had included human rights abuses, a revocation of civil rights, increased sectarian division and needless deaths. Whether due to a desire to maintain the Irish-American vote or the Catholic vote, or both or neither, U.S. involvement could do nothing but help, pending of course that the Administration did not try to play the hero, and turn the issue into another Grenada or worse.

Frannie had been running on virtually no sleep, staying at the Southie house and losing any semblance of his own life. Eileen was only a blip on the radar screen, and they'd been together only twice in three months.

It was 3 a.m. on Wednesday—four days into the final agreement. Six of them had spent five hours in the kitchen in Southie in a cloud of tobacco smoke, mulling over the options after having spent the evening receiving the latest information from cops, bartenders and God knows who else who'd gotten word from home. With all of the pieces of the jigsaw assembled, they were making deals and plans to ensure the success of the ceasefire on both sides of the Atlantic. Frannie had worked so hard in July during the meeting in Chicago with the leadership of the major Rah groups around the U.S. just to get them to come to the table. Finalizing trans-Atlantic agreements were virtually impossible yet in their final hours of coming to fruition.

Lying in bed, Frannie, pumped by the energy of the evening, was between his sheets, alone, holding an erection in his right hand. Suddenly, he focused on comments that the boys had been thrown around in jest between the otherwise stress-filled discussions of allaying fringe groups and negotiating with the antagonist after years of animosity.

"Fran, you need a woman. You've been giving us your fucking attitude for too long. Get out of here and get rid of that tension."

"Nuala, I think Frannie is looking for someone just like you."

An I.R.A. cease-fire is not the place to play the dating game. It was comic relief in the heat of battle. But he was there, alone, unable to sleep. He noticed the light coming under the bedroom door, turned the linens back from his body, swung his feet to the floor and could see only the door knob on the opposite wall. Given its age, the door should have creaked when he opened it. If it did, he didn't hear it. His heart was pounding too hard for him to notice.

Frannie approached the door to Nuala's room where she'd been staying and knocked quietly. If she did not answer, he would return to his bed. Nuala also was awake in the middle of satisfying herself. Opening the door, her eyes met Frannie's bare chest, scanned down to see him in only a pair of black Umbros, then looked up at his face. He didn't see her. He only saw her body, covered in her white T-shirt, barely hiding her hard nipples, and her legs exposed to the very tops of her thighs. Knowing why he was there, she opened the door fully, and reached for his hand when Frannie stepped in, simultaneously pulling her to him.

Even after the initial tension of the impending ceasefire, they continued their almost nightly meetings, alternating bedrooms. Fran continued to call Eileen during the day, tell her how wonderful she was, and then disappear to Southie. Eileen had no address or phone number to reach him. This was supposed to be for her protection, now it was for his convenience. Nuala stopped staying at the house in South Boston. Fran drove to Nuala's apartment in Allston, arriving at just past midnight to engage in sexual gymnastics.

He never learned anything about Nuala, and she would never learn that he found supermarkets confusing and preferred specialty stores, or that he loved country music, or that he found relaxation and gratification by cleaning his bathroom until it sparkled. She would never know that he only ate his salads with oil and red wine vinegar, and ate extra spicy buffalo wings for lunch on Thursdays at his favorite restaurant. Eileen knew all of this. Nuala knew that Frannie got off on having his earlobes sucked, and that he got especially aroused by entering her apartment and finding her spread-eagle on her dining room table in the form of a human all-you-can-eat buffet. One evening she'd even turned herself into a hot fudge sundae, placing dollops of whipped cream on her nipples, chocolate fudge down her torso, vanilla ice cream just above her pubic bone, and a cherry between her legs.

The most recent golf shirt had been a result of a meeting in New York, three weeks before Eileen found her business card. Shortly after the meeting, on a gray, humid afternoon, Nuala had sent him the golf shirt with the logo from the newly launched subsidiary, her business card, and a note inviting him to do her 'six ways to Sundae.' Frannie received the package on a Thursday morning by express mail at his new home. The card inspired him to masturbate on his couch despite the background noise from the talk show emanating from the television, but he subsequently pitched it in the garbage and hung the shirt in the bedroom closet.

Eileen had envisioned a small, blonde woman emerging from his bed, after dinner, a movie, and sex, and leaving her card on the pillow next to his like a corporate whore. She wondered if Frannie thought of Nuala when he made love to her. She wondered if all of his "busy weekends" were actually spent with Nuala. She wondered if the I.R.A. had been a lie—a perverted excuse for his unavailability. After all, he was a politically minded Irishman, and the stereotype had been established years before. A hoax like that, while extreme, would be believable. Then again, Eileen said to herself, he could probably convince me the world was flat if he tried hard enough.

18
November 1997

Fran had been in Chicago for almost a year, and their time together was less frequent, but his disposition had changed dramatically. He'd been more expressive with her and was telling Eileen how much he needed her. Nuala had lasted little more than two months and the thought of her became nearly repulsive. Fran continued to work with her but spent no more time than necessary working with her and the boys. Calls to Eileen were more important. Their relationship had gone from a certain comfort level to one of renewed excitement. He sneaked off to spend a weekend with her in Boston. If the boys had known he was in town, they would have been all over his case. He and Eileen drove to Kennebunkport for the day, just to check out the coast line. "Fran, you look so tired."

"I am. I can't keep doing this, Leen. They're all after me. I'm fucked."

"Frannie, tell me what is going on. You always say that I am smart enough to make decisions on my own and that my life is my own," she was yelling at him in frustration. "Well, I've thought long and hard about this. I've known you what, 10 or 11 years, and this has been a part of our lives the entire time."

"I know." He looked shameful.

"I want to help you. Talk to me. You don't have to tell me everything. You don't have to give me details but how can I feel like I'm supporting you, and you obviously need someone to lean on, when you tell me nothing? Frannie, I am asking you, please, let me in."

"Stop the car."

"What?"

"Pull over." She got off at an exit near Haverhill and pulled into a parking lot.

"What is it?"

Fran didn't look at her. He stared at the floor and kept both hands on the dashboard. His voice began softly, then escalated into rage, "Do you not think that I thought over and over again about how badly I would like to tell you what is happening? Do you not think that I would like to let you in?"

"Yes. I believe you have thought of that." Eileen's voice was a quiet monotone.

"I have thought about this, Leen, but I can't do it! I can't! And it's not because people would know about you. I've watched people crack up over this. People who aren't nearly as close to this as you are. They can't take the pressure. I cannot risk doing that to you. I will sooner die than let this hurt you." His jaws were clenched as he forced out the words.

"But Frannie, it already is hurting me! I sit here, useless, watching you go through one torment after another. It's tearing me up that there is nothing that I can do. You will not let me do anything and I can't stand it." Her monotone evolved into reserved anger.

"I have to go to Belfast next week." He shifted the conversation to a less emotional topic.

"Why?"

"I don't know. But, they told me to get a ticket and get on a plane, so I'm going."

"How long will you be gone?"

"They say a week, but I don't know."

"Eileen, there is a really good chance that I could be recalled."

"What do you mean?"

"I mean, there is a chance that they could call me back home. It was mostly my plan to get the ceasefire going, and it all backfired. There are people looking for my head now." The attempt to maintain rational talk did not last.

"Fine. If you're going then I'm going with you. If they want you at home, then we're both moving."

"No. It doesn't work that way."

"It does in my book. I will be damned if those sons-of-bitches are going to take you from me. If they want you home, then they get me too. I'll be patient for so long, but this is bullshit Frannie. They might have your life, but I will not let them take mine. You are my future and they cannot have it."

"Yes. They can. Look, I'm not saying that this is going to happen, but there is a very good chance and I want you to be prepared.

Eileen slumped over the steering wheel and cried uncontrollably. "I can't do it without you. I waited too long for you. Don't, don't," she was looking at Francis, grabbing at his shirt begging him, "Please don't let them do this Frannie. Please, I'll do anything. Money. We can leave and start a new life somewhere. Anything, just please don't make me do this without you." She was crying so hard she hardly could catch her breath and the muscles around her eyes were sore. Fran held her against his shoulder for a few minutes, whispering to her, telling her that they'd be fine, and that they'd be able to handle whatever happened. Nothing would keep him from her. They would be together. They might have to wait a while, but they would be together. After she'd calmed down, she climbed over the center console into his seat. Fran walked around the car and drove it back to Boston. Eileen continued to cry a little, but eventually fell asleep to the white noise of the tires rolling over the skips in the asphalt on the highway.

Before he left for Southie, they talked a bit more about his trip home. "I don't have a clue as to what this trip home will entail. I'll call you as soon as I can." He kissed her, holding her like he wanted to remember every detail of her body and took a taxi to the house. He told his friends that he'd just arrived in from Chicago and took an earlier flight than expected, thus the taxi, rather than being collected at the airport.

Eileen had become hooked on the Internet subscribing to a number of email lists, mostly Irish and Irish Republican news. Two days after Fran left, there were rumors in the news of an Army Council meeting scheduled to take place. The following day, all reports were denied. Three days later, news was that a meeting had already occurred and had wrapped up the day before. Fran called Eileen nine days after he'd departed for home.

"I'm so glad you're back, Babe."

"Me too. I'm knackered. Absolutely exhausted."

"How'd it go," she asked.

"Fine." She knew that he would not and could not say a word.

"I heard there was supposed to be some meeting, but then it was all confusing. Other than that, I didn't see much fun stuff happening around the world."

"Yeah, a meeting. I'd heard that too. Wouldn't be surprised if they'd had one. But, the good news is that I'm not going back, for now."

"Thank God." Eileen rolled over in her bed and switched the phone to her other ear.

"Yes, thank God, for now, but man do they have some plans for me. This is going to be really busy Babe."

"Well, don't forget about Valentine's Day."

"Sorry. Can't do it."

"You have got to be kidding. Okay, who's the asshole who says you have to work on Valentine's Day? For cryin' out loud Frannie, it's a Friday? Have you men no fear of your women?" She was trying to sound lighthearted about the situation but was mad as hell, and disappointed to lose another holiday. That made it three Valentine's days, two July 4ths, two Thanksgivings, two Christmases, and three of her birthdays spent apart.

19
March 1998

Frannie phoned her in the first week of the month and said, "I know it's short notice, but can you come out here this weekend?" Eileen booked a flight, paid $900 for the last-minute ticket and was at O'Hare by 3:00 PM the following day. He took her to Gibson's, one of the most traditional steakhouses in Chicago and home of the Gibson cocktail. He was taking her on a date, and showing her off to everyone in the place. He could not kiss her enough and they sat in a circular booth so that he could be right next to her. Eileen had plans of her own and was nervous. She'd had three glasses of wine and still felt stone-cold sober, unable to loosen up enough to broach the subject.

At home, in bed, she turned to him, "Frannie, I want to ask you something."

"What?" They were lying on their backs and her head rested against his chest with his arm around her shoulder.

"Will you marry me?"

"What?" He sat up and looked at her.

She continued, "Now, before you look at me and say, 'I can't, and you know I can't,' let me pose a few ideas to you. First, I am not saying that I want to do anything immediately. Second, we've been doing this for just over two years, and I think we've got things down pretty well." She was spitting out her soliloquy at 100 mph, nervous and shaking. "Third, naturally, I'd like for us to live in the same place, but we can work on it. I don't want to lose any more time with you. We've given up a lot of control. Much of that has had to be done, but maybe not all of it. Let's work with this. Keep your life; keep your business. We've gotten that routine down pretty well, and I don't want to know anymore. I doubt if you would not be the only man in your position to have a wife— oh my God, what a weird word—and if you tell me that none of your friends are married, well, I'd have a difficult time believing you. As it is, you tend not to bring your work home, so what's the problem there? And, even if you do work out of the house, we'll get two phone lines, set up a separate room; hell we'll even get a separate entrance if you want it. It'll be your secured space. We've already got the basement apartment at my place. I'm not conceding, I'm trying to find a way that we can work with what we have and not be forced to make too many sacrifices in the process."

Eileen did not notice the empty expression on his face; not shocked, blank. She took a deep breath and delivered her wrap-up, "Frannie, I love you. I adore you. I respect you. You excite me. You thrill me. You give me cause to worry sometimes, but I suppose that's a given in any relationship. I trust you in a way that I have never thought I could for anyone. Please say you'll marry me. I love you. I love everything about you. Someday, I want to be your wife, and so I'm asking again, will you marry me?"

He was devastated and dumbfounded. "Eileen. I can't. I want to, but I can't. It wouldn't be fair to you, and to be honest, people in my position do not have families. The lower level guys do, but we can't. It's too dangerous and it's not fair. Aw Honey, I wish we could. God knows I wish we could, but I simply don't have a choice on this one." He lay back down, looking at her but not making eye contact.

She knew that would be his answer, and so the shock of being turned down wasn't as great as the emptiness of knowing that for at least the next few years there would be no change.

20
April 1998

Three weeks after the marriage discussion, Eileen lay in her bed watching the Oscars. Somewhere between Best Actor and Best Film, the I.R.A. kidnapped her soul. Fran called, a week later than he was expected back from Belfast, and uttered three words, "I've been recalled." Three words, and a sense of panic that shattered everything. He said, "We knew it could happen, Babe."

"Why," she asked, "Why are they taking you? You're from the 26 counties, not the six?" It was all rhetoric. She knew the answers.

She lay in bed with the phone to her ear, crying. Tears ran down the side of her head into her ear, mixing with his quiet, guilt-ridden words. She cried for herself, and for what was to become of him. She heard his fear as he said, "Just let it out, Babe."

"When do you have to go," she asked fearing his response.

"Sunday."

She wailed, "That's five days!"

"I know...I know," his voice deteriorated to a whisper.

Eileen only could say, "I'm sorry. I'm sorry I'm not strong. You have so much ahead of you, and I am just not being strong."

She tried to make light of it in order to keep up his spirits, "Honey, if you really didn't want to get married all you had to do was say so." It didn't work, and they both cried.

They talked for hours. Eileen offered to fly to Chicago and be with him before he left. She offered to sell the house and go with him, but those ideas were out of the question. He had things to do—quit his job, get out of his lease and meet with the local boys. They were the same people who had stolen his time from her. People may come home to find their houses burglarized their VCR and PCs gone, she thought. These robbers walked into my bedroom and took my soul; the VCR and PC left in their places. No fingerprints. No forensic evidence. She went from being a woman in love with the man who'd been able to complete her, to a woman who was planning a funeral with the corpse's help. Three days later he called and they talked some more, trying to ignore the impending deadline.

He told her that she would know if anything happened to him. A "contact" would reach her. She told him that she wanted to know more about him. "I want to know if you get a cold. I want to know if you sneeze." He told her that she wouldn't believe whom the contact was, if he told her. Naturally, he didn't tell her, though Eileen thought of possible hunches.

"I've sent you something by FedEx. You should get it tomorrow." He was speaking gently, almost inaudibly into the phone.

"What? What is it?" She hesitated then said, "Please Frannie, I can't bear many more surprises right now."

"It's just a small gift for you. Call me as soon as you get it."

"Okay. By the way, you should be receiving something tomorrow as well. I didn't know what else to send you, but I hope you like it. It's just a small little thing."

FedEx delivered to each of them by 10:30 that Friday morning. Eileen opened her package and removed a gold, 8x10 frame containing Seamus Heaney's poem *Scaffolding*. For as long as he could remember Heaney had been her favorite poet, and she'd told him that *Scaffolding* was her favorite one by him. She said it reminded her of the two of them and all of the obstacles they'd managed to overcome or circumvent. She ran her fingers over each of the words, written in Frannie's script, smiling and crying through the verses.

Fran received Eileen's package and tore open the envelope removing a small box and a letter.

Dear Frannie,

I wish I knew what to say or how to make this better for both of us. I admit it. I'm scared. I'm scared for you, and I'm scared for me. Funny, when we were younger, wasn't this the point in our lives where we had planned on having everything all figured out? Ha. Good thing we're both creative because we have a long road ahead of us now, I suppose. Darling, I just want you to know that I am proud of you, and I love you, and you always will have my heart. You are my heart. No matter how long it takes or how difficult things may become, you always will have me. No matter what changes or challenges you face, know that I always am on your team. I love you. The enclosed is a small little something that I hope you will keep with you. It will keep you safe and will give you a little piece of me to always have with you. I'll be strong. Don't worry about me. I have just one request, please, please don't let go of me.

With all of my love,

Eileen

He opened the box and pulled out her gold Celtic cross necklace. He'd given it to her in Dublin when they were kids, and she still wore it everyday. The etchings had almost rubbed off from so many years against her neck. He'd never known her to take it off. He held it between his fingers and cried, knowing what he had to do. He picked up the phone and called her for one of their final conversations of plotting and scheming as to how they would keep it all together.

Their last conversation came at 8 AM the following morning. Eileen had cried only a little during their chats throughout the week and struggled to keep herself together. She did not want him to leave with the image of her being a puddling mess. She'd neither slept nor eaten in four days. She couldn't keep track of time and couldn't focus her mind on anything other than the idea of being without him. She wailed, holding the phone. She hadn't told anyone that he was leaving. How could she explain it? "Oh yeah, Fran's decided to move home. Yup, he fucked off back to Europe; got a screaming job in Paris." That was to be her alibi. She lay on the kitchen floor at 11 AM in the same clothes she'd been wearing and sleeping in since the morning after the first call days earlier. FedEx made a delivery to her just after lunchtime. Eileen ran her fingers over the envelope and touched Fran's handwriting. She opened it and removed a note and a small box.

Dear Leen,

Thank you for your gift. I can't keep it, Hon. I can't keep anything that could tie me to anyone. I'm going to miss you like all hell. I have always loved you. I always will. Know that. I'll be okay.

Always yours,

Francis

She opened the box and put the cross back around her neck.

21
June 1998

The slam of the brass mailslot in the door resonated into the living room where Eileen sat on the floor paying bills. The mail delivery had become a daily dose of manic-depression. She kept hoping for some bit of news from Fran and began playing mind games with herself. If the mail were on time, then a letter would come. Early delivery was a sure sign of correspondence from him. Late delivery equaled prolonged foreplay, which surely would lead to something indicating his whereabouts. This rollercoaster dominated her days and nights. Emails were torture as well. No sign of Fran. Had he forgotten her? Was he alive? Was he safe? She tried to stifle her anxiety, walking to the foyer to pick up the mail; a Pottery Barn catalog, two offers for new credit cards, the electric bill and a sealed, unaddressed envelope. Her heart raced as she turned the envelope over in her hands. No stamp so it wasn't mailed from Ireland. Had it been hand-carried? "Stop analyzing and just open it you fool," she yelled at herself.

A single piece of paper fell from it. A hand-printed note written in all capital letters: MOLLY DARCY'S. 3 PM TUESDAY, THE 5TH."

No name. Could Fran be back in town? He would have given her some indication. The 5th was tomorrow. Eileen grew nervous and frightened. This would be the meeting where she learned of his fate. So, a contact does exist, she thought. A strange sense of elation washed over her. I am not anonymous. 12:47 PM. 26 hours and 13 minutes 'til lift-off.

Molly Darcy's was a newly renovated pub on Broadway in South Boston. She'd been there once before the new management rescued it from completely decaying into a run-down Southie bar. She parked two blocks from Molly's and was settled on a chair at the bar by 2:55. She ordered a Guinness and surveyed the room. Three men dressed in faded jeans and old t-shirts sat at the table by the window. They looked like construction workers who must have worked the 6-2 shift. Two other men, each on their own, sat at the far end of the bar reading the *Boston Herald*, smoking Marlboros. They didn't seem to know each other but looked like a set of twins with their matching papers, matching smokes, and matching pints.

Eileen downed half her Guinness by 3:03. For a non-Guinness drinker she had no trouble putting it away. She saw a bottle of Paddy whiskey on the shelf above the cash register. She thought, Paddy had stopped being imported to the U.S. in 1988. What was it doing there? Eileen forced herself not to order a shot for the sake of nostalgia. She and Fran drank it in college. Back then, it was his favorite. No, better to remain clearheaded for whatever lay ahead.

She checked her watch; 3:06. "Hello." A voice spoke over her left shoulder. Eileen looked up disappointed not to see Fran. The man, 5'8" with light brown hair, solid build and grey eyes was one of the three men from the table by the window. She looked at him, then noticed that the other two had left.

"Hello," she answered. What is it, Eileen thought. Where's my Fran? How is he?

"It's nice to meet you, Ms. Eliot." He spoke with a brogue that she could not place. Definitely not bog, not a northerner and not Dublin.

"And you are?"

"It's best if I don't say, but call me 'Francis'." Message received, she thought.

"Okay Francis. What brings us to Molly's? May I buy you a drink?"

"No, thank you. How about if I buy you one?" He gestured toward the barman who began pulling two pints of Guinness. He placed one in front of Eileen, and one before Francis, then walked to the far end of the bar. "Thank you for meeting me."

"I assume you sent the note."

"Perhaps."

"Look, don't play games with me. What do you want?" The Guinness was not alleviating her anxiety.

"Sorry. I'm sure you are quite confused by this. Frankly, I'm pleased to see that you came down here. This isn't necessarily a great neighborhood compared to where you live."

"Why are you surprised I'm here?"

"May I call you Eileen?" He reached into his front pants pocket and pulled out a pack of Camel Lights, lighting one with a miniature Bic disposable lighter.

"Sure." She waited a few seconds, "Not to be rude, but could you cut to the chase?

"Eileen, we've known about you for a long time. No matter what your man thinks. He's fine, by the way, but that's all I'll say."

"I have no idea what you are talking about," she lied.

"You are a handful, aren't you," the man commented. "Well, the man of whom you know nothing is fine. Eileen, we require your help. You do not have to agree, but we are in a bit of a bind and need some assistance."

"How? Why me?" She forgot about Fran, and focused on 'Francis" request.

"We can keep it so that you know nothing, but we need a new place. Too many of us are moving around with all of the changes that are going on." He leaned in next to her putting his arm around her shoulders until his lips were against her ear, like a date whispering dirty fantasies to his girlfriend. "Your basement flat. We can work out a system for getting them in and out. You'd never see anyone."

She followed his lead wrapping her arms around his neck and whispering into his ear, "You are asking me to harbor criminals. It could ruin me. Why would I help you, and how would you protect me? After all, you bastards took away everything that mattered to me." She leaned back then kissed him gently on the lips to maintain the charade.

He ignored her questions. "There's a back entrance to your flat. A colored card will go through your mail slot a day before a package arrives and the morning after the package is collected. Arrival notices will be purple postcards for Maeve's Cleaning Service. Collections will be marked with yellow cards for Maeve's. It will let you know when to leave the door unlocked and when not to go in. Can you do that Eileen?"

"You haven't answered my question. Why would I help you?"

"Because dear, you have no choice. Besides, your Fran would be disappointed if you couldn't help him."

Eileen did not allow any emotion to come over her face but felt her heart stop. So, now he's pulling me in. This is his idea of letting me know that he is okay. She sat silent for a moment then reached for her cigarettes. This man, this 'Francis,' this complete stranger who knew about the locks and set-up of her home was asking her to run a B&B for the I.R.A.. Frannie never would have asked her to do this. Or, had his life become so desperate that he would? "Francis, I want to say yes, but I need some time. Must I give you an answer now?"

"No. Meet me tomorrow in the Black Thorn around the corner. Same time. And Eileen, don't get it into your head that these are 'secret' meeting places. They were selected so that you could find them. That's all."

They agreed to meet again, same time, different location. Eileen got into her car realizing that the I.R.A. knew who she was. Fran might not have known of their infiltration but the fact remained that she was on their list. More than likely, they knew the car she drove and the life she lived. Probably, they knew how many empty bottles of whiskey she threw out in her trash every week, and that she only ate frozen dinners. If she were to regain control of her life she would have to follow the adage, "keep your friends close and your enemies closer."

Eileen met 'Francis' at the BlackThorn promptly at 3 PM the following day. He'd arrived before she did. She strolled up behind him, all smiles as though they were life-long friends, "Well, hi," she said.

"Hello!" Francis responded by extending his arm then wrapping it around her waist. "What would you like to drink, Dear?"

"Just a Guinness." The bar was dark, illuminated by a television and a few neon beer signs including a shamrock with a Budweiser logo over it. It reminded Eileen of the year when Guinness began brewing Bud in Ireland. It was stronger over there than in the States. The place was much more crowded than Molly's had been the day before. Was the beer cheaper or had

Francis brought more friends? "By the way," she added, "I will take you up on your offer." She had no choice.

"Good girl." He raised his pint glass to hers.

She did not drink her beer, and continued, "Given a few caveats and if you cross them, I will see to it that your entire endeavour ends immediately."

Francis looked at her concerned but impressed. She was separated from the business but Fran Sullivan had trained her well. "Tell me your 'caveats,' woman."

"I will run a house for you, but I am not pleased to know that you have cased my home. I don't know how you found me, nor do I wish to. That said, slip me your cards when necessary but no one, and I mean no one is to know who I am. No one follows me. No one watches my home, and nothing other than the package being delivered is to be in my home. No deliverymen, no weapons. Nothing. If I sense one inkling that you are violating any other aspect of my life, I will bring you down without a second's hesitation, even if it means that I go down with you."

Francis stubbed out his cigarette in the black, plastic ashtray. "Your life will be yours. Your basement flat, however, will be ours."

"Fuck you." Eileen stood up from the barstool kissed Francis on the cheek the way an old friend would, and giggled, "I love your letters. Please be sure to write. Otherwise, I'll have to change the locks." She exited the bar and ran to her car.

On the drive home she beat on the steering wheel. She never bothered to turn on the radio. She kept the windows closed and ranted at the top her lungs, "Frannie you son of a bitch! Oh sure," she imitated his voice, 'I'll know yer okay. Oy'd sooner doy dan let dis touch you.' You cocksucker. You fucking terrorist cocksucker. How dare you pull me into this." Eileen knew that she had no choice. They would have followed her, fucked with her accounts, messed with her house or used a thousand different methods of letting her know that her life would be a nightmare without them. "Congratulations Sullivan, you fucking Rah sick fucking bastard," she exclaimed, surprised by the string of words that had left her mouth. "Oy'm in. Oy'm on yer fookin' team now Frannie. Oh yeah Baby, I love you, it's always been you. I'll look after you." She raced from the car, slamming the front door of the house and grabbed the Bushmills without reaching for a glass.

Two days later a purple card fell through her mailslot. She had no idea who would be coming or for how long. The yellow card at the end of the tour would be her only signal. After she picked up the card, Eileen unlocked the door to the basement apartment. No one had been down there since her brother had stayed for a week last year. He was between jobs and on his way to Seattle to find his fortune working for a software company. "The place could do with a bit of a clean-up," she said out loud. Wait a minute, I'm cleaning the house because the I.R.A. is coming to visit. This has to be a joke. Joke or not, Eileen turned on the heat, vacuumed the carpeting, put clean sheets on the full-size bed, and stocked the refrigerator with Coke, Diet Coke, four cans of Guinness, a six-pack of Sam Adams, milk and orange juice. Hell, she thought, this place is more nutritious than my own house. Something in her felt complete. She felt needed for the first time in weeks. At 6:00, she unlocked the outside door to the back entrance of the apartment, walked upstairs to the kitchen and bolted the door between herself and whomever would be living with her for the next however many days and nights.

For three days she never heard a sound from downstairs, but she noticed that she was quieter, trying to be conscientious of the person living beneath her feet. On the morning of the fourth day, a yellow card for Maeve's Cleaning Service landed on the floor of the foyer. Like a child on Christmas morning, Eileen unbolted the lock to the apartment and ran downstairs to survey the area. It looked untouched. She couldn't even smell the remnants of anyone having lived there. Had it been a test? The other 'Francis' had not contacted her, and she had no way of finding him. When that thought crossed her mind, she realized that she risked twisting in the wind should the police or FBI ever come to her home. She had no contact. No excuse. She had allowed herself to become a willing participant in an illegal game with no method of protecting herself in a real emergency. Even though she knew the danger involved, Eileen got a rush from it. Was this why Frannie had joined? Did he get that same rush? No. She had seen the terror in his face when he talked about it and knew that he would sooner die than pull her in. She had allowed this to happen, and she liked it.

A week later another card came through the mailslot. She moved a TV and VCR down to the basement, re-stocked the refrigerator and added a turkey sandwich to the repertoire. The previous guest had consumed one Guinness and two Cokes even though the empty cans were nowhere to be found.

22
January 1999

"What are you doing tonight?" Jack sat in his office on State Street talking to Eileen over the speakerphone. He was sorting through notes he'd taken during the morning's conference call with the Commonwealth's Attorney.

"Sitting on my couch, getting loaded and feeling sorry for myself."

"Nonsense. Eileen, tonight you are re-joining the world. You've been in mourning long enough. Sullivan may be gone, but you most certainly are not dead."

Eileen's chest tightened at his comment. She wasn't dead. She only wished she were. In the months without Fran, she'd learned how to drink her dinner, forego green vegetables, and had developed an empathy for every character on every soap opera on NBC. "Why Jack? What do you want?" Her voice resonated against the window behind his desk.

"Throw on one of your little black numbers, and call in a 911 to your hairdresser for an appointment this afternoon."

"Why?" Eileen was not pleased about going out but Jack piqued her interest.

"We're going to dinner with Congressman Michael Norton."

"Who?"

"Michael Norton. The Representative from Winchester. It's a small group, only eight of us, at the Ritz. We have seven right now and I want you to finish the table."

"Finish the table? You mean like, fill the empty parking space? Jack, I don't know." Eileen, on her cordless phone, stood in her closet eyeing her dresses.

"Eliot, I'm only going to say this once. I will be at your front door at 6:45. Dinner is at 7:15. If necessary, I will carry you to the car and into the dining room, so getcher ass all dolled up, and I'll see you in a little while. You need this, Leen. Consider it your coming out party."

"Okay. Okay. Message received. Who else is gong?"

"George Parks and his wife. David Stearn, you remember him from the firm's golf tournament last fall; Janine Wells, my new assistant counsel; you; me; the Congressman, and his chief of staff."

"So, it'll be a pool of legal sharks, two politicians, and me. Have I done something to offend you," she asked sarcastically. "I'll see you at 6:45. Is it okay if I wear sweatpants and heels?"

"Don't be smart. Goodbye." Jack pressed the speaker button on his phone to disconnect the call and looked at the woman sitting in the chair across from his desk. "You'll love her," he said to her.

"Jack," Janine replied, "I think you're doing something wonderful. If it were me, I'd kill you, but I'd want to have you on my team anyway."

Eileen looked through her closet remembering the nights with Fran when she'd worn one outfit or another. She cried her way through the wardrobe, sitting on the floor, cradling assorted shoes as she begged God to let her wake up from the emptiness.

Jack stood in the foyer at 6:45. "Wow. You clean up nice."

Eileen stood on the stairs in a short, black v-neck dress with spaghetti straps. A 20-inch strand of pearls accentuated her cleavage. She'd curled her hair and pulled it back in an antique rhinestone barrette. Black, silk stockings hugged her calves, ending at black suede heels. "Thank you. I tried the sweats, but the pearls and shoes didn't quite go with them."

The group met at the bar in the Ritz-Carlton Dining room overlooking Newbury Street. Jack introduced Eileen to Janine and made re-introductions to the rest of his colleagues. The Congressman had not yet arrived. Before she'd finished her first chardonnay, Chris Lawson, Representative Norton's staff person crossed through the entry to the dining room. He approached Jack first, made his acquaintance with the legal team then stopped at Eileen. She shook his hand when he extended it to her and felt a shock of chemistry in his grip. "It's a pleasure to meet you, Mr. Lawson."

"And you." The Congressman followed close behind him, completing a call on his cell phone. Michael Norton was a two-term democrat who'd won in a close election after his predecessor died in office. He was an insurance agent by trade, third generation in his family's business. He entered national politics after serving eight years on the local Board of Selectmen.

Eileen greeted the Congressman, but focused on Chris. He had worked for Michael's predecessor, and joined the new Representative's staff before Norton had even arrived in Washington. He'd inherited his father's 5-foot 10-inch athletic frame which he maintained playing pick-up basketball games. He had green eyes, strange for an Irish-American male, Eileen thought. She only knew green-eyed women. His dark brown hair, though short, had an almost Joe Kennedy curl to it. He looked nothing close to his 42 years.

Richard, the maitre'd showed them to their table. The Representative pulled out Eileen's chair for her and handed her her napkin, as Richard did the same for George's wife, Maureen. Eileen smiled up at him, following his face as he lowered himself into the chair on her left. Chris sat to her right with Jack across the table. Was it his way of affirming that Eileen was flying solo? She would not have put it past him.

Most of the evening's conversation focused on environmental legislation proposing to limit the impact of the Big Dig, the new tunnels and infrastructure under Boston, and on water supply quality in the surrounding areas. Halfway through the entrée Janine asked Eileen about her book.

"What book?" Maureen Parks' ears perked for the first time all evening. She'd been a little disappointed that the Congressman was sitting so far away from her. Her business dinners with George allowed her to eat well, but this brush with greatness was too much. She felt like a naked cake whose bowl of icing was sitting on the opposite end of the kitchen counter.

Eileen was startled by the focus on her work. "Well, it's fine. I believe it's being printed as we speak."

"What kind of book have you written Ms. Eliot," Chris asked, thankful not to be talking about politics.

"Oh, it's just a little fictional tale. My hope is to see one or two people reading it on the beach when I'm in Eastham this summer."

"One or two my foot," Jack chimed. "She's already had it optioned for a movie." Eileen did not respond, but shot Jack a look to let him know he was going overboard.

"A movie!" Maureen was sounding like Janet. No wonder Eileen had never enjoyed her very much. Eileen did not like being the center of attention. She could see George Parks' concerned look that the Congressman was no longer the focal point. "Michael," she began, "Tell me about Congress. Do you enjoy it? We always hear so many complaints about politicians that I have to wonder if it's worth the stress you must face."

Chris put his hand on her naked shoulder as if noting her deliberate move to put the Congressman back in the spotlight. She did not hear Michael's response, thinking only of the warmth of the palm of Chris' hand. She could not remember the last time that the human touch made an appearance in her life. The rest of the table burst into laughter, cueing Eileen to do the same. Michael continued on about the differences between Washington and Boston, of which there weren't many, except for the fact that the Cape was so far from DC.

"Oh," Eileen responded, "When I lived in New York I hated being so far from Eastham. It is too easy to become spoiled once you've lived so close to it for so long."

"Eileen has a beautiful little house just steps from a private beach." Jack was doing his best to give her some much-needed attention.

George was impressed that such a young woman would own property on the Cape. "Eileen," he asked, "How long have you had the house?" Translation: did you inherit it? What's a girl like you doing with a property there? Maureen had been hounding him for years to snap up a house in Orleans, but the prices had been going too high lately to make it worth selling the cottage on Plum Island.

"I bought it two years ago. My family has had a place there for years, just about a mile away, and when my house came on the market, it seemed the gods were smiling on me. It was one of those times when you just know that everything is right, and you have to take the opportunity. Chris, do you spend any time on the Cape?"

He answered that his family tended to take weekends in Cape Ann, and that Congress' schedule didn't allow him much time to vacation anymore. "When I have the chance, I go to my sister's place in New Hampshire."

After dinner, David recommended moving to the lounge for a nightcap. The wine and the meal exhausted Eileen, but Jack needed to stay and she didn't feel right cutting his evening short. Twenty minutes later, with a Bushmills single malt flowing through her, Eileen knew that she could no longer keep up with the boys. She should have followed Maureen's lead and had a decaf coffee. She stood up at an appropriate break in the conversation, "Ladies and gentlemen, I must take my leave and call it an evening."

David asked her to stay, announcing that they would be leaving shortly. Jack asked if he should take her home. "Oh, no, no. Jack, stay here. I'll catch a taxi. I'm sure you boys have critical things to discuss, like the Celtics." She smiled as she reached for her wrap from the back of the chair.

Chris stood to help her drape it over her shoulders. "Eileen, it has been a pleasure meeting you. Thank you for joining us this evening. I hope we meet again."

"Thank you. Me too. I'm sure your schedule is quite jammed, but perhaps our paths will cross again." She extended her right hand. Chris took it in his, looking at her.

"Please, take my card. If Mike or I can help you with anything, don't hesitate to call."

The Congressman interjected, "Yes, I'm usually in my district office Mondays and Fridays, so please drop in if you are in Winchester." He extended his hand, then gave Eileen one of his business cards.

"I will. Thank you." Eileen turned to the group, gave Jack a kiss on the cheek and said goodnight. She rode home in the back of the taxi, drunk from the whiskey and wide-eyed from the rush of the evening. "I'm alive," she whispered to herself.

"What was that, lady?" The cab driver thought she was talking to him.

"Nothing. Sorry. Just thinking out loud." She looked at Chris' card, then the Congressman's and grabbed the handle on the door of the cab. Michael Norton was a member of the House Appropriations, and International Relations Committees. Oh my God, she thought. Well Mr. Congressman, if you only knew whose hand you've been shaking. Eileen paid the driver, walked up the stairs to the front door and draped her shawl over the banister. She leaned on it with one hand, pulling her shoes off with her other and carried them up the steps to her bedroom.

23

She woke at 6:15 still wearing her pearls, earrings and barrette. Waking up fully accessorized was not a good sign. Shit, she thought, what stupid things did I say last night? I'm sure Jack will recount all of them in vivid detail. Oh my God, it was a business dinner. Please God, do not let me have jeopardized his standing at the firm. Eileen put on her robe and walked downstairs to the kitchen, stepping on the Congressman's business card halfway down the staircase. It stuck to the ball of her foot the way Nuala's had the morning she discovered it in Frannie's bedroom. She reached down and removed it from her left foot. The shawl fell to the floor when her hand slid down the banister.

The automatic timer on the coffee wouldn't begin for another 20 minutes. Eileen cancelled the timer and pressed "start." She retrieved a Diet Coke from the refrigerator while she watched the machine pee coffee through the filter into the pot. It occurred to her that coffeemakers were more reliable than men. Even with the seat down—the top of the pot—it always made a straight shot into the container. Even the pause-n-serve feature permitted her to interrupt the machine mid-stream, fill her cup, and then return to a perfect pour into the pot. Men, she thought. Can't live with them, can't kill 'em.

She took her coffee to the study and flipped on her PC in search of information about Chris, and Congressman Norton. The House of Representatives website had a link to Norton's home-page. Not only did he serve on International Relations, he also was on the Ad Hoc Committee for Irish Affairs and had co-spon-sored every bill and resolution urging the end to the use of rubber bullets and marches through Catholic neighborhoods. Eileen knew that this meant Chris was heavily involved in Michael's work for Ireland. Chiefs of Staff are like clones of their bosses, oftentimes having better recall on issues than the Member for whom they work.

Jack phoned at 10:15. "Well good morning, bright eyes!"

"Oh God. What?"

"What do you mean, 'what'?" He imitated her. "You left before we did."

"How late did you stay?"

"Janine left just after you, with George and Maureen. She couldn't handle any more decaf, and Maureen kept trying to engage her in conversation about shoes. David, Mike, Chris and I stayed for two more rounds, cigars, and an intense discussion about your legs."

"Jack, please, tell me you are kidding." Eileen, still in her bathrobe, ran her right hand up her calf trying to sum up her legs in her own opinion.

"No, I'm not kidding. By the way, the Chief of Staff asked about your vitals."

"What about me?"

"Nothing," he changed lanes and spoke into the microphone built into the cell phone between the front seats of his Infiniti J30. "But I gave him your number."

"You didn't!"

"I did, and he probably will be calling you for lunch today so get in the shower."

"How do you know I haven't showered?"

"Eileen, how long have I known you? It's time to get back on the horse m'dear. What's the saying, 'The best way to get over one man is to get under another?'"

"Jack, you are a pig."

"Yes, but you love me."

"Yes I do. Now let me go get in the shower and if he doesn't phone, I'll be beating down your office door by 2:00."

"Good, because I'm expecting Lawson in my office at 2:15. Leen, I swear, this is for real. Have a good time."

"Thanks." Eileen took her coffee up to the bathroom to begin the ritual of primping. Jesus, she thought, standing in the shower, I haven't been on a first date in years. Hell, I haven't even been asked. Settle down, Leenie. She heard the phone ringing when she turned off the shower. She reached over the tub and picked up the cordless, "Hello?"

"Miss Eliot?"

"Yes."

"This is Chris Lawson."

I'm naked and talking to a virtual stranger, she thought. "Oh hello. Please my name is Eileen. When you call me Ms. Eliot it makes me think you're going to ask me to switch my long distance service."

"Gotcha. Okay. Eileen, I really enjoyed meeting you last night."

"Thank you. As did I." Silence ran between both phones for a few seconds.

"I was wondering if you were available for lunch today. I'm at Jack's office as a matter of fact."

Jack, you dick, she thought. He'd failed to mention that small detail. "That would be terrific. When would you like to meet?"

"I can pick you up at your house if you like."

"I'd like that very much. How about if we have lunch here?"

"That would be perfect. Having commandeered the Congressman's car for a little while, Chris arrived at her door at 12:45. They feasted on turkey club sandwiches, potato chips and Diet Cokes that she'd picked up at the deli around the corner.

"So, you like working in Congress?"

"I enjoy it very much. The trick is working for the right Member. Campaigning is exhausting, and the hours are long, but I absolutely love it. In D.C., the Chiefs of Staff are as sought after almost as much as the Representatives. Of course, that's due merely to our being more accessible. Sometimes I'd like to be anonymous, like when I'm sitting in a restaurant trying to enjoy a conversation with a beautiful woman." He raised his eyebrow at her.

"Ah, so Congress cramps your style with the ladies."

"No! No, that's not it at all. I was trying to pay you a compliment."

"I know. Thank you." She sipped her Diet Coke and smiled.

At 1:45 they stood in her living room overlooking her patio. Chris stopped her mid-sentence. "Eileen, I would really like to kiss you."

Without answering, she turned, put her hands on his shoulders and pressed her lips to his. "I really would too," she finally replied. "I hope I haven't ruined your image of me."

"Not at all." He kissed her again, this time holding her against him with one hand on the back of her head. "I have a dinner on Saturday night and would really like it if you would go with me."

"Will this be another evening of lawyers?"

"No, it's a fundraiser for Project Children. Mike is devoted to Irish issues and likes me to be at the events with him. It's a program that brings Protestant and Catholic children from Northern

Ireland to the United States every summer. It's black tie. And hey, this may be your big chance to meet Ted Kennedy."

"Oooh, well, if the Senator will be there then how can I refuse? Saturday is only two days away. Will it be a problem if I show up on such short notice? I'm sure someone has spent weeks doing seating arrangements."

"You are a stickler for good manners aren't you? Do you read Amy Vanderbilt every day?" His arms still were around her. He tweaked her nose with his right hand while his left arm remained around her.

"Noooo!"

"I'll tell you what, I will call the organizer and ask if I may bring you. I'm sure they will say yes. They like to keep us happy. It's one of the perks of my job. I will call you later today and let you know what they say."

"Thank you. That would make me feel like less of a party crasher." They separated and Lawson put on his suit jacket as he headed for the door. He kissed her lightly before going down the stairs to his car and back to Jack's office.

Eileen spent the rest of the afternoon rifling through her closet for an appropriate dress for the event on Saturday. Project Children. How ironic. Will I ever truly be away from Ireland, she thought. A young woman called her at 3:00. She was with the Project Children events committee. "Ms. Eliot, Congressman Norton's office called and asked me to extend an invitation to you for Saturday evening's dinner. We would love to have you join us."

"Thank you." She'd never had anyone call her before on behalf of her date.

Chris rang 20 minutes later. "I checked with Project Children and they said that they would be thrilled to have you attend. It was touch and go for a while, but when I mentioned that you were a soon-to-be famous author, they asked if they should send a limo to pick you up.”

“Stop it.” She liked his sense of humour. “I’m not sure who they’ll seat us with, but they usually try to spread us politicos at tables with the big contributors. And, I’m sorry to say that there will be a few moments during the evening when I probably will have to shepherd Mike around. I hope you won’t mind if I have to leave you alone for a little bit.”

“No. Not at all. It’s your job. I’ll be fine. Thank you for the invitation. I’m really looking forward to this.”

“Me too.” He hung up the phone and looked at Jack. “She’s going. Jack, I can’t thank you enough for introducing me to her. She’s really amazing. I only hope she’s half as interested in me.”

“Eileen is a terrific woman. Once you get to know her, she will be under your skin. She’s one of those rare women who tells you what’s on her mind and listens to every word that comes out of your mouth. Sometimes that’s a blessing. Sometimes it’s a curse.” Jack laughed and turned to Mike, “Now, let’s talk about your next fundraiser.”

Eileen phoned Ron, her hairdresser, to schedule an appointment on Saturday afternoon to get her coif done before the dinner. She was on the phone when she heard the mail arrive. A purple card was included in the cache.

24
Friday

"Eileen, I need you to come to my office as soon as possible. It's important." Jack left the rather terse message on her answering machine.

Eileen was parking her car outside the house pulling shopping bags from the back seat. That morning, her shoes told her that they were tired and needed to be replaced. New shoes, naturally, require new handbags and new pants. New pants need new shirts. The staff at Ann Taylor on Newbury St. had no clue what they were in for when she strolled in looking for navy loafers. Eileen didn't know either. It was impulse buying at its worst, and the $900 spree felt good. It was a subconscious reward for not crying in four days. Fran was still all over her mind, as always, but the sporadic bursts into tears were subsiding. She dropped the bags in the foyer and hung the pants and shirts in the hall closet before playing Jack's message. What the hell, she wondered. He didn't sound good, nervous almost. She phoned him immediately and spoke to his secretary, Anne. "Anne, it's Eileen. Can I speak to Jack?"

"Oh, Eileen. He's in a meeting and I cannot interrupt him but he wants you here ASAP."

"Why? Is he okay?"

"I'm not sure. He's in a mood though."

Perplexed and nervous she answered that she'd be right over. Eileen grabbed her handbag and hailed a taxi outside her door. She didn't want to be bothered with the hassle of looking for parking off State Street. Anne sat at her desk taking a phone message when she recognized Eileen. "Hi. I haven't seen you in a while. How are you?"

"I'm well. I think. Where is he?"

"Hold on." She pushed her chair back and walked to Jack's office door. Eileen leaned against the desk and bit her fingernails. Anne returned, "Go on in. He's ready for you."

Ready for me, she thought. She cradled her handbag against her chest and walked into the office. "Jack?"

David O'Brien from Empire Publishing and Kelly Evans, a publicist for Empire sat on the couch in the corner of the office. "Thank God you're here," Jack answered. She turned to David and Kelly and said hello then asked if something was wrong. "Only this." Jack picked up a book off of his desk and tossed it at her. She caught it and looked down at it, realizing that she was holding a published copy of *Accidental Terrorist*. Running her hand over the jacket, flipping through the pages she glanced at Jack and smiled.

"Congratulations, kiddo. You are officially published." He burst out laughing, clapping his hands together as Anne carried in two bottles of champagne and five glasses.

"I can't believe you! What a wind up!" She put the book on his desk then motioned as though wrapping her hands around his neck.

"I wanted to surprise you!" David interjected to explain about the book's distribution and release date, then turned the floor over to Kelly. They gathered around the coffee table as she wrote on a white unlined tablet, jotting down remaining tactical plans for Eileen's book tour.

"Eileen, we want you on the road from June through August. You want to be beach reading, so we're going to make you 'beach reading.'" Eileen forgot about Chris and the basement, but she heard Frannie's voice in her head, whispering to her, "Well done, Babe." They went over logistics and planning and cities and radio stations. Eileen nodded her head to all of it and uttered one requirement. The tour, she stated, would conclude in Eastham at Tidal Page Books, if they'd have her. "Done," Kelly answered, "I'll call them tomorrow. They'll love it. Peak season and a local. I can see it already."

"Yes!" Eileen smiled, fantasizing about the visit. "And I want you all there. We'll finish with a clambake on my beach."

"No!" Kelly raised her hands in front of her as though she'd had an epiphany. "Let me see if the town will let us have a clambake AND a signing on the beach. If it's going to be 'beach reading,' why not buy it on the beach?!" Her mind was reeling with the marketing possibilities. Eileen's mind was reeling with the prospect of being all over the country, getting media exposure. Surely, Frannie would see some piece of her achievement, and concluding in Eastham would mean that, even if only in spirit, the memory of Frannie Sullivan and the site of their first meeting, would be at the pinnacle of the tour.

25
Saturday

Chris arrived at Eileen's place at 6:00 Saturday evening. A black, Lincoln Town Car driven by Robert, a 24-year old legislative assistant sat at the edge of the curb by her front steps. Robert worked in the district office and had the astute responsibility of keeping Mr. Norton on schedule for his events and appointments. Chris commandeered Robert's services before he had to pick up the Congressman. Robert waited in the car while Chris walked to Eileen's front door. He was playing with the radio and did not notice the woman coming up the sidewalk toward the house. The dark haired female carried a small bag over her left shoulder, glancing at the numbers on each house. She noticed the car parked outside, then Eileen's open door. A man in a tuxedo stood in the doorway with the woman in a long navy blue gown, wearing a pearl and diamond necklace that shone in the light over the door. They walked down the steps into the waiting car. Robert put the car in drive and pulled away toward the Westin Copley Plaza Hotel and the dinner. Nuala opened the gate to the back of Eileen's home and entered the basement.

She turned on the light and surveyed the place, completely aware of who her hostess was. Not a bad set-up, she thought. Better than most of the other places she'd been in. Every member of the Boston crew had been instructed to stay away from their homes and usual hangouts for the next two nights. Rumors of an I.R.A. Army Council meeting back home abounded, but the fact was that three of the leadership was coming into Boston. Fran was one of them. He was back for only four nights. His first time in the U.S. in six weeks.

It felt good to be in Boston, but it was desperation not to be able to go back to his old ways. He had a whole new life now with no past and not much of a future. He was staying those few nights in Dorchester. No home he'd known before. The ceasefire was coming apart. Peace was coming apart, and the militants wanted to end it all in one fell swoop. The idea of seeking assistance from the few volunteers in the U.S. and planning against the will of so many of the South Armagh crew could have been suicide. Until everyone had met, made their decisions and returned home to Ireland, no one could spend any bit of their time according to their normal routine. Fran got into the waiting car at Logan Airport and headed down Route 93 alongside of Southie and into Dorchester. So many nights he'd parked his own car in the Copley Center garage, picked up another vehicle, and driven himself to Southie for the weekend.

As he passed Gerard's, he remembered how many times he and Eileen had gone there for a good heart-stopping Irish breakfast. She always read the front page of the morning paper first, and drank her coffee black. He always went first for the comics, drinking his tea with only a hint of actual tea disguised under heaps of milk and sugar. Fran was exhausted from the flight and in his normal state of nervous tension at being back and working with the boys who'd sent him home. That didn't stop him from focusing on those Gerard's breakfasts. They were the best in Boston, and Frannie loved taking Eileen there. Her first morning in the place she thought he had to be kidding. She'd never seen a darkened, cigarette and beer-stale bar packed to the gills with neighbors in search of the holy grail of breakfast. He saw the way her eyes popped out at him in sarcastic disbelief when his fork reached over her plate and attacked her black and white pudding. "Don't worry Dear," he'd said. "You wouldn't like it anyway."

"May I at least try it," she asked like a woman scorned.

"Sure."

She cut a piece of the white pudding and put it her mouth. Fran watched her with a stifled smile on his face, waiting to see if she'd swallow it or spit it out. Eileen would not give him the satisfaction of being right, and swallowed it. She said nothing to him and only pushed her plate closer to him as she gulped down her coffee.

"I won't tell you what's in it," he said.

Frannie's car arrived at the house in Dorchester. None of the lights were on in the front, and they entered through the back door off the kitchen. Four of them were there. Fran knew two. All of them were male. Two digital phones and two pagers sat on the table but rarely were used. It was too easy to trace a cell phone call. They were good for quick tip-offs, but not for actual business. Fran took his gym bag, the same black one he'd used for years, and tossed it on the floor at the end of the couch before going up to the bathroom to wash his face. He was half-way up the stairs when Martin, the man Eileen had met in Molly Darcy's and the BlackThorn, spoke to him, "Everyone's fine. They know all they need to and we'll meet tomorrow."

"Where did you manage to stash everyone," Fran laughed in disbelief.

"You'd be surprised. By the way, your wife is fine."

"Oh." Fran continued up the stairs suddenly feeling exhausted and uninterested in anything they had to offer him, or required of him.

26

Chris and Eileen arrived home by cab. "Chris, thank you for dinner." Eileen crossed the living room turning on the lights at either end of the couch. "It was amazing. Truly. I am thrilled to see how many people support the effort, and the children there tonight were so eloquent. I swear, every one of them is a future politician." She laughed a little as she slipped off her shoes. "Would you like anything to drink? I can put on a pot of coffee, or I also have tea, whiskey, port, anything?"

Chris removed his tuxedo jacket and hung it in the hall closet, before sitting on the couch. "Coffee would be terrific."

"Regular or decaf?"

"Either. Doesn't matter to me."

Eileen put on the decaf and continued talking to him from the kitchen. She was pulling two mugs from the cabinet, arranging the creamer and sugar on a small serving tray. Her mother would have been so proud of her high-brow manners. "Chris, I can't get over it. And that Maggie Daley is such a nice woman. So dedicated." Maggie organized the dinner and sat at Chris and Eileen's table. "I was so pleased for her that the night was such a success."

Chris joined her in the kitchen leaning against the counter next to the sink. He opened the two top buttons of his shirt and was rolling up his sleeves. "Granted, I haven't known you very long Eileen, but I'm really surprised by how excited you are about this evening. So, what is it about you and Ireland?"

"Will you be revolted if I smoke?" Eileen held up her box of Marlboro Lights and shook it a little in front of him.

"No. Of course not. I quit three years ago, but I'm not one of those anti-tobacco zealots. Besides, your house, your rules." He opened his arms as if showing off the kitchen appliances to a game show audience.

"Good answer." She held the cigarette to her lips, then shook the match putting it out as it fell to the ashtray. "Ireland. Well," she exhaled smoke into the center of the room. "There isn't much to tell. I learned about it as a kid, watching the news. I guess you could call me a child of the Bobby Sands generation," referring to the 1981 I.R.A. hunger strike that Sands led in Long Kesh prison. "I was about 13 when he died. A very moldable age, you know. The whole thing made no sense to me, and made me sad too." She walked around the kitchen and handed him his mug of coffee as she envisioned Frannie sitting at the table. "It was the first time I remember being truly touched by news. You know, something outside of my own little world. So, I learned and learned and studied the history and managed to get through college pretty much specializing in US policy on Northern Ireland and the sociological affects of the "troubles"—God, that word irritates me—on women in Northern Ireland. After school, I kept up with everything through the news, books, people I'd meet, etc. etc." She rotated her hands in circles, personifying the etceteras.

"So, it's a hobby of sorts?"

"Kind of. More like a special interest. Here in Boston, everyone seems to know about the Irish conflict, but when I was in school in DC, I was on my own in terms of knowledge and interest. The end of the Cold War was big then, so I think my professors liked knowing that I'd give them something different to review. Besides, when your prof specializes in Russia and you specialize in Ireland, it increases the likelihood that they won't identify errors in your work, so the grades don't get hit so hard."

"What!"

"No. I shouldn't say that. I just like to think that I taught them a thing or two."

"So," Chris asked, "What do you think of the IRA?"

"'Scuse me?" Eileen felt an imaginary bright light shining in her eyes. The question smacked her the way most normal people would respond to a questions like, 'where were you on the night of the 23rd'.

Chris rested himself against the countertop to the right of the oven. "What do you think of them? You've followed the issues for years, you must have an opinion."

Eileen crossed her right leg over her left and rested her head in her right hand with her elbow on the table, "Honestly, I'm not sure." She took a deep breath. "That probably is why so many people cannot come to agreement on how to resolve the problems there. I mean, on the one hand, their activities are inherently wrong. On the other, if you're treated as a second, third or fourth class citizen all your life, how do you not feel compelled to retaliate." In her mind, she heard her real answer. They're dirty, amoral, bastards who have done nothing to help the situation. They stand for prejudice and labeling and use God and country as their defense. They cannot function successfully without draining their members of basic humanity.

Chris was speaking his own opinion to her. Eileen stared at him but kept talking in her head. They're a cult. Give up free thought. Treat those you love like yesterday's news. Do it for 'the cause.' Fuck your fucking cause, she wanted to yell. Her voice screamed across her forehead's interior. They stole him! They took him from me!

Chris startled Eileen from her thought when he put his hand on her head. Eileen looked up at him. "You're crying," he whispered. "What's wrong?"

Eileen half-lied. "It's so sad. I was thinking of the people—the women, the children, and the people who have no affiliation with a group on either side—who have suffered because of the violence. The violence on both sides. It's a tragedy and no one can seem to find an answer. It breaks my heart."

"Wow. Beautiful, smart and empathetic. Is there anything else about you I should thank a higher power for," he moved to a seat at the table. "You know, in all seriousness you might be able to help the Ad Hoc Committee."

"You're kidding. How could I help Congress?" Eileen stubbed out her cigarette and reached for another.

"Easy. We don't have full-time staff for the committee. The legislative staffs follow Ireland as part of their international relations assignments. It might be good for them, excuse me, us, to meet with you." He was looking for a way to bring her to DC.

"And say what?" She suddenly saw herself in a room of 25 year-olds telling them about life as a Rah girl. She'd say, "Now you kids listen to me. I don't know jack about the business, but I can sure tell ya that professional terrorism does a number on your sex life. Any questions?"

Chris brought her attention back around to their conversation. "Give them a little history. Hell, I don't know. It's just a thought, but you seem to know so much, and it might be helpful if a non-politico, who's not asking for anything, got them in a room and hashed through a few issues. I'm brainstorming."

So, she thought, I would be advising congressional staff. Frannie would flip if he knew about this. Mr. Speaker, we need

more funding for Semtex training in the western counties. I rec-
ommend $30 million, and an incentive plan of a free trip to
Disney World for every volunteer who can shave over 30 seconds
off of his bomb-assembling time. Her mind was reeling. "Well, if
you want me to, then sure. It sounds like fun."

"Hey, did you hear that?" Chris looked toward the basement
door.

"What? Eileen felt the color drain from her face. She pushed
her chair back trying to scrape it against the tile floor and camou-
flage the sound of the ringing cellular phone downstairs.

"I swear I heard a phone ringing. It was coming from downstairs." He stood and walked to the door. Nuala had been sitting
on the stairs listening to their conversation and left the phone in
the kitchen, the room with the most resonant acoustics. She leapt
down the stairs on tip-toes, grabbing for the phone, then shutting
out the light in the bedroom and gathering her bag as she spoke.

"I didn't hear anything." Eileen stood against the sink running
the water and rinsing out her coffee mug, making more noise.

"Come on. Appease me. Let's check it out. Besides, I haven't
seen your entire house."

"Oh Chris, the basement is just a little apartment. There's nothing much to see. I'd be embarrassed for you to see it without my
cleaning it first."

"Eileen, allow me the honor of caring about your safety. Please,
let's go check. Besides, English basements always have great character. I'd love to see yours." He was holding the doorknob, turning it
back and forth in his hand.

"Okay. Okay. Let me get the key for the deadbolt." She
unlocked the bolt and opened the door saying, "See, this lock is
enormous. Even if someone wanted to get in, they'd have a devil
of a time. These stairs can be dodgy. Let me go ahead of you." She
spoke louder as she stepped onto the stairs, praying that her guest

was trained in the art of hiding or departing quickly. Eileen walked him through the apartment, fearful every time she turned on a light.

"Very nice," he said. "Eileen, the place is spotless. There's no need to worry about cleaning"

"Oh," she giggled, "You know how it is. When you haven't been in a room for a while, you never know what you might find. I tell ya, the place could have been overrun by dustbunnies, then I just would have been mortified." Dustbunnies, she thought. Where the hell did that come from? I've never even used the word before now. "See? Nothing here." Nuala was under the bed, hidden by the bedspread draping to the carpet. She watched their feet moving from between the fringe.

"Yes."

"Good," she smiled at him. "I want more coffee. Let's get back upstairs."

He kissed her cheek, "Okay, you win." After locking the door, Eileen turned on the dishwasher to muffle any other sounds that might come from below them. Plus, the concept of Congress in her kitchen and the I.R.A. in her basement made her wonder if she wasn't putting him at some risk or harm. Would they decide to send more and more people to her if they knew that there were a chance of listening to Chris talk about his work? Eileen, she thought, shut your brain off for two seconds, go have a smoke and chill out.

They moved to the living room and talked until after 2:00. Shortly after her second cup of coffee, Eileen switched to Fonseca 20-year port. Chris joined her. She sat next to him, leaning sideways against his shoulder as they talked more about her possible work with the Ad Hoc Committee. "Eileen, the Committee has no official legislative influence, but works to convince the rest of the

House to endorse bills and resolutions that would help Ireland and Northern Ireland."

"I know," she answered quietly.

"Somehow, I should have known that." They remained silent for a minute. "Eileen," he almost whispered.

"Yes." She knew what was coming and felt a tightness brewing in her jaw.

"Are you tired?"

"Exhausted." Her whole body was growing increasingly tense.

"Can we go to bed?" He was nervous using the words "we" and "bed."

Eileen sat up and put both feet on the carpet. She rested her cheek in her hand, supported by her elbow on her right knee, and turned her head toward him. "Chris, I would really like for you to spend the night."

"Great." He reserved his elation.

"But, I'm not ready to sleep with you." She sat up, putting her hands out in front of her, "That's not to say that I don't want to at some point, but if you wouldn't mind, I'd prefer if you slept in one of the guest rooms."

He laughed a little. "Doll, that's fine. I'm in no hurry. I'd like to think that we'll get there eventually, but I'm happy knowing that we can have breakfast in the morning. Besides, nice girls are, well, nice." He ran his hand through her hair then down the side of her face before leaning to kiss her.

"Come on. I'm spent," she said.

He kissed her outside of her bedroom door, "Goodnight, fair maiden," waited until she closed the door behind her, then went to the room down the hall, emotionally and sexually frustrated.

The three of them, Eileen, Chris, and Nuala slept in their respective rooms as the dishwasher continued its cycle.

27

Jason called two days after *Accidental Terrorist* was released. Chris and Eileen were having breakfast when the phone interrupted them. Eileen pulled her hand from Chris' to reach for the cordless phone on the table. "Hello."

"Eileen! So good to catch you. It's Jason, Honey." She rolled her eyes at Chris then put two fingers in the air gesturing that the conversation would be brief.

"Well Jason. To what do I owe the pleasure," as if she did not already know.

He made small talk about the importance of keeping up good relations with one's ex-wife, then cut to the chase. "Dear," don't 'dear' me she thought, "I'm phoning to congratulate you. A book. You've written an honest-to-goodness book. A big step up from those little articles.

"Yes, I have." She sipped her coffee, trying to keep from laughing.

"They must have given you a nice advance. I heard about you at the office."

"I'm impressed. You've done your homework. Is this a congratulatory call, Jason? Afterall, we haven't spoken since long before the divorce was final." Chris looked at Eileen, stood up and began kissing the back of her neck. Eileen wrapped her free hand behind her head, holding Chris against her.

"Actually, Babe, we've got a great new fund coming out, and I wanted you," he emphasized, "to have a shot at getting in early. What d'ya say?"

Eileen held the phone to her ear and replied, "Jason, it is so kind of you to want me to have a shot at what I'm sure will be a terrific investment."

"Uh-huh." He had the investment forms in front of him, half-completed for her.

"But, and I say this with the most sincere intention, you have got to be kidding me."

"What?!"

"Jason, please take my advice. First, do not ever call me again. It's bad karma. Second, find yourself a nice, wealthy, young man and get stuffed." She turned off the phone and laughed.

"Get stuffed?" Chris looked at her perplexed by the term.

"It's a nicer way of saying 'fuck off,'" Eileen answered. "Is there any more coffee."

28
February 1999

Chris was attending an annual Democrat retreat in Charlottesville, evaluating and strategizing on the status of the party's legislative agenda. Eileen stayed in Boston for her first weekend home in almost a month. She spent Saturday shopping Newbury Street, buying three outfits, one casual and two formal. She and Chris had been attending so many events lately that she was taking on the fear of being seen in the same thing twice. No big plans for the evening, though Jack would be coming over for their traditional viewing of *Now Voyager*. She couldn't believe the first time he'd recommended that they rent it. She never took him for a Bette Davis fan. By now they'd seen it at least six times. Jack brought the film and a bottle of Silverado Reserve cabernet. Eileen made popcorn. Wearing sweatpants and a T-shirt, she had long ago abandoned the self-consciousness of wearing her Mickey Mouse slippers in Jack's presence.

Sunday morning arrived without a nasty hangover or concerns about visitors in the basement apartment. Things had quieted over the last few weeks. The front page of the *Boston Globe* carried an article about privacy and the Internet, or lack thereof. It detailed just how much one could find out about a person by using a few basic websites or search engines. Eileen ripped the article from the paper and left it next to her PC. The temptation to search out Fran was almost too much to bear, but she'd promised him that she would not try to find him. He had asked her not to, fearing that she would put herself in dangerous situations. She threw a load of laundry into the washer then got in the shower.

"They already know me," she spoke to the shampoo bottle in her hand. "What more of a threat can I face?" Without drying her hair, Eileen returned to the PC, just wanting to know where his mail had been forwarded after he'd left Chicago. She knew everything about him. His birthplace, mother's maiden name, birthdate, places of employment, last six addresses—everything. She wanted to test the web sites for their accuracy, and, she admitted to herself, to find out his very last address. His final utility bills had to have gone somewhere. It would be her very last and most recent link to him. She logged on to a people search site, entered his name, birthdate and last known address, then her credit card number to cover the $39.95 charge for the search. Results were guaranteed in 48 hours. A part of her felt like she'd done something awful. Another part felt as though she deserved to know. Nothing would come of the report. She promised herself that she wouldn't do anything with any new information.

After she hit "enter" she exited out of the system, dried her hair and went to the Black Rose. The tourist chat would be good for her. She liked being in a bar where she blended in with the crowd and could lose herself in eavesdropping over touristy conversations full of misinformation about the city. Three of the patrons were reading the day's newspaper discussing the disturbing nature of the Internet article. Eileen sipped her Guinness and buried her head in *Pride and Prejudice*. She was reading it for the fourth time. Jane Austen always made her feel better. At 6:30, she returned home and focused herself on *60 Minutes* and *Masterpiece Theater*.

Chris called from DC at 9:30 that evening. "How's your weekend been?"

"Terrific. I've missed being home. I know it sounds crazy, but it's been a long while since I've spent three straight weekends out of town. That, of course is not to say that I haven't enjoyed every single minute with you. Jack came over last night." She was propped on the couch with her feet on the coffee table. Wads of cotton divided each of her toes and the open bottle of geranium pink nail polish was waiting for her to apply the second coat.

"Well, I hope you've missed me at least a little bit, because I've been thinking of you all weekend."

"You are very sweet. Of course I miss you. It's been weird not having you around this weekend. I believe, Suh," she said in a mock-southern accent in honor of his being in Charlottesville, "That I have buhcome accustomed tuh bein' with yah." She snapped back to her normal voice, "We're still on for next weekend, right?"

"Absolutely."

"How was the meeting? Any big plans to re-take the majority?"

"Eileen, it was unreal. I always feel like such a little kid when I go to those retreats."

"Why?"

"Because, the senior Members are always armed with these amazing plans and I sit in awe." Chris told her about some of the plans to try and push through health reform and new education policies. The budget surplus was priming them for a fight with the Republicans to either cut taxes or create new programs. "No matter how many years I've worked in Congress, I never am bored. Plus, Mike is doing really well for being a freshman member."

Eileen loved being clued in on political strategy but also was pre-occupied by her toenails. She usually paid for pedicures and the job she was doing proved that it was well-worth the money.

29

Eileen woke at 7:00 and noticed that as usual, she hadn't waited long enough for her toes to dry before getting into to bed. Her sheets left little imprints over the nail polish. She was spitting out her toothpaste when the prospect of getting the Internet report on Francis struck her. Eileen wiped her face, grabbed a mug of coffee and sat in front of her PC. She saw the message saying that she had mail, took a breath and clicked on the mailbox icon. There was one message from the people-search site, with a file attached. She read the message: Attached are the results of the report you requested. It is an ASCII text file. If you wish any additional searches or information on the subject you requested, please call 1-800…The price list of available searches was included. Eileen downloaded the file renamed it "Frannie" and put it in her PC's folder of passworded documents.

She hesitated to open and read it. What if there was something in there that she did not want to see? What if Nuala was his last known address? An empty sickness in her gut told her that Nuala would be in there, somewhere.

She spun her chair around and reached for her cigarettes from the end table. She wasn't ready to read it yet. She opened the file, but couldn't look at it. Eileen stood up, pressed print, lit her cigarette then walked to the kitchen for more coffee as the 19-page report slid out of the laser printer. Her heart raced and more caffeine probably was not the best thing for her, nor were more cigarettes, but she rationalized that there's a time and a place for healthy living. "Okay," she told herself, "You knew this could bring bad news and you ordered it anyway. Your life will be no different 10 minutes from now."

The papers rested on the printer. She put her Marlboro Light in her mouth and picked up the report. No Social Security Number provided. Well, that's good, she thought, at least some things are sacred. Birthdate, yes that was correct. Former addresses were correct. Jesus, who are these people? Streams of names came back. For every apartment building he'd lived in, the names of every one of his neighbors were included.

Page eight stabbed her. He had a current address in Wakefield, and Nuala Sullivan lived there too. "Nuala SULLIVAN?!" Eileen yelled. There was an asterisk next to her name and a notation at the bottom of the page: " * Indicates possible relative." Oh my God Frannie, how could you do this? You married her, you son of a bitch. When? She fingered back through the pages, checking his list of neighbors to be sure that her name did not appear anywhere else. It didn't. According to the report, they owned one car, registered in her name only. Her family lived in New York. She later found that Nuala's her brother even had a homepage on the Internet. Her stomach clenched sending a sour taste of bile and tobacco up her esophagus.

Eileen sat on the couch, unable to determine what she felt, stuck in a limbo of emptiness. She picked up the phone and dialed information.

"What city," the voice asked.

"Wakefield," Eileen responded, shaking.

"Name."

"Sullivan. 214 Arlington Drive."

"I have two listings at that address, ma'am. An N. Sullivan and a Francis."

"I'd like both please." She took down the phone numbers, her right hand steadying the paper as the pen shook across it. "N. Sullivan. N Fucking Sullivan. Somehow, I'm not surprised." She stared at the paper, talking to herself, then decided to twist the knife in her own back just a bit more. It took another 10 minutes before her head cleared enough to realize that Frannie and Nuala lived in Michael Norton's district.

Eileen pulled on her jeans and a T-shirt off of her bedroom floor to retrieve her book of street maps out of her car. She figured out Fran's exact location, just up 93 north then over to 495 and off to the East. There was an Episcopal Church just down the road from his neighborhood. He was a 35 minute drive from her. "I'll be sure you're okay," she remembered his saying to her the day he left, "I'll know how you are," and "Please don't try to find me." Two phone numbers and one car. One car was odd for living so far from the city. Maybe it really was a business set-up. Maybe he never was around. Eileen thought of phoning him or driving to Wakefield, but had promised herself that she wouldn't do anything with the information.

The phone rang, jolting her attention away from the report. "Hi there." It was Chris, calling from his office on Capitol Hill. He was looking at a photo of the two of them from a dinner at the National Democratic Club last month.

"Hey. You're in the office already? It's only 8:15?"

"Mike has a breakfast at LaColline in 15 minutes. I'm going with him, but I wanted to say hi."

"Well, hi." She was struggling to pay attention as the street map blared at her from on her lap.

Chris asked her to fly to DC on Wednesday. "I know it's short notice, but I have a surprise."

"What kind of surprise?"

"There's a dinner for the new Irish ambassador on Thursday, and the White House protocol office would like the Ad Hoc Committee members to attend. Senator Mitchell will be in town on a break from the peace talks in Ulster, and the President wants to rally the troops and show the Senator how much we appreciate him. He's been getting his ass kicked in Stormont for months, still trying to help them through the process, and he could use a good pep rally. If I were him, I would have run screaming from the place after the Good Friday Agreement. What a toll that must have taken on him. I never could have done it."

"I hear ya on that. Chris, are you asking me to join you for dinner at the White House?"

"Well, not exactly. I'm asking you to join me for a cocktail reception at the White House. Committee members and staff are invited to the reception, but only the Members and their guests will stay for dinner."

"Gosh. I was thinking of washing my hair that night, but I suppose I could change my plans," she joked. "I'll grab the 3:00 flight to National and meet you at your place on Wednesday. What should I wear? I mean, Chris, I've been to some interesting dinners with you, but this is too much."

"That navy gown from the Project Children dinner will be perfect. Besides, it'll be a small affair. Consider it a warm-up."

"A small affair. So, we're going to a small cocktail soiree with the President, the First Lady, Senator Mitchell, the Irish ambassador, and just what the hell kind of warm up is this for? What's next? Tell me we're having tea with Queen Elizabeth and I will pass out."

"No. Sorry, no queen. I'm talking about the dinner on St. Patrick's Day. The White House always has us and all of the Irish politicos for a big to-do. John Hume and the G. Man have been invited so this one should be a humdinger."

"The G-Man? They're inviting G. Gordon Liddy for St Patrick's Day?"

"No silly. Gerry Adams, the republican leader."

"Oh. Yes. That should be interesting. I look forward to it." Eileen ran her finger over the top of her coffee mug envisioning her meeting Gerry Adams, "Why Mr. Adams, it's a pleasure. I know you have nothing to do with the I.R.A., but are you perhaps familiar with Maeve's Cleaning Service? That Maeve. That Maeve. I tell ya. She leaves my basement clean as a whistle." She returned to her chat with Chris, "I'll rifle through my closet and come up with something. "

"Excellent. Hey, the G-Man thing is still up in the air. The rumors abound everyday as to whether or not he'll actually be invited to dinner, but I thought I should warn you, given your book and all."

"Thank you. I appreciate that. Hey, this could be fun. Hon, you better hurry or you'll be late for breakfast."

"Yes Dear."

Eileen turned off the phone and channel-surfed through talk shows and game shows until lunchtime. She didn't bother showering, pulling her hair into a barrette, throwing on some eyeliner and lipstick and drove to the BlackThorn with the report and the morning paper. The phone numbers were tucked in the back pocket of her jeans.

As she pulled away from the house, the mailman made the daily drop. An hour later, a purple card from Maeve's joined the pile on the floor in the foyer. Few people were in the Thorn. Eileen had been back there four times since her meeting with "Francis."

Something about the place made her feel at home. She knew that she did not have to talk to anyone or be remotely social, but the barmen always treated her well. They spoke to her when she wanted to talk, and left her alone when she wanted to be alone. Plus, she knew that she never would run into anyone she knew. Her friends would never think to venture to Southie. The Thorn might not have been a republican bar, per se, but her meeting with "Francis" made her feel closer to the entire disgusting effort. Today, she needed to remind herself of what it was like to be a Rah girl.

Eileen thought about how well this whole experience would have fit in her book. She'd kept Frannie's trust since the night in the New York hotel so many years ago, but within months after he'd left, she had to put it on paper somehow. Even though Mark Mullen was fictional, she'd created him almost as a surrogate Francis. Mark and Sophie helped her get through the first months without him. It was cheap therapy. Since Jack had shopped it to Empire, she waffled between feeling like the accomplished writer she knew she wanted to be, and feeling as though her medical records had been emailed around the world with the subject line: "Inside the Flake's Mind." Some nights she'd written for hours, smoking and drinking so much that upon review she didn't remember drafting certain paragraphs. Then again, some of her best scenes came through in stupors.

Married. How could it have happened? Eileen sat at the barstool, crossing her legs, then uncrossing them, then switched the cross to the other leg. The Jameson mirror posted on the wall ahead of her had two clocks—one showing "Our Time" and one showing "Dublin Time." The "Our Time" one had stopped but the Dublin clock ticked along its merry way. U2's *Until the End of the World* played from the jukebox in the corner. She smiled at the pathetic irony of it all. Sitting in a dark bar, at the end of a string of months when every day and night had been a manic fit of concern and worry. I'm in a nice house. Is Frannie cold somewhere? I'm eating well. Is Frannie safe? I'm proud of myself for getting through the day. Is Frannie thinking of me? Good days without him had left her feeling guilty. Bad days without him felt a hundred times worse.

In the back of her mind, she'd wondered too often just how much of a sick joke Nuala was. Had she always been real to him? How scary was she? Eileen had berated herself over the months for even thinking that he might have been cheating on her. Her living room furniture had heard the discussions she'd had with herself so often they could recite them pending of course that they could speak. The stack of postcards and the greeting card came screaming back at her. Rick, the barman pulled another cap off of a bottle of Miller Lite interrupting her train of thought when he put the bottle in front of her. The brief shift in her attention didn't last long.

"Oh man," she'd said to Fran that night two years ago. She sat in his living room with the postcards on her lap. "You know, if she's going to send you stuff, the least she could do is get her postmarks right."

"What do you mean?" He spoke over his shoulder, while he was bent over the television, running through the channels.

Eileen held a postcard in each hand, flipping them back to front. One was from Minneapolis and one from San Francisco. "Well gosh, let's see," she read a sentence, "'Tomorrow morning I leave for San Francisco to see my family. I can't wait, but I miss you so much.' Puke," she'd added.

"Yeah, so what?" Fran sat on the couch next to her and held her right foot in his hands.

"The San Francisco card is post-marked in Minneapolis. How could she mail you a card of San Fran before she's even arrived there?"

"Jaysus. Thank God you're not a forensics specialist." He grabbed the card from her and tore it to bits before throwing it in the kitchen garbage can. The postmark validated her trust in him. A stupid little circular stamp on a 50 cent postcard reassured her that perhaps Nuala truly was a front for his side work.

"Why don't we put in a call for rain and stay in bed." Eileen almost threw up when she saw that card, which Fran had so prominently displayed on his book shelf. She pitched a fit at him when she saw it. "Frannie, what the fuck is this?"

"What?" He walked to her and looked at the card.

"Oh, another piece of evidence of my 'social life.' It's nothing, Babe."

"Fuck you 'it's nothing.' Francis, this shit stops right now! I don't care about you and the Cause," she dragged the word out and raised her hands making quotation mark gestures. "If you need to put up some sort of front, then fine, fucking do it, but have the decency to take this crap down when I am here." She started walking in circles in the room holding her head in her hands. "Jesus, I can't believe I'm putting up with this. I can't believe that I am telling you to keep this up, but to just make sure I don't see it. Oh yeah," she stared right at him and pointed her finger, "anything to keep you safe Frannie. Anything to hide your secrets. Well fuck you. Fuck you for making me put up with this. I am patient. I am understanding. I give you all of the time you need, and you can't get rid of a few postcards, and a card that has some mysterious woman talking about wanting to stay in bed all day with you? Try living in my world for a few days, pal!" Her throat was sore when she'd finished yelling.

He stood, dumbfounded and ashamed, a look he'd often given her when he knew that he had been neglecting her. "I'm sorry. You're right. I'm sorry. This isn't fair to you. I will make it stop right now. I will get rid of everything, and I will tell them this weekend that the cards are to stop."

"What will you use as an excuse?"

"I don't know. But, there is no reason for you to be hurt by this any more than necessary. This is something that I actually can do for you, Leen and I will do it. It's done. Over. No more."

She lifted the beer to her lips recalling those moments. Son of a bitch. Son of a bitch. The phrase rolled over in her brain. No other words could come to her. "I'll know you're okay." "Please don't try to find me." Sure Frannie. Whatever you say.

She left the Thorn at 5:45 and cried her way back to Beacon Hill. She knew what she was going to do, realizing that it was going to have to happen sometime. She had allowed Frannie to hold all of the cards in their relationship. This was her chance to take a little bit of control of her life. He might never speak to her again but after months of silence, how much was there to lose? WBZ gave news and traffic reports over her car radio. Eileen still was unable to listen to music since he had gone. Music made it too easy to cry. She only listened to it these days when she and Chris were at dinners, dancing.

Chris was a good man. Eileen enjoyed him and he adored her. She sometimes felt badly not being able to return his affection with the same intensity he showed her. Jack was right; getting over one man by getting involved with another certainly helped ease the pain. She loved being the center of Chris' attention and the excitement of going back and forth to Washington, but she was not as attached to him as Jack and her other friends would have expected. The old Eileen, the pre-Fran Eileen, would have fallen for him within two hours of their first date. By the third date, she would have had dreams of their wedding.

She arrived home, opened a beer that she did not need and got on the Boston real estate homepage. She clicked on "recent sales," then entered Fran's address. It had been purchased four months ago for $280,000. "That fucker is living in a $300,000 house," she yelled. "Son of a bitch. Where'd ya get the money, Frannie?" She wondered if they'd made him liquidate his retirement accounts. Suddenly, she felt sad for him for everything that they must have taken from him. But hey, she recollected, he got a wife out of the deal. Hell hath no goddamn fury.

At 9:14 she picked up her phone, staring first at the key pad then glaring at the phone numbers on the table in front of her. She pressed "talk," dialed *67 to block her phone number on a Caller ID box in the event he had one, and dialed the number assigned to Francis Sullivan. No answer, just an automated voicemail system that didn't even have his voice on it. She did not leave a message. So much for the big confrontation. Eileen didn't bother to check the mail until 10:30, before she went to bed. She held the purple card in her hand and whispered, "Here we go again." Not knowing what time her guest would arrive tomorrow, she went down to the apartment changed the sheets, stocked the refrigerator with whatever she had upstairs and left a note. This was the first time she'd made any contact with whomever would be staying. She knew it was the wrong thing to do, but was not in a state to care.

"Welcome. Will be leaving town Wednesday. If you leave before Sunday, be sure to lock the doorknob and pull the door shut." She did not sign it.

30

She was in the shower when the basement door opened. Fran looked around, touching the white pillow case, sickened that Eileen had been pulled into the mess. He didn't care when they told him that he couldn't stay in Wakefield for a few days. He was glad to be out of there. It was the address they'd given him that sent him into a panic. On the drive over, he sat in the backseat trying to count the number of nights he'd spent in that house. He used the bathroom then noticed the note when he entered the kitchen. Her handwriting on the page made it nearly impossible for him to remain downstairs. He wanted to race up the stairs and bang on the locked door separating them. He wanted to see her face, hold her, and beg her to stop opening her home to the animals. Who had been using her this way? She never would have gotten involved unless someone had given her the impression that he approved of it. He punched the pillow then left the house, not caring if anyone saw him.

Fran stood on the street looking up at her bedroom light. He waited for a minute to see if she might walk past the window, but only saw the light go out and the hues of blue change on the television set glaring from the foot of her bed. He walked across Beacon Hill to the Park Plaza Hotel bar. If they needed to find him, he had his cellular phone. He had to get out, away from her house. His body shifted from left to right with the subtle swagger he'd always had. The orange tip of his cigarette swung with his arm, then move toward his mouth in the darkness. He was biting the filter as he inhaled. Distress and anger urged him to walk faster. Ten feet into the hotel lobby, he knew that the Park Plaza would not do. Fran had intended to sit in the bar where they'd spent an evening a year ago. He would have his alcohol and he would have a sense of her. A smart compromise at first, he'd reckoned. His mood would stand out too much in a hotel lounge. He wasn't 25 feet inside the lobby before he changed his mind. He kept walking, stewing, until he found his way to the Pour House; a small downtown pub popular with the locals. He used to go there years back when he'd first moved to Boston.

Frannie threw his Marlboros on the bar. The cellular phone was clipped to his belt. He ordered a Guinness and a Bushmills. It had been months, months of thinking about her, seeing her face in his mind, remembering the way she stifled her crying into the phone when he left, and the way he knew that he had betrayed her over and over again. "I'll know you're okay." He heard himself saying those words on their last conversation and knew he'd failed her. He knew nothing of her life. If he had, he could have protected her. Who had gotten to her? Who had pulled her in? He reached for the Guinness then opted for the whiskey and knocked it down his throat. When they were young he used to tell her, "You don't knock it back. You drink it." Not tonight. He heard her laughing at him in Nineteen O'Connell in Dublin when he'd said that. God, he pressed his hand into his knee as though holding pressure over a deep cut, why can't I let you go, Leen? How did you get to me so deeply? He prayed that he never would let go of her. She had to stay with him, no matter how crazy it made him.

Someone wanted him to know that Eileen was in the fold and that he was powerless to it. Hurting her, forcing her to live according to his responsibilities was his sentence for being one of them. Smoking his cigarette, he uttered to himself, "If there is a hell, I am living in it."

31

Newbury Street was jammed with shoppers. It was one of the last warm Saturdays of the year, and everyone wanted a piece of the last bits of summer-like weather. Chris and Eileen sipped grande lattes at a table outside of Starbucks, both facing the sidewalk. "Oh my goodness," she whispered over her coffee cup. "Eleven o'clock. Purple shirt and silver knit pants."

"Jeeze," he replied. "Does she think that's attractive?"

"Honey, I'm sure she thought it looked good on the mannequin at Armani, and ya know, it probably did. But my what a unique look she's mastered."

Chris was really getting into it. "The sunglasses," large gold ones with rhinestones on the arms, "are the piece de resistance."

"Very good Dear! Now you're getting into the spirit of the game." Eileen added a congratulatory clink to his coffee cup for a job well done.

"Do you think they realize we're sitting here like Olympic judges assessing fashion sense?" He referred to the tables around them.

"Nah. They're probably doing it too. Besides, it's all a matter of remaining inconspicuous, and I must say that you blend well."

"Why thank you. I learn from the best. We'd better get a move-on. The game starts in 20 minutes." They left Starbucks and hailed a cab to Fenway Park for the last Red Sox-Yankees showdown of the season. Eileen was thrilled when Chris managed to get tickets for the game. Her excitement grew even more after receiving Maeve's postcard the day before. Maeve had not contacted her at all over the last few weeks and her announcement was almost shocking to Eileen. She'd been spending so much time being normal, being a girlfriend, shoving Fran to the back of her mind that Maeve felt like an intrusion.

Shortly after the card came, Eileen recommended that they go to Chris' place in Winchester for the rest of the weekend. He liked the idea of waking up in his own bed with Eileen next to him. Congress was in recess for the week and she'd even agreed to spend Monday in Mike's district office learning more about his staff and helping out wherever she could. She'd become quite a wordsmith answering some of the constituents' letters on Mike's behalf. It had taken her only a few hours to learn how to write in a manner that sounded exactly the way he spoke. Mike's staff checked all of her correspondence before it left the office to be sure that she was conveying the correct opinions on the issues she addressed.

32
September 1999

Eileen was spending the week in DC with Chris as she had begun
to do once each month. "Hon," Chris leaned across the table at
Capital Grille, "pack your bags."

"Excuse me?" She stopped spearing an oyster with her cocktail
fork. Twice during the meal, and they'd only just gotten their
appetizers, lobbyists had stopped at their table to say hello trying
to remind him of some of their issues. Chris thanked them for
stopping by and finished nearly every conversation with, "Give
me a call and we'll talk."

"We're going to Ireland."

Eileen dropped her fork. "What are you talking about? When?
Why? Do you want to take a vacation?"

"No," he answered drinking his Stoli Doli, a Capital Grille sig-
nature drink of vodka and pineapple. "The Ad Hoc Committee
has been invited to go over to Belfast to meet with the representatives from each of the parties in the new government. I'm one of
three staffers who will attend. Even though Mike is new to the
Committee I'm what you might call the ranking staff member, in

terms of my own seniority. They've had some problems with the peace talks and the President thinks that we might be able to help move things along with a goodwill mission. Plus, we're also considering a financial package to assist business development in the north, so they want us to go over and take a few corporate prospects with us."

"So, the Committee is going over to make the parties feel important and to dangle the carrot."

"Your blatant observation is correct, madam. We can bring spouses, and I want you to go with me."

"But, I'm not a spouse."

"A small detail Sweetheart, that's a small detail. Besides, with your book and your knowledge, you can educate some of the Members more in 20 minutes than they'd learn in two months of studying."

"Honey, stop sucking up," she smiled. "What will you have to do? I thought only Members went on these things."

"Not this time. I've had about 30 plates in the air for the last few weeks."

"Like?" Their bleu cheese salads arrived and Eileen picked at hers while Chris continued.

"Leen, I wish I could tell you all of it, but I can't." Where have I hard that before, Eileen thought to herself. "It's been a lot of juggling schedules and waxing diplomatic between the White House, the State Department, the Secret Service, the Irish and British embassies, and all of the political parties in the peace process." Chris explained the need to keep three governments and corporate America happy. "We've convinced six manufacturing conglomerates and possibly two hotel chains to send representatives with us, the trick will be to get them to sell sell sell to the parties in hope of motivating them to advance the peace process."

"It's going that poorly?" Eileen asked him as though she hadn't followed the news for the past few months.

"Eileen, come on. I know you. You've been reading the news on the Internet. They can't speak to each other without a mediator. We need to help even if that means throwing around some financial incentives."

"That sounds so sleazy."

Chris put down his fork and sipped at his drink. "Hon, you have to understand that, okay, I shouldn't say this, but the White House needs this process to work. It's a matter of legacy, hope, ego and desperation."

"Desperation?"

"We took a leap on this. Congress, the President, everyone. No other Administration would touch this with a 10-foot pole. Go up against a tiny portion of a small nation not only overrun with terrorists, but that also is considered the homeland of 40 million American voters? Get serious. Reagan went into Grenada. Not exactly a hotbed of a voting bloc. We've gone into Belfast and Derry—Londonderry, depending on your perspective—brought Sinn Fein and the Ulster Unionists into the U.S., etc. etc." Chris added, "This is one of the President's goals. He wants it, and we're going to give it to him."

"Chris," Eileen put her hand on his, "I'm blown away by your passion for this. Why haven't we talked about this before?"

"Too busy, I suppose. I do what I have to when I have to. Otherwise, I don't think about it." His job saddled him with every possible issue area in some respect. His recall for names and issues was almost frightening. For as much as he knew about legislative topics, he kept an even closer attention to Eileen's likes, pet peeves and anecdotes.

"Eileen, please say you'll go."

"Belfast, huh?" She thought of Frannie. *I'd be on his turf, and he wouldn't even know it.* Then again, she thought, *maybe he's been sitting with his feet up living the quiet, suburban life in Wakefield.*

Chris noticed a change come over her face. It was an expression he'd never seen in her before, and it almost scared him. She wasn't hearing him. She was somewhere else. "Hello? Are you in there?"

He startled her, and she looked around the restaurant at all of the lobbyists and businessmen cutting deals in the dining room darkened by the cherry wood and green leather décor. "Of course I'll go. It will be an amazing opportunity. Plus, it might help me with my next book. Will it be okay if I do a little of my own research on the side?"

"Sure. The spouses will have some lunches and tours to attend but for the most part, you should be able to find a little time to yourself. Maybe we can even find some for ourselves." He reached across the table and held her hand.

Eileen was settling into the idea of going with him, "When do we leave?"

"Five weeks from now. Tuesday the 11th."

"I'll start making out my list of things to pack. Chris, thank you so much for inviting me, but I will pay my own way."

"Don't be silly. I'm picking up everything. Hell, the hotel is already covered, so it's just a few meals and your airfare."

"No. Chris, I insist. Please let me pay for at least the airfare."

He knew that her pride in taking care of herself ran very deeply and was not going to battle with her over a few hundred dollars. "If it will make you happy, then fine. You can cover your airfare, but I will get everything else."

"Deal."

33
October 1999

Georgeanne Carney, Representative Bill Carney's wife, sat next to Eileen in the Dulles terminal waiting to board the British Airways flight to London. The spouses, all women, were thrilled to be going to Ireland, but their apprehension about going to Northern Ireland had grown clearer in the terminal. Elizabeth Bennett kept looking at her boarding passes, studying the one from Heathrow to Belfast. She leaned over to her husband, Representative John Bennett, and put her hand on his elbow. "John. John. We'll be in safe places, right? And, it'll be safe to shop?"

He put his hand over hers, "Yes Lizzie, we'll be fine. We're staying at the Europa, a lovely hotel, and will be going to marvelous dinners. Besides, the Secret Service is here if we need them. Remember, the Speaker is with us, so security will be overseeing us. We will be fine, Dear. We'll have a wonderful time filled with work, dinners and shopping. I promise."

"I know." She let out a sigh, half-reassuring herself.

Chris and Eileen were with the group, listening to the chat. The "ghosties" as Frannie called them were assaulting her. The announcement reminding the airport population that *"Dulles International Airport is a smoke-free airport"* taunted her. Boarding would begin in 55 minutes. She wanted a few minutes outside before boarding the tram to the remote terminal. "I'm going outside for a smoke," she whispered to Chris. "I'll be back in a few."

"Want me to come with you?"

"No. No. Stay here." She patted his shoulder and kissed his cheek. "Watch my bag, please." Her pace quickened the closer she got to the airport entrance. Skycaps milled about with handtrucks, asking passengers if they needed help with their luggage. Eileen fired up a Marlboro Light exhaling like she'd taken in her first breath of fresh air in months. A woman stepped out of a baby blue Cadillac Eldorado. Far too much jewelry, Eileen noticed. She surveyed the woman's exchange with the skycap she'd flagged-down, before the car's trunk finished it's elegant, slow, automated opening. A young man got out of the driver's seat to help the woman who must have been his mother. The skycap removed two large suitcases, a wheeled wardrobe bag, and a carry-on make-up box. "Oh Honey," Eileen whispered to herself, "overkill with the get-up. Where are you going, a Joan Rivers fan club meeting? You must not travel much, and for fuck sake, are you running away from home with all those bags? Unbelievable."

The woman, in her sixties, sported jet black, obviously dyed hair choked back in a huge gold barrette and drowning in hairspray. Her foundation make-up was a shade too light giving her a Morticia Addams complexion that exaggerated her false, thick eyelashes and hooker-red lipstick. The lipstick reminded Eileen of all of those Sunday dinners at her grandmother's when she'd have to go through the gauntlet of kisses and hugs from each of her grandmother's friends. Every last one of those women, lovely as they were, left her cheeks looking like a psychedelic clown's. The colors were always accented by the imprints left by the women's thumbs as they'd each try to rub off their Estee Lauder calling cards from her cheeks.

"Love the gold studs. Do you have enough of them, dear?" Eileen was whispering to herself as she watched the curbside drama play out. The woman wore a black knit sweater with large gold and crystal-looking studs around the neckline and down the front of the buttonless cardigan. Each sleeve was bejeweled with four rows of gold studs. Black pants hugged her legs, and her waist was strangled by a thick leather belt with a large gold buckle. Naturally, the belt had the same gold and crystal studs to match the sweater. Her presentation concluded with stiletto-heeled gold pumps. Real travelers wear flat heels or sneakers to get through airports. Eileen wondered if the woman's sweater would clear security or if she'd have to undress and send half of her wardrobe through the scanner.

It didn't take long for the ghosties to come back. Eileen lit another cigarette. She could not return to the group with visions of Frannie dancing in her head. Fran Sullivan. Francis "married fucker" Sullivan. "Well Frannie, I'm going to your town. Imagine, it took Congress to get me there. Yup Frannie," she said, "not only am I going, I'm going with Secret Service escorts. What a hoot." She shook her head at the irony and twisted her foot over the cigarette butt. "Well, off to duty free." The automatic doors slid open, inviting her back into the terminal.

Eileen boarded the plane wondering where the over-dressed woman flew off to, and remembering the taste of those last two cigarettes. The free drinks on the flight elevated her desire for nicotine, but alleviated her anxiety about facing Belfast and having to face it with Chris. He'd been talking up the trip for weeks, mentioning how they could escape from the group one night for a little time alone. Eileen couldn't focus on that. She wanted to keep her head down and keep moving; follow the itinerary and take a few moments to herself. Sleeping in the same bed with Chris, in Belfast, would be difficult enough.

34

As the plane landed in Belfast, Eileen looked out the window watching acres upon acres of farmland pass below them. First, it was five or 10 sheep below, then 20, 50, 100. There must have been a thousand furry, white bodies dotting the dark green land under the plane. Thanks be to God, she thought when the night and morning of travel were over. Despite British Airways' hospitality, Eileen just wanted the journey to be over. Outside the airport, she grabbed a smoke, ten feet from the delegation of non-smokers, unless they were offered a cigar with a good single malt scotch. She'd watched the members of Congress do it all the time, even after the Health Ball. This time, she was not a 19 year-old girl walking into the welcoming arms of the man she loved, still loved. This time, she was a 35 year-old woman flying by the seat of her pants. How, she thought, did I get to this place?

The van took them from the airport into Belfast, via Ligonier Street then through the Shankill Road. Shortly after, she noticed one of the signs indicating that she was in Shankill. The van passed a mural for the Ulster Volunteer Force and Eileen felt her senses constrict. Not 20 minutes in the country and already she was in a place where she should not have been. She clutched her Celtic cross necklace as if hiding it. Chris made small talk with the driver, asking if he lived in the area. The driver said no, that he lived closer to the airport, then began to talk about the weather in Belfast and some of the events occurring in town over the coming week. The rest of the group listened intently to the quick-speaking driver, and exchanged pleasantries about the cities he'd been to in the US. Eileen watched out the window at the murals painted in homage to the Ulster Volunteer Force that sparked her attitudes and her nationalist opinions. Then, she felt scared. Despite her nationalist leanings, she just wanted to get the hell out of there. This would be one long week. Secret Service or not, the ghosties were lining up around her, ready to tap her on the shoulder at any time.

Thursday was deemed "free day" for the spouses, and Chris was running back and forth tying down some final plans. The Secret Service was taking Speaker Gilman's wife shopping in Donegal Square then up to the Botanic Gardens. The men were off to Stormont to meet with Senator Mitchell and representatives from the leading political parties. Yesterday, they had met with industry leaders, including those from the Republic who could benefit from bringing business into the North, given the proposed financial package that the President was prepared to sign to assist the peace process. American computer companies and pharmaceutical factories were lining up to pursue opportunities. Luring in the hotel chains was the hardest sell.

The other women joined Mrs. Gilman, but Eileen chose to take the day to herself. She made the excuse that a little touring could help her with research for her next book and bid them a pleasant afternoon. She walked from the Europa to the West Belfast taxi stand, almost directly across the street. The grey sky looked like it wanted to let forth rain at any second but withheld its inventory for later. It would come shortly, for about an hour, then let up for another three. The black taxis were lined up in columns according to the neighborhoods they served. She walked toward one column where two men leaned against a car. One asked her, "Can I help you, miss?" Eileen asked him for a tour of the neighborhood. The first driver looked at his friends and said, "I'll take Dorothy." Eileen sat in the back of the car and thought, Driver, take me to Oz.

Henry, her driver, was a pleasant fellow and invited Eileen to sit in the front of the cab while he drove her down the Falls Road and through every little nook and cranny of the neighborhood in the area. He stopped at the murals explaining their meanings, then pointed out the green "peace line" fence dividing the Catholic and Protestant neighborhoods. They stopped at Milltown Cemetery where Henry showed her the graves of Bobby Sands, the other hunger strikers and the Gibraltar Three. He walked around for a few minutes while Eileen stood in the misting rain, her head bowed over the markers. So many years later and the markers still shone like they had been put in just days before. Fresh tri-colour sashes decorated some of the stones, while imitation carnations adorned others. She remembered the news stories about Bobby Sands on television, had read his writings and poetry, and thought of all of the families affected by loss who were represented in the small area of the cemetery dedicated to republican volunteers. She whispered a Hail Mary, and a Glory Be, crossed herself and met Henry back at the taxi.

They stood on the gravel not far from the grave sites and had a cigarette while Henry told her about some of the other neighbors who were buried in Milltown. His old barber who died of cancer, the woman who'd babysat him when he was a child, some of the nuns who had taught him in primary school—all regular people with regular lives. No grand stories behind them, just a few color-ful memories they'd left behind so that the neighbors wouldn't forget they'd been there.

"What are those towers," she asked, referring to the metal scaffolding in the near distance. From where she stood, they looked as though they were springing directly from the statue of the Blessed Mother.

"Video cameras. The RUC—Royal Ulster Constabulary—likes to know who's visiting the dead," Henry told her wryly.

"Lovely." She followed him back to the car and continued her tour. "Henry, where's the Felons Club?"

"See that flag?" Henry asked.

"Yes."

"That's the Felons." Henry pointed to the pub almost directly across the street but a bit further from the cemetery.

"Great. Thanks. A friend said I should check it out, and honestly, I want to be sure that I can have a few minutes peace where no one will find me."

"Are you not traveling alone?" Henry was taken aback by her comment.

"No. If you must know, I'm here with an American group. Kind of a goodwill mission." She probably should not have told him with whom she was traveling but Eileen truly did not care. Driving down the Falls she felt her shoulders relax, and years of wondering what Oz was really like came to a graceful close. She felt completely comfortable.

"A mission huh? Like the Blues Brothers," he joked, "we're on a mission from God," quoting the movie and laughed.

Eileen reached into her handbag and put on a pair of sunglasses, "Absolutely." As they headed back up the Falls to the taxi stand, they talked about his family, where his wife worked, his five children and the trouble with 11 year-old boys. "Henry," she finally confessed, "I'm with a group of members of the U.S. Congress. They're doing all sorts of meetings and I'm here as a guest of one of the staff. I hate all of the protocol and would like nothing more than to find a nice pub, grab a newspaper and a pint, chat with the locals and be real for a few minutes. The political bullshit is killing me. I've only been here two days marching around to lunch and dinner parties like a beauty pageant contestant. If I last the rest of the week, it'll be a miracle. I am no beauty queen and couldn't give a monkey's about ball gowns and smoked salmon."

"So, you're AWOL from Congress."

"Well, yes, I guess you could say that I am. And the Secret Service. Ain't that a hoot!" She slapped the dashboard, giggling.

"Brilliant! Fuckin' brilliant! God, everything they say about American women is true."

"What do they say about American women? Oh hey, could you slow down for a second? I'd like to take a few photographs." Henry stopped the car, and Eileen got out to snap two murals and a rickety bicycle leaned up against a brick wall.

Henry continued when she returned to the car, "American woman think. They are risk takers. They're fuckin' intimidatin'." He laughed and shifted the gears.

"We are not intimidating." Eileen smiled. "We are merely entertaining."

They arrived back at the taxi stand and Eileen handed him a 20 pound note. "It's only 10 ma'am."

"So what," she answered. "You've really helped me figure this place out a bit. Thanks so much. Have a great day, Henry."

"You too, Miss."

"Eileen."

He nodded his head, "Eileen."

After the drive, Eileen walked back down the Falls and veered off into St. Peter's Cathedral. A few other parishioners were in there and a priest crossed back and forth between the sacristy and the chapel next to the main church. The stone cathedral felt like any other church in the U.S.; dark wood floorboards, worn with age but still shining in some areas of the church, supporting creaking pews of matching wood. A rosetta window over the altar caught intermittent rays of sunlight, illuminating the center aisle of the church. Stained glass windows ran down both side walls catching indirect sunlight. There were no lights on. Eileen stood in the back of the church and took a picture trying to capture the serenity of the pews in the natural light. It had been a longtime since she'd gone to church. Since Frannie left, her relationship with God had been difficult, trying, if not overwhelming. For months, she'd considered talking to a priest but could not bring herself to betray Fran.

Eileen walked to the front pew, listening to her shoes echo throughout the cathedral. She rested her hand on the pew. It creaked under her grip and got even louder when she slid onto the seat. She looked up at the enormous crucifix over the altar, wondering what kind of fear Jesus must have felt during his last days. What loneliness must have come over him, and what enormous trust he must have had that God would take care of him.

She thought of her own fear and loneliness, wondering when God was going to care for her. Eileen knew in her heart that God had been caring for her and that she had not been alone, but the pain of emptiness still had been so overwhelming for so many months, she wondered what worse things could have happened had He not been there to help her through. Tears ran down her face, and she tried not to make any noise. The slightest cries would have echoed through the church. She sat, with her hands folded in her lap, looking up at the cross, whispering, "God, I'm here. I made it. God, please take care of my Frannie. Oh God, I still love him so dearly. You know that. There is so much that I do not understand and I just don't know what's right and what's wrong anymore. I know that I have to move on. I cannot live like this anymore. Please God, care for him. Care for me. Help me to get through this loss. I still don't know if I can." She dabbed at her eyes with her jacket sleeve. "God, some days I don't know if I can make it. I had so much in me, and now I am numb. Chris is a wonderful man. Thank you for him, but God, he cannot replace the emptiness and loss that I still carry. Sometimes I wish You'd make it all go away, and sometimes I hope You never do. If I were to stop missing Frannie or thinking about him and hurting like this, it would make him further from my heart, and God, I'm just not ready for that. I don't know if I ever will be." Eileen finished her conversation with Him, and sat quietly for a few minutes listening to the silence around her, before she said a decade of the rosary, finishing as she always did, with a Glory Be, her favorite prayer. She'd learned it when she was six, and it summed up everything to her: Glory Be to the Father, to the Son and to the Holy Spirit. As it was in the beginning, is now, and ever shall be, world without end, Amen.

She left St. Peter's, knowing that she had to keep moving. It was only 12:30 in the afternoon, but she had to keep going. This was her day. She'd needed and hoped for it for far too long. She stopped in the Sinn Fein bookshop and browsed through the book selections, not seeing anything of particular interest that she did not already own but bought a few hair clips for herself and her mother. As she got further down the Falls Road, nearer to the Felons, a taxi drove by and honked the horn at her. Henry waved at her and shouted "Hello." I'll be damned, she thought, not two hours in this town and already the locals are recognizing me. The Felons was a long walk from the taxi stand and made for a good workout. She snapped a few photos of kids kicking a soccer ball in Beechmount, women pushing prams in front of one of the murals, an older man and his dog leaning against a shop front— shots of daily life in an unreal location. She reached the Felons, noticed the closed-circuit camera, and pushed the button on the gate as Henry had told her she'd have to do.

The man at the desk asked her to sign in. She obliged, then stepped into the pub realizing that she was the only woman in the place and the gentlemen seemed disturbed by her presence. They looked up from their jars of Guinness and Harp, staring at her as though one of the nuns from their third grade class had caught them all smoking in the bathroom, and was about to yell, "Put out your hands." Eileen walked to the bar and leaned to the barman, "Pint of Guinness, please." When she spoke, they were even more perplexed to find a lone American woman in their pub.

The barman placed the glass before her and said, "You're the woman Henry met this morning, aren'tcha?"

"That would be me," Eileen replied as she was lighting her cigarette.

"Welcome." Frank, the barman, introduced himself and extended his hand to her. Frank was, like most men in the pub, roughly 5'8" and physically fit. He looked like any guy in Boston, with light brown hair and blue eyes, but unlike most of the guys she'd met in Boston, he was quiet.

"Thank you." Then she leaned toward him and whispered, "I can't tell if I'm making everyone uncomfortable or if I'm just a temporary shock to their system." She looked around the place. The Felons had a reputation as a republican bar run by former I.R.A. POWs, as they called them. No matter who ran the place, it was a lovely little pub with a good-size, dimly lit but welcoming dining room, and a pub in the front with a few tables, a jukebox, a brightly lit bar, and a pool table. There were virtually no windows. Eileen didn't bother to ask but assumed it a safety precaution. The place, as she'd learned on the Internet, prior to the renovation had been attacked numerous times, and a pub can't stay open if the punters keep getting shot. There wasn't a single reference to republicanism. The same promotional beer signs hung on their walls as in Southie, Eastham, downtown Boston and New York.

Frank wanted Eileen to feel welcome but wasn't sure what to say, except for his occasional calls for "language" when one of the punters used words he deemed inappropriate in the presence of a lady. After his second admonition, Eileen turned to Mickey Donnell, the man closest to the her and said, "Please boys, don't worry about me. Say whatever you like," then laughed out loud.

Mickey and his compadres were startled when she spoke directly to them. His friend, Tommy Phelan, answered for them, "So Miss, what brings you here?"

"I wanted a drink."

"No," he replied, "why did you come to this place?" Without trying to frighten her his eye contact made it clear that he and the rest of them were suspicious of any tourist who happened to wander into the pub. Few tourists would want to go to a place surrounded by gates and cameras, and ask you to sign in.

Eileen sipped at her Guinness and said, "A friend from Boston said I should check it out."

Tommy clinked his glass against hers, "Well sweetheart, that's all you had to say!" The three other men engaged her in a conversation about the US, New York City, did Chicago really dye the river green on St. Patrick's Day, etc. Politics were never discussed, nor was she asked her opinion of Belfast. She learned that one man had spent years in prison—long enough to earn a college degree and a doctorate, and now he was a history teacher. Between conversations, Eileen kept eyeing the pool table. A few transient punters had been playing during the afternoon. Finally, Tommy asked, "Would you like to play?"

Eileen's eyes widened with her smile and she said, "Would you be willing to be seen playing pool with a woman? That doesn't seem to be the done thing here."

"Don't say another word." He reached for two cues while Eileen set up the rack on the table.

They played two games, and the boys at the bar were surprised to see how closely Eileen kept up with Tommy's game even though she lost both of them. She never noticed them pushing pound coins back and forth to each other on the bar, betting on her chance of sinking a shot. After she scratched on the eight-ball, Eileen looked at her watch and saw it was already 4:15. She and Chris were supposed to have their "night out" tonight. She excused herself to the ladies toilets and called the hotel from the pay phone next to the bathrooms. He answered on the second ring. "Chris?"

"Eileen, where are you? Everyone else came back about an hour ago."

"Oh Chris, I'm having the best time. Come meet me." He heard a change in her voice inflection. She sounded lighter, happier than she'd been in weeks. He was upset that she hadn't had that same sense of fun with him, but got over those feelings when she asked him to come and meet her.

"Where are you?"

"The Felons Club."

"The what?" He'd never heard of it, and had no idea how far or near she was to him.

"Chris, it's a local pub. Go to the black taxi stand and tell them you need a lift to the Felons. Oh and please come by yourself." She looked around the doorway at the nearly empty dining room, and listened to the crack of a cue ball breaking up a fresh rack on the pool table.

"Everyone else is going to the dinner at the Wellington Hotel. So, no one will be around, except for a couple of Secret Service guys."

"No. No one else. Just you. Come and be with me. Just the two of us and the locals I've met. Oh, and don't be intimidated by the front door to the place. I'll tell them at the front that you're here to see me."

"Eileen, what the hell kind of place is this?"

"Just a pub." She looked around wondering how Chris would fit in. What would his reaction be to entering a place with such high security and a less than favorable reputation? She stopped caring about protocol, "Come casual and prepared for a few pints and a couple of games of pool. Tonight, we're kicking back."

Eileen returned to the bar and ordered a bottle of Budweiser. For some reason, being away from home made her appreciate American beer more. She liked being an American and didn't mind being completely blunt about her citizenship, even if she showed it through the beer she drank. Plus, after a while, Guinness makes it damn near impossible to lean over a pool table without feeling as though you'll fall over. Frank lit her cigarette, "So, what do you do in Boston?"

"I'm a writer. Other than that, I do nothing." The evening news was running on the television over the bar and Ian Paisley's image took up the entire screen. Hissing noises could be heard from a few punters in the bar, as the ultra conservative unionist bellowed from the television.

"Sounds pretty good to me." Frank leaned on one of the taps and smoked his own cigarette. "What do you write?"

"So far, I've published one novel. I'm working on a second one, but it's not coming as quickly as I would have hoped."

"Ah, writer's block."

"You could say." He asked her what she'd written just as Mickey asked her if she'd like to play another game of pool. She nodded yes to Mickey, then turned to Frank and said, "*Accidental Terrorist.* I doubt if it's made it over here, and if it has, I tend to wonder if this crowd would still like me."

"No you didn't."

"Yes, I did." She was holding the pool cue, half looking at the table and half looking at Frank.

"Well, fuck me," he said, "you're Eileen Eliot. Jesus, that book has been a big seller around here."

"You're kidding. I don't believe you." Mickey broke up the balls on the table. One of each dropped and he decided to play the solids. Before he took his fourth shot, Frank called him over and told him and Tommy who Eileen was. Both were impressed by her notoriety. Mickey made a joke about how he was competing with greatness. "Yes, and I'm losing badly," she replied gesturing to the pool table.

Chris arrived to see Eileen, still the only woman in the place, sinking a shot on the pool table, and Mickey, Tommy and Frank quietly applauding in cynical support. "Oh hey!" Eileen leaned her cue against the wall and met Chris with a hug and a kiss. "I'm so glad you're here."

Tommy joked, "She's been greeting the boys that way all afternoon! We're thinking of hiring her as the Welcoming Committee. Business will go through the roof." He extended his hand to Chris and introduced himself. Chris was still recovering from the shock of entering a place that was locked down like a fortress and absorbing the sight of the woman he loved looking happier and more at home than he could remember.

Chris mixed in well with the others and almost gave in to having a cigarette, but fought the urge. He and Eileen played three games of pool. She didn't even know that he liked the game, or that he was so good at it. She lost every game and ultimately handed her cue to Tommy so Chris could have at least one good opponent.

"So Chris, you live in Boston too?" Tommy continued, "I was there years ago. Brilliant city."

Chris wasn't sure how to respond, and looked at Eileen for guidance. She smiled and nodded her head in the affirmative, then took a drag on her cigarette. Chris leaned over the table, took a shot, banking the four ball off the far center edge of the table until it rolled back into the right corner pocket in front of him. "I live in Washington, DC. But I split my weeks between there and Boston."

"What do you do for work?"

"I work in Congress."

Tommy looked over at Eileen. "The US Congress? He's an elected official?"

Chris sipped his Guinness. "No. I'm not. Merely staff. My boss is here for the week, and I'm accompanying him and his colleagues."

"Cool." Tommy sank the eight ball off of a bank shot into the left side pocket ending the game.

"I suppose. You want to play again?"

"Nah. Let's take a break." They returned to the bar for another round. Chris bought Tommy a drink.

Chris quickly understood why Eileen enjoyed the place so much. The locals took to her, as most people did, and he fell right in with the small crowd. They told him and Eileen places they should be sure to visit while in town. "I wish we could," Chris answered. "Unfortunately, we're here for business and don't have a whole lot of free time. We're cutting school tonight, so to speak."

"Sorry?" Frank asked him, placing a bowl of stew in front of Chris and then one for Eileen.

"God, this is heaven," she exclaimed, digging her spoon into the bowl. "I'm famished."

"Hon," Chris joked, "I think you've got the munchies. The beer's making you hungry."

"Don't I know it."

Chris answered Frank, "We were supposed to go to a dinner tonight, but decided to bow out. I'd planned to take the fair maiden," he pointed at Eileen, "for a nice meal and a few drinks. Next thing I know, she phones from here, and well, the rest is history."

"Fair play t'ya both." As they ate their dinners, Frank took a candle from one of the dining room tables and put it in front of them. "A little atmosphere for ya," he winked at them, then refilled their drinks.

"Thank you." Chris smiled at him. After Frank took away their bowls, Chris turned to Eileen. "Sweetheart, I haven't seen you so happy in ages. Has something been wrong?"

"No! No. Oh darlin', it's just been so busy lately. Preparing for this trip, and my book isn't working the way I'd hoped it would. It's been taking up more of my brain than I'd have hoped. Today has been a marvelous escape. Thank you so much for coming down here tonight and not complaining that I changed our plans. It just feels good to be away from all of the protocol and bullshit."

"Don't be silly dear." He rubbed her shoulder, then stood up. "Miss Eliot," he took her hand, "Eileen, this isn't exactly how I'd planned it."

At that, the men around them, including Frank, stopped their debates and watched him. Eileen looked up at Chris and held his hand tighter. "What are you talking about?"

"Leen, I'm crazy about you. I love you."

"I love you too. Chris, you're scaring me. Is something wrong?"

"God, no." He reached into his left front pocket, and removed a small box. "I've been carrying this with me since the day before we arrived here. I thought it would be the right place given all of your work, and your novel. Have I told you lately how proud I am of you?"

"Chris, what are you saying?"

Frank checked the refrigerator to be sure he had a cold bottle of champagne. No one ever ordered champagne in there. He knew what was coming. It would be a first for the Felons history books.

Chris opened the box revealing a 1.25 carat, round-cut, diamond ring set in a platinum band, accentuated by two emerald baguettes. "Eileen Eliot, would you please marry me?" Eileen sat dumbstruck, staring at Chris, forgetting about the audience surrounding them. Chris kept looking at her waiting for her answer. "Please?" He smiled at her, nervous.

She put her hands to her cheeks, realizing that she hadn't answered him. "Yes. Yes, definitely." She pulled him to her and kissed his right cheek, then his lips. Frank popped the cork on the champagne bottle as Chris put the ring on her finger.

They stayed another two hours, accepting good wishes from everyone in the pub, then left at 9:00, hailing a black taxi back up to the rank by the Europa. The rest of the group was still at the dinner up the road, but due back by 10:00. Chris had told the other staff members that they would meet them in the hotel lounge at the end of the evening. Chris and Eileen took the hour hiatus to properly celebrate their engagement in the privacy of their hotel room.

35

"Jesus." Congressman Bennett pushed the paper across the table to Chris during the morning buffet breakfast. "Chris, what the hell were you up to?" Mike looked up from his plate confused.

He and Eileen looked at him unsure of what he meant. Chris took the copy of the morning's *Belfast Telegraph* from John and nearly choked on his toast at the photo and headline "US Closes Deal in Felons." The story detailed Chris and Eileen's night in the pub, the way he'd asked her to marry him and had a photo of the two of them leaving the place with an inset photo of Eileen's ring on her left hand. Brief biographies in the article described Chris as lead congressional staff on Irish issues, and Eileen as an I.R.A. novelist.

"This is bad, Chris. Really bad." Bennett continued, "We're to meet with the multi-party reps today and the unionists will not be pleased to see this."

The group sat at the table unsure of what to say next, or who should say it. The wives sat at the table fearing the worst, envisioning doors being slammed shut in their faces, and the Secret Service being forced to actually protect them as opposed to just escorting them about the city. Mike was silent. Eileen finally cut the tension, "Mr. Bennett, it's all my fault. If you want, I will go to the meetings as well, or you can mention me as the scape-goat. I'd gone down there yesterday. I was doing research for my book and wanted to gather some of the local flavor. I wound up enjoying myself so much that I invited Chris to meet me. Honestly, there was nothing more to it. Chris had no idea of the place's reputation."

"Did you know," Georgeanne asked her, almost panicked.

"Well, yes, I did."

"But the article says it's a republican pub. It says it's run by I.R.A. supporters! Weren't you scared?!"

Chris put his hand on Eileen's knee under the table. He was reassuring her and also begging her not to irritate Representative Carney's wife. Eileen speared a piece of sausage from her plate then drank her coffee. "Frankly, Georgeanne, walking in there was very intimidating at first, but as I said, it was a fact-finding mission of sorts. I mean, look at you, look at all of us. I'm sure Congress has never been a walk through the park and I know that some of us weren't necessarily thrilled about coming here. Let's be honest, wouldn't some of you have preferred to have spent yesterday strolling the Champs Elysee in Paris?" She laughed a bit, uncomfortable, yet hoping to sway her audience. "I was nervous, at first, but soon I learned that they're just people. Enjoyable, fun people. Right, Chris?" She turned to him and put her hand on his forearm, fearing that she'd cost him his job.

He was almost embarrassed at her laying herself before them in his defense. "Absolutely, and I doubt if the news would have been worth it's salt if I hadn't let the romantic fool in me get the better of me."

"Chris," Speaker Gilman added, "We'll find a way out of this, and she just might need to be our fatted calf. Eileen, do us a favor and stick with us for the rest of the trip, okay?" He sounded so much like Eileen's father.

She remembered the way he'd caught her when she was 10, after Mrs. Gilroy from next door came over and said that Eileen had picked all of her yellow tulips. Mrs. Gilroy had seen Eileen walk home wearing a necklace made of her tulips woven together. Her father met her in the living room with the necklace he'd fetched from the backyard fort in his hand and said, "Dear, I appreciate your creativity. So does your mother, but the neighbor's haven't quite caught up yet with your talent. Let's keep it within the family from now on, and do not pick anyone's flowers again. Ask first." The discipline came through in the tone of voice.

The entire group left for Stormont for another all-party meeting, including the spouses and Eileen who would be participating in separate discussions. During tea, Eileen was seated next to the Sinn Fein representative's wife. They'd met before in Washington at a reception. The two chatted endlessly while the other spouses hesitated to speak with either woman. Eileen left the meetings branded as the unofficial envoy to the republican contingent. That of course, did not stop the other women from admiring and asking about her ring.

"Jack," Eileen phoned him from her hotel room, "You're not going to believe it."

She'd woken him, forgetting it was only 4 AM in Boston "Eileen, where are you?"

"I'm still in Ireland. Jack, Chris proposed."

"I know. Or, at least I knew he wanted to. That's great, kid. What did you say?"

"I said yes!"

He sat up in bed surprised at her good news. "Leen, that's terrific. You finally landed a normal one."

"Shut up!" she slapped the bedspread. "Yes, you're right. I've landed a normal one. Now, I just need to be a good wife."

"Stop it. You just had a run of bad luck for a few years. Okay, so maybe like, eight years. Have you set a date?"

"No. We haven't even talked about it. Oh, but wait until I tell you what happened this morning."

"What did you do now? Eileen, I knew you'd get into trouble over there."

She switched the phone to her other ear. "I didn't get into trouble. Not really, but I'll show you everything when I get home next weekend. We're flying back to Dulles on Tuesday and I'll be at Chris' in DC until Friday morning." After she finished her conversation she fingered through the five copies of the newspaper she'd picked up across Great Victoria St. Buying them in the hotel seemed somewhat conspicuous to her. The hotel staff already was making glances her way as she walked through the lobby. The Europa was the most bombed hotel in Europe compliments of the I.R.A.. The staff had been so proud to have President Clinton there a few years ago and now a contingent of Congressional representatives. They didn't know what to make of the group now that two of them had been seen not only drinking in the Felons but getting engaged there. Eileen didn't either. The previous day had been her time to face the demons, then she'd wound up with a fiancé.

36

Fran was back in Boston and he'd already heard the news about the engagement. The boys had a right laugh about it when the story had reached them. He knew before the story had made it into the paper. It hadn't taken long for the gossip to spread from the pub to the whole of West Belfast. When it hit the paper, they reveled in the disgust it must have registered on the faces of the opposition. She and Chris had become the I.R.A.'s flavor of the day merely for their shock value.

Fran was staying in Wakefield with Nuala and tried to show the same thrill at the notion as she and the boys drank to the good Congressman and his bride-to-be. "Gosh," Nuala joked, "should we send them a thank you note and a political contribution? Fran, you should pay the dear man a visit the next time you're in DC." Nuala gloated to herself imaging Frannie's intestines twisting as they all joked around him. Boo-hoo, she thought, dear heart's love has found another. She watched him walk into the kitchen to get a mug of tea when she knew his emotions—the ones he pretended not to have—were rioting in his head. Keep the leash short; that was Nuala's mantra. It had served her well through the years and her husband had responded well. She knew Frannie was strong-willed and it was important to tug the leash every now and again to keep the upper hand. Besides, a man full of tension was a good thing when she wanted satisfaction.

"Right," he answered sarcastically and sick to his stomach. The conversation changed to sports, then work, and then back to sports. Fran stood in the renovated kitchen, tapping his foot on the vinyl flooring, remembering his nights in Eileen's basement. When he knew she'd left town, he'd broken a cardinal rule of the organization and found his way into the main house. Eileen was never very concerned with security. She had no alarm system, and Fran had learned over the years to pick a lock or two.

He entered through the patio door, listening for any signs of humanity. When he confirmed he was alone, he crossed through the living room picking up photos of her and Jack. He never liked Jack. He didn't cross his mind very often when he and Eileen were together, but anytime she mentioned Jack's name, Fran would utter, "Babe, you know he wants you." That would lead to brief debate about how wrong Frannie was. "Sweetie," she'd say, "He's the older brother I always wanted. That's all. Now, shut up about it." He stopped raising the issue when Eileen finished her admonitions with "How's 'Post-Card Bitch'?"

Her house still displayed the cluttered lifestyle she'd never managed to conquer. He picked up her sweater from the back of the kitchen chair and held it to his face. He could smell her skin and remembered the night when she wore it when they went to see the Pops. He'd told her to bring it in case she got cold. She said she wouldn't get cold, yet wound up wearing it all night.

He ascended the stairs to her bedroom. His eye caught her perfume bottle and hair brushes on the vanity. He was pulling pieces of her hair from the brush when he looked just to his right and saw three framed pictures—all of the two of them. He picked up one. It was of her laughing, sitting with him on her patio. Jack, of all people, had snapped it three years ago. She was holding his hand, and he was making a mock-surprised face as though he was thrilled by her touch. He was. "God, I miss you Leen." Fran spoke out loud and wiped his eyes before replacing the picture to its place on the tabletop and left the house.

Now he stood, still tapping the floor, looking at the woman, the demon in the living room, convincing himself that this was his life and he'd better accept it. The Felons, what the fuck was she doing in the Felons, he thought. His network had crawled under his skin, taken his soul, and pushed the one piece of his remaining sanity into their arms. For a moment, he considered suicide.

37
December 1999

Eileen was staying at Chris' apartment for the week sorting through wedding plans and trying to figure out when they could schedule a ceremony between the House's schedule, fundraisers and the upcoming election cycle. She'd just arrived back from Old Town Alexandria, and a shopping spree of flowers, wine and cheese at Sutton Place Gourmet. Tonight was a rare evening when they did not have to be anywhere after 6:00, so she also picked up two of Sutton's pre-cooked bistro dinners. She opted for peppered tenderloin, mixed grilled vegetables and garlic mashed potatoes, complemented by a large salad. She justified the purchase by determining that their weekday time was so precious that surely she shouldn't waste a moment of it by cooking or having to clean dishes. She remained the champion of avoiding domestic skills at any cost. How did I get so lazy, she thought driving down the GW Parkway back to Capitol Hill. Then again, she joked to herself, when haven't I been a domestic slacker?

She was looking through menus from a number of potential locations for the wedding when the phone rang. "Hello?"

"Hi Doll," Chris spoke to her.

"Hey, how ya doing? I've got a great dinner planned, and I've been cooking all day."

"Liar," he laughed.

"Okay, so I blew a fortune at Sutton Place, but tonight we're going to eat well and channel surf. What are you up to?"

He was at the Democratic Congressional Campaign Committee's headquarters on Ivy Street, just two blocks from his office. "I'm here at the DCCC for a quick strategy lunch and well, how would you feel about having dinner a little late tonight?"

She could feel the air deflating from her imaginary balloon. "How late? Chris, please tell me that I don't have to dress up tonight."

"No dear, no dressing up. But, we're having a meeting here around 6:00, and I need to be in on it."

"Is something wrong?" She put down the menus and listened to him.

He explained that the campaign would be heating up shortly and that it was going to take a lot of his time. "Why don't you come with me? I promise. It won't take too long. We'll be home by 7:30. Is that okay with you? Somehow," he sarcastically mentioned, "I'm sure that dinner will still be salvageable. Unless of course, you have some wicked sauces brewing on the stove as we speak."

"Chris, we both know that culinary delights are your job. I kept with tradition and got take out, but great take out. Okay, I'll meet you at the DCCC at 5:30."

"Thanks. Leen, I love you."

"I love you too. Now, go make the country a better place for all of us, Superman."

"I'm hanging up the phone and jumping into my telephone booth. Bye."

Eileen returned to the menus, some from locations in DC and some from places around Boston. They still hadn't decided where they'd get married let alone when, but the date looked to be somewhere in the vicinity of mid-November when the election would be over and Congress would have wrapped up the session. Eileen hadn't given much thought to the campaign, but now it was starting to creep into her mind.

The DCCC staff led them into a conference room on the second floor. Dry-erase whiteboards hung on the walls around the room detailing races considered to be the most vulnerable around the country. The Democrats were counting on this election to take back the House after the agony of losing control of both the House and Senate in 1994. Kyle Foster, the staffer overseeing the New England races, led the meeting attended by Mike, his DC-based campaign staff, Chris, Eileen, and Mike's Winchester-based staff, who joined by conference call. "Thank you all for being here on such short notice," Kyle began.

"Well," the Congressman responded, "We're happy to be here and frankly, we hope that you can help us move from this war room to one with less tense races," he joked uncomfortably. Eileen sat in silence listening to the discussion.

"Congressman," Kyle began, "Charlie Tate has decided to get into the race."

Michael leaned over to Eileen, "I beat Charlie in the last election, but the point spread was so close that they actually counted the votes by hand."

"Yes," Kyle continued, "and we don't want to run the risk of having to win on another 92 vote difference this time around, sir."

"Nor do I."

Kyle outlined Tate's actions to date. "He's working with the grasstops, the businesses, the local party, etc., but it won't be long before he starts hitting the grassroots at full throttle. We're expecting him to begin working with the local media, the school boards, and every other group that might offer its endorsement."

Eileen listened for another five minutes about the need to begin a telephone outreach campaign, bring constituents to DC to testify at hearings, and hold local hearings in the district to increase his recognition. "Excuse me," she interjected, "I always thought Massachusetts was a die-hard Democrat state. Honestly, this is a completely new world for me. How is it that Tate came so close last time in such a Democrat region?"

"Ms. Eliot," Steve Williams, Mike's campaign manager added, "The district has changed quite a bit over the last 10 years. The number of businesses in the area has skyrocketed, not to mention the health industry. They have been running scared by proposals like health care reform and limitations on business tax credits. The voters work for those companies, so they are feeling the concerns of their employers. Mike, and Chris for that matter, have done a great job of straddling the fence on issues that directly affect the district, but in general, he could be branded a typical tax-and-spend Democrat. Many business-owners have the notion that without a Republican Congress to protect them, they would have paid dearly by now. We need to appeal to the residents, the school boards, and the people who have benefited from programs like subsidized day care. It's not going to be an easy race, but if we get out of the gate early enough, and behave ourselves, we should be okay. Incumbency is on our side too."

"Thank you." Eileen sat back in her chair, putting weight on only two of Steve's words, "behave ourselves."

Kyle and Steve tag-teamed throughout the meeting, talking about what the DCCC could do in terms of offering phone bank space and coordinating PR efforts, while Steve ran through a draft timeline of local events, media interviews, and increasing television coverage on the Boston news affiliates. "Mike," Steve concluded, "I'm warning you, this could get really ugly. Once Tate announces, the press might have a field day trying to unravel every intricate detail of your life. Look at what the *Globe* did to Mayor Flynn," referring to a story in the *Boston Globe* criticizing the former Mayor. "We don't want one of those experiences. Or at least, if it does, we want it to happen to Tate, not you."

They wrapped up the meeting at 7:15, and Steve walked next door to the National Democratic Club with Chris and Eileen. They sat at the bar and had cocktails while some of the regulars watched the tail-end of *Wheel of Fortune*. Steve sipped a Guinness and said, "Look, we've got most of the campaign covered and should be fine," he put his hand on Chris' shoulder. "Granted, we'll have to be prepared for the first shot which more than likely will be the photos of you two outside the pub in Belfast and a re-run of the media frenzy. Tate will do anything he can to taint our campaign. Eileen, can you handle that?"

"You mean, am I willing to be the fatted calf?" The concept made her very uneasy.

"In so many words, yes."

Chris became almost agitated at the thought. "No. I do not want her being thrown into this race for the opposition's fodder."

"Fodder? Where the hell did you get a word like that?" Steve burst out laughing.

"He's been hanging around with me for too long." Eileen finished off her wine and ordered another.

Chris and Steve debated options for public appearances and local hearings to boost Mike's exposure while Eileen found herself becoming engrossed in *Jeopardy* with the rest of the regulars. Half way through her second glass of wine, she remembered that Maeve had sent her a guest earlier in the week. She hadn't been home for their arrival but got the note on Sunday before flying down to DC. She had no way of contacting 'Francis,' and knew that the campaign could be the downfall of many people, including herself, unless she was extremely careful. "Leen," Chris touched her shoulder, interrupting her mental score keeping on *Jeopardy.*

She spun toward him in her barstool, "What's up, Sweets?"

"Steve wants to go to the Lounge. Are you interested?"

"Capitol Lounge? But Chris, I got great stuff at Sutton Place."

"Honey, it's wing night."

"Say no more." They finished their drinks and walked up Pennsylvania Avenue to Capitol Lounge which was jammed with other regulars clamoring for ten-cent Tuesday night chicken wings.

38
January 2000

Eileen drove to Winchester, rehearsing her speech in the car. She did not want Chris to come to her place for the discussion. Traffic getting out of the city was heavy as normal, with each vehicle bobbing and weaving through the construction sites created by the Big Dig and other revisions to the city's infrastructure. "Come on!" she yelled, banging on the steering wheel engulfed in anxiety. "Son of a bitch! It's 1:00 in the afternoon. Where did all you people come from?!" Once she made it out of Boston, the traffic moved too quickly taking her closer to dropping the axe. The weeks since the meeting at DCCC had been gnawing at Eileen's brain, infecting her thoughts with visions of closet doors bursting open from the force of skeletons and Maeve's Cleaning cards whipping around in the air. She'd practically forgotten about the emptiness and angst that Frannie had left in his wake.

Chris had the table set and two chicken breasts marinating in his "secret" red wine-based concoction. He kissed her as soon as he let her in the door. "Hello Bride. Where are your things?" He held out his hands waiting to take her duffel bag.

"Don't worry about that." She stepped into the living room then followed him to the kitchen. Chris' home reflected strong family ties; furniture from three generations and a host of family photos, some from the mid-1800's. The house used to be his grandmother's and hadn't changed much since her death eleven years ago. He kept it almost to her standards, with nothing out of place and every throw pillow fluffed. Rather than go to the sterility of a hotel or restaurant, many of Mike's fundraisers, and those for some state representatives, had been held in Chris' home. Eileen touched the dining room table and recalled the last fundraiser six weeks ago when she steered the caterers throughout the party. She'd referred to herself that night as "the rudder."

He poured her a glass of Ravenswood Monte Rosso zinfandel in one of his grandmother's crystal glasses and handed it to her. They were separated by the open refrigerator door as he pulled out a plate of cheeses and grapes for her. Once, Eileen had told him that she enjoyed autumn and winter because it signaled the time for cool evenings with a good red wine and a sharp cheddar cheese. Chris banked her comment in his mental vault of her likes and dislikes. She watched him put the plate on the coffee table and listened for the voice in her head to say, "Go," but it took its time. She spun her engagement ring around on her finger then spoke. "Chris, I need to talk to you."

He moved closer to her and put his arm around her shoulders, "Sure Hon, what's up?"

Eileen sat back on the couch holding her wine glass. "Chris, I've been doing a lot of thinking and, and," the voice still hadn't said 'Go' but she proceeded all the same. "Chris, I can't marry you."

He pulled away from her, numb. She knew he felt the same knife in his gut as she had when Fran's Internet report came off of her printer. "What? Eileen, you can't be serious. Why?"

She was holding her wine glass to her lips but not drinking the wine, just holding it there. "Chris, I just can't. Your schedule, the election, my past. Everything. It's all too much. I thought I could handle it, but I can't."

"Eileen," he answered in desperation, "I will quit my job if you want. I want a life with you."

"No. I can't ask you to do that, and I wouldn't be able to live with that if you did." She stood up and looked down at him for a second, but he stood to face her. "Chris, I am afraid of marriage. I've hardly had time on my own. I do love you but I can guarantee you that I would make you miserable. Chris, photographers and reporters are outside my home. Some follow me during the week while you are in DC. I can't live with this. " Literally, she thought. Too often the vision of the headline "I.R.A. in Basement While Congress Sleeps" had been waking her since the DCCC meeting.

"Eileen, I'll do anything."

At that, she began to cry realizing that her dream of a man who made her his top priority stood within arms-reach. "God, Chris, please, please, I've thought about this."

He fell back on the couch, sobbing. "I'm begging you to change your mind."

She sat down next to him and rested her hand on the back of his neck, feeling his hair brushing against the edge of her finger. "I can't. I'm sorry, Chris."

"Can we just put off the wedding and stay together?"

"I don't think so. Chris, it's all too much for me. I cannot continue this way. I'm so sorry. I wish there was more I could say." Eileen struggled through her words, crying harder. "I have to go," she whispered.

"Please. Please. Eileen, don't."

"I have to. It's better."

He grabbed her and held her, sobbing into her shoulder, asking, begging her to stay. He only made her cry harder, and she cursed the life she'd chosen. Destiny is no accident, Jason had told her once. Despite their failed marriage, he had ingrained that one true statement on her mind. The Rah took Frannie, and now it was stealing Chris too. "I'm going home now. It's best." She kissed him on the cheek, "Goodbye, Chris." White-knuckling her hand-bag, Eileen walked quickly from the house to her car, got in and slammed the door shut.

She drove for five minutes through Winchester, screaming and crying, yelling "Fuck you, Maeve! Are you happy now, Maeve?! Are you fucking happy?" Maeve had sent a tenant to Eileen's the day before. Eileen's anger and frustration raised the risk of her going home, running down to the basement and killing whomever it was that was sleeping in her house. She took a deep breath before getting to the on-ramp for I-93 and called Jack from her car. He could hardly understand her but managed to make out the words, "I'm coming over."

Jack held her as she rambled on about why she had to leave Chris; the stress of the campaign, not wanting to be a wife, want-ing a life of her own, fear of screwing up another marriage. "Leen, I don't get it. You love the guy, and he's crazy about you. Even you said you'd finally gotten it right."

She jumped off the couch, wiping her nose with a tissue simper-ing, "Jack, I can't do it. I just can't do it. Please don't make me. Please, please just let me stick with my choice, and don't pressure me."

"You're thinking of Sullivan, aren't you?"

"No." She cried harder.

"You think he'll come back to you and that if you are married to Lawson, that you won't be able to be with Fran the way you've always hoped."

"No. I don't know," she wailed. "But Jack," she sat back down and rested her head against his shoulder, "If any of that is the case, doesn't that automatically make it wrong for me to marry Chris? I mean, how can I pledge my life to someone if my heart is not completely in it? It wouldn't be fair to him, and God knows it wouldn't be fair to me. I haven't thought of Frannie in months," she lied, "But, but this is too big a decision for me to make if he is still hanging around in the cobwebs of my soul."

"Okay. Okay." He poured her another whiskey and pulled a blanket over her, sandwiching her between the flannel and his body. He rubbed her head as she sipped at her drink. "Eileen, I will never understand some of the ways your mind works, but I will never judge you."

"Thank you." She fell asleep on him until 1 AM, when he nudged her a bit and put a pillow under her head, leaving her on the couch before he went to bed.

39
August 2000

Jennifer MacLean from AOS called Eileen just before Labor Day Weekend, desperate, "Eileen," she questioned into the phone. Eileen was packing her duffel bag to spend the rest of the week in Eastham; anything to get out of Boston and back to where her head felt as close to clear as possible. "It's Jennifer."

"Hey! How's it going?"

"Uh! Don't ask." Jennifer was nervous. "Eileen I feel kind of stupid calling you."

"Why? Jen, I'm thrilled to hear from you. Is everything okay?" She hadn't heard from her in over a year.

"Well, I followed your book tour and I just am so proud to know that we worked together at one time."

"Jen, we're friends. Spit it out. Do you need me?"

"Yes. We have a meeting coming up in New Orleans next month and one of my reporters is on maternity leave. All of my other freelancers are booked. I know it's been a while, and if you're busy, I understand, but—"

"When and where? I'd love to."

"Really?" Jennifer's sense of relief was too obvious.

"Eileen, if you want, I'll get you a book-signing session in the exhibit hall."

"Jen, do it, and I'll kill you. Just fax me my assignments and get me a decent hotel room. That place the last time I worked for you wasn't fabulous."

"Really?" Jennifer sounded concerned.

"Yeah, no mini-bar. What's up with that?" Eileen giggled into the phone, thinking back to her last assignment in San Diego and Fran's surprise visit three years ago. She couldn't have cared less about the mini-bar on that trip. Having him with her for just one night was all she needed. "Come on, I'm kidding. I'll be there with bells on."

"You can't be serious."

"Okay, I'll leave the bells at home, but it's been so long since I've been a normal person. This will be great!"

Without paying attention to Eileen's 'normal' comment, Jen answered, "Thank you so much! I owe you."

"You owe me nothing. I need to get out of Boston for a few days. I owe you."

"Good. Then, will you meet with my staff and talk with them about publishing and stuff?"

"Done, but only over dinner at Commander's Palace. We always work so hard at those meetings you guys throw. Let's make sure that this is a fun portion of the program."

They talked for a few more minutes catching up on the soap opera that is AOS; reorganizations, leadership changes, legislative nightmares, and who's sleeping with whom.

Four weeks later, Eileen was in the New Orleans Convention Center, working the floor so to speak, traipsing over cheap carpeting laid out over 20x20-foot squares of the exhibit hall delineating each company's "show space." She was covering the meeting, free-lancing for their daily onsite newspaper. The sign hanging from the ceiling sent a grenade exploding from her stomach, catapulting shards of anxiety to that space behind the eyeballs where the little man with the drums began to pound. Ophtech. Ophtech. Ophtech. The word had been thrust upon her once before on the business card next to Fran's bed, with her name on it. He'd always claimed she was one of the brethren, one of "the boys." Now, in Eileen's mind, she was the wife. She didn't care if Nuala was expert at fundraising or at weapons proliferation. She had his name now. Not much else mattered.

I can't be concerned with this, Eileen thought, I've too much going on here. There are meetings to cover and deadlines to meet. She did it anyway. Eileen checked the list of registered exhibitors and sure enough, Nuala had the nerve to work her meeting. A rational woman would know not to stick a key in a light socket. Eileen's mother said she'd done it loads of times as a child. Eileen grabbed her keys, and made the 200-yard trek down the cheap carpeting, seeking the socket. Her feet hurt. Her little toe in each shoe was jammed into the front edge of her Easy Spirits. Easy my ass, she thought.

Under the Ophtech sign, sales reps reeled in physicians looking for the latest technology. It isn't easy to subtlely read a name badge from 20 paces, but the colors of the exhibitor badges made them easier to discern from the doctors. Eileen moved her badge down to her waistband just under the hem of her jacket.

There she was. The only female in Ophtech's exhibit area. Five-feet seven-inches of surety and confidence. Eileen didn't care about her black eyes or her dark hair. She was the woman "fronting" as her Frannie's wife. The bitch had the nerve to wear his last name on her badge: Nuala Sullivan, Ophtech, Inc., Framingham, MA.

Nuala approached Eileen like a white-collar pimp looking to give her the best 10 minutes she could spend with an ophthalmic laser. Eileen extended her hand, "Hi, I'm Eileen Eliot, with the Association. I handle Medicare payment for new technologies and wanted to stop by and see what you have, how the meeting's been treating you, etc." She flashed her sincerest smile and lied through her teeth. Freelancing had taught her enough of the right lingo.

Nuala blabbed on as Eileen heard herself saying in her head, "So, your husband tells me you're a scary bitch. He mentioned that after I found your notes on top of his refrigerator. Oh, did I mention that I was fucking him two months before he married you?"

Eileen never heard Nuala blabbing on about the great new Ophtech 2000, the laser of the future. It slices, it dices, it corrects your vision, eliminates wrinkles around the eye, and cooks dinner. She waxed poetic. Eileen gave in. "I once dated a Frannie Sullivan. Funny you should have such a similar name. Then again, it's pretty common too, I suppose."

"Really," she answered, "Frannie Sullivan?"

"Yeah, a lovely Irish guy, he was living in Boston. Gosh, that's not far from Framingham. Anyway, you were saying about the 2000." First rocket fired.

Nuala introduced Eileen to her regional manager, Ted. Ted told her about the 2000 and about how new payment policies would help cover the cost of the machine, not to mention expand sales. Eileen lied about having to get to a meeting, shook Ted's hand, thanked Nuala for her help and disappeared out of the side exit to the nearest ladies' room where she vomited her continental break-fast into the toilet. She paged the press office to report her food poisoning and found the nearest bar. At 10:00 AM, one is bound to find an open bar in New Orleans. She chose O'Flaherty's pub near Jackson Square.

In a stupor of beer and Bushmills she found her way back to the Omni Royal Orleans at 10 PM. Eileen paid no notice to the wall of mirrors in her room that only yesterday had introduced her to the backs of her thighs. Not as much cellulite as I would've anticipated, but I need a better bikini wax, she thought. Sunlight blinded her at 6 AM, but failed to shroud the flashing red message light on the phone by the bed. "Fuck." She picked up the phone and hit the message button. The automated voice said she had one message. I hope that "woman" gets royalties, Eileen thought, because she's on every voice mail system in the country.

The message began to play, "Eileen, it's Fran." She bolted up and sat on the edge of the bed. "I called every hotel in New Orleans to find you. I understand you met her. You shouldn't have done that. You're playing with fire. I'll be at your hotel at 8 AM. If you won't be there, leave me a message where I can reach you." He finished with his cell phone number and, "Eileen, I swear, it's not how you think."

So, what is it, she thought. "Tell me Frannie," she said as she paced back and forth making hand gestures at the mirrored wall in a T-shirt and no underwear. "Just what the hell do you—man, my legs really aren't too bad—what the hell do you mean Frannie?!" Her eyes were puffy, cheeks blotchy and her heart pounded so loud in her throat speaking was difficult. It'd been two years since the Oscar night phone call. Two years, 10 pounds on, 20 pounds off, probable liver damage, sleepless nights, frightening days, anger, abandonment and more sleepless nights. "He's going to show up here, cry terrorism and protection, and try to get me into bed." The mirror agreed.

The face in the mirror squinted her eyes and pointed at her, "Don't you think for a moment that he's interested in your welfare. He's covering his own ass. He's afraid that you'll blow everything. For all you know, he's crazy about her. He may writhe over her body every night, breathing heavily in her ear while his cock is blasting away inside her." Eileen was stunned by the mirror's realism. The phone by her bed rang. The phone in the bathroom rang. The message light vibrated on and off. Even with the chandelier's 12 lights resonating in the mirror and the curtains open, the message light was glaring with each ring of the phone. She crossed the room to the phone on the desk and picked it up.

"Hello?"

"Eileen?"

"Yes."

"It's Francis."

"I know." His accent hadn't changed.

"What room are you in?"

"You're two hours early. I tend to think you should sit downstairs for a while. Maybe you should go see your wife."

"Eileen, please. Please, let me see you. We need to talk."

Her curiosity got the better of her, "I'm in 475." Eileen put the receiver back on the cradle and reached for her jeans. She watched the door, but with the heavy carpeting in the hall, no warning of Frannie prepared her. The rap came. She looked at the mirror, ran her fingers through her hair and approached the safety catch above the doorknob. Fran stood before her, in a worn-out golf shirt and faded jeans, shifting his eyes to the floor then back to Eileen's.

"Hi," he spoke so quietly.

"Hello." His hair was a bit grayer, but his 34-inch waist remained. Maybe a few more wrinkles around the corners of his eyes, but the blue of his irises still grabbed her, commanding her attention.

"May I come in?"

"I suppose." Eileen smiled a little bit and pulled the door back, wedging herself between it and the wall. She watched Fran's body in the mirror as he crossed the room. He stood at the foot of the bed with a look that seemed to ask for a hug. Two years. The two years could've been two hours. Why did he always do that to her? A piece of her wanted to fall against him and cry. She was so tired of carrying herself, and the weight of her own emotions for these two years. The rest of her was wounded and mad as hell.

"You're looking really, really well."

"Thank you," he said. "You too." Truth was, he was looking a bit haggard. She'd never imagined he would be seen in a worn-out anything. Fran was no clotheshorse but he always cared about the way he presented himself.

He came toward her and gave her a hug. "God, I've missed you," he said in her ear as his left hand crawled up the back of her head. The tears congregated in her throat until she backed away. "I've been thinking about the day I'd see you again since the moment I left. You look better than I've imagined. I just didn't think we would meet under these circumstances."

Eileen gestured toward the chair in the corner, against the wall, "Sit down." Frannie walked to the chair. "So, why are you here?"

"Wha-,"

"Frannie, why are you here?"

"I'm frightened for you."

"I find that hard to believe."

"Eileen, I am. I heard that—,"

"No, let's cut to the chase. Fran, everything you've done has been in order to protect me. You never introduced me to your friends, never mentioned anyone to me, left me with seemingly stolen weekends, and found it hard to say 'I love you' unless we were between the sheets. You left me with no formal good-byes and said I'd be cared for, and that you'd know how I was." Eileen glanced at the mirror and saw the face looking back at her proud and supportive. "In return, I wound up running a hotel for your 'boys', and I've spent two years in silence. No phones, no emails, no nothing. Christ, I ran an Internet search only to find that you married her. You son of a bitch! You married her. She wears your name. No wonder you said you couldn't be a father. I lost that baby."

"You wha-???"

"Yes, I went to a doctor and verified it. I was pregnant, but the baby and I spared you the hassle of parenthood. And for what? So that your girlfriend wouldn't know? I've loved you. I sacrificed for us. What do you want from me Frannie? Blood?! What's the big threat now?" Eileen was pacing again, hardly paying attention to him. The face in the mirror raised its fist in pride.

Fran stood up, came toward her and grabbed her shoulders. "Jesus Eileen! I've thought of you every bloody day since I left. I had no fuckin' choice. Do you know what it's like to get the call, to have four days to bundle up your life and cancel out everything you know and love?" His accent was exaggerated in his rage. "They didn't just come for me. They fookin' came t' get me. I'd one mahn who said he'd luke out fer ya and obviously he didn't." She thought of how when they first met, everyone said they couldn't understand him, but she never missed a word he said. "There's no one on my side. Next thing I know, they're telling me I'm to marry the woman. It was fuckin' horrible. In a back room in a pub in Southie. They took everything I had. You, my money, my pride. Fuck. I could feel your tears on my face as I said the vows. I've spent every day thinking of you. Call me a pig, but I've been in bed every night wankin' myself and thinking of you! Your face. The most beautiful face I've ever seen. Hearing your voice and the way you'd say 'Hello Darlin.' How was your day?' How was your fuckin' day. That's all it took to make me hard."

"Yes, I married her, and I've hated every minute of it. I do not sleep with her. I can't bring myself to go near her. She's fine I suppose, but I gave up myself and all I am for the God-damned company." He justified his lies as trying to protect her still. The sex had happened; just not since the wedding. "Jesus Eileen, it's been a rotten time, but if staying away means keeping you safe, then I'll do it every day of my life. You don't know the half of what I've done."

"Try me." Her patience had run out months ago. Frannie had moved on in Eileen's mind and her own sanity was all that she had left. He could've said he'd been with the Pope and a band of leper Rah men and she wouldn't have cared.

"When I saw you'd been in Belfast my heart sank." Frannie walked across the foot of bed toward the TV and lit a cigarette. He turned toward the mirror, his right hand resting on the minibar and looked at her in the mirror. "There was the bomb scare at the town hall, when you were there. That was me. I should be killed for telling you this, but you have to understand." He walked to the window with his hand over his eyes. She felt a change and looked at the mirror. The face shrugged her shoulders and raised her eyebrows. "I was there. There we were in the same place, wandering the same streets and I never saw ya. But, I nearly killed you. God, it would have destroyed me if I'd known you were there."

"Shut up!" She jumped to her feet. "Shut up! Shut up! Shut up! You come marching in here like you're going to save the goddamn day. Do you want some sort of absolution?" Her arms were flailing out to her sides, up toward the ceiling. She felt like a dervish. "Am I to say, 'Oh Frannie, thank you for letting me live on that fateful morning in Donegall Square? Thank you for leaving me with nothing but my wits. And thank GOD for a vibrator that cries out my name while I dream of endless nights on my own!' Is that the personification of lasting love?!" She fell back on the bedspread, half-crying, half-laughing. All at once, her tears stopped and she shot into a 90-degree seated stance. "Maybe I should phone INS. 'Hello, INS? Yes, I sponsored this I.R.A. fucker for a green card many moons ago and now he's scared chicken-shit that I'll crack and turn him in. What d'ya say? Should I believe his words of Shakespearean desperation or should I have you send his ass over to his I.R.A. wife's hotel? That's right, it could be a two-for-one hit today!'"

"Eileen, stop it! Christ. I love you. Now. Before. Always. I lay in bed at night and can taste you, smell you. My fingers can feel you."

"Why are you here?" Her mind was on another plane. From the moment she saw him she felt like the Rah girl she'd always been whether she liked it or not. She wanted to bury her head in his chest, kiss his neck, half-breathing, half-panting and say, "I need you." This was the way her life had been for 14 years. The secrecy and the fear felt normal. She saw the eyes of the 20 year-old boy she'd met after her freshman year of college. The same one who held her hand in the grocery store, taught her how to make good two-cup Irish tea, let her teach him to drive on American roads with the reverse round-abouts, and whose body had fallen over top of hers so many times as she'd learned the thrill of having an orgasm during intercourse. This was the same man who'd cried to Eileen about his need for her love, yet had chucked her own needs to the wind while she rifled through his pockets to find boarding passes telling her how he'd spent his weekends. "Leave me alone." Eileen whispered it into her chest where her chin and collarbone met. "You left me to feel this way, and she has your name. That's all I need to know."

"No Eileen, please no. That's not it. I'm getting out, I swear. I'm getting out."

She looked him in the eye as he now sat next to her on the bed. "Fran, please. What's that movie line we used to joke about? 'Yer neyver owt.' I thought you'd got out years ago."

Here it came—tears, wailing, the whole lot. "Either you're here or you're not. I can't keep living this way. Every day is a 'Frannie and I did this,' or a reminder of a conversation we had. You're telling me you're getting out. So, what does that mean for me? Do I wind up the winner for holding on while you chucked me to the side? Christ, Fran. Damn you. Goddamn you for doing this to me. I want to fall against you and beg you to tell me that it's all over, but I know better. You'll say, 'Eileen, I luv ya Dear. God knows I've missed ya, but dere's woork ta be dun. I'll be wit ya soon. I luv ya. Please, give us a kiss."

"Okay, so you know me pretty well, and you've got the stereotypical thing down too. Fair play to ya. Eileen, I swear I'm getting out. I'm within weeks of it. That's why when I heard you'd met Nuala I came jetting down here. I couldn't let anything mess up my coming back to you. I've been dreaming of taking you out for a meal, treating you the way you deserve to be treated, staring at your face and holding you in my arms. No more phone calls. No more stolen weekends. No more secrets. I want to make love to you from now until forever."

She was breathing out of her mouth with each exhale forcing her facial muscles into various stages of crying. She bit her lower lip and felt her eyes fill up. The left side of her mouth wouldn't stop twitching. As she pulled her right hand to her mouth and closed her eyes she whispered, "No." This time, Eileen's lips tensed and water ran down the side of her nose, "No." She hardly could speak. She wanted to let him hold her and bring it all to a succinct, unemotional "there, no matter" close, but she gave in to the water and the emptiness. He put his arm over her shoulders and held Eileen against him. "Oh Frannie," she said, wiping her left hand across her face. Her cheeks were hurting from holding it all in. She didn't care if she had eyes like a basset hound. "Frances Sullivan, you son of a bitch. I gave you everything I was. Granted, the company was there before I was, but you sacrificed me to those wolves and never looked back. I've been through every stage of this game. I found you and your wife, and I laid down the gauntlet that brought you here. I can't let you make me cry myself to sleep any longer, making me wonder what's next. I asked you to let me in and you kept me on the periphery. Then, you had the balls to marry her. You could have done just about anything, and I would have found a way to justify it, but marrying her, her of all people. That was the knife you twisted in my back. You almost, almost, destroyed me. I can't wait for you anymore. Get out of the business if you really can. Lose your wife if you want. Get a real job and a real life with normal hours, but until you've been at this whole real-life thing for a while, stay away from me. Damn you, Sully. I love you. Fuck. I'm sitting here mad as hell, humiliated, and I still say I love you. I've tried letting you go and I know it doesn't work. I'll never let you go from my heart, but please, don't come back into my life unless you can give me what I deserve." Eileen knew she'd cowered in the end but it was the best she could do. With that, she stood up, ready to face him.

Francis stood in front of Eileen looking at the floor, looking at her, then looking at the floor again. The grey print carpet didn't command that much attention. He hugged her before she knew what'd happened. He ran his hand up the side of her head, through her hair. His back was shaking against Eileen's arms, and for the first time since she'd met him, Francis Sullivan was crying and allowing her to see it. He turned his face to hers and kissed her. She'd kissed him so many times before but this was the first time that she felt desperation in his lips. He didn't even attempt to let his tongue move into her mouth.

Their noses were touching and he pressed his forehead to hers as he said, "I love you, Leen, my sweet beautiful girl. I love you.

It's always been you. I promise you with my last breath, I'll see you again."

She was left again, with no assurances, no assumptions. The hotel room door slammed shut and the hallway carpet gave no clue that he was heading for the elevator. She almost opened the door after him but couldn't. Until the Rah was gone from him, she always would be nothing in his life, persona non-grata. Eileen knew she needed more. The face in the mirror looked at her, wrapped its arms around each shoulder in a fake hug, and Eileen fell to the floor.

40
October 2000

"You know what you call an Ulster man in suit? A solicitor. You know what you call a catholic in a suit? The defendant!" Eileen met Ciaran the day she walked into Sullivans. She had to stop in the pub for the mere fact that the sign over door carried Frannie's surname. She was a sucker for sentiment. Eileen had flown down to Alexandria checking on the rental property in Old Town. She loved that house and the current tenant was moving out. Mrs. Rutstein had lived there for the last three years. She was a sweet woman, a widow, in her early seventies and kept the house in immaculate shape. Eileen would have to give her not only her security deposit but extra money for all of the work she'd done on the garden out front. The house was in the Yates Gardens section on Franklin Street just a block from Sutton Place Gourmet. Eileen bought it while she was married to Steven, Husband #1, considered selling it during her second marriage but loved the house too much to let it go. Washington had been good to her after college and relinquishing all ties to the area just didn't feel right to her. Jason's short existence and colorful departure from her life guaranteed her the chance to keep the house and an excuse to continue venturing down to Old Town.

Sullivan's was a new pub off of King Street. Jimmy O'Neill, the owner had taken over the property previously occupied by numerous other restaurants that never could seem to match the local clientele. He owned two other pubs in the area and each one was decorated to replicate a different area of Ireland or Irish culture, or at least the American perception of the "Old Sod." Sullivan's, Sully's to the locals, sought to recreate the feel of a tiny west village pub. Dimly lit lanterns hung on chunky, floor-to-ceiling, dark wood beams against the white washed walls. Jimmy had collected musical instruments over the years and hung them throughout the place. A small harp hung on the center wall behind the bar, with hurling sticks lining the side edges of the mirrors that were mounted on the wall behind the top-shelf liquors.

Ciaran, Sully's daytime barman, was making small talk with a few visitors from Belfast and his sense of humour did not amuse Eileen. Even though he hadn't been speaking to her, she heard all of it but tried to immerse herself in her newspaper and some of the rental applications that Marty Egan, her real estate agent at Pardoe, Inc. had collected over the previous week. Eileen was sure that the applicants all were lovely, responsible people. Most people wouldn't pay $4,000 a month for a three-bedroom townhome. The high rent was Eileen's way of weeding out the types of people who wouldn't take care of her home, and catering instead to those who would use it for elegant dinner parties. Ciaran leaned over toward her, holding on to the Budweiser and Harp tap handles. "Would you care for another Bud?"

Eileen looked up at him only briefly and nodded her head while uttering, "Yes please. That would be very nice."

He put the bottle in front of her and took away the empty, dead soldier. "Are you okay? You're very quiet."

"Fine thank you." She did not look at him. "Frankly, I found your joke offensive."

"I apologize." He tipped his head toward the opposite end of the bar where the Belfast group was laughing amongst themselves. "They're northerners, and I suppose it's just an old underlying reflex for me to want to please them."

"Why?"

Ciaran laughed, and extended his upper body between the tap handles until his hands were parallel with his shoulders, "Because Dear, it's important to appease the customers. Know your audience."

"Gotcha. Well then, I rescind my initial desire to kick your 'arse' but please, go easy on us poor punters." She introduced herself and extended her hand to him over the bar.

"Ciaran Miller," he said.

"Keer-ahn," she replied slowly pronouncing his name. "Is that with a 'K' or a 'C'?"

"A 'C'."

"Very good." Eileen returned to her paperwork, but raised her right eyebrow and looked out of the corner of her eye as he walked to the other end of the bar. She finished her drink, left $10 on the bar and left.

Two days later Eileen left her hotel room at the Embassy Suites and went for a workout at the Sport and Health Club. On the treadmill she decided to reward herself with twenty minutes on the tanning bed then a visit back to Sullivan's. She walked into the pub, crossed the dining room and sat down in the same seat she'd been in the other day. In her better days, she would have opted not to go into a pub, and instead to spend a few hundred bucks on a pair of shoes and some underwear, but this day was, well, hell, Eileen wasn't sure what the day was. It just was. Ciaran stood behind the bar, smiling and pulling that "Oy'm Oirish, welcome to moy pub" crap. The tourists ate that shit up, but she just didn't want anything to do with all that. She wanted reality, a conversation, but was not prepared for the chat or what it would stir.

Eileen sat with a post-workout Marlboro Light in her left hand, holding on to Stephen King's *The Stand* with her right. Normally she wouldn't read Stephen King. He unnerved her too much with his talk of "redrum" and battery-operated aliens, but on impulse, Eileen had picked up the book in the bookshop two blocks away.

"How 'ya," he asked as he pulled her third pint of Miller Lite. It was a simple question but struck her nerves like air on an untreated root canal. It was the first time that she'd bothered to look at Ciaran. My God, she thought, what a face! Had he always had those wrinkles from smiling too much or had they appeared in the last two days? He was a very good looking man who didn't fit the typical persona of a barman. The ones she'd known tended to be overweight, jovial men who displayed too many years of standing behind a bar making small talk about sports and keeping the tobacco industry in business. Ciaran's face was chiseled, framing a near-perfect nose and small, expressive brown eyes. The short sleeves of his Sullivan's Pub polo shirt gave a hint of the definition to his upper arms. The definition matched the "V" formed by his chest and small waist, and was accentuated by the way his bicep and tricep would flex then relax with the pull and release of the tap handle. It'd been months since Eileen had bothered to pay attention to a man. She'd decided that she didn't have time for them. It was all she could do to get herself out of bed in the mornings, let alone think about men. Frannie and their New Orleans discussion still usurped her energy. This rare occasion when she'd dropped her guard felt good.

"Well, it's been a devil of a day, but other than that, I can't complain." Ciaran was a recent arrival in Alexandria. He had a no-nonsense approach and an accent that still hadn't been invaded by terms such as "ya know," "yada yada yada" and "whatever."

"Really." She was curious, "Can you tell me about the devil in your day or would you rather keep to yourself?" Jesus, she was engaging the guy in conversation and it had nothing to do with work or politics or both. Her eyes lifted and widened as she spoke to him. She thought she was smiling but the concept had been so foreign for so long that she wasn't sure.

"You know. The usual stuff. People not showin' up for work, people asking me where everybody is. Nothing major."

Hmmm, she thought, nary a yada yada yada in his verbiage. They began to talk about books, writers, places to visit along the East Coast, and their families. It all was such trivial stuff but it was like someone had walked into a dark room and grabbed for the string hanging from the ceiling. She wasn't Eileen the writer, Eileen the former fiancée, Eileen the I.R.A. man's former girlfriend and apparent lackey. For a rare moment in too long a time, she was just Eileen Eliot, woman.

Ciaran leaned over the bar to her at one point and put his hand on her face. He said, "You're a beautiful girl. One with far too much on her mind if you ask me."

"Yeah well, maybe," she laughed. You bet your life sweetheart, was what she wanted to scream. "Nah, it's no big deal. People say that I think too much. Maybe they're right, but I've always been this way." She was getting philosophical. She hated that. She thought she should've said, "I do think too much. It's silly. How 'bout those Redskins?"

"What?" He looked at her perplexed, but very interested.

"Nothing. Just a funny thought that struck me. Please, you've given me such a nice day. Let me buy you a drink."

"That'd be nice. Thank you." He poured himself a coffee, took a Marlboro, from the pack he kept in his front pants pocket, lit it and clinked his mug against her beer bottle.

41
November 2000

"Eileen, you can't be serious." Jack was following her from the living room across the foyer to the dining room. He was carrying a folder of contracts in his hand.

"Jack, I am completely serious. It's not forever, just for a while."

"Dear, I know it's only for a while, but I can't bear to think of what it will be like without you here." Jack Marston, one of Boston's top poker-faced lawyers was showing his cards.

Eileen was pulling a Diet Coke from the refrigerator, yelling through the kitchen back to the dining room. "Jack, you're being silly. I'm sure you'll be just fine without me. I need a change of scenery. Besides, it'll do you some good to get out of Boston and fly south every now and again. You will come visit me, won't you?" She sat at the table next to him and put her hand on his knee. It was Saturday, and he was in navy pants and a white Ralph Lauren oxford shirt. "Plus, I fully expect that you'll be in Eastham on the fourth of July. Afterall, I wouldn't be able to start the grill without you." She laughed and lifted the can to her lips.

"You know I wouldn't miss it. So when's the date? Your tenants here won't be moving in until November 1."

"Mrs. Rutstein is leaving the 27th. I'm going to help her move into her new place. She bought a house on Fairfax St. just a few blocks from me. It's perfect for her. Once she's gone, the movers should be bringing my stuff on the 30th. I'll be at the Embassy Suites until then."

"Are you going back to Lawson?" Jack was rounding the table to the brandy carafe on the sideboard.

"Jack, brandy at this hour? Isn't it a bit early? And no, silly, I'm not going back to Lawson. For God's sake, cut me some slack. Jack, what is going on with you? You're so squirrelly today." Her voice was growing heavier with sarcasm and disbelief.

"Nothing. Will you need help with this place? Getting it packed?"

"Hell no-O," she sang. "That's what movers are for. I intend to be in the living room in a beach chair with a nice bottle of Saintsbury chard, a cheesy novel, and maybe even a paper umbrella in my hair." She twirled around with her arms out to her side and finished with a pirouette. She was in her finest Doris Day regalia; black pedal-pushers, a long white dress shirt knotted at her waist and canvas Tretorns. "Oh Jack, it's going to be so great. I've already got ideas and scenes for my new book racing through my mind. It will do me so much good to get out of Boston for a while and focus on new experiences."

"I know. But I'll miss you, Dear. Now, how 'bout a little dinner? Come on, let's celebrate." He walked to the door and put his hand on her back guiding her through the foyer.

She turned back and looked at him, "Il Panino," her favorite trattoria in the North End. "I feel like Italian."

42
December 2000

"What are you doing?" Ciaran leaned over the bar peering at her spiral notebook with over-exaggerated curiosity. For days, he'd been watching her wander into Sullivan's with smokes and a notebook, writing for hours without looking up except to order another beer.

"I'm," she put both hands on the edge of the bar and leaned back exasperated, "I'm working on my fucking book, excuse my French."

"Your book? A book? Really?" Ciaran was surprised. "I thought maybe you were keeping a journal."

"No," Eileen let out in an almost whiny breath. "It's my second, and I'm to have the completed project to my publisher by June."

Ciaran came around the bar and sat next to her. He picked up the notebook but did not read any of it. "You're a writer?"

"Yup." They each had a cigarette as Eileen told Ciaran about *Accidental Terrorist*, then about Chris and the break-up, but not about Fran. Though an avid reader, Ciaran had not read her book. He stuck mostly non-fiction.

"So," he summarized, "you wrote a book, realized a dream, met a great guy but the wrong guy, and this new story of yours isn't coming forth because you still feel guilty about breaking the nice guy's heart."

"I'm sorry," Eileen responded, "did you get the number of the cement truck that just drove over me?"

"Oooh," he answered and put a hand on her knee, "guess that was a bit of a harsh comment."

"No. No. Not at all. Well, yeah, maybe, but no one has ever put my life history in a tiny box with a nice ribbon around it and handed it back to me." She teared up a bit.

Ciaran put an arm around her, and like most men, panicked at the sight of a woman in tears. "Leenie, shhhh, what's up with ya? What are you cryin' about, woman?"

She leaned back upright on her barstool, wiping her eyes, then reached for a bevnap. "It's nothing." It's Fran, she wanted to say. "You have no idea how long it's been since I let my guard down. I left Chris to protect him. My past is full of skeletons, and if I hadn't ended it, the press would have had a field day. I've had lousy taste in men, then meet a good one, but I had to give him back because of my stupid youth. Fuck. When is it my turn? When will I find a good one who won't have to be the porter for all of my emotional baggage?"

"Huh?"

"Never mind," she laughed, "an American term." They sat in silence for a few seconds watching CNBC on the TV above the bar. Still staring at the TV, she spoke, "Ciaran, you're a good man. You gave me a dose of reality that I needed."

He'd gotten up and fixed himself a cup of tea. They were the only two in the bar, as usual for that time of day. "Dear, we've been talking over the bar to each other for weeks now. I was wondering when you'd let me into that head of yours. If you guarded yourself any better, you'd be wearing armor and carrying a sword." He spoke louder and laughed through his words, "Bejaysus, the woman has feelings!"

"Fuck you," Eileen smiled then went back to her notebook.

"Is that a threat or a promise?" He put another beer before her. "So, you ever going to let me read some of that," He wiggled his eyebrows as though mimicking a bad pick-up line.

George walked in, sat at the other end of the bar and gave Eileen a half-wave hello. "Tell ya what. Tomorrow, I'll bring you a copy of my last book. Read that, then maybe I'll let you read some of this draft."

"I'll plan on it," he answered as he delivered George's white zin down the bar, then came and talked to her again. "I'm there too," he said cryptically.

"You're there where," she asked him.

"Eileen, I'm hard on the heels of a nasty break-up. I don't want a relationship. I need air for a little while, but a bit of fun wouldn't be bad either." He took a breath. "I'm attracted to you and I know you are attracted to me."

"You think so, huh?" She was trying not to show her cards.

"Well, I think so. And I hope so."

Eileen had wanted him for too long. It was the same sort of heated chemistry she'd shared with Fran, but without the emotional bond. "Okay, be at my place by 8:00. Here's the address." She handed him a piece of paper with her address and phone number.

"I'll be there by 7:45."

Eileen walked home to watch the clock as she was known to do, until Ciaran's car would pull up in front of the house. She tidied up the kitchen and dining room, putting scattered papers in piles on the dining room table. Eileen noticed a white postcard face down on the floor. Turning it over decide if it was a 'trash-or-keep,' she threw it back on the floor in a panic.

Maeve's Cleaning Service stared back at her. Maeve had never sent a white card. It couldn't have moved with her from Boston. The card must have been in a pile of papers Jack had given his secretary, Anne to copy for her before the move. Anne's diligence would have led her to put the copy through the paper cutter to keep its original size. She knew that Anne had to have done it. Within weeks of moving to Alexandria, Eileen had had a security system installed. The Franklin St. house was locked down like a fortress.

Ciaran arrived a few minutes early and hugged Eileen within seconds of stepping inside the door. Their first kiss was almost aggressive as they each held and touched each other as though tearing the wrapping from an enormous Christmas gift. She walked him to the living room, introducing him to her surroundings while also patting down her hair from his fingers having just run through the strands. He sat in the leather chair while Eileen went to the kitchen for drinks. She returned holding a Guinness and a Miller Lite. Ciaran was squatting before her stereo with his back to her. "What are you doing?"

Ciaran pressed the play button then stood and faced her. *Ain't No Mountain High Enough*, from Disc 3 of her Motown Singles Collection began to play. Ciaran swung his hips from side to side as he approached her, placed the two beers she was carrying on the end table and reached for her hands. Eileen giggled when he swung her arms in sync with her hips, but quickly followed his lead and danced around the furniture with him, doing twirls in the foyer. Ciaran pulled her to him with his right arm tightly around her waist. They sang along with the CD. When the tune ended he kissed her, "That was great!"

43
February 2001

The house was coming together and *Accidental Terrorist* still was selling well. The FBI never called around again, but even if they had, there were no remnants of evidence to discover. Eileen spent the day unpacking the boxes that contained mementos she never looked at, but was unwilling to discard. After six hours of figuring out where to stash photo albums from the sixth grade, she chose to reward herself with a walk to Sullivan's.

Ciaran was working the bar, as usual. Did he ever not work, Eileen asked herself. Either she had become a fixture in Sully's, or Ciaran lived there. Over the weeks it'd reached the point where the chicken and egg debate came into play. Approaching the door to the pub she decided to make the pitch. Ciaran might or mightn't be prepared but her gut told her it was time. Actually no, her inability to remain silent said it was time. She never had been very good at keeping grand plans to herself, especially those that were so obvious to her.

Thankfully, Eileen didn't have striking thoughts very often. Typically, they were grand schemes reeking of stupidity. This one sat comfortably inside her.

The rain had stopped but it still made for a bad hair day. Eileen wore her barn jacket and slapped a baseball cap on her head. She tilted her head toward the ground on the walk over. It kept her cap from flying away and let her mind focus on the issue at hand. He was going to think she was crazy but so what. She pulled the door toward her and entered the halls of Sullivans' white washed walls.

Ciaran was in the far corner of the bar clearing away an empty coffee mug. He looked at her when he heard the front door creak. "Hey, Leenie, how are ya'?"

No one else was at the bar. She threw her files down on the bar and draped her jacket over the seat to her right. "Hi there," she smiled. "How's your day been?"

"Dead."

"Lovely."

"So, what brings you in here so early today?" He put a Diet Coke in front of her. Today, it came with a slice of lemon.

"Ciaran," she leaned over the bar toward him, "what the hell is the Unicorn Song?" She pointed to the sign over the bar, "Unicorn Song. 11 PM nightly."

"Oh bejaysus," he laughed. "You don't know the U-nee-corn?" Sometimes his accent and actions were almost a caricature. She wondered if he was purposefully aware of it, if it was just his nature, or did the occasional act to please the punters sometimes bleed through to moments of reality?

"I don't think so."

He began doing the motions and reciting some of the lyrics each time stopping to see if she recognized it. "You know, there were green alligators," he extended his arms clamping them together

like an alligator's mouth, "long-necked geese?" More gestures. He
twirled his finger above his forehead and said, "The loveliest of all
is the unicorn? Are you not familiar with it?"

"Guess not."

"Oh well. It's popular here. The weekend crowd really gets into
it. Once the band starts playing it, the staff disappear outside for a
smoke. We love the little ditty." He smiled and winked at her.

Ciaran had been showing up at her house for coffee and long
chats. Jack had been her friend for years, but still he knew nothing
about what really went on in her head. Ciaran was real, and spoke
what came to him. Eileen would sooner release Fran's secret to
him, the one that had been the weight around her ankles, than
ever ponder talking to Jack about it. It made no sense on the one
hand. On the other, it was perfectly clear, or at least, pleasantly
translucent.

Eileen put her right hand on her Diet Coke and said, "Oh, you
know. It's a dreary Wednesday, and I grew tired of the grey haze
coming through my windows."

"O-kay."

"What?!" Eileen waved one of the two red straws from her
drink, then placed it on the napkin.

Ciaran had one foot up on the beer cooler with his hand on his
knee. "Tired of the grey haze coming through my windows?
Please woman, can't you just say, 'The weather is lousy, and I
thought I'd wander in for a pint'?"

He was right. "Sorry," she laughed. "I've been thinking about
my next book. Guess the storyteller in me won on that one."

"I'll say." Another wayward punter approached the bar. Ciaran
excused himself and went to the man's aid.

The butterflies were circling in her stomach. Eileen tried to
remain composed. Ciaran crossed the bar and went into the
kitchen, talking to her as he left. "What's up?"

"Nothin'." Eileen looked down at her file containing plumbing proposals for the master bathroom renovation.

Ciaran was fixing himself his sixth mug of tea, dumping one sugar packet after another into the drink. "Eileen, you know you can say anything to me."

"I know." It was a quick, almost defensive response.

He came around the bar and sat in the seat next to her. The other punter had thrown back his shot of Bushmills and left. Ciaran rested his head against the palm of his hand with his elbow on the bar. He put his other hand on her knee. "So, what is it?"

"You're going to think I've gone off the deep end." She giggled, a little from her nerves and a little from the fact that she was opening the dialogue in a completely public place, subject to interruptions at any time.

"Say it."

"Okay," she lit a Marlboro Light. "I want to preface this by saying that I thought of this weeks ago. You need to understand that when something grabs my attention, I dissect all of the details. I've always been that way. I thrive on information."

"That's great. Now, say it."

"Okay! I'm getting there." She took another drag from her cigarette then returned it to the ashtray. "Look, you want to stay here and get a green card, right?"

"Of course."

"Well, as it turns out, your best bet likely would be to marry me." Eileen proceeded to detail the facts she'd uncovered. Ciaran's visa was set to run out in two months.

"But you have to prove the marriage is valid."

"I know. But that shouldn't be a problem. All you need are utility bills and bank statements in joint names, and photos." The night staff was coming in and made small talk with Ciaran. He followed them into the kitchen, then returned behind the bar across from Eileen.

"Leenie, why would you do this?"

"What?" She was whispering now.

"Is it just to help out another human being? Because, you know that this is something I will think about. It's an intriguing option. But why? Why would you?"

Josie came through the doorway from the kitchen. "Ciaran, Brian needs you in the back."

Over the weeks, she'd been researching the laws for her new book, thought of Ciaran's reaction to the proposal—literally, it was a "proposal." He'd walked off before she could answer. The bar quieted and the staff sat at a table in the corner rolling silverware into napkins.

"You want to know why," she asked when he returned.

He leaned over the bar and looked right into her eyes. "Yes. Why?"

"Because, and take this however you please; because my gut says so. Because so often we make decisions and have a gnawing sense in the back of our minds that says, 'Is this the right thing.' And because for all of the time that I've spent looking into this, and for all of the times I've made decisions that carry that gnawing feeling, this decision sits very comfortably in my gut. Because I can sit here and look you in the eye and talk about this and I don't have a nanosecond of hesitation or doubt about what I'm doing. Frankly, it would make me happy. Now, may I have a beer please?"

Ciaran slid open the top of the refrigerator and put a bottle of Budweiser in front of her. "Okay. It's good to know."

"I hope I put that correctly. I don't want to sound stupid."

"Eileen, you're not stupid. But, what if you meet someone and you're married to me?"

"That's my problem. Please, silly man, let me deal with myself.

"Are you sure this will work? I mean, why isn't everybody doing it? I know of so many people who want green cards."

Eileen was shifting into lawyer-mode. She focused on Ciaran's eyes. Her hands gripped the edge of the bar, occasionally waving in the air to accentuate her points. "Finding an American to marry is not a simple task, thank you very much. If you're with an American, your paperwork should be good to go in a few months, otherwise you have to go home before your visa expires, get into the immigration pool, and wait about 100 years before you're called." She took a sip of her beer and reached for another cigarette. "Look, whatever you want to do is fine with me. There're no ulterior motives at play. I want to be clear on that. I know what I want to do. I want you to do what will make you happy. If this is what you want, then I'll speak to a lawyer just to make sure that I'm protected. But, I happened to run into a friend of mine at a reception last Thursday. She's very well connected."

"And?"

"Well, I floated a trial balloon. I told her that a woman I know phoned me and was rather upset. I said that she's involved with a lovely Irish guy, but his visa will run out soon, and that they're nuts about each other and want to get married. Mary gave me a few attorneys' names and then she said, 'Send them to me. I'll take care of them.'"

"Eileen, where do you find these people? Do you have connections to all of the world's great problem-solvers?"

"No. Just yours." She smirked at him then returned her focus to the pictures she'd been doodling on one of her files throughout their chat.

"Woman, tell me one thing," he took a drag on his cigarette and whispered in jest, "do you have mob ties too?"

Eileen moved closer to him until their eyes were separated by only a few inches, "Dearie, I could tell ya, but I'd have to kill ya."

"Roger." Her directness struck and exhausted him too. This was his sixth straight day of work with three days of double-shifts having just wrapped up the night before. He was not in the best frame of mind to have the idea slapped on the table even if it was something to consider. "Leenie, what about the validity of the marriage?"

"Eileen, are you sure this is legal?"

"Pretty much. Truly, we'd only need to show that we are legally married, the marriage has been consummated, and that we share a real home and a real relationship. As for the consummation thing, I don't know if INS wants home videos or what, but I think we should be able to deal with that hurdle without problem. Anyway, in answer to your question, it would be legal. Listen, I may push the envelope but I would be sure that everything we do is completely above reproach. This is too important"

"Lady, I would hate to be on your bad side."

"Why?"

"Because, if this is how you investigate something you want, you must be a pit bull in an argument."

"Eh, it depends. Though a good fight does give me a rush." She was on her fourth cigarette and the file was covered with lines, squiggles and poorly-drawn flowers. "Thank you for asking me why I'd do this, and all that. You could have been a complete louse and either 'taken the money and run' so to speak, or laughed in my face. Your reaction to this reminded me why this is such a no-brainer, in my mind. But, it's a big decision so take your time and deal with whatever you need to consider. If you say no, that's fine, but," she stood up from the bar stool, leaned toward him and whispered, "we might make a pretty good team. Who knows?" Eileen winked at him and sat down.

The happy hour crowd began to trickle in, casting calls for pints of Guinness, and gin and tonics. One woman, clearly from out of town, rambled on about the, "known fact that Irish bars are popular because the bar tenders make those little shamrocks on top of pints of Guinness." No one in her band of co-workers had the heart to tell her about the bright pink lipstick on her teeth as she droned on. It matched her New York accent and her Stoli martini with two olives.

Eileen left $10 on the bar to cover her one Bud and two Diet Cokes. She was tired; pleased that she'd finally shared her idea with him but tired from the stress release. The rest was up to Ciaran. The rain had started up again, but only in a mild shower. Eileen watched the odd raindrop fall into puddles ahead of her feet. Her head was down. The bill of her cap kept the water out of her face, but she felt the rain land on her neck and slide down her back. The heels of her shoes beat into the bricks, taking quick steps toward home with the file tucked in her jacket. She felt good that she'd told him. There were no butterflies, no gnawing senses.

44

Eileen entered the house, hung her cap on the hook inside the closet door but left her jacket on the end of the banister in the hall. No matter how much her mother had tried to drill it into her head since she was a child, she never mastered the art of hanging up her coat.

The red light was flashing on the Caller ID box in the kitchen. She pressed the recall button to see who had phoned and when. "Unavailable, Unavailable," she said aloud as she paged through the list, "Fucking telemarketers. Unreal. Oh hey, Jack called. Cool." The last was a number she did not recognize, but she'd received so many wrong numbers since her reappearance in DC that it didn't surprise her. She lifted the phone from the cradle on the wall, and dialed her voice mail access number. Eileen was in a very good mood, and almost enjoyed mocking the automated system. She spoke along with it in the monotone computer voice, "You have one," the system said she had two new messages, not one. "Hmmm, wonder which organization wants me to consider buying their knives or donating my car."

She pressed the "1" button to retrieve her messages. Jack was first. "Hey doll, it's Jack. How're you doing? I won a huge case today and wanted to tell you all about it. I hope everything down there is still good for you. Call me at the office when you get in." Eileen deleted the message.

The automated voice came back on, "Second message. Delivered at 4:25 PM..."

"Hi," then there was silence and the phone on the other end hung up.

Eileen pressed "2" to save the message. She recognized the voice but couldn't be sure. She replayed it four more times until she had to walk away and clear her head. It was Fran. She knew it had to be. They hadn't spoken since New Orleans, and he shouldn't have known that she'd left Boston, but somehow he'd found her.

"Fuck off." Eileen reached for her cigarettes and crossed into the living room. She hated that she was doing it, but she opened her china cabinet, removed a crystal cocktail glass and poured herself a large Bushmills 10 Year single malt whiskey. He didn't have to say who it was. She knew the voice. Hell, she knew the way he breathed. It was not going to start again. She would not allow it.

Eileen sat in the leather armchair, one of her most flamboyant purchases and her favorite piece of furniture. The chair cradled her while she watched television or worked on her manuscripts. It partnered with a mahogany side table, equipped with a brass reading lamp and the crystal ashtray. She kept her cordless phone on the table just so she wouldn't have to leave the chair. She could feel the angst brewing. So much for her walk home feeling as though she ruled the world, not to mention her gut. "Fran, don't even try it. Just—" she jumped out of the chair and pressed her hands against the window frame, "just stay away from me. Let me go!"

The phones throughout the house rang at four different rings and chirps. Eileen picked up the cordless phone and checked the Caller ID. It was Jack. "Hello."

"Hey! Why didn't ya call me?" Jack was laughing.

"I just got in," she lied, "and just got your message. What's going on? What big case did you win? I want to hear all about it." Jack could hear her smiling into the phone. He couldn't hear her knocking back the whiskey. Her father had taught her that a good single-malt never should be bastardized by ice.

Jack recited each step of the case and each of his ingenious motions and arguments. "So, what's going on with you? How's Old Town? I need to get down there."

Eileen walked to the kitchen, with the phone pressed into her shoulder, the ashtray in one hand, and the glass in another. She emptied the ashtray into the garbage then leaned against the counter, lighting another cigarette as she answered, "Oh, it's great here, Jack. It really is. I can't tell you how happy I am to be back. I'm working on re-doing the master bathroom. I'm gunning for a two-person Jacuzzi, marble counters, marble sinks, the whole nine yards."

"Two person, ay? Anything I should know about?"

"No." Eileen laughed at him. "You nut. I want plenty of space for my candles, smelly oils, books and all of that other girl-stuff. I'm flying solo these days, and very happily." What was she supposed to say? *"Well Jack, I've met a guy who I really enjoy. He's a hellcat in the sack. It's a casual thing, but I'd like to help him and that might mean marrying him. By the way, Frannie phoned today but didn't leave his name. I recognized his exhales. I'm expecting him to show up any minute. Did I mention that I'm coming unglued at that fact? Nah. Nothing's happening here."* She kept her mouth shut and listened.

Jack talked for another 15 minutes, hitting the highlights of his closing arguments while Eileen roamed the house picking up little pieces of trash and straightening items that were out of place. "Okay you," Jack said, "I'll call you in a few days. Stay out of trouble."

She laughed into the phone. "Don't you worry. It's just me and a bunch of marble samples down here. I'll call you soon. Hey Jack, congratulations. I'm really happy for you." Eileen shut off the phone and stepped outside on the bricked-in patio. It was warm for February. They'd had no snow so far this winter, only a few rainy days. Eileen looked up at the sky, watching the stars overhead. It was silent. Sutton Place Gourmet had closed. The traffic had disappeared, and the neighbor's dog burrowing through a pile of dirt was the only noise she could detect.

"Oh hell," she said out loud, "I need to buy Valentine's Day cards. Fuckin' Valentine's Day. This holiday has to be a cruel joke mastered by married people who hate the fact that their single friends can do whatever they want whenever they want. Yes, a night to myself is the big payback for having my freedom while those of the ball-and-chain set are out for mandatory nice dinners with requisite flowers and chocolates." The whiskey was kicking in.

She got another call, shortly before 8:00. The Caller ID box flashed "unavailable." Eileen picked up the phone, but there was no voice on the other end. She waited a few seconds to see if it might be Frannie trying to be smart, then detected the oncoming sound of a siren through the phone at the other end. Eileen replaced her phone to its cradle, then heard the same siren of a police cruiser pass her house heading north on St. Asaph Street.

At 8:15 her doorbell rang. "What the hell?" Eileen considered not answering it but headed toward the foyer anyway. She looked through the peephole to see Ciaran standing on the front step. Eileen opened the door, pleased to see him. "Hi."

"Hey ya," he said to her. "Listen, I hope it's not a bad time. I was on my way home and wanted to stop by."

"No. No. It's fine. Come on in. Would you like me to put on some coffee?" She walked back toward the living room without looking at him. She was almost embarrassed to have her whiskey glass in full view and considered hiding it.

Ciaran was comfortable in her house now. He knew where pretty much everything was, and didn't hesitate to hang his coat in the closet. Eileen's still rested on the banister. A small difference in personalities. "Yeah, coffee would be great." He followed her into the kitchen. "I hope you don't mind if I stopped over."

"No. God, don't be silly. I always enjoy having you here. Of course," she laughed, "a two-minute warning so I could clean up a bit would have been nice, but whatever. I suppose now you're getting a glimpse of the real me."

"Looks good so far." He walked to her, put his arms around her and pulled her to him. Eileen tightened her arms around his shoulders, holding on to him and breathing in the smell of his cologne. He ran one hand up her neck into her hair then moved back and pressed his lips to hers. They spoke between kisses.

"I'm so glad you're here," Eileen whispered.

"Me too. I wanted to feel you. I was nearly crazy today looking at you." He was almost biting her lip.

Eileen pressed him into the counters and drawers, and wrapped one leg around him, "Mmmm, I like this."

Ciaran stopped her, "I know. But, let's sit down for a minute. God knows I want to take you up those stairs, but let's sit for a just a minute."

"Isn't the girl supposed to say that?" She smiled as she kissed him.

"Maybe. But, it's been a big day."

"Okay. Go sit down. I'll bring you your coffee." Ciaran headed for the leather armchair and pulled a Marlboro from the pack in his shirt pocket as he sat down. Given his seriousness, Eileen assumed their immigration discussion was on his mind. She ran through her mental laundry list of things to tell him that she'd forgotten earlier. The phone rang again. Eileen saw it was the same number as before. This time, she would make sure that Fran was clear on how she felt.

"Hello."

"Hey. It's me." The fucker. Even after all of the crap he'd put her through he still had the gall to use the term "it's me."

"Yes, I know."

"How are you? I miss you." In all the years they'd been together he never ever revealed emotion so early in a conversation.

"I'm fine. Fran, what do you want?"

Even though four months had passed since their conversation in New Orleans, the chill in the phone stunned him. "Leen, I'm out. I told you I'd do it, and I did. Please, I want to see you."

Eileen's knees were weak and she grabbed the edge of the countertop to steady herself. She leaned around the kitchen doorway and motioned to Ciaran that she'd be right in with the coffee. "Frannie, I can't talk. I'm glad you've moved on from everything."

"Eileen, please, you are all—"

"Francis, I have to go. Be well." Eileen hung up the phone and rested her head against the microwave door. "Okay, okay, you're okay," she said to herself. "Come on. Take a deep breath. It was just a call. Things are no different than they were five minutes ago. Now, go on. The years of analysis were paying back in spades. She carried the two coffee cups into the living room.

"Ah, I caught you," she laughed at Ciaran. He was channel surfing with the remote control.

"What?"

"I thought you didn't watch television."

"I didn't," he picked up his coffee, "Until I bought one. That Judge Judy is one hot babe." Ciaran thought that comment was hysterical and let out a huge laugh.

"Very funny." Eileen sat on the ottoman next to him, her legs crossed tightly at her ankles.

"Are you okay?"

"Fine," she smiled.

"You just seem as though you're not here. Are you sure I haven't come at a bad time?"

"Don't be silly. I'm fine. I just," she pulled the ottoman closer to the leather chair and put her hands on his legs. "I, well, I got this very strange phone call just now from an old friend, and it really blew me away."

He smiled and raised one eyebrow, "A friend?"

"Kinda."

"What?" She dropped her head to her chest. "Come 'ere t'me," he stretched out his arms toward her. Eileen moved onto his lap and put her head against his right shoulder. She inhaled the scent of his cologne on his neck and her body relaxed against his. "Now, what is it," he asked.

"Remember how we talked once about how we'd each been completely in love with someone?"

"Yeah."

"Well, the guy I told you about just rang."

"And?"

"I didn't want to talk to him. I cut him off and hung up the phone."

"Why?"

"I don't want to talk about it. Maybe later, but not yet."

"Okay." Ciaran kept his right arm around her waist and stroked her hair with his left hand. "Leenie,"

"Yes."

"I hope you're not making decisions because of me. I mean, I don't know what's going to happen."

Eileen sat up and looked at him. "Christ. Sometimes you are such a *guy!*"

"What?" He was confused.

"I mean it," she laughed. "I have a lousy moment and I tell you about it, and you think that I'm digging myself into a hole because of you."

"Wait a minute."

"No, Ciaran," She wasn't mad or defensive as she would have been months earlier. She didn't jump off of his lap and pitch a fit. She stayed where she was, comfortable, relaxed, though her voice was a bit higher, and continued, "Sweetie, this has nothing to do with you. This is all me. As much as I hate to be blunt, I have a life outside of you. Oh shit, I'm sorry. That sounded awful." She pressed her hand to her forehead.

"No. Go on."

"Ciaran, I've been on a wild ride and it ended before I met you, but, a piece of it came back and shook me up. God, I wish we weren't having this conversation. Can we just stop it?"

"No."

"Excuse me?"

Ciaran shifted in the chair and lit a cigarette. He handed her her Marlboro Lights. "No, we can't. You've got something to say and I want to hear it."

"Fine." Eileen's voice rose even higher, like a defiant teenager's. "We hang out together. Man," she laughed, "we're too old to use that term. But anyway, I enjoy you immensely, hell, I'd be lying if

I were to say that I didn't care for you. I love our times together, and just because I get angry or upset does not mean that it's because of you. I don't want to scare you but your being here really makes me feel better in spite of my situation. Jeeze, Ciaran, sometimes I think I could shock you with the way things have gone for me." Eileen stood up, leaned toward the ashtray and flicked her cigarette against its edge. "At some point, nothing would make me happier than to let you in on my twisted mystery. For now, though, let's just leave it alone."

"Okay."

Eileen was waiting for him to stand up and leave. "Okay? That's it?"

His eyes were direct, clear. "Eileen, what do you want me to say? It's okay. You've made your point."

"Fine." She smiled a little, then stood in front of him, unsure of what to do next. Ciaran reached for her hand then stood up. He put his arms around her, gently dragging his tongue over her lips. She followed his lead. He moved her to the couch, pressing against her torso as they pulled each other's shirt out of their pants and over their heads.

45

Eileen woke the following morning craving a raspberry croissant. She pulled her sweatpants and T-shirt off of the bedroom floor, walked downstairs and put on a pot of coffee. Sutton Place was open so she walked the two blocks to satisfy her need.

Walking back home with the croissant in a small bag and the morning's *Washington Post* under her arm, Eileen stopped dead 50 feet from the house. Her pulse began to race and she considered walking in the opposite direction. She thought of heading for Sullivan's but wouldn't be able to explain to the staff why she was there at 9 AM, had no money, and no underwear beneath her clothes—not that they'd necessarily be aware of that detail. She knew she had to talk to Frannie and kept walking toward him. He stood up as she got closer. This time, he was in black jeans, a clean pressed golf shirt and he'd cut his hair very short. He looked much more human that he had in October.

"Morning," she said as she put her key in the lock, trying to be non-chalant.

"Leen, I need to see you." Fran stood on the bottom step looking down at her. He gripped the railing with his right hand.

"Thanks for the advance warning." Eileen struggled not to make eye contact with him. Only a few months ago she'd fallen to the floor in a fit of tears and exhaustion after he'd left her hotel room. "Excuse me."

"Wait. Eileen, please wait. Talk to me." He turned to face her as she stood on the landing, opening the front door.

"I don't want to." Lie.

"Eileen, we can't talk out here. You know I can't."

She turned back to face him. "Fine. Come in. Five minutes."

"That's all I need."

He followed her into the kitchen where she poured herself a cup of coffee. "What Fran? Have you been watching the house? Or, have the boys been watching the house so that you could get a restful sleep?"

"No." He looked away from her then focused on her coffee cup. "I tried to tell you. I'm out of that. I've filed for divorce, and left the whole outfit. I'm done. Totally. Please Eileen, I'm clean of it all. You've been my reason for getting out."

Eileen put her coffee down and took a deep breath. "Frannie, I'm happy for you. I hope you're getting divorced because you want to. If not, then maybe you and the little woman can both get out of it and have a nice life together. After all, you always enjoyed fucking her, didn't you?"

"No! Jesus, it's you. It's always been you. I told you I had to marry her. It was for work! You are my sanity." She used to feel special when he'd said that, like he absolutely needed her.

Eileen handed him a cup of coffee. He never used to drink it, but she refused to heat up some water to serve him his preferred cup of tea. "Frannie, I'm not going to relive New Orleans, so let me cut to the chase. I loved you. Perhaps I still do, but I am not going to go back to a life that is in any way tainted by what you've done. I want no part of it no matter how big or small. You say you are out, but I'd be the one dealing with you and your nightmares. I'd be the one hearing the occasional funny anecdote about what some guy did in the middle of a plan, but you wouldn't be able to say what that plan was. I would be the one watching you zone out on me and not tell me what you're thinking because you can't. I'm not going to stand on the sidelines anymore even when I'm sleeping next to you. Once, I thought I could, but now I know that I cannot."

"I'm sorry. I tried to protect you." His hands shook as he spoke.

"Yes, I know but you also left me behind. Fran, what the hell did you expect of me? You call me, say 'I've been recalled. I'll be in touch,' and then you disappear. Then, you marry the woman who I always felt sure you were screwing while we were together. You pushed me to my limit. I'm not getting back on your bandwagon."

Francis walked into the dining room and sat in the chair in front of the bay window overlooking the patio. He put his head in his hands, and rested his elbows on the table. "Eileen. My God, I've loved you since I was a kid. All I wanted was for us to be together. I didn't want to hurt you or put you in danger, so I stayed away. So often, when we were together, I wanted to tell you everything but I knew that it would only put you at risk. Please, forgive me for what I've done. Forgive me for what I did to you."

"Fran, you always said you'd never be out. What happened? Why should I believe you now, when years ago, I and all of my money could have bought your freedom?"

His left thumb and forefinger slid back and forth along the edge of her kitchen countertop. "My necessity has outlived its time. Eileen, you never could buy my freedom."

Eileen threw her coffee mug on the kitchen floor, startling them both. "Tell me the truth! You never left for me. You never left! Let me guess, your time has come. Oh sure, 'Leen, I'm close. I'm getting' out.' Fucker. This isn't because of me, is it?"

"No," he started but grabbed her shoulders so she'd have to listen. "The last three years have been a punishment. A means of showing me where I fucked up. It could have gone on longer, but better, younger guys came up through our ranks. They knew I was too much of a peace advocate. Peace might only be a dream now, and I don't fit the plan. I'm fucking USELESS, okay? This is my chance to lead me own life, do me own thing, for us to start again…Fuck." He rubbed his forehead.

"Okay." Eileen sat down. "I knew this wasn't because of me. I needed you to say it."

"Honey, I may have been given my gold watch," he laughed a bit, "but coming back to you has been the only thing that's kept me going. I've spent fourteen of the last twenty years watching my back, hoping that if I stayed alive and got out of this mess, we still would have a chance. You always were with me."

Eileen stood in the kitchen, refilled her coffee cup, ran a sponge over the counter, and gathered her thoughts until she was ready to join him at the table. "You are going to think I'm making too much melodrama out of this, Fran, but I don't know of any other way to explain it."

"Okay."

"How many times did you call me your 'sanity'? I never wanted to be your sanity. I wanted to be your girlfriend. I only wanted to love you and for you to love me. I was glad I never knew more than I did. I pity you for the life you chose. I am indebted to you for not dragging me into it. Thank you for standing by that decision. But Fran, it's always going to be there. No matter how far away from it we both are it always would be in our heads, polluting our hearts, and it would be the elephant in our living room. I will always love you, but I cannot be with you. I'm sorry. I don't know what else to say."

"Okay. It was a risk I took, and I'll have to accept the consequences." He was a champion at shutting off his emotions. "I'll make sure you always know where I am in case you change your mind." That would be a first, she thought. He was walking to the front door. Eileen followed behind him. Fran turned to her and put his arms around her. She wrapped hers around his neck. At times like this, in the past, they always wound up going to the bedroom, instead of his leaving. He pulled away a little then kissed her, deeper than he had in New Orleans.

Eileen returned the kiss, letting her tongue find its way into his mouth. "Wait. No." Eileen pulled away. "I'm not doing this. I'm not going down that road. You have to leave."

Fran opened the front door and kept his hand on the doorknob. "Okay. I'm going." He kissed her cheek and brushed his hand over her chin. He spoke the same phrase they'd uttered to each other at the end of each college rendezvous; "I'll see you again."

"Maybe." Eileen hardly could speak. Her words came out in forced whispers.

"I love you Eileen Eliot. You know I always have, and you know that I will wait for you the rest of my life if I have to."

"Uh-huh," she whimpered. Francis Sullivan left her house, walked down the front steps and headed to a black Saab 9000 parked on the corner of Franklin and S. Pitt, just at the end of her street. When he started the engine, she closed the door.

The raspberry croissant sat in the bag on the counter, but she didn't want it anymore. All semblance of hunger disappeared, replaced by violent nausea. Eileen scrambled to the bathroom down the hall with her hand over her mouth. Leaning over the toilet on her knees, she ran her hands through her hair and wiped her eyes. "No more of this," she whispered to herself. She remembered the last time this happened, and how it was the beginning of her letting go of him. "This is a good thing," she tried convincing herself. "It's going to suck for a while, but it's a good thing." She cleaned herself up, put on a pair of shorts and her Nikes and went for a long run around Old Town, starting at Jones Point, getting down past the Giant at First Street and circling back.

Standing in the shower trying to remember if she'd washed her hair, she looked at the small battalion of assorted hair products. Eileen picked up a bottle of Suave shampoo with conditioner deciding to knock both steps out of the way. After she rinsed the suds from her head, she sat in the bathtub with the water teeming from the showerhead above her. Her conversation with Fran replayed in her mind, but it was followed by visions of his clothes in her closet, his CDs in her living room, and him outside on the patio reading a book as she worked in the den. "Stop it," she yelled. She leaned toward the faucet, turned off the shower and reached for a towel.

Eileen dressed in a pair of jeans and a grey, short-sleeve, v-neck T-shirt. She combed her wet hair but didn't bother to dry it. In a little while, she'd pull it back in a hair clip and make it another baseball cap day. It was only 10:40, but she wanted a whiskey. She fought the urge and poured a glass of lime Perrier instead. Her new manuscript, nearly completed, sat on the dining room table. She knew she was in no mood to be creative, and opted for making edits and revisions to what she had with a red felt-tip pen.

At 4:15 Eileen was itching to leave the house. Physically she still felt raw, but her mind was surprisingly clear. She knew she'd made the right choice, but it still didn't feel very good. She pulled her barn jacket off the banister and went on autopilot to Sullivans. Yesterday's puddles were gone and her tennis shoes made no noise on the bricks of Pitt Street. Sully's was a straight shot, six blocks, from her house. Between Eileen's and the bar, housing prices varied from $300,000 townhomes to the million dollar period homes and their historical plaques denoting their presence during the late eighteenth century.

Eileen entered through the side door of the pub off of Royal Street. Ciaran, was serving a cheeseburger to a man at the middle of the bar. Eight patrons were in there, staking out property for co-workers who shortly would be joining them. Eileen took a seat under the television nearest the door. She opened the binder containing her manuscript and 10 blank sheets of paper. Perhaps a spark of creativity would reveal itself. Ciaran walked up to her and tapped on the front of the binder. "Planning on taking notes on my punters?" He winked at her.

"No. I'm writing my will."

"Huh?" She'd caught him off-guard. For once, she'd pulled the first punch. "Yup. I'm detailing all of my secret offshore accounts. You know, a million in Barbados, four mil in Switzerland, and, oh yeah, my Internet gambling racket in Costa Rica."

"Well, aren't we in a mood today. So, what'll it be, Mrs. Hoffa?"

Eileen leaned toward him and spoke through tight lips, "Soda water, rocks, and a slice of lime. Hold the vodka."

"Ooh, we're living on the edge."

"Yup."

Ciaran placed a pint glass under the soda gun, squeezed a slice of lime over the ice and hit the button for soda water. "There ya go ma'am."

"Thanks, but my mother is 'ma'am.' Call me that again and I'll make you cry."

He pursed his lips and squinted his eyes at her, "Ow."

Eileen smiled at him as she opened her binder. She looked around the bar to see if any new potential characters were in her midst. George, a regular who drank white zinfandel, was watching CNBC on the far television. White zin. Gross, she thought.

Harry sat three seats away from George. Harry read the *Boston Globe* and drank half-n-halfs. He was a mortgage broker, around 62 years old. His wife Janet occasionally joined him. She was a sweet lady, soft-spoken, around his age. She drank Guinness; never more than one a day. The four seats next to George were taken by a variety of people. Most were smoking. Eileen didn't bother trying to sort out each one. She would have been accused of staring.

Her manuscript helped her pass the time, and also pushed Francis to the back of her brain. On the walk over, she'd given herself another pep talk about how things were so much better now, and how strong she'd become, how she'd be all right and that he would bring her nothing but heartache and hardship. She knew all of those things were true. The most disturbing fact was accepting that she'd done something she never thought she would. She had pushed Fran away, and she had hurt him. She never thought she could be capable of hurting him. Over the years, she'd always compromised or given in, so as not to hurt him. She'd never complained. She'd never told him how much he took from her. Hurting him had bothered her the most. The storybook romance of the star-crossed lovers battling to be together in a terrible environment ended with a swift blow, and she wasn't the one who'd gotten hit.

"Oh Mr. Barman," she spoke in an exaggerated accent and batted her eyelashes at him.

"Yes, miss?" Ciaran was putting a bottle of Heineken in front of one of the four men sitting near George.

She switched accents, "Towwws me a bee-ah, would juzz? I'm doyin' ovah hee-ah."

He grabbed a bottle of Bud from the cooler and walked over to her. "Miss," his face was deadpan, "is there something I can do for you? It looks as though a variety of personalities have taken control of you. Shall I phone for a doctor?"

"No!" She laughed at him.

"If you prefer, you may also attempt to entertain us all. There's a stage just over there. Help yourself."

"Shut up. No, I'm just feeling a little silly today. I'll be right back." Eileen got up from her seat and walked toward the ladies' room. The patrons at the bar were all situated with their drinks and snacks. She was the only woman in the place. He followed her and waited outside the ladies room, looking up at the bulletin board. When he heard the door open he turned to face her.

"Well, look who it is," he whispered to her.

"Don't I know you?"

He gave her a quick hug and a kiss. "I couldn't wait. Hope you don't mind being stalked throughout the bar."

"No," she whispered back through a smile. "Though it does tempt me to want to find a broom closet somewhere and live out a few fantasies of you, me and furniture polish."

"Stop woman, you're killing me. Come on, we should get back." He turned away to leave, and Eileen grabbed the back of his left shirtsleeve.

"Hey, one quick thing."

"What?"

"Why don't you come on by tonight. Last night, you seemed as though you had something you wanted to talk about and we never got around to it. I promise, there will be no interruptions. The floor will be yours."

"Okay. I'm off at 7:00. I'll try and be by around 7:30."

"Great." They walked through the hall toward the bar and she whispered, "Okay, how ridiculous do you feel plotting our meetings between stolen chats outside the bathroom. Sometimes this feels so juvenile."

"Yes, and sometimes it only adds to the excitement." Before they reached the open area of the dining room, he smacked her on the ass.

"Stop it. You know what that does to me." She rolled her eyes at him and walked back to her seat.

Another patron had arrived and sat at the end of the bar opposite from Eileen. She didn't notice him until she heard Ciaran ask where he was from. Ciaran usually only asked that of people with Irish accents. Typically the response led to something relating to where someone's family member grew up, where someone went to school or worked, etc. He always got a little louder with fellow Irishmen. "Dundalk," he blurted. "I lived in Newry for a year with my aunt." Eileen, horrified, saw Fran at the bar talking to Ciaran. She didn't think Fran had seen her, but she leaned over and put her cap back on her head. Eileen wondered if she should leave or stay around to see what transpired. She couldn't call Ciaran over to ask for her check, and leaving without making some notice to him wouldn't be normal for them. She bowed her head and stared at her manuscript. Am I being paranoid, she asked herself. Is he following me, or is this a sick coincidence? Ciaran came back down the bar toward the punters nearest her. Eileen said quietly, "Hey, Egg," she'd told him about her chicken/egg debate.

"Yes Chicken?"

"I forgot. I've got a plumber coming over in a few minutes. What do I owe you?"

"What? You can't leave now." He leaned in with a sarcastic look on his face, "Hey, there's a hot one down there for ya. How 'bout a nice paddy for ya for Valentine's Day?" He tilted his head toward Fran.

"Get stuffed."

"I should be so lucky," he laughed.

"Come on, send me home. I've got to go."

"Okay, three dollars please, miss." Eileen handed him a five. He took it from her, but held her hand with the bill in it for a second and winked at her. Eileen grabbed her coat off the back of the chair and ducked out the side door. She ran two blocks before stopping to put on her coat.

Ciaran rang her doorbell at 7:25. She knew that it was he ringing at the door, but she almost hesitated to answer. She opened the door, let him in, locked it behind her and turned out the porch light outside. If anyone were watching, she would not provide a well-lit view. Ciaran was walking toward the doorway leading into the living room when she stopped him. Eileen tapped him on the shoulder as she slid her arms around his body with his back against her chest. She kissed the back of his neck the way he'd done to her before and licked his ear. Ciaran turned around and pulled her closer to him. "Hello Chicken," he said between kisses.

"Hi Egg," her smile almost stopped their kiss but they managed to continue. Eileen backed away a little. "So, how was your day?"

"The usual."

"I'm sure. Oh, thanks for playing 'Love Connection' this afternoon. I really appreciated it. Who was that guy?" She wanted to know if Fran had let on to why he was there.

"Aw, come on! I was just playing Cupid. Ha! He was some tourist. Said an old girlfriend lived in town and he needed some courage to go see her."

"Oh, and wouldn't I just love to have some re-bounding fool to write home about."

"Your man liked you."

"What?" Did he know? "My man who?"

"Your man. In the bar. The tourist. He asked me about you."

"Tell me you're kidding."

"No, I'm serious. He asked who you were. I said, 'Why that's Eileen Eliot, the writer.' And he said, 'Try as she might, but a baseball cap can't hide her beauty.'"

Eileen's body went numb. "Oh, I hope he leaves town soon."

"Why? What's wrong with a man thinking you're attractive?"

"Nothing, I suppose. But sometimes it makes me feel a little weird."

"Silly thing."

"Okay, something was on your mind. You still want to talk about it?"

"Wow. That was a swift end to that chat. No mincing words with you, huh?" His arms were still around her waist.

She lightly smacked her hand against his shoulder. "Come onnnn! Jeeze." She rolled her eyes. "Give me a break, pal."

"I know. Come on let's go," he took her hand walked to the living room.

Eileen settled into the corner of her couch and put her feet up on the cushions. Ciaran did the same at the opposite end. They were propped up on throw pillows facing each other. "So," she started, "What's up?"

Ciaran reached for her right foot and ran his hand back and forth from her toes to her ankle as he spoke, "It's the visa. I was listening to you yesterday, but really only took in about half of what you said. Now, tell me about this again."

"Well, it wouldn't be a walk in the park, but honestly, it might to be your only option." Eileen held her pack of cigarettes in her hand, turning it end over end. "Basically, it looks to me like the government is big into family unity, pending that it is an American citizen and his or her spouse or children."

"But, what would that mean?" He was looking at her and playing with her toes. Eileen replied detailing the differences between marrying in Ireland or in the U.S., the types of paperwork that would be required, and timelines.

"Are you always this thorough?"

"Hell no. It was on the Internet with all of the other info. In the worst case, we go back to Dublin, get married there, and then go to the embassy and get your papers started."

"But, what would I get after we got married?"

"Lucky, every night of the week, if you play your cards right." She laughed. "I'm sorry. You gave me an opening and I had to take it."

"No, I mean, could I work?" Eileen tried to detail the ins and outs of what she'd found.

"I don't know Leenie. There has to be a catch."

"On some level there is, so we'd definitely have to talk to a lawyer to be sure. Stop it!" She pulled her foot away from him. "Do you want to suck on my toes or talk, because I can't talk if you're going to do that."

"Sorry," Ciaran took her foot out of his mouth, and shifted his body to lie against the back of the couch. His body was behind her, and he put an arm under her neck. Eileen lay on her back and turned to face him. "Continue."

"Okay," her hands were waving in the air, quietly expressing her comments. "If you want to play this totally above-board, we can go the fiancé route. It doesn't matter if we met here or there. For cryin' out loud, they're giving these things out to people who met on the Internet! It's unbelievable." Her understanding of the process was limited.

"Eileen, I'm still trying to figure out why you'd be willing to do this. It would be great if we stayed together, but, realistically, what would you get? What's in it for Eileen? You can't tell me that the warm fuzzy feeling of doing something nice is enough."

"Well," she looked at him then back up at the ceiling, "Aside from the warm fuzzy feeling, I'm in it for the jewelry. Afterall, wouldn't you be so indebted to me that I'd get great presents on every major holiday?" She looked at him with complete seriousness. Ciaran was dumbstruck. Eileen let out a delayed howl, grabbing her stomach as she laughed.

Ciaran rolled over on her with his face only a couple of inches from hers. "Oh, yes, yes, you are so very funny. Little do you know that I own a South African diamond mine. It was to be a surprise, but I guess I'll just go ahead and sell it now." He kissed her then rolled back on his side. "Leenie, I'm serious. Come on, no more jokes."

"I know. Shut up. No. I don't know." She waved her arms in front of her. "Honestly, I'm offering you this option because I want to. Because I have no hesitation of doing so. This is something I would be proud to do. Plus, I cannot stand the idea of your having to go home, or of your staying here illegally. Please, is that enough?"

"Is it me or did someone just slap a brand new wall in the room?"

"Ha." Her face was against his chest but she looked up at him to finish. "Right now, I'm asking you to trust me. Believe me when I say that I know what would be involved and that I'm ready to jump in both feet first, with a big fat smile on my face."

"Alright Dear, I'll take you off the hot seat," he rested his right hand around her waist. "Look, I don't want you to get hurt. You need to do what's best for you."

"Uh-huh." Eileen had heard this from him before and was not at all surprised by his comments. She'd have been shocked if he'd said anything different.

"Let's wait and see how things go. It's a lot to think about, and I've got loads of other stuff to deal with right now."

"That's fine. I told you, take your time, and do what works for you." They were quiet for a minute. "Do you have plans tonight?"

"No, but I'm exhausted and am on a double-shift tomorrow."

"Great," she slid her leg between his and pressed her lips to his chest just above where his shirt opened.

He put his hand against her back, under her T-shirt, "Let's go to bed."

"I thought you'd never ask." He pulled her up the stairs into the bedroom, stepping on her shorts and shirt from the morning's run.

Ciaran left at 9:10. At 9:25, her phone rang.

"I'm outside," it was Fran.

"Francis, go home, wherever that is now."

"Please, can I see you?"

"No, Fran, let me know where you are, keep me informed. That's fine, but go home. Please. I always respected you when you told me not to call, or when you'd disappear for days and I'd never ask where you were. Please do me the same courtesy." Eileen hung up the phone.

47

Eileen drove to Fredericksburg the following morning for its annual antique fair, searching for a small sideboard for the dining room. All of the other ones she'd found were suited for enormous homes with twelve-foot ceilings and grand formal dining rooms. They wouldn't work in her 11-by-12 foot area. It was Friday the 13th. She'd forgotten about Valentine's Day; V.D. as she and her friends called it in high school. They thought it was comical that the initials for the holiday o' love also stood for venereal disease. Fredericksburg proved to be a bust but at least the radio stations played good music during the trip.

Eileen pulled into the driveway and carried a bottle of cabernet and a bouquet of stargazer lilies to the house. Two floral arrangements sat outside her door. Eileen unlocked the front door and put her parcels at the bottom of the stairs. She leaned back outside the door, picked up the flowers and set them on the dining room table. She expected one was from her parents. They always sent her flowers on Valentine's Day. She was removing the tissue paper from one arrangement when the phone rang. She leaned around the doorway and picked up it up. "Hello."

"Eileen?"

"Hi Mom. How are you?" She'd spoken to her mother only two days earlier and had no new "news" as they called it, to report.

"Oh, I'm fine Dear. Dad and I are on the Cape," as her mother had previously indicated they would be. They were in semi-retirement and already Eileen could see that they needed either hobbies or new jobs. It wouldn't be long before her mother would be calling from the car to say that they were driving to Eastham and how the traffic over the Sagamore Bridge was treating them.

"I wish I were there. Nothing compares to the beach in February. It's so peaceful. What are you two up to this weekend?"

"Nothing. We're taking it easy. I convinced your father not to do any work on the house. He's always working so hard."

"Very good. You two should enjoy the weekend. Enjoy each other."

"Oh Eileen, we've been so busy lately. Your grandmother has been keeping me on my toes. She needs so much help these days."

"Well, I'm glad she's doing better, but I hope you're also doing things for yourself."

"I'm trying, but I've neglected the house so much. I need a week just to clean it."

"Mom. It's Valentine's Day. Forget about the house. Remember the saying, 'It's more important to have sex on the kitchen floor than to have a clean kitchen floor'?"

Her mother laughed. "Oh Dear. Leave it to you to remind us of life's priorities."

"Sorry."

"No! I'm sorry."

"Why?"

"Because, that's why I'm calling. I completely forgot that Valentine's Day was this weekend. I remembered to send cards but forgot everything else. By the time I tried to send you flowers it was too late." Eileen looked at the arrangements on the table. "I wanted to be sure that you had some lilies in the house for the holiday. They smell so good."

"Mom. Don't worry. If it makes you feel any better I bought a bunch of them this afternoon."

"Oh good. I'm so sorry, Sweetie."

"Mom, forget about it. Thanks for your card." She spoke with her mother for a few more minutes then returned to the flowers in her dining room. The first arrangement, a mix of red, white and pink roses with baby's breath and eucalyptus came with a card attached tied to one of the white roses by a white lace ribbon. "*Let's talk.*" It was unsigned. The second, a mixed bouquet of roses, carnations, daisies and lilies, was accompanied by a card attached to an artificial sunflower, "*Whenever you want.*" Again, unsigned. She poured herself a glass of cabernet and lit a cigarette. "This has to be a joke." Two bunches of flowers; two unsigned cards. Eileen looked at both of them and thought, Fran, you're trying too hard. This is overkill, and so typical.

She shook an empty can of Guinness before tossing it in the trash as her mother continued her small litany of family news. Ciaran had two the last time he was over. Eileen grabbed a Miller Lite from the refrigerator. One can of Guinness remained in the fridge. She knew Ciaran had had two, and could not recall if she'd had one since. Eileen briefly contemplated giving up the booze altogether. She'd never forgotten drinks she'd consumed. Why the hell would I have had a Guinness, she thought. She never drank it at home.

Maeve's card and the roses came to mind. Eileen felt sure that she hadn't drunk the Guinness. She raced though the house rifling through drawers and papers, trying to find anything else out of place. Nothing. Everything remained intact; no doors or curtains altered. She sat on the edge of her bed and rubbed her hands up and down over her face. "Snap out of it!" The walls and pillows did not respond. She reached for the phone on the antique pine night table and dialed Jack's number.

"Hello."

"Jack?"

He heard her consternation in the way that she uttered his name. "Leen, are you okay? Whatsa matter, Dear?"

Eileen lay on her side with the phone between head and the pillow sham. "Jack? Am I crazy?"

He laughed, "Eliot, that's a loaded question."

"No I mean, you think I have my wits about me, right?"

Jack sat up with his butt on the edge of his couch. He looked at a framed photo of her on his coffee table. "Yes Eileen. You are perfectly sane. Why? Has something happened?"

"No. Well, I don't think so. Jack, I keep finding weird things. Things that don't fit, or that I don't remember. Flowers at my door, empty beer cans in my kitchen," she didn't tell him about Maeve's card for fear of sounding completely crackers.

"Leen, when is your manuscript due?"

"Next month," she answered.

"And have you ever before faced a book advance and a deadline?" His voice rose a bit for emphasis.

"No."

"Ei-leeeen. You are suffering from stress. Welcome to the club, Sweetness."

She sat up on the bed picking at the ripples in the bedspread. "Do you think so? Really?"

"Yes." Jack sipped at his iced tea. "Eileen, if something is frightening you and you want me to, I will be on the first flight out tomorrow. Honestly, I think you are just feeling a bit overwhelmed."

She took a deep breath. "You're right. It's a new kind of stress. Hell Jack! If a man isn't involved, I don't consider it stress. Thank you for pulling me back to reality."

"You're welcome."

"And, for as much as I love and miss you, I am okay down here on my own. Once the manuscript is in, let's plan a long getaway to Eastham. Laptops will not be permitted. Work will be defined as a comparison of the amount of time we spend making sandwiches and getting the boat launched at the town landing, versus the time we spend cruising the bay."

"You've got it. It's lonely up here without you."

"I know. I love Old Town, but it's not the same without having you a few blocks away. I miss my best friend."

"Well," he moved back into the couch cushions, "I miss you too. Getcher ass back up here Eliot, before I have to go down there, throw you over my shoulder, and kidnap you to Brendan Behan's."

"Jack, ya big tease. I'll be there soon. I promise." They hung up their phones, and Eileen picked out an outfit to wear for the evening, a no chocolates, no hearts and flowers girl's night.

Eileen went to Carolyn's, a high school friend who lived over in Arlington. They spent the evening swapping Valentine's Day war stories. Carolyn won with her story of V.D. 1991, when she'd tried to surprise her boyfriend at the time only to find him in bed with her personal trainer and his secretary. Eileen didn't feel so bad about both of her husbands blowing off the holiday when she heard that one. Carolyn was always good for besting her in "you think you've got it bad" stories.

Saturday afternoon rolled around too quickly. Eileen treated herself to a massage and a pedicure at Serenity Day Spa on Union St. Spa services were her reward for getting through the week not to mention her own Valentine's Day gift to herself. Eileen left the day spa and stopped into Sullivans. Ciaran was making small talk with a couple from Knoxville, Tennessee. Eileen took a seat in the center of the bar and took out her journal where she jotted down ideas for her book.

"Good afternoon, miss." Ciaran said to her. He was turning up the volume on the pleasant-barman persona. Anything to please the tourists and add to the tip.

"Well hello there. How are you today?"

"Just fine thank you. May I get you something to drink? And how about a menu? We have a lovely cream of asparagus soup today."

Oh for crying out loud, Eileen thought, turn it down a notch, wildman. "Just a bottle of Bud please, Sir."

"Very good." Five minutes later, Ciaran went into full tourist mode. He did that sometimes. It was his stress release after double shifts. "Oh bejaysus, it's Valentine's Day!" He came around the bar and hugged each woman. When he got to Eileen, he hugged her, dragged his tongue up the side of her face and kissed her quickly. He was on a roll. Eileen looked at the tourists, swatted his shoulder and laughed, then went back to her journal. New ideas had surfaced during her pedicure. Ideas came so easily when she was relaxed. She wondered if she could deduct spa services from her taxes as a business expense.

After her second cigarette, the tourists had left and Ciaran spoke to Eileen over the bar. "Happy Valentine's Day."

"You too, Sweetie. Happy Valentine's Day." She held her journal with both hands. "Come 'ere," she gestured for him to lean over the bar. He did so, and Eileen held his face in her hands and planted a dramatic, comical kiss on his lips. "Mwa," she said as she delivered her kiss.

Ciaran looked at her and whispered, "Did you like the flowers?"

"Oh, yes, so much. Thank you. I was shocked," She whispered back through her smile. Why would he have sent anything?

"And how about the chicken and the egg?"

"What?"

"The chicken," he said. "The egg. Weren't they there?"

"No."

"I'll have to call the florist and beat the shite out of him. It was supposed to have a chicken and an egg, like you see in Easter plants. I thought it would have been funny."

"Oh. Even if they weren't there, I compliment you on your creativity."

"Well, as long as you got the posies."

"They're wonderful. You completely blew me away. Thank you."

"No problem. You deserve them, Dear." Four patrons, all male, entered the bar. "Woops. Duty calls." Ciaran left her to tend to the new flock, leaving her wondering which bouquet, if any, he'd sent.

48

Eileen left the bar shortly after their chat. Too many questions were running around her head and she needed to be at home to sort through them. The walk down Pitt St. only exacerbated her imagination. Despite Ciaran's talk of having sent flowers, it did not seem possible that he would send such a suggestive note no matter which one might have been his. It was not his style. She threw her notebook down on the dining room table and grabbed a Perrier from the refrigerator. The Caller ID light was flashing. Eileen scrolled through the calling record. Fran had left DC. He had a new number in suburban Boston, a 508 area code. It was a different number from the one for his home with Nuala. Eileen still had that number memorized even though she had dialed it only once two years ago. He had phoned twice in the last hour. "So, Francis is on his own again." Her curiosity got the better of her. It always did. Eileen turned on her PC and connected to the Internet. She was giving in again. She had to know. Her search took three minutes until she found that he had taken an apartment in Woburn, only 25 minutes north of the city. Eileen logged off the system, stepped back into the kitchen and retrieved the messages he'd left. She stood next to the speakerphone drinking Perrier straight from the bottle. The dry bubbles swirled in her mouth as she listened.

"Hey, it's me. Listen, I've moved. I've got a new place. I told you I'd let you know where I am, and I meant it. Please Leen, any-time you are ready, let's talk. I hope you liked the flowers. I'd give anything to hear from you. It's all different now. I swear it is. Leen, please, call me. Whenever you want." He finished the mes-sage with his new phone number.

Second message. "Leen. Sorry. I know you must think I'm a lit-tle off my rocker calling you twice. I promise, after this, I'll stay away and leave everything up to you. I had to tell you. I under-stand now. I understand how hard everything must have been for you. Here it is Valentine's Day and I'm so lonely thinking of you. I've been thinking of you all day praying that I'll hear from you. Now I know how it felt for you. The birthdays I missed, the Valentine's Days and Christmases that I missed with you. Eileen, I am so sorry for having done that. You never deserved that. You deserved better. I'm probably too late, but please call me. We'll talk it over, and I promise, you never will be alone on a holiday again."

So, she thought, both arrangements were from him. She knew he wanted to talk, and now she knew that he wanted to hear from her "whenever you want." Ciaran's flowers, if there ever were any, had never made it to her. She tossed the empty bottle across the kitchen into the trashcan. Had he lied to her? Son of a bitch, she laughed, you were winding me up. That would be so typical of him. He'd wanted to make her squirm, and she'd played right into his hands. She could not be mad at him, but began trying to figure out for how long she should let him keep up the mystery.

49

She invited Ciaran to come over for lunch three days later. He had the day off and appeared at the door with a bottle of Diet Coke for her, and two packs of cigarettes for each of them. "Well, thanks for the presents. You know, they say the way to a woman's heart is through her caffeine and tobacco addictions."

"Actually, I've heard that Philip Morris is now saying that smoking is an aphrodisiac." He gave her a kiss on the cheek. "Mmmm. They must be right. I suddenly feel a little bit crazy."

"Quick, light another one before we lose the moment, goofball."

He sat at the dining room table as Eileen was amassing sandwich ingredients on the counter in the kitchen. "Oh hey, the flowers are nice." He noted the mixed arrangement. "Still too bad about the chicken and the egg."

"Uh-huh." What? He was really getting a lot mileage out of the joke.

"I meant what I said on the card."

Okay, Eileen thought, Ciaran, that's enough. She wanted to tell him that he'd exhausted the joke, but let him continue anyway. "Well good. I'm glad about that. You're too kind."

"Ah yes, Dear," he walked behind her and put his hands around her waist. "Whenever you want." Her eyes exploded open. He had sent them. "Whenever you want to show me that manuscript of yours, that epic you've been creating before me, I will read every word. There's no need to be shy." Suddenly, Eileen remembered their chat in the pub three weeks earlier. He had been asking her what the new book was about and she wouldn't tell him, but she'd shown him a few random pages. He'd asked to see all of it, and she said she was afraid to release it to anyone yet, but would let him see it in good time. His response to her that afternoon had been, "Whenever you want." Her shoulders relaxed and she began to feel a little stupid. She put down the package of ham that she had been unwrapping and laughed. "What is it?"

"Nothing," she answered. "I've just been under a bit of stress lately, and I realized that I have been making mountains out of molehills. I swear, somedays I am amazed that I don't think more stupid things than I do. I'm just waiting for my head to explode one of these days, and everyone will stand around the wreckage; wag their heads and say, 'Well, if she'd only stopped worrying and planning for two minutes, this never would have happened.'"

"What are you talking about?"

"Okay," she turned to face him. "You want to hear something really funny?"

"Sure."

"I totally misunderstood your message."

"How?"

Her face was turning pink inflaming to deeper shades of red. "I hope I don't upset you, but I thought you wanted to get married. To me."

"Wha-?"

"I was thinking of our talks about the green card, and then you said, 'whenever you want,' and well, I put two and two together and got six."

"Oh God. Eileen, I'm sorry." Ciaran saw the embarrassment and a hint of disappointment on her face. Eileen was laughing, trying to shrug off the misunderstanding, but he was smart enough to know that women do not take mentions of marriage lightly. He'd learned that using the "M" word, no matter what the context, was a walk on dangerous ground. "I must have really thrown you for a loop."

"Well, maybe a little." She reached into the upper cabinet and pulled out a loaf of bread. "No matter. Let's just forget about it." She opened a bag of Doritos and leaned it toward him, "Chip?"

50

ER was almost over and the cordless phone had been staring at her all night. She knew that before she went to bed, she would talk to Fran and was afraid of how the discussion might go. She held the phone in her hand, pressing 'talk,' then pressing it again to turn off the phone. At 11:05 she dialed his number and her body shook as the phone rang. In the old days, he would not be home. He would have called her over an hour later, exhausted, but revealing nothing about what he'd been doing. It was always, "I was in Southie." Third ring. She was preparing to hang up. "Hello?"

"Fran?"

He recognized her voice, turned on the light next to his bed and sat up. "Leen?"

"Yeah. Did I wake you?"

"No. No." He could have told her that he'd been lying in bed thinking of her, but talk like that would not have been right for this conversation. "I'm glad to hear from you."

"Are you really out? I mean, really, no chance of ever going back?"

"Yes. Completely."

"Thank God. Fran, I need you to tell me why. Why did you leave it all? I have to know." Tears ran down her cheeks, but she would not allow him to hear her cry. She was not ready to let him know that he had a chance of coming back to her. Her fantasy of him sitting on the patio reading a book had been overtaking her imagination since Valentine's Day. He still had a hold on her, and she wasn't sure if she wanted him to loosen his grasp. Everything had been easier when he wasn't there.

"I couldn't do it anymore. It's wrong Eileen. It's always been wrong. I didn't have a choice. I had to stay. But everything changed enough in the organization, and I saw a chance to get out. I wanted you to be proud of me. I want to be with you, and I want to be the kind of man you deserve. When I left, I told you it could take years, and I did not expect you to wait for me; but Leen, I had to take the chance. I had to see if there was any hope that you would have me back. I can't tell you how happy I am that you called."

"Frannie. I don't know what to tell you. I want you to be happy. You did the right thing by walking away from it all, but Fran, you walked away from me too. I'm not sure if I can forgive you for that. I'm not sure if I can ever get past it. I know you had no choice at the time, but that didn't make it any easier for me. I'm different now."

"Oh, I don't know how different you could be. Eileen, we went for five years without seeing each other and managed to come right back to each other. Remember?"

"Yes, Frannie, I do." She let him hear her crying. There was no use trying to hide it anymore. "But it's not the same. Back then, your work wasn't between us. It wasn't until later that I became low man on your priority list. Fran, I know you loved me, but I don't know if I can just wipe away that emptiness. Your marriage is a real problem for me."

"I told you, I've left her."

"I don't care. You might think I'm being unreasonable, but I'm having a very difficult time getting past that. I mean, we never could have a life together because of work, and then you go off and marry her because of work. I was alone, coming unglued, worrying about you and bawling my eyes out everyday over you, and you went and got married."

"I'm sorry." He began to cry. "I love you. I never told you enough. I love you. I'll tell you a million times a day, every day, until the day I die if you want. They took everything from me. I have nothing to offer you. I'm broke."

"I don't care about your money. I never did. I only wanted to hear your voice. I only wanted you to listen to me, but you couldn't do that. I know you wanted to, but you couldn't do it." She walked to the kitchen and poured a whiskey into a juice glass.

"Eileen, I will listen. I want to. I need you, Hon. I always have." He walked naked into the living room and sat in his recliner, holding a cigarette. Fran took a drag and continued, "Whatever you want. You know, I read your book. I'm Mark, aren't I?"

"Duh." She laughed. "I was afraid to write it. I felt sure that you'd never speak to me again. I had already expected that I would never hear from you, and I had to let it out somehow. Sometimes it's easier to lose yourself in someone else's life rather than live your own. I'm glad you liked it. I hope it didn't get you into trouble."

"Nah. But I have to say that for a few weeks we looked like a fucking book club, sitting around the kitchen in Southie talking about it. At one point, there were three copies of it around the place. You really know how to capture an audience." He was laughing hard, "Always did."

"Shut up," she finished the whiskey and poured another.

"Hey, you've managed to capture my attention for 14 years. Honey, you cut through a family of 10 in a three-bedroom house, 3,000 miles, college exams, high-intensity jobs, an international conflict, and I hate to mention it, but, a marriage, and you still are all I can think about. How do you do it? You took me over and I never even saw it coming."

"Francis. Please, stop. You, you did the same to me."

"I miss you."

"I know." She hesitated. "Me too."

"Can I see you?" He couldn't let her off the phone without asking.

"I'm not sure Frannie. I just don't know yet. Truly, I don't want to hurt you, but I have to protect myself. I still need to think about this, but I swear to you that we will talk again. Please leave it to me to call you. Maybe after a little while you can phone me, but I need to get my bearings. I'm doing really well, Fran. I've almost finished another book."

"That's terrific! I can't wait to read it. What's it about?"

"I'm not telling, but I can assure that you Ireland will not even be mentioned. Woops. No, I lied. There is a vacation scene in Donegal. Other than that, I'm through with Rah stories."

"Good girl. I am too." He smiled and looked at the picture on his coffee table, the one of the two of them in Nineteen O'Connell. Eileen had sent him copies of all of her pictures from the holiday. Fran had destroyed everything before they came to take him back to Belfast, but he kept a safe-deposit box in the Orleans, MA branch of Citibank. He'd hidden his prize-possessions in the bank on the Cape, never allowing the organization to pollute his core. The box had contained a photo of his mother, one of his niece Clare, $28,000, letters Eileen wrote him in college, and their picture.

"Okay, I'm going to hang up now. But we will talk again. I can't make you any promises Fran."

"I'm not asking you too. Eileen,"

"Yes."

"I love you."

She sobbed into the phone. "I love you too. Goodbye."

"Bye."

Eileen slumped down in the leather chair and let the phone fall to the floor.

51

Eileen did not go to Sullivan's for two weeks. She wanted to finish her manuscript, and her phone call to Fran kept re-playing in her head. If she saw Ciaran, she knew she'd crack and tell him about what was happening. It wouldn't be fair to dump her troubles on him. Why, she reasoned with herself, would I dump all of this on some unwilling participant? It was better to protect him from it all, from her troubles, and telling anyone about her history with Fran would require letting it all out. She'd convinced herself that telling anyone, especially a northerner, about her life on the fringes of the Rah would have turned her into a social pariah. She trusted him so much. If she told anyone, he would have been the one. He knew how things worked at home; how they used to work. He would have understood the logistics of it all, but it was too close. Eileen knew him well enough to know that this very well could be a boundary that, if crossed, would backfire in her face.

After her second Wednesday away from the pub, Ciaran stopped at her house on his way home from work. Eileen sat in the den, editing the chapters she'd just completed and was unnerved by the sound of the doorbell. She was expecting Pizza Hut, but not for another 20 minutes. She looked through the window on the edge of the door and saw Ciaran with his hands in his pockets, looking from side to side.

"Hey," he said when she opened the door.

"Hi. To what do I owe this pleasant surprise?"

He stepped into the foyer. "It occurred to me that I haven't seen you in quite a while, and I guess you could call this a welfare check. "

"Huh?"

"I wanted to be sure you were okay."

"Oh. Oh yeah. God yeah, I'm fine. I've just been busy. Loads to do," she said lighting a cigarette and tossing the pack back on to the coffee table.

"Good." He gave her a hug and kissed her cheek. "I was beginning to think I was off the team."

"You are so funny. No. You're still on the team, doll. I'm just on the DL."

"The what?" He still was learning baseball terminology.

"The DL. The Disabled List. I'm off the team for a bit. Wrapping up a few loose ends, and it's taking me longer than I expected."

"Okay. You almost finished?"

"I think so," she answered. "How about if I pop in tomorrow afternoon?"

"How about if I pop over here tomorrow afternoon? I'm free until 6:00. I'm filling in for James tomorrow night.

"Sounds good to me. 1:00?"

"Perfect." She brushed his hair with her hand and kissed him. He always smelled so good. Eileen liked touching his neck and his hair so that after he'd gone, she could still smell him on her. "I'll see you tomorrow then, sir."

"Excellent." Ciaran walked down the front stairs to his car. Eileen closed the door and held the back of her hand to her nose.

52

Mass. Eileen woke from a less than healthful sleep at 8:35 on Tuesday morning with one thought, I must go to mass. Nominal Catholics typically attend mass on four occasions; weddings, funerals, Easter and Christmas. Even then, Easter and Christmas are not a guarantee. She'd joked with Ciaran a month before that "When the 'nominals' are in trouble they say a Hail Mary either before scratching off the lotto ticket or doing the pregnancy test." Today, she called St. Mary's recorded line for the schedule and walked into the 12:35 mass in the small stone church located halfway between her place and Sullivan's. She could not explain the need for religious intervention knowing only that one little crawl space in her brain needed the connection with God, Jesus, His Mother, and the apostles.

Twenty some-odd of the faithful, most over 60, sat dispersed throughout the church saying rosaries or praying in silence. Eileen took a seat fourteen pews back from the altar with the confessionals to her left. She fingered the missalette and hymn book in the cradle before her then twisted her head taking in each wooden carving depicting the Stations of the Cross. It was two minutes before the priest, minus the Sunday morning pomp and circumstance of the bellowing organ and processional of altar boys, emerged through the sacristy door. "Peace be with you," he began.

Eileen listened to his opening remarks and the readings, then he began the homily. "What is peace," the priest asked. "When we seek peace, do we seek it in the world, in our communities, in our homes, our hearts, our minds, or in our spirituality?" Father continued and his opening question grabbed Eileen in a tidal wave. She drifted away in thought just as she used to when she was a child.

Peace, she thought, had smacked her against the sharpest jetty. Keeping the peace with Steven when he'd called her a slut. Seeking peace, twice, in marriages that proposed to make her a good peaceful wife. Sacrificing inner peace for Fran's love and his search for supposed community peace,. Giving up Chris in order to allow them both a piece of dignity.

"Peace is where you make it," Father finished. "Spiritual peace builds the peace within our hearts, minds, communities, and ultimately the world." Eileen remained in the pew for a few minutes after mass concluded. A few parishioners lined up for confession along the wall next to her. She watched the older women, with varying shades of grey hair, and thin legs from countless rounds of golf. They each stood quietly, some saying another decade of the rosary, some just watching the light over the confessional door to see when one confessor would emerge and another could enter.

Eileen glanced at them wondering what their lives were like. They each wore wedding rings that spun on their thin fingers. One woman rested left her hand on the edge of the pew where Eileen sat. Her platinum wedding band was thin from so many years on her hand. The woman's knuckles were a bit enlarged from arthritis guaranteeing that the ring, no matter how much it slid back and forth on her finger, would not come off.

Eileen enjoyed the walk home from St. Mary's. Like most winters, they'd gone without snow in Alexandria but the air remained brisk and dry. She pulled the sleeves of her barn jacket and turtleneck down over her hands as makeshift mittens. Eileen pulled out the mail from the brass box mounted on the front of the house before entering her home. After hanging her coat on the banister she picked up the mail off the bottom stair and picked up a box from the pile, likely her new checks. It contained the booklet of liner notes from Disc 3 of her Motown Singles Collection and a purple card from Maeve. "Nice place," was typed on the back.

53

She was in Sully's, editing her book with the red pen until she couldn't see straight any longer. "Hey egg."

He looked at her startled that she'd said that. "Yes chicken?" He looked at her.

"Do you like to play pool?"

"Yeah. I haven't since I got here, but I used to play every weekend back home. Why? Are you weaving a vicious game of snooker into your story?"

"No. I love to play, and I haven't in ages. Would you like to play sometime?"

"What? A woman who enjoys billiards?"

"Aw Honey! I don't play no refined game of billiards! I'm talking a game of rack 'em up, kick-yer-ass nine ball."

"Put a tenner on it, and you've got a date."

"Excellent. Now, it's been a while–," her wrists were moving in circles as she spoke.

"Oh sure, here come the excuses."

"No! I'm just tellin' ya it's been a while, so I can't promise a fabulous challenge, but it'll be fun. At the very least, you'll go home with a few bucks in your pocket."

Ciaran put another beer in front of her. "Okay. Tuesday afternoon. I'll be at your house at 1:00, and I'm driving."

"Okay." She looked confused.

"I'm not going to give you the advantage of subjecting me to your NASCAR approach to cruising through Old Town. The shock to my system would be an unfair advantage."

"Very funny. I think there's a guy down there who actually WANTS your attention." Ciaran left her and tended to the wayward lawyer in search of a Dewars on the rocks.

They kept a standing Tuesday afternoon date with a few nights thrown into the mix. For their third night out, she took the bold move of inviting him over for dinner. "I'll cook."

"I'm scared," Ciaran said into the phone at the end of the bar.

"Ha. Ha. Seriously, do you like Indian?"

"Sure." He hadn't been able to find a decent curry place in Alexandria. They might have been good by DC standards but didn't match up to London or Dublin.

"Well, I love it. Though I must warn you. I cook according to color, and my curry will take the paint off your house. If you're looking for a good tandoori meal, well then I guess we'll be getting take out."

"No. No. Curry is great."

"Excellent. I'll pick up some more cayenne pepper on the way home."

"Cayenne? Who taught yow how to cook?"

"No one. But the first time I tried it, it didn't look yellow enough, and I thought the cayenne would give it the color it was missing."

"Okay. How about if you cook, and I supervise?"

"What does that mean," Eileen was in her car with a marble table for the porch from Upscale Resale hanging out the back of her car.

"I add the ingredients and you stir."
"You big chicken."
"Yup."
"Take the skirt off."
"No."

54

On Thursday, the 14th of March, Eileen sat in the leather chair holding the cordless phone. Agent Lloyd's business card sat on the end table next to her. She sipped her coffee and stared at the television, though it was not on. She recalled her conversation with Fran in New Orleans, and her flippant comment about turning him and Nuala in to INS. The *Washington Post*, which she read religiously every morning, sat untouched on the couch. The crease in the paper wedged into the cushion. Eileen pressed the phone's "talk" button, held it to her ear checking for a dial tone, then entered the numbers on the phone. A woman answered, "Counterterrorism."

"Agent Lloyd, please."

"May I tell him who's calling?"

She thought of hanging up the phone, but changed her mind, "Eileen Eliot."

"One moment. I'll see if he's available."

Hurry, Eileen thought, or I might not be here. "Lloyd."

"Agent Lloyd, this is Eileen Eliot. We met about a year ago at my home in Beacon Hill."

"Yes, Ms. Eliot. I enjoyed your book, by the way. I am not sup-posed to say such things during an investigation, but I truly enjoyed it."

She was startled. "Uh, thank you."

"What can I do for you?"

"I'm not sure how to say this."

"Yes." He sat up in his desk chair and reached for a pen.

"Well, I've moved to Alexandria, Virginia, near Washington, and I need to speak with someone in foreign counter-intelligence, but am not sure who to go to."

"Is this for another book? Because we have a public informa-tion section that might be able to–"

She interrupted, "No, Mr. Lloyd. This is for real."

"Ms. Eliot, I have to warn you that this conversation is being recorded."

"I expected as such," she reached for her coffee, took a sip and continued, "I'm not comfortable having this discussion on the phone. Frankly, I am not comfortable having it in my home either. Should we meet, I can fly to Boston, or is there someone in Washington I can talk to?"

"Ms. Eliot, I'll need a few details first."

You have got to be kidding me, she thought. "Sir, what if I were to tell you that my book was actually an autobiography and that I am prepared to lead you to 'Mark Mullen's' den of thieves. They're only about 40 minutes from your office."

"I'll call Washington. Hold the line please Miss, and I'll try to conference in one of my colleagues."

"Fine."

Stuart Lloyd put his hand over the mouthpiece and leaned toward his partner, "Get Washington F.C.I. on the line and con-ference them into this call. Now." Lloyd's pulse was racing as he spoke into the phone, "Ms. Eliot, are you telling me that," his partner gave him a thumbs-up sign. "One moment Ms. Eliot. Go ahead please."

A deep, soft-spoken voice interrupted the discussion, "This is Special Agent George Stearn. With whom am I speaking?" The three talked for a few minutes about Eileen's book and her admission of its truthfulness. Special Agent Stearn agreed to meet Eileen at his office in the J. Edgar Hoover Building on Pennsylvania Avenue at 2:00. She hung up the phone at 9:53 AM.

At 10:30, she drove to Sullivan's, parking in the Pitt St. garage under the pub and walked up to the side entrance. The lunch crowd wouldn't be expected to stream in for another 45 minutes. Eileen walked to Ciaran and gave him a hug. "Hey pal, how are you?"

"I'm great." He looked up and down at her. "You're looking very smart today." She was in a beige pantsuit, dressed to the nines. He'd never seen her in formal clothes. She hadn't bothered to wear them in six months. "What? No files or binders with you today, woman?"

"No." She sat on the barstool closest to the service station. "Listen, can you sit down for a minute? I need to talk to you."

He looked at her for a second and wondered if she might be pregnant. "Sure, let me get a cup of tea. You want anything?"

"Just a decaf coffee, please." She leaned her elbow on the bar. "It's too early for beer," she smiled. The rest of the staff milled back and forth between the kitchen and the dining room setting up for lunch. Ciaran sat down in the seat next to her, nervous.

"Ciaran something's come up."

"Yes." He took a gulp of his tea.

"I have a meeting in two hours and wanted to talk to you first."

"What is it?" Please tell me you're not pregnant, he thought.

"Look, I don't want to put you in any jeopardy and I hope that we can talk about this later, but I'm not sure what's going to happen." Eileen's hand rested on the mug of coffee, but she didn't drink it.

His mind eased then shot back to attention. "Jeopardy? Leenie, what are you saying?"

Eileen whispered back to him, taking his left hand in hers. "Sweetie, I cannot say much right now, but I trust you. I'm glad that I don't know what it is that tells me when to drop my guard, 'cause you snuck under my defense systems and have been nothing but good for me. I wish we'd met years ago. Then again, I would've been a total head case back then." She laughed a little.

Ciaran tilted his head down a bit and raised his eyebrows at her, "Leen?"

"I know. I'm sorry. I'm rambling. My emotions always have ruled me—so much so that I've trained myself not to use them very often. You've knocked me for a loop. Thank you. I really just wanted to see you, and tell you that I've got this meeting in a little while. I suppose I needed a little courage, so I'm here buggin' you. I could be making a huge mistake by going. I can't be sure. I want you to hold on to this." She handed him an unmarked letter-sized envelope. "If something happens, read it. I trust you not to open it otherwise."

"Oh Eileen. Come on. You know how I am with unopened mail. It'll never last. WHAT is going on? You're getting weird."

No more talking to bathroom mirrors she thought. She faced the demons, pulling her seat closer to him until their shoulders were touching. "I'm afraid to say it. I'm afraid of losing my friend; losing you. I can't get the words out." God, I sound like Frannie. "I have information about the I.R.A., and I'm going to the FBI. That's all I can tell you. I'm sorry. I'm scared, but I know I'm doing the right thing." Ciaran said nothing. The look on his face reminded Eileen of the way she felt the night Fran had told her everything in the New York hotel. "Take this if you want it." She pushed the envelope over to him. "If you don't, I understand. It's okay. I should go." She stood and reached for her overcoat.

Ciaran took the envelope, folded it in half and put it in his shirt pocket. He helped Eileen with her coat and faced her, keeping his hands on her lapels. "I'm still standing here. I've got your letter, and I do not intend to open it. I expect you to tell me what it says when this is all over. We're friends. I'm not going anywhere."

"Thanks." Eileen wiped her eyes.

"Why, Ms. Eliot, are you crying?" Ciaran smirked at her.

"Shut up," she laughed. "Yes. Yes, I am. O-kayyy?" Her eyes opened wide as she glared at him and smiled. "Yes, the Ice Queen has feelings. Keep it to yourself, or this place'll be crawling with TV trucks."

"What last time?"

"The last time you asked if I was crying. The day when we were talking everything over. Yes, I was."

"I thought so. Why didn't you say so?"

Her left, middle finger dragged under her lower eyelids, "I was afraid that if I said yes you'd ask why, and we'd talk so much that I'd frighten you, and you'd bolt out the door before I could pull on my sweatpants."

"Tell me you're joking. That's ridiculous."

"No. There was so much I wanted to say, and I wasn't sure where to start. I knew that if I let out one little bit I would have gone to pieces. You wouldn't have recognized me. Okay? Can we leave it at that?"

"For now."

"For now," she said back to him. "I'll plan to see you soon. Maybe even before dinner time."

"Call here when you get back, and just let me know how it went."

"Sure." She put her handbag over her shoulder and turned for the door.

"Hey. Come here a minute." Eileen walked back toward him. Ciaran hugged her the way he did when they were alone in her kitchen.

"What are you doing," she whispered into his ear, wrapping her arms around his neck. "Everyone is watching."

"Who cares." He kissed her cheek, then her lips. Eileen forgot about the staff despite the sounds of chairs sliding across the floor and silverware hitting tabletops coming to a distinct halt. Elizabeth, holding silver meant for table 21, reached into her apron and handed James a dollar. James handed Gary a fiver. Rachel stood in the kitchen doorway looking thoroughly confused. "Go get 'em." Ciaran patted Eileen on the ass, and she left out the side door down to her car in the parking garage.

Eileen noticed a man leaning against the Volvo parked next to her Audi A6. He was smoking and paging through a day planner. Eileen assumed he was early for a meeting at a local office. He looked up at her when he heard the chirp signaling her car door locks' being deactivated. "Hello," she said.

The man responded, "Hello, Miss." Eileen did not see him turn toward her as she opened the car door, sat down and pulled the seatbelt around her body.

"Eileen," he asked, with his hand on her doorframe. She was trapped with the belt around her and his body blocking the door. "Did you like the flowers? Yer such a luvely womahn."

Her hand was on the ignition key with her right foot ready to hit the accelerator.

"By the way, I have a message for you."

Eileen looked up at him. "A message? What's that?"

He leaned his face inside the car and whispered, "Your Fran died an hour ago."

"What?" Eileen knew what was next.

"Yes. Your Francis. A pity. Wrong place. Wrong time. Like you." He took the silenced Glock 18 from behind his back and pulled the trigger. Blood splattered out of her back soaking into the leather interior. Eileen's lifeless body was pinned into the seat by the belt. The man pumped the trigger two more times then left up the stairs and entered the back of the pub.

At 11:55 sirens and police officers interrupted the early lunch crowd in Sullivan's. Ciaran sat in Jimmy's office on the phone with the linen company arguing that the bill and the delivered goods did not match. This was not the first time they'd tried to short-change them. He did not hear the commotion in the other room. Rachel crossed through the door and told him to come into the dining room. "What's the problem," he asked putting his hand over the phone.

"The police are all over the place. Someone was found dead downstairs and they want to talk to everyone."

Ciaran's face went pale. He couldn't speak to the cops. If they asked him for identification they would know he was illegal. He sat in the cold metal chair mulling over his options. He wondered who'd died. Some stockbroker from next door must have had a heart attack. He calmed himself and realized that a few questions from the cops shouldn't be a problem. Better to face them than to disappear. They stopped in the bar all the time. He hoped they were officers he knew. He pushed back the chair and walked to the kitchen. James stopped him before he reached the dining room. "Ciaran, I need to talk to you."

"I've got to see what's going on out front. Can it wait?"

James put a hand on Ciaran's shoulder to stop him. "No man, that's what it's about. A woman was, well, they found a woman dead in her car in the garage." Ciaran stood looking at him half paying attention.

"A woman? That's awful. Have the cops talked to everyone else?"

"Man, it's Eileen."

Ciaran steadied himself against the wall. "What?"

"It's Eileen. She was shot in her car. I'm sorry, man. I know you guys were friends."

"Are you sure it's her?"

"Sounds like it."

Ciaran entered the dining room, stunned, and met the police officers. When the detective described Eileen and how a man leaving the garage had found her, Ciaran ran out of the pub and down to the garage. Six police cars surrounded the area near her car. Two forensic specialists were taking photographs and dusting the area. Eileen's body was gone already. Rachel and James followed him until they found Ciaran sitting on the stairs talking with a detective. They could not hear the conversation, but saw his hands moving in frustration as he spoke. He told him that she had a meeting at the FBI later in the day but did not know what it was about. They asked him the nature of his relationship with her. No one had ever asked. Not even his co-workers. "We are, were, we were friends. Very close friends. She was a good woman."

The officer closed his notebook and looked at him. "I'm sorry Mr. Miller," he said. "I know how hard it is to lose a friend."

"Thank you," Ciaran stood.

"If you like, we'll keep you posted on our progress."

"Please do. She has no family here. They're all in Boston." The detective handed Ciaran his card. "I'll phone you if I hear of anything."

In the pub, he sat at the bar smoking a Marlboro. The business card was in front of him and he thought of his conversation with Eileen earlier in the morning. When he put his lighter in his shirt pocket, he remembered the envelope. Ciaran unfolded it and held it in his hands. "Well dear," he said to himself, "I guess I should open this." He looked up at James. "Hey, watch the floor and answer the phone for the next few minutes, would you?"

"Sure." The dining room was empty and George was the only one at the bar. He sat reading the *Boston Globe* and had a half-drained beer in front of him.

Ciaran slid his finger under the envelope's seal. A letter and another envelope were inside. The envelope was addressed to Agent Lloyd. Ciaran unfolded the papers that accompanied it and began reading.

14 March 2001

Dear Ciaran,

Well, I suppose something has happened, otherwise, you wouldn't be reading this. I want to come clean with you, but first I need you to do me a favor. Please post the enclosed envelope. It's all set. You need only to drop it in a mailbox. Yes, it is addressed to a Special Agent at the Feds. I never told you because I was afraid, but for a long time I have had information about the I.R.A.. I stood on the edge of a dirty secret. Keeping silent was the worst thing I've ever done. I won't go into the details. There is no need to put you at unnecessary risk. This has been bothering me for years, and I've decided to clear my conscience. I need to rid myself of it and going to the government is the only way I know how. Since you are reading this, it is clear that someone found me out. Please, don't push to find out who did it. It's best to leave it alone. Just know that I am confident in the choice I made.

A few years ago I learned that people need to be told when they've done something well or that they are a good person. I'm sure you've heard it all before. If not, then someone's neglected you something awful. Ciaran, you are a good, smart man who deserves nothing less than all of the best that the world has to offer. I believe that we were meant to meet. From the day I walked into Sully's and saw you behind the bar, I knew that we would become great friends. You have only reassured me that my hunch was correct. You have meant the world to me and you reminded me that caring about someone does not have to mean sacrifice.

I've made a few arrangements for you. I hope that's okay. You need to contact Jack Marston, my friend and attorney, in Boston. He's at 617.676.7198. I went to see him a few weeks ago. He doesn't know anything about why I am writing this, only that you are a very dear friend to me.

I've deemed two accounts for you. One is cash, and one is a mutual fund. As of this evening, they are worth a total of roughly $2.85 million. Most of it is in the stock fund. They are trust accounts, so the tax burden should be as minimal as possible. Jack can help you with that. The stock market treated me very well, and I guess I have a knack for investments. The house on Franklin St. is also meant for you. Keep it or sell it. Do whatever you please. It's yours now.

I did some checking and with the accounts, you should be able to settle your visa situation without a problem. Contact Mary Sweeney at 202.437.9641. She's the woman who I said would get you sorted. Tell her I sent you and that you want an entrepreneur visa. You'll need to complete an Immigrant Petition by Alien Entrepreneur form. It's for people with over a million dollars who want to start a business, so pick an industry and go nuts. I'm digressing. Sorry. You know I get mired in details. Granted, getting married might have been loads more fun, but I think this route will suit you as well.

Be well, Ciaran. Follow your dreams and set no limits. You've given me so much. These small actions of mine cannot begin to return my gratitude.

Oh, before I forget, I finished my next book. It went to the publishing house. There's a copy of the manuscript for you on the dining room table. Use the key in the geranium pot on the patio to get in the house. It'll be a month or so before Jack can get the house transferred to you.

Thank you thank you thank you.

With loads of love and friendship,

I remain,

Yours,

Eileen

Ciaran looked up from the pages. James stood across the bar from him. "You okay," he asked.

"Yeah. Fine. Listen, I've got to get out of here. I'll see you tomorrow."

"Sure. No problem. I'll let Jimmy know. Take it easy."

Ciaran headed toward the front door, "You too." He walked down Pitt St. holding the envelope in his left hand. He clutched another cigarette between his right thumb and index finger. At Pitt and Prince Streets, he stood before a postbox. For a second, he considered keeping the letter to Lloyd, reading it, then posting it to him in a new envelope. He couldn't do it. She'd trusted him to do this one thing for her. Ciaran put the cigarette between his lips and pulled the mailbox open with his free hand. The envelope sat on the mailbox's door. He stared at the address then released the handle. It slammed shut echoing on the street corner. The letter detailed everything she'd planned to tell Lloyd and Stearn; Fran's history, everything he'd told her, the house outside of Boston. Every last morsel she could recall of her time with him fell on top of electric bill payments and Publishers Clearinghouse sweep-stakes entries.

The house on Franklin St., his house now, didn't look any different. He walked around to the patio, retrieved the key and rounded the street to the front door. Ciaran almost pressed the button for the doorbell as he had done so many times before. Using the key didn't feel right. He slid it into the lock and opened the door. The echo of his shoes on the hardwood floors disturbed him. Eileen's voice was supposed to be talking over the noise. He entered the kitchen and made a pot of coffee. He didn't notice that he actually did know where everything was.

He poured the coffee into a mug, took the manuscript into the living room and sat in the leather chair. The binder lay across his lap as he lit another cigarette and set it in the crystal ashtray.

He took her book in his hands and opened to the title page, *Mortal Whims*. Ciaran turned to the next page, read it and sobbed. Eileen had left him a house, almost $3 million dollars and her words. "For Ciaran. For your friendship, your honesty, and for telling me that I need a good editor. Egg, the Chicken is more than thankful."

About the Author

Kim Colman Moore resides in Alexandria, VA with her husband Steven and their Labrador retriever, Bear. This is her first novel.

0-595-20925-4